PRAISE FOR DAMYANTI BISWAS

"*The Blue Bar* will assault your senses as the setting comes alive in this intricately woven mystery. It examines the gritty, corrupt politics of Mumbai as an inspector tries to solve cases of dismembered women when he doesn't know who to trust within his own ranks. A tale of loyalty, love, and revenge, this sophomore novel by Biswas is not to be missed."

—Jaime Lynn Hendricks, author of *Finding Tessa* and *It Could Be Anyone*

"Immersive, propulsive, and beautifully written. In this gaspingly authentic police procedural about a missing dancer and the inspector who cannot forget her, Biswas transports us to India—not only to investigate a grisly and sinister series of murders but to explore the dark and disturbing life of Mumbai's bar girls. With its heartbreaking love story and Biswas's revealing social commentary, *The Blue Bar* will change you, haunt you, and have you understanding the world in a different way."

—Hank Phillippi Ryan, *USA Today* bestselling author of *Her Perfect Life*

"*The Blue Bar* is one of those books that tattoos itself onto your bones—the luscious language, the glorious sense of place, a mystery that draws you in deep, so deep that you forget there's a world around you. Best of all is Inspector Arnav Singh Rajput, the tender, lionhearted man at the story's center who will stop at nothing to see that justice is done. I'll be thinking about this one for a long time."

—Jess Lourey, Edgar-nominated author of *Unspeakable Things*

"An intense, visceral thriller that . . . will leave you breathless!"

—Lisa Gardner, #1 *New York Times* bestselling author

THE
BLUE
BAR

OTHER TITLES BY DAMYANTI BISWAS

You Beneath Your Skin

THE BLUE BAR

A BLUE MUMBAI THRILLER

DAMYANTI BISWAS

THOMAS & MERCER

Published by Thomas & Mercer, Seattle

www.apub.com

Amazon, the Amazon logo, and Thomas & Mercer are trademarks of Amazon.com, Inc., or its affiliates.

ISBN-13: 9781662503917
ISBN-10: 1662503911

Cover design by Faceout Studio, Amanda Hudson

Printed in the United States of America

For Swarup, without whom I might never have dared write my very first stories

You are pale, friend moon, and do not sleep at night,

And day by day you waste away.

Can it be that you also

Think only of her, as I do?

  ~Subhāṣitāvali

CHAPTER ONE

TARA

2002, Borivali Station

Endings are overrated. There's only one true, certain end—everything else a load of bullshit, or how you call it, *bakwaas*. Beginnings, though. Beginnings are everywhere. It all began with that midnight-colored saree, thick with dark-blue sequins, its endless sea of shimmering dots stitched by hands that must have cracked and bled over the months of needle in and out of taut cloth in some dingy, godforsaken hole in one of Mumbai's stinking alleyways.

The saree, draped well below Tara's navel, scratched against her skin. The low-necked silver blouse scraped her shoulders, but she tried not to think about any of this, or the sweat trickling down her back while she maneuvered through the crush of bodies.

It had rained that afternoon, cooling the air, but not enough for the wide, dark shawl Tara had worn as per instructions. It was never cold enough in Mumbai for shawls. Especially not on a platform at Borivali Station during rush hour, which swarmed thicker than ants on a dead beetle. The voices of hundreds of men and women rose around her, red-uniformed porters yelling at everyone to stand back, squalling children, announcements of all the trains departing from or arriving in India's city of dreams.

To reach the end of the platform, Tara elbowed her way through the milling passengers. Many regional languages. Body odor. Perfumes. She pushed back against the women, stepping aside for the children and the men who hustled toward her in their rush to leave the platform. If she didn't give way to the men, they'd shove her at the shoulder if she was lucky; lower, if she wasn't.

She reached the finish line, where she could step no farther without falling off the platform. A little stretch of emptiness in a cramped city. In the distance stood slums with their tin-and-tarpaulin roofs. Towering above them, shiny billboards advertising refrigerators and televisions, with posters featuring building-sized faces of film stars, the drunken-eyed Shah Rukh Khan, dewy Aishwarya Rai, and the tall, lean figure of the heartthrob all girls swooned over, the sweet, baby-faced Karan Virani.

At seventeen, Tara had learned enough not to swoon over a man, not even Arnav, the police constable who made her heart beat faster these days. She dismissed the posters and did as asked. Stood facing the tracks as if poised to jump down and sprint after departing trains through scattered debris.

When she'd been brought to Mumbai on one of those trains four years ago, the stench of the city had overwhelmed her: a mix of rotting vegetation, frankincense, urine, perfume, frying fish, and the hopes and despair of more people than she'd ever seen gathered in one place. She didn't notice it anymore. Just like she took for granted her own changed smell—talcum powder and flowery perfume borrowed from the other bar girls. She could never leave, nor did she want to.

She dug in her heels instead, the expensive, pointy-toed silver shoes paired with her blue outfit, and ignored the passengers stepping off the train and navigating their way out of the mob of others waiting to board. A black-coated ticket checker gave her a quick once-over but continued his frenzied rush, sticking charts beside each of the compartment doors.

Tara shifted her weight from one heel to another. She usually got lost in crowds. Most men and even a few women towered over her. Not anymore. She felt tall, and these were absolutely the most glamorous clothes she'd worn, despite the whiff of dry cleaning each time she received them. She'd never looked better. Pity she wasn't allowed to wear these when gyrating at the bar, where they'd have fetched her a shower of hundred-rupee notes.

Her boss never explained why he paid nearly as much for each of these weird trips to the railway station as she made in a month dancing to lewd Bollywood numbers. Sometimes she wished for more of these trips in a week. *Don't be greedy, Tara,* she scolded herself, the way her mother used to, in another life.

The vibrating phone felt like a live thing in her hand. Shetty, the hefty, dark-skinned owner of the bar, had given it to her a month ago, saying she must take care not to lose this toy with its cracked screen and tiny beetle buttons, or else. She pressed the green button he'd showed her, raised the phone to her ear, and said a shaky *hayylo* into it. *Now,* said a voice at the other end. She didn't recognize the speaker but knew what to do.

Dropping her shawl, she posed as per Shetty's instructions, and counted off the seconds for the phone to buzz again. She donned her I-don't-give-a-damn look, while all the male passengers, vendors, and policemen noted the drape of her blue saree, the way it left most of her slim midriff exposed, called attention to her breasts. She paid no mind to the breeze at her back, bare but for the two silver strings that held her blouse together. Her breath steady, the same as before going onstage, she longed for the swig of alcohol that helped her through the first part of each evening's catcalls and groping.

Several low-throated lewd comments and snatches of Bollywood songs followed, but she bit back her litany of swear words. She focused on the rail tracks as if another train were on its way, one she alone knew about.

When the phone shivered in her sweaty palm, she didn't let her relief show, nor pick up the call. Instead, as instructed, she snatched up the shawl without wearing it, and headed for the stairs leading up to the bridge. An ebb in the crowd after a mass exit of passengers allowed her to make good time. She'd practiced running in these heels.

Breathing hard, she stumbled once at a crack in the platform pavement before she took the stairs as fast as the crowd and her saree would allow her. The slanting afternoon sun caught the sequins, lighting her up. Blind to all but the gaps she slipped through, and the bodies she must kick or elbow past while not losing her balance, she kept up her pace. She must exit the station in precisely three minutes. Her boss had never told her what might happen if she didn't. Forgetting her resolve to give up on prayers, she sent one up to Ma Kaali and raced on.

From the sixth-floor window of a nearby high-rise, a pair of binoculars stalked her progress as she ran.

CHAPTER TWO

ARNAV

Present day

Stuck in a traffic jam far away from the crime scene that would upend his life, Inspector Arnav Singh Rajput scanned the packed Chowpatty beach.

Ravan Dahan. At six stories tall, the demon Ravan awaited being burned to the ground during the popular festival of Dussehra—his cartoon-pink skin, ten heads, and golden crown glowing in the afternoon sun. Arnav sent Ravan a rueful smile. In his twenty-year career, no real-life demon from a Mumbai slum or skyscraper had ever tarried quietly for death. In five days, a crowd would watch this one explode in a bloom of firecrackers and celebrate the victory of good over evil while munching on spicy *bhelpuri*, as men in khaki uniforms made sure no one lost a wallet, a child, or life.

The thought of *bhelpuri* reminded Arnav he'd skipped lunch while trying to reach the Mantralaya, the seat of Maharashtra government. The Home Minister wanted to review security arrangements after a heightened alert, and Arnav's boss had picked him for the lengthy trek downtown to attend the briefing afterward. Arnav sighed. Now he had to race all the way to Madh Island, near his office, the Malwani Police Station, in response to a call. Laborers had stopped working at a new construction site close to a scrub-forested area. The excavator had dug up what they suspected was a dead body.

Arnav had asked the driver to lower the windows of his white police jeep. The salty air clung to Arnav's thick dark hair and mustache. He could switch on the siren and make the traffic part, but after a morning of long-winded speeches by the bigwigs, including Home Minister Namit Gokhale, Arnav craved a breather. He sent a message to his assistant, asking her to get ahold of a constable and meet him at the scene. Taking off the black-banded cap of his khaki uniform, he let traffic noises and the tinny song on the jeep radio wash over him, grateful none of his phones had rung for the past fifteen minutes. He'd reached home past 1:00 a.m. every night for the last week. His brain craved sleep.

His reprieve from work calls on his listed and unlisted numbers didn't last long. He negotiated Dussehra arrangements. Coaxed informants. Withheld curses while noting impossible court dates. Hammered away at ongoing investigations. The scenery outside his window changed from crammed roads flanking iconic art deco buildings near Mumbai Central to the windswept length of the Bandra-Worli Sea Link, which stretched across the Mahim Bay, to claustrophobic high-rises towering up in Bandra and then Andheri.

When the jeep hit the New Link Road in Malad and raced on to Madh-Marve Road, Arnav breathed deep. The air on Madh Island, a peninsula drooping off Mumbai's western coastline, was cleaner. Also a few degrees cooler. Mumbai's unforgiving sultriness remained, but trees flanked the road, providing shade. It looked pretty and innocuous, but local auto-rickshaw drivers spoke of hauntings on this road past midnight. Stories of a woman in a red-and-gold bridal *lehenga*, hitching rides. When Arnav had first heard the tale, he'd felt sorry for that bride, picturing her—kohl and lipstick smudged, her eyes wild.

Maybe she was indeed a ghost. It wasn't entirely uncommon to find dead bodies washed up on the beaches and in the surrounding mangrove forests, though this was the first time in Arnav's three years posted at the Malwani station that he'd heard of a body buried at a site. Mumbai's gangs disposed of their *ghatis* and *bhaiyas*, troublesome peers and victims alike, in the coastal mangroves. They expected the tide to carry the bodies out into the waters. Sometimes, they miscalculated the moods of the sea, and decomposed remains turned up on the local beaches.

In what seemed like less than two minutes, Arnav's jeep pulled up next to a large pile of bricks not far from the Aksa beach. A line of coconut palms swayed in the distance. A board in front of the site declared that Taneja Estate Holdings was building a sea-facing luxury spa for an established hotel chain.

When Arnav stepped out, the weak October sun lit up the straggly bushes under a few large trees. Assistant Sub-Inspector Sita Naik emerged from behind one of them, camera in hand. His assistant's face looked haggard these days—shadows under her eyes—but her khakis sat crisp on her fair, squat figure, her hair neatly tied beneath her cap. Unlike his own occasionally rumpled appearance, Naik dressed professionally at all times.

"Set up the perimeter?" Arnav said.

"Good afternoon, sir," she responded with a bright smile that clearly took effort. "Yes, we have."

It had been anything but a good afternoon, but he stopped himself from snarking at her. He returned her greeting and nodded, striding up the gravelly slope toward a cacophony of raised male voices.

A faint breeze wafted in from the nearby sea, but Arnav's shirt stuck to his back with sweat. Since this site was never a graveyard, the case could only be homicide, long concealed. He already struggled with a punishing workload, and didn't need another case right now.

The site felt isolated, with no other buildings nearby. Naik introduced Arnav to the site manager, who had rushed up to meet them. A pasty young man in a suit with a British twang to his English, totally out of his depth with the grumbling knot of laborers.

Arnav raised a hand and asked the men to step back and take a break. He'd call them if necessary. A tall, thin man, who seemed to be their leader, stepped forward and spoke to Arnav.

"They wouldn't have called you if we hadn't made a ruckus, *saab*. Get rid of it or we'll have to find work elsewhere."

Arnav reassured the man, and the flock of laborers left.

"Let's see what you've found." He gestured to the fancy-suit manager.

"This way, Inspector."

Fancy Suit stumbled, but righted himself and walked on toward an excavator that might have once been red, but was now an unrecognizable mud-splashed color.

"When did you hear of this?"

"The laborers showed it to the supervisor this morning. He called me."

"When did Taneja Estate Holdings start working at this site?"

"This week. The land ownership was contested for many years, but we started building as soon as they won the case."

"Do they know what's going on?"

"Yes, sir. I was on the phone with Mr. Taneja himself. He wished to understand how soon we can resume work. Once we build a basic structure, the other party won't be able to appeal the court decision. The architect's plan has been approved, and we've already ordered all the materials."

"How long has the lawsuit been in the courts?"

"More than twenty years."

"That's quite a while."

"Some local organization said this land belonged to the protected coastal mangrove forest area, and brought up stay orders each year."

"I see." Arnav handed the manager his card. "For now, it's a crime scene. We'll let you know once the investigation is done."

"We've already hired these workers, Inspector. You saw what an issue this could become."

"I understand, but this is a murder investigation, from what I can tell so far."

Arnav turned to Naik, who had followed him, effectively dismissing the site manager. "You've called Forensics?"

"Yes, sir. Dr. Meshram is on his way."

"Check the manager's story about this land's ownership. Does Taneja Estate Holdings own the land, or does it belong to someone else? If it was under litigation, verify all the details."

"I'll get a constable on it right away, sir," Naik said.

Disputes often led to dead bodies—this wouldn't be the first time a land dispute led to murder. Those who had dumped the body had assumed that the place would stay undisturbed for a while.

Right beside the excavator, Naik's scene markers and yellow tape surrounded a rectangular pit. A constable stood beside it, and upon their approach snatched away the kerchief he'd been holding to his nose. Arnav had worked at similar crime scenes before. When Tara disappeared more than a decade ago, this had been his immediate, panicked thought—he'd one day find her dumped somewhere, exactly like this.

From the heap of mud, stones, and stray twigs, he spotted a bone sticking out, and a dark leathery material. Desiccated skin and flesh, looking eerily at home in the soil.

CHAPTER THREE

Cut. One. Two. Three. He hummed the words while the razor traced lines on his thigh. Inhale. Two. Three. Cut. He kept the pressure even. It stung hard enough to satisfy, light enough he didn't flinch. The hum rose and fell with each line. Red bloomed on his parted skin, the halves gently taking leave of each other, the barely-there metal smell a soft lull that kept him floating without water in his bathtub. He closed his eyes and leaned back on the cool marble wall, letting darkness take him. He wouldn't let her win.

It didn't last long. A soft knock, and cheap aftershave in the air.

"Adults don't do this, you know." Bilal's harsh voice broke the quiet. "You can't come apart each time some little thing happens."

This was no little thing. And what did Bilal know? He pictured Bilal, looming over the tub, his short-sleeved shirt neatly pressed and buttoned, shining bald pate, the belt a little too high on the waist, pant creases sharp enough they could hurt anyone they touched. His eyes filled with reproach, and that terrible thing. Pity.

"Come on now. Sit up," Bilal's tone was peremptory.

Maybe he still thought himself an adult in charge of a teen. Exactly how old was Bilal? He didn't know, nor did Bilal. He'd asked Bilal the first time the man had taped up the shallow, hesitant cuts. Bilal had been there, not young, not old, solid like a load-bearing wall each time the roof caved in.

He heard Bilal leave and return scant minutes later, like he knew his trusted housekeeper would. Ice clinked in a glass, and when he opened his eyes, there it was, dark amber held right beneath his chin. He accepted the crystal glass of single malt, let Bilal help him sit straighter, relishing the way that made the cuts unfurl in pain.

"I'm not cleaning up after you again." Bilal picked up the gauze and the antiseptic, and perching on the edge of the tub, patted at the cuts, his hands deliberately brisk.

Bilal would take care of his wounds. Always had.

"You'll be sick again. This has to stop or I'm leaving."

"This is better than the other thing, you keep saying."

"It is the other thing I'm talking about. The last time had better have been the final one. No more. I'm here only because of your father, and he hasn't been alive for years. Remember that."

"Not even if they deserve it? If they exceed the time? If they want more money?"

This one had exceeded her time, was not afraid, coveted his money. Granted, it wasn't Diwali yet, but she met the conditions, and he'd been upset. Quite upset.

Bilal couldn't understand the amount of control it took not to give in. The pain of gazing at them from a distance. Being that close, not closer.

"One more time, I'm out." Bilal stood up, his job done. "You'll be on your own."

CHAPTER FOUR

Arnav

Arnav had known the portly Dr. Meshram for years. The quiet man with his soft, kindly features looked more like a benevolent priest than a forensic officer who examined dead bodies and recorded the results for a living. He smiled, introduced a white-coated man as his new assistant, shook hands with Arnav, and busied himself with thermometers and his camera. A constable followed him, making notes for the *panchnama*—a precise, detailed account of the scene signed by two witnesses from members of the public, without which there would be no case. Courts tended to believe the accused rather than the police.

Meshram hadn't said yet if this body was male or female, but Arnav couldn't help imagining this person's last moments. Did they see it coming? Did they suffer? Did they know the person who did them in? His training and decades of crime scenes had failed to inure him to those first moments of empathy and suffering before the mask of professional calm and feigned indifference set in. And that twinge of fear. Would it be a familiar face? Heaven forbid, a loved one. Soon, it would be twenty-three years since he'd seen his sister's lifeless, bloated face. In the intervening decades, it had endured in his nightmares. Solidified, instead of fading away. As clear in his memory now as in the moment he'd found her.

Arnav watched Dr. Meshram wield a small trowel to remove soil from around the cadaver and place it in a bucket his assistant held for him. He wore a mask and a pair of gloves, and alternated between a brush and the trowel to uncover as much of the body as possible without causing damage. Soon, he gestured to Arnav to use a mask from the forensic examination kit and step closer.

"The head is missing."

Arnav slipped on the mask and leaned into the pit. He could see the leathery black-and-brown shoulders, but only a blackened stump where the neck should have been.

"This will take me some time to uncover. Delicate work, all of this, *kya*?" Dr. Meshram stood up with a groan. He tagged a *kya* at the end of his sentences whenever he wished to emphasize a point. Literally, *what*, but meaning, *don't you agree?*

Arnav agreed, and nodded to show he appreciated the skill required for the task. "Any details on the victim?"

"Based on the shoulder bones, it is either a woman or a teenage boy. My money is on a woman, because the shoulder is narrower, and has less bone development at the muscle attachment site."

"You can't say for sure?"

"Only after I've uncovered the pelvic area. For a woman, the inlet will be open, circular, and the subpubic angle wider."

"Any idea when this body was buried?"

"Could be months or years—the rate of decomposition depends on numerous factors: ambient temperature, the soil, moisture, the body's fat content. The topsoil has already been disturbed here. Impossible to tell the duration of decomposition unless I'm able to extract and transfer the body for a proper postmortem."

"How long will that take?"

"This is a cold case. I sometimes have to buy gloves and masks with my own money—do you think my bosses are going to agree to a rush on this?" Dr. Meshram shrugged, and sank to his knees again.

Cold cases held relatively low priority. "No priority" would be more accurate, unless the case was high profile in some way.

A memory stirred at the back of his mind. Many years ago, he'd helped out on another case around Dussehra. It had rained. That body had remained underground for a great while, but on the basis of the bones, it was a woman. No skull, no hands and feet. In her twenties. They hadn't been able to solve the case. At the time, Arnav was a new constable on his probation at Dadar Police Station.

His brain felt foggy from hunger and lack of sleep, but the details would come back to him.

He turned to Naik, who was taking pictures of the site for the department's record.

"Get someone to look up all unsolved cases involving bodies that were buried in and around Mumbai. Check if any of them were decapitated. Go back twenty years. I think I remember a case that was registered at the Dadar station."

"That long, sir?"

Arnav held back a sigh. Naik meant to ask whether they could spare a constable's hours for cold cases. Another assistant sub-inspector might have raised more questions, but not Naik, the best at her job and at following orders.

"Yes, but keep it quiet for the moment."

These perished women deserved for someone to take notice. His boss would likely throw a fit at the "wasted" police hours, but Arnav had never let that stop him.

"Right, sir. I'll leave the constable here in charge of the scene?"

"For now. We can decide next steps based on Dr. Meshram's input. Take the jeep back with you."

Naik nodded and left. If they could connect this cold case to others, he could advocate for them to receive higher priority.

"Interesting." Dr. Meshram stared at where the assistant had brushed away the soil along the arm.

Arnav craned his neck to figure out what had caught the attention of the pathologist, while trying not to grimace and hold his breath. The putrefying flesh and leathery skin was split at the elbow, from which a bone stuck out. Dr. Meshram was slowly removing soil from where the hand should have been. Instead, there was only a stump at the wrist.

Arnav tamped down the thrill of excitement that being on the right track gave him.

"The bone here doesn't seem naturally broken at the wrist. Someone used an instrument to sever the hand."

"What sort of instrument?"

"I'll need to examine this under better light, and maybe a microscope. You still want to stick your neck out for this case? This is not some fancy western TV show, *kya*? We don't even have goddamned basic protective kits."

"I can't ask you to work against your boss's orders. Totally up to you."

Forensics didn't answer to the rest of the police force. The police called the technicians, who showed up in a van for a consult, collected evidence and the body for postmortem, and left. They took their time. Arnav could only hope for Dr. Meshram's natural curiosity and drive to win out, as on previous cases they had worked together.

Dr. Meshram rose. "I know this isn't what you would like to hear, but we might find more bodies at this site."

"How do you figure that?"

"Consider the vegetation. If you notice that clump"—he pointed to a thriving shrub to the right of where he stood—"it is far greener than the ones beside it. Sometimes a decomposing body enriches the soil, making the vegetation flourish."

"Are you sure about this?"

"Not until I remove the topsoil, but I'd suggest digging there. Better make sure there are no more bodies rather than have these people call us again, *kya*?"

"Excuse me, Inspector."

Arnav turned at the sound of the manager's voice.

Beside the lanky Fancy Suit stood a suave man in casual but exquisitely tailored office wear, feigning patience. The sort of man used to bowing and scraping from others.

"Rahul Taneja." He offered his hand. "Taneja Estate Holdings. I heard about the unfortunate discovery and came to check how I could help. Can we talk?"

Taneja's smile seemed to invite Arnav into a sleek office instead of across the uneven ground of a damp building site in Malad, where a fetid corpse burdened the sea air. They walked away from the others, and Arnav hoped that the breeze would lift the clammy stench.

Taneja owned more than one private jet and must keep a team of lackeys, an entire law firm, to clear any blocks in the path of Taneja Estate Holdings. Why was the man himself here? And on his own?

"Thank you for coming here, Mr. Taneja. I'll inform your manager as soon as the investigation is finished."

"The manager should have mentioned this—we'd like to have some of the foundation in place by Dussehra. You know how these labor forces are—our team will struggle from now until Diwali to get any work done."

Diwali was the festival of lights, but it was also the festival when most of the labor force stayed home.

"I can understand. The forensic officer says we need to make a thorough examination of this site."

"What do you mean? More bodies?" Mr. Taneja lost his urbane, relaxed act.

"I can't say for certain yet."

"Inspector, this is serious business. If we don't move fast enough and end up receiving a stay order from the courts, we'll run into huge losses."

"This is a murder investigation."

"My manager tells me that the person has been dead for a while. Surely we can come to an arrangement?"

Arnav let that pass. He'd vowed not to be provoked if he could help it. Mr. Taneja's "arrangement," the polished version of the usual *chai-pani*, involved a briefcase filled with cash that no doubt sat next to an assistant right now in the back seat of his car. Arnav marshaled calm and put on the expression that served him well while conducting interrogations.

"I think you'll agree that the dead deserve justice." Arnav paused to clear his throat. "We'd want that for our own dear ones."

"All that's fine. You can remove the body—continue your examination in peace. Let us do our job."

"This site isn't far from the mangroves, Mr. Taneja. Is that why you're anticipating a stay order on the construction? Has the State Mangrove Cell been involved?"

Land-grabbing mafia had made inroads into Malad. Political corruption ran rampant, eating into the mangroves every year. This site, a short walk from Aksa beach, could easily be part of such a racket. Arnav resolved to follow up with Naik about the site documentation.

"Inspector . . . ah . . . Rajput, there's no need to threaten me with the officials from the Mangrove Cell. You'll find that I have contacts far beyond your reach. Vacate these premises and we won't have any trouble. Good evening."

Taneja turned and was about to walk away, when Arnav said, "You'll find that your contacts know me already. We'll remove the police tape once we're done. From the way you've come running, this place might have a few other things buried here besides dead bodies, Mr. Taneja."

"You'll regret this," Taneja said, without turning back. He stalked off, dialing on a phone the size of a tablet.

Returning to Dr. Meshram, Arnav recounted his chat with the no-longer-affable tycoon. After Dr. Meshram promised to do what he could, Arnav instructed his constable to set up a large perimeter and arrange for help from the station to secure the site.

Arnav sent the preliminary findings to Naik, his head growing heavy with the stench. He strolled toward Aksa beach, hoping the sea air would clear his muddled thoughts.

A long beach amid a city, Aksa was clean and well maintained despite its ill repute of being haunted by demons from both worlds after nightfall. Regular police patrols urged civilians to not linger by the seaside in the late hours. For this moment right before sunset, though, Aksa put on a family-oriented, welcoming face.

Letting his shoes sink into the sand, Arnav dialed a coded contact on his phone, sending out feelers to his team of *khabri*, informers he trusted to bring to him the pulse of Mumbai's so-called underworld. The dons who once financed Bollywood in order to get their black money laundered to white had mostly reinvented themselves. They ran businesses now, having turned corporate—alternately extorting or facilitating successful businessmen of Taneja's ilk. The underworld, a parallel hell on earth brimming with crime and filth, hadn't faded entirely away.

If the dead body Dr. Meshram had uncovered with such care had secrets to tell, one of his *khabri* could have heard snippets of relevant information. They were small-time criminals, ex-criminals, their relatives—the fringes of the city's criminal activity. Some of them were teens, and answered with fake accents at his first ring, and said *hayylo*. Like that girl-woman entwined in his life long ago. Tara.

Arnav flinched from that strand of thought. He focused on his surroundings instead—a few children in rags chased each other, their shrieks rising in the salt-laden air. Arnav was named after the sea. Despite its waters slick with oil and refuse, and the noise of the city muffling its soothing wave and crash, the Arabian Sea was one of the few things he loved about Mumbai.

He checked his private phone. A text from Shinde.

Get here now, you wrinkled prune. Your girlfriend has cooked a
feast, the kababs are ready, but we can't eat till you're here. The
kids are starving.

He'd forgotten. Nandini was cooking for his friend and colleague
Hemant Shinde and his family this evening. The stench from the body
seemed to have entered his lungs. He had no appetite left.

I'll be late, he typed in. Body offense case came up. It wasn't a lie.

Hurry up and get your ass here, you fucker. Your girlfriend and
my wife will poison us if you don't reach home soon.

Genteel as ever, his childhood friend, with no dearth of swear
words. For once, Shinde was right. He should hurry. It was already an
hour after he was supposed to reach Nandini's place.

He didn't feel up to a happy evening of feasting and laughter.
Evening joggers and young couples holding hands thronged the shore,
where so many of Bollywood's famous movies had been shot—this was
a place he'd walked with Tara, holding hands, chased her when she ran.

He turned away and found himself stopping under the light of a
pao bhaji stall, the soft *pao* and fried potatoes spicing the air. Maybe
a plate of *pao* would set him right, ground him in the present. The
families gathered at the counter spotted his uniform and made way as
he approached.

He bought himself a few *pao*. The band of children who were playing tag earlier roamed about, selling pink cotton candy, droopy red
roses, key chains. They seemed to range from six to twelve years old, but
their undernourished bodies and grown-up eyes made it hard to tell.
They wouldn't come willingly if he called them, having learned early not
to trust a khaki uniform. Arnav thrust some money at the befuddled
stall owner and asked him to call the children and serve them their fill
of *pao bhaji*.

"Don't tell them it is from me. I don't need the bother."

His sister had done this from time to time, much to the annoyance of his parents. He accepted his own warm paper plate laden with the gleaming *pao* buns fried in butter, and spiced *bhaji* made of potatoes and vegetables, but couldn't bring himself to eat. He returned it to the stall owner, assuring him the food was fine—he'd remembered he had an appointment.

He must head toward Nandini's place sooner or later. The later he went, the longer Shinde's tirades. He might as well try to enjoy a good dinner before he forgot all about decent meals for the next few days of madness leading up to the Dussehra rallies. He tapped on Nandini's address in Bandra among the favorites in his app, and called a cab.

Before walking off, he turned to watch the children gather over their plates, laughing. His older sister used to laugh like that—all noise and no grace. His parents had named her Asha. Hope. She'd begged him to bring her *pao bhaji* and *sevpuri* the last time he'd seen her alive.

CHAPTER FIVE

MUMBAI DRISHTIKON NEWS

Business Section

Real estate tycoon Rahul Taneja tops Siparu list, gains 26.4 percent in net worth

9:30 PM IST 6 October, Mumbai.

Siparu, India's most authoritative rich-list and philanthropy-list provider, has released its report on the real estate sector this month.

The biggest gainer in rank this year was Rahul Taneja, the founder and CEO of Taneja Estate Holdings (TEH). His net worth went up by 26.4 percent to ₹45,723 crore (more than 6.1 billion USD). The 50 percent rise in TEH's share price supported the growth in Taneja's wealth, the report said.

According to this report, India's top 100 realty developers' wealth rose by 20 percent year-on-year, and Rahul Taneja now tops the list. The list is based on the valuation of real estate businesses owned by the entrepreneurs as of September this year, although their personal liabilities, or debt, were not considered for calculating the net worth.

The news of Taneja's topping the Siparu list has come as a welcome reprieve to TEH because Taneja has been in the news for all the wrong reasons this past year. TEH stocks tanked following the uproar during the MeToo movement, with several B-list Bollywood actresses accusing Rahul Taneja of making physical advances during the lavish parties he threw at his Malabar Hills mansion. Taneja responded to the allegations with pointed rebuttal and has filed defamation suits against several accusers.

The rise in his Siparu listing and the news of his engagement to Kittu Virani, mother of the Bollywood movie star brothers Karan and Rehaan Virani, has indeed helped TEH stocks, which rallied 17 percent to their highest level in nearly two years.

CHAPTER SIX

ARNAV

Once Arnav reached the tall gates of Nandini's apartment complex in Bandra, he dismissed the car so he could make calls without anyone listening in. On a given day, he fielded more than two hundred calls, about fifty from his *khabri*. He'd just missed a call from his best, and most expensive, source.

When he called back, a hoarse voice answered. *"Ji, saab, boliye."*

It belonged to a man who identified himself only as Ali. Arnav liked these conversations. Basic and to the point. No attempt at a greeting—straightaway *please tell me, sir*.

Arnav spoke about the body and offered to pay for relevant information. He also asked about gossip on Taneja, and any connections he might have with the less savory parts of Mumbai. The call was brief and ended by the time he reached the door to Nandini's apartment. It stood ajar. He could hear Shinde's children, a boy and a girl, laughing out loud.

He pushed at the familiar carved door knocker that spelled WELCOME, hoping to walk in unannounced and freshen up before he met anyone. Nandini opened the door, paused for a second, and broke into a smile. Most times, Arnav found her face ordinary—her eyes not large, her eyebrows thin, her nose snub, her jaw square—but when she smiled one of her rare, full smiles, she was almost beautiful. Other women in her place wouldn't have smiled right then, but Nandini wasn't any other woman.

"Hemant Shinde is hungry and making more noise than his children." Nandini smirked. "He's gone to wash his hands. We were about to start."

Shinde was older than him, his childhood friend and mentor. The man took his role seriously—not withholding any insult whatsoever when they sparred—whether at the karate dojo, or the chess table over strong cups of tea. He was the one responsible for Arnav joining the police force.

"Sorry I'm late. Tell him I'll join you soon." Arnav shut the door behind him. "I need a bath. It was one of those days."

She knew what he meant by *one of those days*, because he said it often enough. Proximity to a dead person. He sneaked into the master bedroom. The crime scene stench clung to his clothes, and he didn't want it to creep onto the children.

Arnav kept spare clothes in Nandini's closet, and some of his toiletries sat in a haphazard pile in the bathroom closet. Tara wouldn't have stood for such mess. A wry smile hovered on Arnav's lips as he shed his clothes.

Tara cooked and cleaned for him because it had pleased her. She'd enjoyed playing house with him—a pretend game of domestic routine that lasted months without any promises, or words even, until one day, she vanished. She had left years ago. That dead body was not her. He had to stop letting her wander into his mind. Arnav stood under the shower and let the warm water sluice away his memories.

When he stepped out of the bedroom in a fresh set of T-shirt and jeans, Senior Inspector Hemant Shinde made as if to rise from the dining table. "Look who is finally here. Welcome, Avi *saab*!"

Shinde appeared his usual sarcastic self, curly hair cropped back into a severe crew cut, twinkling eyes, salt-and-pepper mustache. Arnav smiled back at his friend and then ignored him altogether, saying namaste to Shinde's wife and exchanging fist bumps with the children, the girl a teenager at thirteen, and the seven-year-old boy full of mischief. They seemed to have finished their dinner, and asked if they could watch TV.

At a scowl from her husband, Shinde's wife took them to the TV and switched on a cartoon channel, and Nandini passed Arnav a plate. Arnav let Shinde's teasing and recriminations wash over him, followed by the nonstop tirade about work problems. Nandini was the one who should have been upset—she wasn't pleased about his tardiness, it was clear, but she hadn't made a fuss about it.

She sat there chatting with Shinde's wife, whom Arnav called *Vaeeni*. Sister-in-law, in Marathi. She wore orange flowers in her long, braided hair, and a traditional, gold-bordered saree. Everyone had forgotten her name, Sujata—all Shinde's friends called her the distant, respectful *Vaeeni*. *Vaeeni's* gaze remained lowered, like most other times, her hands busy serving the table, making sure the glasses were filled. He wondered how Tara would have fit in here, at this table.

"We'll be there the next time this Rasool *Bhai* makes a move." Shinde picked up another leg of tandoori chicken, ready to take a bite. "We'll catch his men red-handed when they are up to their tricks at Versova."

Rasool *Bhai* was Rasool Mohsin. *Bhai*, brother. Except in Mumbai the word held altogether different meanings. A hooligan, a gang boss like Rasool, or a famous don like Vijayan, a part of the underworld, who escaped by either skirting the law or making the evidence disappear.

"Let's not talk about you and your encounters at the dinner table, Shinde," Nandini cut in. "You don't need a journalist on your tail now, do you?"

Shinde had developed the reputation for being an "encounter specialist"—because of the goons he'd shot in his career—a sobriquet made famous by numerous Bollywood movies in which a Mumbai inspector captured a don and his gunmen and staged a shoot-out, executing them before they reached the courts. Shinde had taken over as the senior inspector at the Versova Police Station less than a year ago, and aimed to make his mark in the new jurisdiction.

While Shinde responded with a smart repartee of his own—asking Nandini to set aside her journalism at home—Arnav spooned food into his mouth, the spiced lentils garnished with coriander, the way he liked, the way Tara used to make them. Tara loved the tang of coriander and often bought bunches of the herb, filling his parents' old bungalow kitchen with the refreshing lemony fragrance.

She would insist they eat in bed—fry up a batch of potato and vegetable fritters and make him feed her the warm, crunchy snacks dipped in coriander chutney. He would remind her they were both working out, dieting. As a constable in those days, who was to sit for internal exams for promotions, he needed to be in peak condition. She'd laugh, tell him she'd added mint to the chutney, a digestive. That even her fritters were fried in healthy oil.

"Hold my waist," she'd order him as he helped train her to do push-ups. She hadn't said so in as many words, but she longed to be an actress and followed their diets. He'd lie on a mat and let her practice push-ups on top of him, balancing on his shoulders. A game at first. Then, not a game after they kissed and it all turned into a different kind of workout.

A slap on Arnav's shoulders made him cough, and he blinked. When Shinde spoke, Arnav made himself focus on his friend's words.

"Why don't you answer?" Shinde said. "Your girlfriend has gone to so much trouble, shouldn't you give her a compliment at least?"

"Yes." Arnav gazed at Nandini, who laughed at what *Vaeeni* had just said. He wanted to ask Shinde if he gave his wife compliments, too. Shinde was right, though. Nandini *was* his girlfriend, and deserved all the praise. Tara was long gone. Even had she remained in his life, she couldn't have been here—she was too forthright to be like *Vaeeni*, too unpolished to be Nandini's equal.

It irked him that each time he found a woman's dead body, he wondered if that was the sort of end she'd come to. If it was the reason she'd vanished.

"I'll call you," Arnav said, once he'd helped Nandini clear up. Shinde and his family had left an hour earlier.

"I'm the one who calls you. Stay tonight?"

"Can't right now. Maybe next week?"

"All right," she said, pausing when she spotted the packet of his unwashed uniform on the table.

"I'll get it washed. Come back once you're off duty."

"You know I'm on a case." He picked up the packet.

"All the more reason to leave it here. I'll have it laundered. Come and sleep here when you're not in the office. Stewing by yourself won't do you any good."

"Quit nagging." He moved out of her arms. "You're not my wife."

He regretted the words as soon as they'd left his mouth. She wasn't, but only because he hadn't asked her in the two years they'd known each other.

"I'm sorry." He stroked her waist. "Thanks for dinner, and for inviting Shinde's family. See you soon."

He hated who he'd become: a man with no family, no desire for one. Content to receive without giving anything in return, other than in bed. But by the time he'd taken the lift downstairs and called to check in at the police station, any stray thoughts of Nandini had vanished. All he remembered was the victim, a headless body turning into mud, and the informer Ali, who'd promised to call back soon.

CHAPTER SEVEN

ARNAV

Arnav sipped a cup of strong black tea as he listened to his team's reports. He should have stayed back at Nandini's last evening, not returned to the office near midnight. But as Shinde said, Arnav couldn't keep away from cases involving dead or missing women. He spent each spare minute working them, often to the detriment of others.

He'd combed through his old notes to pinpoint the exact date of the case he'd remembered helping with as a constable at Dadar Police Station—a woman's bones, without the head, hands, and feet.

Once all the officers had reeled off their updates, Arnav passed a slip of paper to Naik. "On the Aksa case, look up the files from Dadar Police Station from August 2003."

"Right, sir. No luck so far, so this will help."

"What about the land deeds for the site at Aksa beach?"

"Land mafia, sir. Vijayan had grabbed the site years ago, heaping it up with debris, but Taneja Estate Holdings bought the land from the state government at throwaway prices instead of paying Vijayan. Taneja has since received death threats, and requested police protection. Someone has been using a local environmental nonprofit to bring in stay orders to prevent Taneja from building on the site."

"Give me the names in the ministries involved with the permission for sale."

"Sir, the current Home Minister, Mr. Namit Gokhale, was in the Urban Development Department then. He signed off on the sale."

Arnav made a note of this. He'd tried to get in touch with Taneja all morning with no success.

"Who else is named in this spa project at Aksa? Anyone we can access?"

"It appears his fiancée, Kittu Virani, won the contract to design and furnish the interiors of the spa. She's mostly known as the mother of her sons, Rehaan and Karan Virani."

Karan Virani was a name from long ago. Tara and her slightly over-weight, much older friend Zoya were mad devotees of that movie star. Zoya—he hadn't thought of her in ages. She'd disappeared the same night as Tara. The other bar girls claimed they had run away. Or at least that's what Shetty, their Malayali hulk of a boss, had said to them.

"We could go, sir?" Naik looked nonplussed.

He should have slept last night. His lack of sleep was showing him up.

"You'll have to repeat that, Naik."

Arnav let a hint of apology seep into his voice. He must focus on cornering Taneja. Naik repeated herself: one of Kittu Virani's interior decoration projects, a restaurant, was opening that night. Her family was likely to be there, along with her fiancé.

The restaurant launch was invite only, but as an inspector of the Mumbai Police, Arnav had his own sources. He thanked Naik and made a few calls until he hit pay dirt. He'd have to break out the sleeker of his two evening shirts tonight, and say hello to Taneja and his fiancée.

CHAPTER EIGHT

BILAL

The boy had been jittery lately, and Bilal didn't like that one bit. It never boded well, especially not this close to Diwali.

Each year, the boy promised him that it would be the last. And Bilal repeated the words to *Bhai*. He didn't believe them himself anymore, but what choice did he have? On some nights it wasn't the boy's nightmares but his own that woke him up, and he threatened to quit. The boy called his bluff each time.

At the end of the day, it was not pity or duty that held him back against his conscience.

In front of the world, the boy leaned on no one, but it was a different story behind closed doors. With no family to call his own, Bilal needed to be needed.

He was terrified of each event, loathing himself for helping clean up after. But when the boy cried out for him at night, in the throes of a nightmare, it made Bilal feel large and powerful, a man who could protect his boy from all menace. The menace he knew about, the ones he didn't.

He used his burner phone to dial the number he'd been given. After brief greetings to an assistant, he was able to speak with the *Bhai* himself.

"We had no call planned today," *Bhai* said. "What do you need?"

The man's boyish, high voice was at odds with his fearsome reputation in many quarters. Bilal wished the *Bhai* a long and healthy life, then broached the topic.

"Of course, it's been taken care of," *Bhai* said. "Are you trying to insult me?"

"No, *Bhai*, not at all."

"You're never late on payments, so I'll let it slide. Never question me again."

CHAPTER NINE

ARNAV

Nursing a drink for an entire evening usually put Arnav in a bad mood. He made it a point never to get drunk, but he did savor an occasional glass of wine. The fresh-lime soda he'd ordered, after a cursory glance at the menu without prices, tasted like dishwater. His contact had wrangled him onto the guest list, but hadn't showed up yet.

Arnav aimed to keep this as casual and nonconfrontational as he could—his boss would not thank him for riling up a tycoon and his movie-star-mom fiancée, which might make headlines. Not the kind of attention he wanted on himself or his career. It called for a lighter touch.

Arnav took stock of his situation—seated on a barstool, holding his drink, returning interested glances from a woman or two. He must fit in—a man on a night out, not a police officer.

The Mediterranean music was muted, waiters appeared solicitous and spoke in hushed whispers as they cleared plates or refilled glasses, the lighting dim and strategically placed to make faces glow.

Kittu was surrounded by Bollywood types, and despite Arnav's complete lack of interest in Bollywood, he thought he recognized a few faces from screens. Nandini spoke often of these events, the air-kissing, the flicking of hair, the exaggerated laughter, the expensive fragrances. Gleaming watches and jewelry.

At a dark corner table right next to his barstool sat a large man, beard and sunglasses covering most of his face, his thick hair tied in a ponytail. His stance seemed to telegraph to everyone to stay away, and they did. He scrolled on his phone and Arnav let him be, focusing on Kittu instead, keeping an eye on the distant entrance for his friend who could take him to Kittu's table.

Kittu Virani was like no woman he'd ever seen. It was impossible to say how old she was.

Under the mood lighting, her rich dark mane glinted auburn, but her face seemed smooth to the point of ripeness, skin taut as a drum underneath a thick layer of makeup. In her tight black dress, she seemed flat where other women were curved, and vice versa—like a grotesque voodoo doll.

Arnav gave himself a talking-to: Women came in different shapes, his sister Asha had told him. All were beautiful.

"You're watching her, too?"

The question gave Arnav a start. Deep and chesty, the voice had emerged from the guest he'd noticed earlier. Arnav didn't know how to respond, so he gave a half shrug and a nod that could have meant anything at all.

"She has no idea what she looks like, does she? All those beauty filters have turned her head," the man grumbled, tossing back what seemed like a large whiskey.

"She is popular and successful." Arnav was not sure where this conversation was going or why he was defending Kittu Virani to a stranger, but it wouldn't hurt to know more about her, especially from someone who was clearly not a fan.

"Those are not qualifications. Most of it lies here"—the guest drew a line across his broad forehead, in the typical Indian gesture that meant fate—"and the rest, all about how low you're willing to stoop."

"She's done a decent job with this restaurant." Arnav sized up the soft lights, the solid wooden tables, the chairs that suggested style and comfort even to his untrained eye.

"She has hired a good team." The stranger waved to a waiter. "I'll give you that."

Once the waiter left with an order of "another of the same," Arnav decided to nudge a little and see where that led.

"Why do you hate her so much?"

"She's a woman, isn't she?" Arnav's new friend barked out a bitter laugh. "What's there to love?"

Arnav kept his expression noncommittal—not many people did well with silences. This brooding patron might prove no exception.

"Don't you ask too many questions?" The man's voice slurred. He seemed familiar.

"I'm not from the press." Arnav leaned back on the swivel barstool. "And even if I were, I have no clue who you are. Your secret is safe with me."

"My job here is done—I can tell the director I managed to blend in, and throw off everyone but you. You know who I am, right? You must be from the police."

The guy spoke with a smile, which faded when Arnav said, "Guilty as charged. Here to meet a friend, who invited me to the opening."

"I see. No wonder. Well, it is no secret. There have been so many blind items. I have no love lost for my darling mother."

A moment later, it all clicked into place. Blind items: the stories Nandini had told him were anonymous hatchet jobs, published by film magazines. Behind the beard and the sunglasses was Rehaan Virani. Arnav let his surprise show and exaggerated it a little. A man who thought he'd gotten the better of you was likely to talk longer.

"Sorry about that. It seems quite impossible, living under such scrutiny."

"Why don't you join me?" Rehaan gestured to the chair opposite him.

Arnav didn't wait. He could not give Rehaan Virani time to change his mind.

"You work in the police? Which station?"

"Malwani. I'm Inspector Arnav Singh Rajput."

"Do you only drink soda?"

"I'm on night shift later, after this event."

"This event will drag on—my mother knows everyone in Bollywood, and all their distant relatives."

"Her fiancé doesn't seem to be here."

If he could not reach Kittu, her son could provide a few details.

"Rahul? Hah. Never around. That's the one thing I like about him."

So Rehaan liked Rahul Taneja about as much as he liked his mother.

"He's a top name in the real estate business." Arnav sipped on his soda.

"He's also fourteen years younger than her. Forty-two."

By all accounts, Rehaan was in his early thirties. Arnav watched Rehaan as the Bollywood star gulped down some more of his whiskey. That might explain why Rehaan was speaking with a perfect stranger. Arnav could have been anyone. Rehaan hadn't asked to see his ID.

"They go on like it's a love match. It is a match all right, but I doubt love has anything to do with it. I can see why she'd go for Rahul, but I don't get what's in it for him. He could have had anyone at all. Women half her age and twice as beautiful."

"There have been rumors about him," Arnav said.

"Not rumors. He did molest women. All the guests here know that, but won't say a word. Maybe that's why he's marrying her. If she decides to quash a rumor, it won't survive."

"She's working with him, as well."

"She is?" Rehaan sat up straighter and signaled the waiter for another drink. "You don't want another soda?"

"No, thank you, I'm fine." Arnav held up his glass, which was still half-full. "And yes, Ms. Virani is doing the interiors for a spa that Taneja Estate Holdings is building on the Aksa beach."

"Ah, that's the one she was grumbling about. She had a row about it with Rahul. I tune her out half the time."

"I wanted to speak to Mr. Taneja."

"What about? Is that why you're here today?" Rehaan leaned forward. "On official business? What's he done this time? A woman?"

Arnav hadn't anticipated the sudden barrage of questions. Before he could answer, Rehaan's phone buzzed on the table, and he dismissed the call. Arnav didn't get a peek at the number, but he soon understood who it was. Rehaan glanced up, and Arnav followed his gaze to Kittu. Rehaan waved at her when she gestured for him to join her at her table, and stood up.

"I must go and do her bidding. Is there a number I could call you on, though?"

Arnav passed Rehaan a business card and left. He'd not been able to speak with Taneja, but he now understood a few things about Taneja's fiancée, and had passed his card to Taneja's future stepson. With more facts in place, he could confront the businessman. Outside the hotel, back in Mumbai's cloying, moisture-laden air, he dialed Dr. Meshram to ask him for updates.

CHAPTER TEN

ARNAV

Scramble around the letters of your name, and you're the demon Ravan, Asha had teased Arnav during their childhood scuffles. He'd definitely worked like a demon for the two days since that afternoon at the Aksa beach. The extra work on Dussehra arrangements on top of his current caseload had kept him on his toes.

The streets had been crowded due to Navratri, the nine days of Hindu celebration and dances that led up to the tenth day of Dussehra. Hindus and Muslims lived cheek by jowl in many parts of Mumbai, but the involvement of political parties raised tensions, and sudden conflagrations emerged during festivals. The Malwani station was located in a "sensitive" coastal area with an 80 percent Muslim population. Militants from international terrorist organizations had previously radicalized local youths.

The constant vigilance on top of his routine duties had taken its toll. At 7:30 p.m., Arnav was ready to pack it in when his phone rang. About to ignore it, he noticed the caller ID and answered.

"Good evening, Dr. Meshram. I called you yesterday, but you didn't answer."

"I'm sorry I saw your call too late, but I have an update on the Aksa case now."

"Yes?"

"We'd discussed exploring other parts of the site. I didn't find anything at the spot I'd mentioned. On a hunch, I checked at a different location a few feet away." Dr. Meshram sounded nervous, and paused.

"Dr. Meshram?"

"I found two other bodies. Similar characteristics. No skull on either, no hands or feet. I would have called earlier, but I wanted to be sure. These might be even older."

Taneja wasn't going to start construction anytime soon. If they'd discovered three bodies, there could be more. Is that why Taneja himself had rushed to the site?

"Any further details?"

"The first victim was a woman, possibly in her twenties. Height about five feet, four inches, but I can't be certain because of the missing head and feet. Haven't been able to do a proper postmortem yet."

"Do we know how long the bodies have been in the ground? An approximate date of death will help me scan missing persons records."

"It will take time. My assistant will go to the site tomorrow to collect more soil samples."

"We'll keep the place closed for now. Keep me updated."

After he cut the call, Arnav dialed Naik's extension and asked her about that old unsolved case file from Dadar Police Station. It would cost him, but it might also bring justice to wronged women. He felt a bleak smile spread across his face. At a world-weary thirty-six years old, few things brought him satisfaction anymore.

Naik entered, file in hand, and Arnav straightened his expression.

"We couldn't find the case from Dadar, but here's one from Azad Nagar Police Station, sir. Woman's body. No hands, head, or feet. Decomposed beyond recognition. Found in a sewer."

Another woman. Three at Aksa, and the one he remembered at Dadar.

"This case was solved?"

"No, sir," Naik said. "It wasn't followed up."

"How do you mean?"

"That body was found in November 2008, sir. On the morning of the twenty-sixth."

Twenty-sixth of November. A date Arnav would never forget. Ten Lashkar-e-Tayiba terrorists had docked at Mumbai, hijacked cars including a police van, and struck Mumbai at five locations simultaneously, shooting dead a hundred and forty Indians and twenty-five foreign tourists. The terrorists executed American and British passport holders in two luxury hotels. Fifteen policemen lost their lives. Naik's husband had lost an arm.

The Azad Nagar station was at the epicenter of the disaster that had brought Mumbai to its knees, but that still didn't explain why the case wasn't investigated later.

"Did they make a *panchnama*?"

"Yes, sir. We have the details here. Inspector Atul Gawde was the investigating officer. The body had no clothes, no head or feet, and was cut up in several places."

"So when you say no follow-up, what does that mean?"

"Still unsolved, sir. Lack of evidence. They couldn't identify the body. And Inspector Gawde was transferred out."

"You're sure there's no mention of a similar case at Dadar Police Station?"

"That case might be from before we computerized all entries. We might need to hunt down a physical copy."

"I'm familiar with that station." Arnav had begun his career as a constable-in-training there.

"We can send a constable, sir. Also, Mr. Taneja called our station. I think he's spoken to Mhatre sir."

"Thanks for the heads-up." Arnav gathered his papers. "I'm done for this evening. I'll head to Dadar."

If he found this file, that would make it five nearly identical cases, spread over decades: Dadar, Azad Nagar, and the remains at Aksa.

"Who's going to Dadar?" Senior Inspector Ravi Mhatre walked into the room.

At six feet two, Arnav's boss Mhatre was easily one of the tallest in the Mumbai Police Force.

"Hello, sir." Arnav stood up and cut a salute, as was expected of him. "I'll be going."

As a matter of procedure, Mhatre summoned Arnav to his room, so this was new.

"Good. I don't have a car this evening, so you can drop me at my event."

"Was there anything else, sir?"

"We can talk on the way."

Arnav drove out of the station with his boss beside him in his trusty old car. Asha was learning to drive it the year they lost her. Ravi Mhatre didn't comment on the state of the beat-up vehicle, letting his expression speak instead. He'd already refused Arnav's offer to drop him home in Bandra after Arnav finished at Dadar Police Station.

In the last three years of working with him, Mhatre had proven to be more of a chess king. An indispensable official, but not an attack dog. Arnav couldn't complain, though. Mhatre had backed him up more than once when he was on shaky ground after his transfer from the Crime Branch to the Malwani station.

For several minutes Arnav's boss kept busy on the phone as he navigated the traffic out of Malad and into Goregaon, then Mhatre leaned forward to adjust the radio knob. Music burst forth. *Akhiyon ke jharokhon se*, of all songs.

The lilting number was about a couple's love, an unlikely pair who married despite the odds. The movie ended with the woman's death. That song had played a long time ago when Tara had flicked on the TV in his bedroom. They were cuddled together under the covers, her soft body relaxed against his, the scent of her freshly washed hair wrapped about him. He'd watched her staring at the screen, dreamy eyed.

"What's wrong?" She was quick to catch on to his changes in mood.

"This doesn't end well. Let's watch another."

He'd told himself he didn't want her to waste time on a sad movie, but even then, he'd known that wasn't the real reason.

"It ends well, I'm sure." Tara's heart-shaped face had seemed at peace for once. "They're together."

"Not in the end." He'd gathered her close and changed the channel, hoping she'd forget about the movie, never watch the heartbreak. She suffered enough at work, and terrifyingly enough, he'd nearly killed her in his bed that afternoon.

He'd woken up to her fists beating against his chest. He'd been in the grip of another nightmare. Joshi. He'd battled to strangle Neelesh Joshi, but in his sleep had ended up grabbing Tara by the throat.

"Joshi sir would not be pleased."

The words jolted Arnav back to where he was, in his car with the senior inspector, who did not look pleased. Joshi sir could be only one man, Joint Commissioner of Crime Neelesh Joshi, a top dog in Mumbai Police. The boogeyman from Arnav's nightmares. Arnav arranged his face into what he hoped was an agreeable expression, and turned to his boss, placing his bet on Mhatre's habit of repeating himself to drive a point home.

"Rahul Taneja is a trusted name in Mumbai business circles. A big supporter of Mumbai Police initiatives. Commissioner Joshi would be quite upset if he knew you've been bothering Mr. Taneja."

During their weekly meeting, Arnav had given a brief on the Aksa case to Mhatre, including the fact that Taneja Estate Holdings was involved in the construction at the site, with no major reaction from his boss. Taneja's call had clearly riled Mhatre up, worried him about the commissioner. Taneja probably kept Neelesh Joshi on speed dial.

The car sat trapped in a traffic jam, and the radio mercifully switched to a peppy dance number. Arnav turned the radio down so Mhatre could hear him clearly.

"Sir, I've spoken to Mr. Taneja just once," Arnav said, "when he visited the crime scene. He hasn't responded to any of my calls. I checked in with Forensics today. Dr. Meshram has found two more bodies at the Aksa site, resembling the first one."

Arnav kept his eyes on the road ahead, but he could feel Mhatre's glare burn a hole right through him.

Finally, Mhatre said, "Your report specified that the land was disputed and had laid abandoned for decades. Anyone at all could be involved with those bodies."

"Right, sir. I've simply followed the standard process of investigation."

"Never forget that we're public servants, Rajput. Our role is to help people, not cause a bother."

Arnav suppressed a smile. Help people, indeed. Mumbai Police was trying to revamp its image, make the force sound more public-facing, friendly, but the macho reputation created by decades of Bollywood movies remained.

"Yes, sir." Arnav moved the car into gear as the traffic let up in front of him. Arguing wouldn't help, so he changed the subject.

"Sir, do you know Inspector Atul Gawde?"

Mhatre switched off the radio. Interesting. Arnav waited for his boss to speak.

"Why do you ask?"

Arnav spoke at length about Gawde, the inspector at the Azad Nagar station, who couldn't close the case with a striking resemblance to the one in Aksa. Shortly after, Gawde was shunted to the Local Arms Division, a low-profile department of Mumbai Police that provided men for security arrangements at various events.

Mhatre's face hardened, and Arnav wished he wasn't driving and could scrutinize the other man's expression. Arnav couldn't say why, but his instinct warned him to weigh each word spoken from then on.

"You're saying someone has been beheading women and leaving them in graves for all these years, in different police jurisdictions? Gawde found a body similar to the ones Dr. Meshram excavated from Aksa?"

"It is possible, sir. I remember another case from earlier, when I was a constable at the Dadar Police Station. We can't locate that case file in the system, so I'll try tracing the physical copy." Arnav paused, easing his car forward from a traffic light. "What happened with Inspector Gawde, sir?"

"That was a punishment posting," Mhatre said. "I heard whispers about not following rules."

Silence reigned in the car until Arnav steered into a lane—the address in Dadar Mhatre had given him.

"For the moment," Mhatre's tone shifted to that arrogant timbre he often used when issuing an order, "I think we have more immediate priorities, Rajput. Let Taneja have his site back. Focus on the mountain of files on your desk."

"This isn't one body, sir. There are several. The killer could be at large and hunting women right now."

"We don't know that. You're not due for a promotion for a while, but you know it all adds up. Consider this a warning."

Fascinating man, his boss. Mhatre had just warned Arnav against conducting actual police work on women's bones being dug up from the ground. Nothing had changed since Asha's death.

Arnav's phone vibrated on the dashboard, but he declined the call. He'd dial back as soon as he dropped Mhatre. It was Ali.

CHAPTER ELEVEN

ARNAV

Arnav parked his car outside Dadar Police Station. Little had changed inside the premises in more than a decade, other than the computers that had sprung up on the desks of the sub-inspectors, who typed their reports in Marathi instead of writing them by hand. Arnav discovered his old friend Tukaram hunched over one such device at the desk farthest from the door.

"On night duty as usual?" he asked the skinny man, who was hollowed out by life and a love of cheap arrack. Sub-Inspector Tukaram's uniform hung off his shoulders.

"Keeps me from the bottle, my wife says." Tukaram looked up and grinned. "Your assistant said you needed a file? You could have sent a constable."

Tukaram paused to arrange for tea for Arnav, and Arnav passed him a note with the year and what he remembered of the case details. "I wanted to see you."

Arnav had missed his friend, it was true, but Tukaram was also an invaluable resource. His remarkable memory helped him recall cases going back decades. He knew what went on with each constable and officer at his station, and many others besides.

"I keep hearing about you, you know. Don't go thinking you're not on my radar." Tukaram took Arnav's note, placed it beside him, and continued typing on his computer, a slow one-fingered tap at a time. "I'll go get it for you after I finish this. Hmm. 2003. It will take some searching."

"Thank you. I'll wait."

"You need to live it up a little, see," his gangly friend elaborated. "It is, what, past nine on a Saturday evening and instead of roaming around Juhu-Chowpatty with a pretty-pretty girl, here you are, searching for dead people. No life in Mumbai Police, I tell you."

"That's true." Arnav laughed. "I'm talking to you instead."

Tukaram liked to tell people what he thought of them, and the more he talked, the chattier he got. Arnav needed his friend to talk today.

"What?" Tukaram's brows shot up in mock annoyance. "Now that you've won two-three bravery medals, become an inspector, and served at the Crime Branch, you're too good for old Tukaram, is it?"

"Not at all. A few minutes ago, my boss told me off for working cold cases while fresh murders pile high at my desk."

"You have no clue when to keep your mouth shut," the older man said. "Shoot first, ask questions later kind of man you are, Rajput. They keep transferring you. How come you've not been transferred these last three years? Ravi Mhatre not giving you any trouble, huh?"

"He's all right," Arnav said. "So far. We'll see. I just dropped him to a whiskey-tasting night."

While turning his car around, Arnav had spotted the large placard outside the restaurant Mhatre had entered, announcing the event in cursive script.

"There's a man who knows his drink," Tukaram said.

Arnav's phone flashed with Ali's number, so he excused himself to step outside and talk.

"*Ji, saab.*" The usual Ali greeting. "Sorry I couldn't speak when you returned my call."

"Tell me," Arnav said.

"I've heard chatter about a regular contract. To get rid of a *lafda* like the one you talked about. Around this time of year. Dussehra-Diwali."

"Are you sure?"

"It is hush-hush. Top-level work. The fellow I spoke to is with *Bhai*'s team, but not high level enough. They have to bury the body so it is never traced, not toss it into the sea like usual."

That did sound like the remains at Aksa.

"You're saying this is recent. You mean your *Bhai* has taken the contract?"

"I don't know for sure, *saab*. This man was drunk and blabbering."

Ali's words brought on a familiar pang of disquiet and ferment. The cadavers at Aksa might make a cold case, but if an established contract for body disposal had been renewed this week, it meant someone had killed again.

"Keep an eye out," Arnav said. "Anything on the other big man?"

Even though he used burner phones and so did Ali, it was safer not to name Taneja now, especially after Mhatre's warning.

"There is, *saab*, I'm sure. Big-time real estate in Mumbai means land mafia. He won't get his hands dirty himself, so it will take a while to dig. I have to be careful. This one is a big shark, much more dangerous than *Bhai*."

"OK, you can count on the usual," Arnav said. "And if your information leads to an arrest, I'll double the payout."

Arnav returned to his friend, keener than ever on the file, only to find Tukaram's seat empty.

A loud clang from the adjacent room startled him. Rushing in to check, he wound up at the door to a hidden room. A weak yellow bulb flickered above. Tukaram called out, and Arnav made his way around steel shelves to find Tukaram under a heap of collapsed files. He rushed over to offer the man a hand.

"The revenge of the files." Tukaram gave a shaky laugh.

"I didn't know about this place."

"It's been there, hidden behind shelves." Tukaram gasped as Arnav helped him up. "They opened it up two years ago and extended the Record Storage area."

No one seemed to have dusted it in a while. Tara would have enjoyed cleaning up the thick coat of grime—he'd often caught her singing an odd tune, face covered with a scarf like a bank robber, holding a stick tied to a broom, getting rid of cobwebs. That girl had a mania for neatness. It cheered her up, so whenever she appeared out of sorts he used to open up a room or two in his parents' bungalow and let her have at it. It embarrassed him now to think he'd been in such a funk for all those months after she left without so much as a goodbye. They hadn't made any promises.

This room would have taken her more than a day. Dust rose, making him cough. That helped him shake off the sudden happy flash at the thought of that young girl. It didn't matter. She didn't matter.

"I think I located your file." Tukaram wiped his face, removing a streak of cobweb from his cheek.

Tukaram was about to give the file a whack, but Arnav grabbed it. He didn't need another dust cloud.

"You go on out." Tukaram seemed rueful. "I'll set these back up and join you."

Arnav walked out of the room, and grabbing some tissues from a nearby table, wiped the file clean. He flipped through it and came upon the details he remembered. The conclusions from the postmortem, which didn't amount to much. He was a constable then, and had merely assisted in making the *panchnama*. His superior, a dour sub-inspector named Rajesh Bendre, was in charge.

Arnav kept turning the pages, and didn't stop when he heard Tukaram come in.

"The team found sequins in the soil along with bones. Discolored. We'll have to get the evidence reexamined." Arnav kept up a commentary as he flipped the pages.

He found a note in Marathi in a margin, from Bendre: *Seems similar to a case at the N M Joshi Marg station last year. Check.*

"If this N M Joshi Marg case mentioned here is verified, it might have been the first. In 2002. This case file is from 2003; the case Naik has listed from Azad Nagar station was in 2008. And now the bodies at Aksa."

"If they are all by the same suspect, that's quite a gap between the murders," Tukaram said.

"We may not have discovered all of them, and we don't know when the women buried at Aksa were killed."

As the officer who had made that note, Bendre might be able to help. At the time, Arnav had argued with Bendre about the rules for a new constable and Bendre had packed him off on probation to a different station. Arnav hadn't seen him since.

"Can we speak to Sub-Inspector Bendre?"

Tukaram paused while offering Arnav a plate of biscuits. "He's no more."

"He died?"

"Yes. Road accident. No arrests made. He left behind a wife and children, but since he died when off duty, they received no compensation. A stinking heap there, if you ask me."

"Why?"

"My wife and I visited Mrs. Bendre, and my wife became friends with her. Sounds like Bendre received threats. Mrs. Bendre couldn't tell us what the threats were about or what the caller wanted Bendre to do, but she said there were several calls before he was killed."

"What year?"

"January 2004," Tukaram said.

Arnav had been in a blue fog all of 2003, the year after Tara disappeared. He had no recollection of the news.

Bendre had died. In the Azad Nagar station case, the officer in charge, Gawde, was handed a punishment posting. Dreadful things seemed to happen to those investigating crimes resembling the Aksa case.

"What's wrong?" Tukaram said.

"I'll need a copy of this file."

Tukaram nodded. "I'll get it done. By the way, your boss was the one who signed off on the statement on Bendre's death, calling it an accident."

"Mhatre?"

"The very same."

With the photocopy of the file in hand, Arnav drank the rest of his tea in a gulp.

"Thanks for all of this. Let's meet soon."

"I no longer go drinking."

"We'll think of something."

"Remember," Tukaram said as they walked to Arnav's car, "this job will let you go someday. Find yourself someone who won't. Maybe a good girl. Get married. Your family will stick by you. Invite me to the wedding."

"I will." Arnav smiled as he lied to his nosy, well-meaning friend. No marriage or family for Arnav Singh Rajput.

"I've known you since you were a green constable, Avi." Tukaram was the only sub-inspector allowed to use the shortened version of

Arnav's name. "Wherever you look, you see your sister. She's gone. You can't bring justice to all the dead women."

Arnav drove away into a light drizzle, his mind on the victims who had ended up at the wrong place at the wrong time. Like Asha, who'd taken a shortcut through an alleyway because she was late for her tutoring sessions.

After her family had made enquiries around the vicinity, having failed to reach her phone, and learned from the coaching center that she hadn't showed up for her classes, Asha had returned home past nine in the evening. Clothes torn, scratches on her face and throat. She rushed into her room and locked herself in. In a radical step during those days when a rape was hushed up for fear of bringing dishonor to the family, Constable Rajput had filed a complaint on his daughter's behalf and made her go through medical checkups, unwavering in his faith in his bosses. Months had gone by, and she'd finally smiled that evening their parents had gone out to attend a wedding. Fifteen minutes. That was how long he'd left her alone to fetch her *chaat* from across the road. It was the first time in months that his sister, who had given up eating, had asked for her favorite savory snacks.

"Get me a *sevpuri* and a *pao bhaji*? Extra tamarind chutney."

Those were her last words.

He'd skipped off imagining how much she'd enjoy, after months, the crunch of *sevpuri*, the sour tang of tamarind. When he returned and couldn't get her to unlock the door, he knew. Dropping the food, he shoved against it with all the strength his thirteen-year-old body could muster, his feet slushing on the chili sauce and tamarind juice on the floor. The neighbors broke open the door when he raised the alarm. He caught a glance inside the room before someone bodily carried him away. The red saree Asha had used to hang herself, part of her trousseau her mother had been gathering for years, the eyes, the bloody nose, the swollen tongue, the wet *salwar*, her bent feet, the mess on the shiny floor.

Arnav braked hard—the reflected shine on the road had blinded him for a moment. While driving in the middle lane, he'd abruptly taken a left. Thankfully, no cars followed close behind or they would've crashed into his. He'd reached the tree-lined neighborhood in Malabar Hill that he'd been staking out for years. The second home of Joint Commissioner of Crime Neelesh Joshi.

When Arnav first met Joshi more than twenty years ago, Joshi was a newly minted assistant commissioner of police. As a clueless thirteen-year-old, Arnav had vowed to destroy the ACP, who was lax on the case filed after Asha's rape. Arnav's father, a police constable, had begged for help, but Joshi had said, "Why was your daughter out at night?"

Ever since he'd joined the police, Arnav had unofficially tailed the commissioner, and watched him from a distance on Republic Day parades, during award ceremonies and memorial services. Joshi rose from case to case and post to post, moving from the peak caps with the silver IPS badge of a senior police officer to the caps of the topmost ranks with gold-embroidered visors. His startling career graph took off thanks not only to his uncanny ability to sniff out criminals but also to his connections with the political party that had ruled the state of Maharashtra for many years.

Decades ago, Arnav was convinced he could bring Joshi down. He was no longer as sure. He watched the house, lights switched on in all its rooms. If Joshi was in touch with any remaining gangs, there had been no outward evidence of it in the past years—no suspicious cars or individuals lurked near him. His personal reputation was blameless.

Arnav started his car. Once home, he left a bunch of instructions for Naik and her team to organize all the connected case files and reexamine the investigation into Sub-Inspector Bendre's death. They required enough evidence to justify interviewing Taneja. That would prompt Mhatre to set up a departmental enquiry on disobedience, but Arnav wasn't new to those. If Ali was right about his *Bhai* signing a contract to bury a body, another woman would die soon.

CHAPTER TWELVE

Through the window of his study at the sprawling farmhouse, he stood gazing at the dense foliage that began right beyond the backyard, green and inviting. Years ago, Dad had taken him hunting in the teeming scrub jungle bordering the property, taught him to fish in the brook that once ran less than two miles away. It had dried up. He felt a longing to watch those silvery fish darting about in dark pools where the water collected in the rainy season.

Turning away, he headed to the wooden table and the task at hand.

He ran his thumb over the round splotches and took a swig of watered-down whiskey. He needed his wits about him for what he had in mind. This table had belonged to his father. For a forest officer, that man sure dawdled for long hours in his study.

From a drawer, he retrieved a key and unlocked the metal cabinet that was once home to his father's magazines, some of them not suitable for children. The cabinet door opened with a screech that must have echoed in the rooms upstairs and through the wide courtyard, but the farmhouse was off-limits to anyone other than him and Bilal, and Bilal was away for the weekend. Piles of notebooks lined the paint-chipped, rusty shelves. They smelled of mold and dust.

He picked up a few of the notebooks—math, but also English and Hindi—and, turning a few pages, read his own scrawl. All his teenage years he had used the same notebooks as diaries, hiding them in plain sight on the shelves along with his workbooks for different subjects. He must get rid of them now, as well as the basement workshop—Bilal's *Bhai* had screwed up. If his hands weren't tied, he would have taught both of them a lesson, the *fattus*, the spineless pussies. How the hell did three rotting packages end up buried in the same lot? No one could connect them to him. Those two pussies wouldn't dare open their mouths. Yet here he was, destroying his old shit.

He sipped his whiskey and dug through the diaries. While flipping through the pages, one caught his eye.

It is a sultry afternoon today, the kind that settles as sweat at your hairline, eyebrows, and above your lip if you're trying to grow a mustache, like I am. Bilal has made sweet kheer, rice, sugar, caramelized milk, cashews, and raisins, boiled the way I like them. He remembers that it cheers me up. Ma used to make it. I need to be full before lunchtime, and the kheer works fine.

That woman is supposed to bring lunch, "cooked with her own hands." She can't cook to save her life, afraid to switch on the burner, the wimp. She's terrified of fire. Dad doesn't know and I can't tell him. He believes whatever she tells him. Since she's late, I want to check if Dad would be up for this new game he's ordered from abroad. Maybe we can shoot up a few stick figures on a flickering screen.

When I get to his room, though, I hear voices, and wonder if he's ogling one of those movies which he says he'll let me watch in a few years, but not yet. I know what to do to sneak in a glimpse or two, so I sidle out into the backyard hemmed in by the forest on all sides. Shuffling through the shrubs, I make for his bedroom window. He's not watching TV, but there's a channel on, with a raunchy Hindi film song.

She's not performing for the cameras. I can see the top of my father's head over the windowsill. She dances to these numbers in short clothes, on shoots where Dad sometimes takes me along. The directors call them "item numbers."

Hair down, she is gyrating to the music from the TV, but unlike a proper item number, she's taking off her clothes at the same time, and soon, the only support for her breasts is her hands. Now this is an Item Number. Or she is. She saunters up to the bed, shimmies up to my father, and kneels over him. I can't see them now, but I can hear him and the Item Number. And then she rises, her hair spread over her bare body, and sinks again, my father grunting in time to the song. I'm about to run away, when Item Number looks up, straight into my eyes.

He shut the notebook. So that's when he'd named her Item Number, decades ago, in these books his man Bilal knew only a little about, but hated all the same.

Last week, the old housekeeper had taken stock of the mess at the workshop, the floor slithery with red, and rolled up his sleeves. "I'm not doing this again. You keep promising me, and it comes to this each time."

"Not true. Most of them get away."

"You know how dangerous it is. What you could lose. Your father told me to keep you safe. I promised him on—"

"His deathbed, I know. Make it all go away this time. It will never happen again."

He liked that Bilal cared more about the word given years ago than the fate of the harlots. They came of their own will—he longed to argue with Bilal—they gave in to their greed, their sloth. They didn't escape the railway station in time. Not even when they were allowed the luxury of not being tied, when they didn't have to watch for who they were running from.

Dad would have been proud of me, he wanted to insist with this family confidant, Bilal, the true servant. He would have loved these clean cuts. See how well I get where the bones join. I can sever a foot at the ankle in a neat line. Like Dad, your *sahab*, who used to butcher some of the animals he was employed to protect. Cutting up a body is an art like any other, Dad once said. You agree, Bilal? Right?

But he hadn't said any of it, because in that moment he'd needed the man.

He stared at the pile of notebooks now. He would take them all out and light them up on a pyre. This was as good a beginning as any, for that end Bilal urged him to aim for.

CHAPTER THIRTEEN

ARNAV

Two days after his visit to Tukaram, Arnav sat at his table at the Malwani Police Station. Having switched off his phone for an hour, he attacked the piled-up paperwork, trying to ignore his growling stomach at dinnertime. When Shinde had dragged him into the police force more than twenty years ago, he hadn't mentioned that his position might one day involve endless meetings and paperwork.

Arnav's last shower had been more than twelve hours ago. He was sure he could smell himself right now. Noise from the rest of the station filtered through into the room he occasionally shared with another inspector—raised voices from the lockup area, honking cars, and relentless drumbeats. Dussehra was in progress, and the neighborhood used it as an excuse to set up drums interspersed with raunchy music on loudspeakers so the teens and aunties could dance the *dandiya* one last time. He glared at the reports to file, applications to sign, and expenses to approve, wishing they'd burn. Sitting at a desk had never made sense to him, not like the karate dojo or the chessboard, where he was able to throw an opponent or be thrown. His father often said, *Play chess all you want, but studies will give you a better life. Look at your sister; be like her.*

All the studies in the world hadn't saved Asha. She would have turned forty-three this year. At a knock on his door, Arnav glanced up.

"It is about the Aksa case, sir," Naik said. "Dr. Meshram tried to call you. After examining the soil from around the three bodies, he's found a few blue sequins."

Sequins. The file he'd read with Tukaram mentioned sequins.

"Did you send him the evidence and the details from all the other old cases?"

"Yes, sir. From Dadar, Azad Nagar, N M Joshi Marg. I noticed that sequins were also found in some of those cases, sir."

His assistant didn't miss much. She'd also wrangled the files and transferred them to Dr. Meshram within days, not weeks, in a police force hamstrung by procedures. Arnav smiled at her. She carried herself better today, her shoulders thrown back, the shadows under her eyes gone.

"Thank you, Naik, that's very well done."

"Thank you, sir." Naik left, closing the door softly behind her.

Arnav switched on his phone—he didn't want to miss other calls. It rang a moment after the screen turned on. Shinde. Arnav considered ignoring it, but Shinde would keep calling till he picked up.

"Tell me," Arnav said. Their usual no-frills greeting.

"Now that you've broken my arm, you owe me."

"You're joking, right?"

"All because of you, you son of a bitch. The doctor sent me home on bed rest."

Shinde was at the dojo this morning, not far from Arnav's home in Andheri. He'd challenged Arnav to a round of sparring, and all through-out, Arnav had seen the disintegrating dead body at Aksa, the delay in the postmortem, the silence from Ali, and his stuck-up boss warning him against investigating Taneja, demanding to know about security arrangements for the Dussehra festivities. His head in a whirl instead of the calm center where karate put it, Arnav had found an opening and come down hard on Shinde's arm.

"You're high on painkillers. Go to sleep. You must be glad I saved you the headache of trying to arrest your Rasool *Bhai*."

"I might get him yet. That's why I called. They've intercepted a van. A few men dumped a body in a suitcase in the Versova mangroves next to the creek, and ran. I'll send an inspector to the crime scene right now."

"So?"

"I want to be there. Rasool's men may be involved—they've been taking hit jobs in Versova. I can call a car because the place is near enough, or ask the inspector to pick me up, but as you said, the painkillers are strong."

"You don't wish to make a fool of yourself in front of your inspector."

"I could also use an extra pair of eyes. You can drive me home later."

"I'm not a chauffeur," Arnav said, exaggerating his annoyance.

"You are going off duty now. You're the reason I'm in bed and not on my way to the scene. A woman, from what I heard—a constable from my team found her."

Arnav checked his watch: 7:45 p.m. His exhausted mind and body craved a bath, dinner, bed. He ought to refuse.

"All right," he said instead. Shinde, the cunning fox, had played the right cards. Arnav knew it made no difference—women routinely suffered violence—but he couldn't refuse to help on a case involving a dead or molested woman. His nightmares wouldn't let him sleep.

Arnav leaned forward, his hands steady on the motorbike. He'd borrowed it from one of his constables. It was faster to take the five-minute ferry from the Madh jetty and cross over to Versova instead of driving for more than an hour all the way out of Malwani and making a U-turn. The ferry allowed bikes, not cars, across the creek. He'd picked Shinde up from his apartment and now negotiated the path toward the Versova mangroves, the bike bouncing away on unpaved roads.

"You had to get a bike, didn't you?" Shinde panted. "Why don't you kill me? You do realize what this ride is doing to my arm?"

"This was quicker. You know you can't lose time once a body offense is reported. Finally, we're the 'Jai and Veeru' they call us at the station."

This was an ongoing joke and debate. The staff at Malwani teased Arnav and Shinde, naming them for the Bollywood blockbuster classic *Sholay*, about two small-time thieves who defeat a gang of robbers. You couldn't join Mumbai Police without hearing of the movie and the actors who were immortalized by their leading roles.

"My inspector must have already arrived on the scene. And you're the worst Veeru I've seen. Veeru's bike had a sidecar."

Jai was brooding, smart, and a great shot, and Veeru the opposite. Shinde fit Jai's mold—he was cranky, too, and manipulative when it suited him. A sidecar? Really?

"Why are you going? We can turn back," Arnav said. "Let your inspector do his job."

"I would have, especially after I saw your bike. But it is not an ordinary dead body. They messaged me pictures right before you reached my apartment. The woman has no head, hands, or feet."

CHAPTER FOURTEEN

ARNAV

When Arnav fought to tug his boot out of the gray, sulfur-smelling mangrove swamp, it sucked back, and for a moment he reached an impasse. Then, like Asha, who used to swing him around and release him with a giggle when he was at his most unsteady, the swamp let go. He would've fallen headlong down the slope had he not grabbed a mangrove branch and broken the momentum.

Arnav had dealt with bodies hacked up and packed in suitcases before—killers found them easy to wheel out without attracting attention. Despite Shinde's constables offering to haul the large black suitcase out of the mud for him to examine, Arnav waded in. He wanted to see the cheap rexine suitcase for himself. His boss had railed at him about cold cases. Well, the constables said this was a decapitated body. That meant that the cases in Aksa might be combined into an investigation to trap an active serial killer. He could afford to miss nothing.

These mangroves in Versova ran alongside the narrow, polluted Malad creek. Cross the creek by boat and you hit Madh Island. Aksa beach lay a short drive farther. Even though Aksa was under the jurisdiction of Malwani Police Station, and the Versova police were in charge of these mangroves, as the crow flew, the two sites were not far apart. Whoever was dumping the bodies was familiar with that area.

Lit up by his flashlight, the suitcase lay awkwardly on the torpedo-shaped mangrove seeds spiking out of the swamp. Mudskippers and frogs scattered at the team's stumbling approach. A few paces inward, and the suitcase would have sunk under the black, boggy water.

Around him, a million crickets sang, and frogs took up the chorus. A constable stepped forward, and together they dragged the suitcase back toward the road. Curved mangrove roots exploded out of the water near the mudbanks, looking like dark, ghostly arms stretching up into the darkness. Small wonder that not many locals ventured out in this area late at night. Arnav spotted a shiny object on a nearby root and leaned forward to pick it up with his gloved hand. A metal watch strap. The swamp was used as a dumping ground and the tide brought in its own debris from the sea, festooning the mangrove with swaths of dirty cloth and broken plastic, but the strap hadn't been there for long.

Back on solid ground, he placed the watch strap into a plastic bag as a constable unzipped the suitcase. The yellow glow of the flashlight showed an unclothed woman's body stuffed in, curled in a fetal position. In place of the head, hands, and feet—dark stumps of dried blood. Arnav tamped down his burst of vindication. The woman had been brutally murdered—bruises flowered at her shoulders—she'd been tortured before she was decapitated. Fantasizing about flinging an "I told you so" at Mhatre could wait.

Shinde rested against the bike, nursing his right arm in a sling. The inspector who reported to him hadn't reached them yet.

"What would you like to do?" Arnav said.

"Based on what you told me about the bodies at the Aksa site," Shinde paused, taking in the dense mangrove trees, "this has been going on for a while. Rasool could be responsible, or not. Let's find out more."

Shinde hailed his constables, and soon they stood in a tight circle around the bike.

"Who followed the vehicle?" Shinde said.

"I did, sir." A tall, well-built constable with a thin mustache stepped up.

"You saw them toss the suitcase out?" Shinde said.

"There were three people, sir—two in the front seat, one in the rear. They flung it from the back seat."

That watch strap could belong to the goon who had tossed out the body.

"You weren't near enough to stop them?" Shinde's voice took on a challenging tone. "Which way did they come from?"

"My bike faltered, sir. I called for backup, but by the time we reached the main road crossing, they were gone. They didn't stop at our checkpoint."

"What make was the car?"

"A big black Maruti van, sir."

"Any updates on the number plate?"

"Came in right now, sir. It was fake."

Arnav listened to the conversation and made mental notes. The suspects were well prepared, possibly professionals. Ali's input was correct. Someone did indeed have a contract for disposal of these bodies. He'd have to call Ali as soon as he finished here. Arnav took a drawn-out breath of air heavy with the smell of wet leaves, and asked Shinde if they could speak alone.

Shinde asked him to wait, and turned to the head constable on the scene. "Get two constables to comb through missing persons reports. And pick up the footage from the CCTVs around the crossing. We must find the black van."

"Yes, sir."

Shinde was on the right track. After the Mumbai terrorist attacks, many CCTVs watched each main road.

"Get everyone to check the surroundings," Shinde added, "for clues related to the suitcase, or the body, which can help identify the victim."

"We'll comb the area, sir."

The constables dispersed, and Shinde leaned back, his face briefly contorted with pain. "Tell me."

"The suspect in this investigation could be connected to the Aksa case."

"You're saying your cold cases might turn warm now, but cold cases are career self-sabotage, Avi. I don't need to tell you that. Focus on the cases piling up on your desk. No dearth of murdered women in Mumbai."

The second senior inspector with the advice to focus on recent murders. Arnav was tempted to scoff at Shinde, but that wouldn't help.

"I could assist on this case. You'll take a few days to heal, and that gap could be crucial. You can lead again once you're better, end of this week."

"Let me think about it. If it points to Rasool . . ."

"I mean only to help," Arnav said. "If we make an arrest and Rasool is behind it all, he's yours."

"All right, I'll drop a note to your Mhatre."

"Who is coming in for forensics?"

"Meshram." Shinde grimaced, and shifted his injured arm.

Made sense. Dr. Meshram took care of the cases from this area: Malwani, Malad, and Versova.

"That's good. He's the one who found the other bodies at Aksa." Arnav watched his friend flinch when his arm touched the bike handle. "How are you feeling? Do you have your painkillers on you?"

"No," Shinde said. "You killed my arm with your mad bike trip, you *khajoor*."

Khajoor. A casual, harmless Mumbai slang word that Shinde used when he was feeling particularly salty. *Khajoor* meant dates, the fruit, but it also meant you were stupid and you knew it. Arnav hadn't realized how bad Shinde's arm hurt until now.

"You want one of your men to drive you home in their jeep? I'll finish up and make a report—if you tell your constables."

"When my inspector gets here," Shinde said, "if he gets here, he will be the lead. That's protocol. You understand that?"

"Yes."

Arnav could not lose this investigation. This killer had been active all this time: killing women, decapitating them, and getting their bodies buried—keeping their heads, arms, and feet. What monster did that? Why?

"You can help, the way you've been threatening to do all evening. I'm going back home. Don't screw this up. You hear me?"

After Shinde left, Arnav flicked on his flashlight and set off on the dirt path in one direction, then another, hoping and fearing that he'd come face-to-face with a woman's severed head any moment. Amid the night alive with mosquitoes, mating bullfrogs, and other, perhaps more sinister denizens of the mangrove, Tara's laughing face rose in his mind, unbidden. Before banishing it, he sent up a wish. Wherever she was, let her be warm and safe, far away from dark places.

CHAPTER FIFTEEN

ARNAV

Exactly four days after Arnav had slipped on a pair of gloves to examine the crime scene next to Aksa beach, he watched another dead body, surrounded by the mangroves this time, light up with the flashes from Dr. Meshram's camera. Not a body, he corrected himself—a woman. The killer had spent quite some time with her, given the extent of bruising, the slashes on her arms, and the decapitation.

"What time did they halt the van?" He turned to the constable.

"At 7:35 p.m., sir."

"Was this your routine checkpoint?"

"No, sir. We only set that checkpoint because of a drug squad alert."

"The suspects didn't know or they wouldn't have taken this route."

Arnav asked the constable to flick open a map on his phone. They peered at it together.

"The men were driving down the STP road from this direction." He pointed out the road they were standing on in the map. "So they might have picked up the body from somewhere nearby—you need an isolated place to do this."

"Yes, sir. We'll look out for any derelict buildings."

"If we abandon this location now, the killers might come back to retrieve evidence. Post four men overnight, and make sure no one enters this area."

Assigning overnight duty to Shinde's constables in a mangrove forest near a road believed to be haunted wouldn't make Arnav popular, but he saw no choice. Locating other body parts could help identify the woman.

Dr. Meshram and his assistant were not able to lift the dead body from the suitcase on their own, and asked for help. The constables came forward, but Arnav waved them off, asking them to prepare a manned post for the night. The body was heavy, and it had stiffened. Based on his experience with scores of postmortems, Arnav knew this meant death had occurred more than four hours ago. The stumps where the head and the limbs had been severed had turned dark. The breasts remained in the posture the body had lain in, and once turned over, the body didn't lie flat. One of the newer constables retched.

Arnav used his forearm to wipe sweat off his forehead. Mumbai humidity was bad enough, but in this stretch of jungle, it was a blanket of wet clamminess.

Arnav watched Dr. Meshram use a pair of tweezers to remove a fiber from behind the victim's thighs.

"What is it?" Arnav leaned closer for a look.

"Nylon thread."

Arnav examined the thread: white, and slightly thicker than human hair. Meshram eased it into an evidence bag.

"This is quite similar to the body near Aksa, right?" Arnav said.

"Yes. Other than the fact that it has not been buried. Same person or persons could be responsible, *kya*?"

"What else can you tell so far?"

"The wounds on the body were made over a period of time. Several look like they're more than a day or two old. And the body has been bled out."

"How did you get that?"

"There is no postmortem lividity that I can see. A few hours after death, the blood pools to the portion of the body touching the ground, and we see dark stains. No such stains, so not enough blood in the body."

"The cause of death?"

"Not sure in this light. The cuts on the throat, wrists, and ankles appear surgical, so the victim was either dead or unconscious—wasn't moving or struggling. No bruising around the amputation sites, which could mean that the heart had stopped by that time. Hard to be sure without a proper examination."

"What age was the victim? Approximate height and weight?"

An age range would help narrow down potential matches in missing persons complaints. This woman went missing some time ago, so any reports filed in the last two months could be a match.

"Between twenty and forty years old, and about five feet, five inches tall. I'll need to examine the bones. With no skull or teeth, this will take a while."

"That may have prompted the decapitation—hiding the victim's identity," Arnav said. He must organize a meeting with Taneja. Rattle the cage a bit and see what turned up. If the same culprit was responsible for all the deaths, and three of the bodies were found at a site Taneja had recently won in a court case, he held useful information, at the very least. And if Mhatre continued to go easy on Taneja, Arnav could employ the media. A well-placed article in a paper like *Mumbai Drishtikon* could make it difficult to ignore this case, especially if they found out that a similar murder had taken place recently.

"My seniors won't begrudge me time spent on this case now." Dr. Meshram broke into Arnav's thoughts. "Once you talk about an active serial killer, they all sit up and take notice. Not a good look, *kya*?"

"Check for sequins. If we find blue sequins on the body or in the suitcase, we'll have a stronger case."

"Yes. Sequins are plastic. Plastic will not decompose for a hundred years. The bodies we dug up near Aksa are not holding up, though. We don't have the facilities to store them properly, and there's no viscera in the condition for further analysis."

"This one?"

"I'll be able to extract the viscera and send it to the forensic laboratory at Kalina. We'll find out about any drug reactions or poisoning."

"If we can connect the Aksa cases to this victim, we could apply the same conclusions to all the bodies. Find a common thread. Maybe even a motive."

"Whoever did this," said Meshram as he glanced up from the suitcase, "not right in the head, *kya*?"

As Arnav neared the Versova jetty, traffic sounds pierced the rustling quiet of the mangroves. Loudspeakers bellowed the last few scenes of the Ramleela play, building up to the crescendo of Ravan's destruction, Dussehra's climactic episode. A much smaller Ravan in this Muslim-dominated area, but he would burn the same as the one at Chowpatty. Somewhere in the city a real-life Ravan prowled, kidnapping women, torturing and killing them.

At a recent event organized by the state's Mangrove Cell, the scientist had said that the mangroves acted as nurseries for fish, birds, and a million small animals. It was also a place where the decomposition of the dead made new life—the fringe between life and death, salt water and sweet. Death itself was an edge, and this woman had been pushed across. Was she, too, doomed to roam the jungles at night, stopping passersby for a lift? She had good reason to be furious at the world and exact bloody vengeance. Arnav dialed Ali as he drove down the allegedly haunted Madh-Marve Road back toward Malwani Police Station, a part of him terrified yet waiting for the distressed woman to bar his way and hitch a ride.

CHAPTER SIXTEEN

ARNAV

At Dr. Meshram's office beside the Bhagwati Hospital morgue, Arnav and Shinde refused an offer of tea. The office in which they sat was damp, a leaky refrigerator grumbling away in a corner on top of a frayed carpet, the walls bare other than a lone picture of the maverick, saffron-clad right-wing leader in his trademark sunglasses, worshipped by all of Mumbai.

Arnav watched the fidgety Shinde, who had not yet been cleared to report for active duty, four days after he was injured. Shinde had no use for rest.

The inspector Shinde had assigned to the Versova case had taken a leave of absence following a death in the family, so he had let Arnav take the lead on the case.

After a few minutes of waiting, Dr. Meshram peered in through the door, in his white overcoat, surgical cap, and gloves, his usual cheerful demeanor faded with exhaustion.

"I know you'd asked to be present at this one," Meshram said before Shinde could speak, "but my assistant had . . . uh . . . already prepped the body, so I had to go ahead."

"Do you have any clue how important the identification is in this case?" Shinde said.

"I'm sure Dr. Meshram has done his best." Arnav stepped in. Shinde's injury had made him ornery, especially after he learned that the bone in his upper arm wasn't healing at the expected rate.

"Thank you, sir, I try." Dr. Meshram offered a weak smile and held up his gloves to show he couldn't shake hands. He turned back to Arnav. "My regular assistant is on leave. With an electrical problem in the ventilation system, and neither of the saws working, the cases had backed up. The man replacing my assistant is new to the job."

"The body is still on the dissection table?" Arnav said.

"Yes. You can take a peek if you want. I'll walk you through my conclusions."

Masked and gloved, Shinde and Arnav stepped into the dissection room. The smell of formaldehyde and disinfectant rode the air-conditioned air. The decapitated body on the steel table was paler than before, and seemed waxier, the cut marks on the arms, breasts, and thighs almost black. A large, deep Y-shaped incision started at the top of each shoulder, ran down the middle of the chest, to below the stomach. It stood out as a welted scar—the stitched-up dissection.

"The subject is between twenty-five and thirty years old," Dr. Meshram began. "We don't have teeth or tooth enamel, so I doubt we can be more precise. I've sent bone samples for analysis as well."

This wasn't good news. The more precise the age, the better the chances of finding a match in the missing persons records.

"Stomach contents show she hadn't eaten in a while. I've taken tissue and blood samples for examination at the Kalina laboratory."

"What about the decapitation?" Arnav said.

"Happened a while after death. She died about ten hours before she was discovered."

Ten hours. Arnav's mind raced even as the pathologist spoke. So she'd died that morning. Whoever had done this had a lot of privacy, some infrastructure to get the body bled out, and help with this ghoulish operation—perhaps the men who dumped the remains.

"The culprit had her for at least a week, based on some of the healed wounds," Dr. Meshram added.

Starved and tortured. Arnav saw daily the depravity of humankind paraded through his files, but this was extreme.

"Cause of death?" Shinde said.

"The culprit may have smothered her, because the lungs show edema, but we corroborate that by examining the nose and lips." Meshram shook his head. There were no nose and lips in this case.

"Sexual assault?" Shinde crossed his arms.

Morgues were cold, but now Arnav felt a different kind of chill in the room. His hackles rose, as if in response to a threat. Someone had committed horrific atrocities for more than a decade, with no one the wiser.

"Yes. But we found no traces of the culprit. Based on the examination of her organs, she has given birth, at least once."

A mother. Who was taking care of this woman's child? Arnav fought for calm. He'd seen mothers on this table before, but the fate of this woman, who had been robbed of her face even in death, distressed him. The chemical whiff layered over the faint notes of rotting cabbage, which came from the bodies, did not help. The last time he'd choked at a morgue was ten years ago. He wasn't about to start now. He stood straighter, fisted his hands.

"Identifying marks?" Shinde said.

"A birthmark under her left breast."

The birthmark could only be used to corroborate her identity, not determine it. Dr. Meshram pointed to it, standing out like a pale shadow under the left breast.

"X-ray results?" Arnav said. "Maybe she underwent surgery at some point?"

It was better to speak than throw up. To Arnav's relief, his voice stayed level. An inspector unsettled by a dead body. Shinde would never let him hear the end of this if he knew. He sneaked a glance at his friend, who didn't look any better than Arnav felt. Like most Mumbai police officers, Shinde faked professional detachment.

"We did an X-ray, but found no supportive device in her body. We sometimes find pacemakers, but only with older victims." Dr. Meshram picked up a ziplock bag. "You'd asked me to keep an eye out for these, however, and I did find them."

Within the transparent bag, tiny blue sequins shone in the white light—the confirmation Arnav sought.

"She's one from the same series of murders," Arnav said. "No other way to determine her identity?"

"Only DNA to go on, unfortunately. Blood and tissue reports might help. It'll take a while."

"Nothing else?"

"She's had laser hair removal done," Dr. Meshram said. "All over her body."

Arnav filed away that piece of information. Shinde thanked the pathologist, and Arnav left Dr. Meshram with a request to keep custody of the body till further notice. As per normal procedure, the pathologist only preserved tissue samples, and sent unclaimed bodies for their last rites within three days of the postmortem.

Once he had dropped Shinde back home, Arnav dialed Ali.

"*Ji, saab.*"

"I need that black Maruti van I told you about." Arnav gripped the steering wheel, his gaze focused on the road slippery with rain.

"I'm trying to get a picture for you."

"Where is it?"

"*Bhai* owns a stake in a cab company near the Andheri-Kurla Road. One of my boys saw a van like the one you described, covered up in the corner of the garage."

Ali's *Bhai* was Rasool Mohsin. Arnav sat up straighter.

"If that van turns out to be the right one, I'll make sure you're happy you traced it."

"I'll do my best, *saab*."

Ali wasn't exactly Rasool Mohsin's right-hand man, but a lieutenant of sorts, and ran a few goons under his supervision. Arnav had saved his life once, years ago, in the course of a police raid. The man hadn't forgotten. He was expensive, but Arnav had never regretted spending on him, sometimes out of his own pocket.

If the blabbering fool Ali had overheard was right, Rasool could have taken the contract for body disposal. It made sense that the black van was part of the clandestine fleet of repurposed vehicles all gang leaders kept at their disposal.

He could tell Shinde now, which might make him turn over the case to another inspector from his station. Rasool was too big a fish for Shinde to leave in the hands of an officer who didn't report to him, even if it was his best friend. Or Arnav could wait till he had confirmation. He didn't care about Rasool. If Rasool had indeed signed a contract, Arnav only wanted to know who had issued it.

Arnav switched on the radio, and another of Tara's old Hindi songs floated up from the speakers, bringing back memories of the smoke-filled restaurant at the Blue Bar, and Tara's seductive yet distant smile amid the flashing lights.

CHAPTER SEVENTEEN

He lay curled up in a corner of the four-poster bed, curtains drawn. It was all too much. Bundles of cash for Bilal's bloody *Bhai*, and he'd still messed up the last package, on top of the other three. All he had to do was spirit the package out of Mumbai. Not get it stuck in the mangroves.

Outside the door, a gentle knock.

The inevitable man Friday with one of his trays, carrying healing potions filled with antioxidants. Good for your skin and your mood, Bilal would murmur.

"Go away."

"There's someone to see you," Bilal rumbled low from beyond the door.

Bilal used to call Dad "sir." As Dad's son, he was *baba*, the male version of "baby"—a term Indian help used for the master's little boys. Bilal didn't call him *baba* anymore, but hadn't shifted to "sir," either. To Bilal, he was still a boy to be coddled. He smiled. Bilal was the one he could count on, more than Dad. Bilal had never hit him.

Another polite knock followed. In Bilal's place, he'd have banged the door by now. But Bilal wasn't the master.

"You must meet him. He has a phone for you."

That was different. Not many people sent him phones. This guest wouldn't hand pass the phone to anyone else. Not even Bilal.

"Ask him to wait."

He let himself out, locked the door with his code, and headed toward the small sitting room at the back of the apartment. A sullen-faced man waited. They were all the quiet sort, but this one seemed not merely unwilling but also unable to speak. The henchman handed over the phone and sauntered out. The door led to the back entrance, which Bilal kept locked. Late-night visitors cooled their heels under a small porch.

The phone in his hand was one of those cheap things with a keypad. It seemed new. When it buzzed, he waited out a few rings before picking it up and saying hello. He hoped it wasn't about what he feared.

"This is an official matter." The gruff voice echoed. "I'm ending our arrangement."

Uhnna. The world called him Vijayan, the man who'd made Mumbai Police lose sleep before he escaped to Dubai. Vijayan was *Uhnna*, the Malayali word for Big Brother—a mafia don—or for a friend of the family. And he was angry. Not just angry, crazy pissed.

"*Uhnna?*"

"I can't deliver your supplies anymore."

"You'll tell me why, of course." He let his voice deepen a pitch. Keep it casual, straightforward. Pretend you know nothing.

"We do a lot of business together," *Uhnna* said, "and I thought you were honest with me."

"I am."

"A package was discovered, with parts missing. I don't make enough with this business for packages to end up like that, and definitely not for the wrong people to find them."

Thank the stars *Uhnna* didn't know about the others. With this new one, he'd taken all the usual precautions. Made sure the woman reported back to her bosses, said she was going away of her own volition. Sent texts from her phone to her family, saying she would be busy, or traveling to another city. But Bilal's man had failed again.

"How do you know that the package was damaged?"

"Only reason I didn't find out earlier was that I trusted you." The voice at the other end grew distant. "This was a favor for old times' sake."

The "old times" part was true. Dad invited him over for a bit of shooting in the forest, followed by a feast for him and his men in those days when Vijayan's word was law in Mumbai. Over the years, *Uhnna* had taken care of matters big and small. Using the wily Item Number's connections, *Uhnna* had thrived.

"*Uhnna* . . ."

"You need me more than I need you. I wish you'd remember that."

He bit back the words he wanted to toss at the don. He would remind *Uhnna* that *Uhnna*'s businesses received special treatment from Maharashtra's state ministers. Now was not the time, though.

"What if I guarantee that the packages will remain intact from now on?" he said.

"I wasn't born yesterday." *Uhnna*'s tone was clipped.

"I'm giving you my word."

"You gave it before. It's clearly not worth much to you. In our line, one's word is everything." The phone went dead.

CHAPTER EIGHTEEN

ARNAV

Arnav stood chatting with another inspector outside Mhatre's office. He was to go in next.

The entire police station was abuzz—Joint Commissioner Joshi was on a visit. No one knew why. He'd come alone. Senior officials toured stations in their zone on a fixed rotation, unless trouble struck, like a bomb blast or shoot-out. It was a formal affair, often with one or more additional commissioners in attendance. Joshi had asked to meet each of the inspectors, with Mhatre present.

Arnav had never been in a direct conversation with the trim, brisk Joshi. As long as Arnav continued to treat Joshi like any another superior, Joshi would never recognize Arnav unless he took the trouble to probe into Arnav's family history.

Arnav turned at the raised voices from inside, Joshi's baritone followed by the lower tones of Mhatre. His colleague sidled off. Arnav was about to leave when Mhatre stepped out and beckoned him in.

In Mumbai Police, it was customary for the senior visiting officer to take over your seat. At much below six feet despite his gold-embroidered peak cap, Joshi looked dwarfed by Mhatre's chair. Joshi carried his fifty-seven years well, and returned Arnav's salute with a crisp one of his own.

"Good morning, sir." Arnav stood beside the seated Mhatre, ready to face queries into his cases. A glance at other chairs in the room had showed him the likely reason for Joshi's visit. Taneja lounged, typing into his large smartphone. Kittu Virani sat beside him in a loose, white, full-sleeved *salwar-kameez*, her head low, her smile demure.

"Good morning, Inspector Rajput." Joshi gestured toward a seat, placed like a patient's chair at a doctor's table.

"Thank you, sir."

"I've spoken to Mr. Taneja, here. He says you've been obstructing his business."

Arnav used the tone he employed when making reports. "Three dead bodies in various states of decomposition have been found at the Taneja Estate Holdings construction site. We'll let him have the site back as soon as we finish our investigations. In fact, I had a few questions for him, and haven't been able to meet him since we discovered another recently murdered woman near the Versova mangroves yesterday."

"I know nothing about the Versova mangroves or dead bodies." Taneja smiled, as if explaining complex Penal Codes to a small child.

"Each body is decapitated and dismembered the exact same way." Arnav kept his gaze trained on Joshi.

Ignoring Arnav, Joshi addressed Taneja. "I'll look into this. It should be possible for you to resume construction soon."

"Thank you, Joshi *saab*. That's all the reassurance I hoped for. I'll leave now, with your permission."

Kittu cleared her throat, and Joshi turned to her. "Ms. Virani, it is always a pleasure to see you. About your request—I'll do my best. Let's see—Rajput, you're trained in karate, right?"

Arnav had no idea where this was going. He saw no point in denying it: he'd been training for far longer than his career in Mumbai Police.

"Yes, sir."

"You are exactly what we require—a fit inspector trained in the martial arts. Rehaan Virani needs a teacher—uh, a consultant, for his next movie role."

"Sir?"

"After all the bother you've caused, you can make time for this, Rajput." Joshi nodded to Mhatre. "See to it."

Arnav wanted to retort that he was a police officer, not a karate trainer. Joshi had no business asking him to work for Bollywood heroes, but pointing that out would lose him a chance to be in regular touch with Rehaan, and through him, Kittu Virani and Rahul Taneja. A man like Taneja had much bigger fish to fry than the spa at Aksa. His presence here meant he had something to hide.

Both Taneja and Kittu Virani rose to their feet, and Joshi stood up with folded hands. "Let us know how else we can help. Our duty is to serve."

Joshi smiled, and gestured to Mhatre to see them out.

Once they'd left he turned to Arnav, his voice reflecting none of the displeasure in his eyes.

"As you're aware, in Mumbai Police, we pride ourselves in taking new steps to improve our performance. The commissioner wants me to come up with new initiatives. I'm counting on your help."

This was a complete change of tack. Arnav remembered himself enough to say, "Sure, sir."

There you go, Arnav, cutting salutes along with the rest of them, he thought. Seemed like the best option till he understood Joshi's motives.

"We've identified officers with good crime detection records and conviction rates. Yours are impressive, even though there are remarks on your behavior with seniors. What do you have to say?"

"I do my job, sir." The longer the question, the shorter its answer. Joshi was here to please Taneja, who clearly did have friends in high places—high enough to make a joint commissioner do his bidding.

Mhatre returned. His expression remained unchanged at what Joshi said next.

"You're the kind of man we want. I'm promoting you to senior inspector at Bandra Police Station. You'll follow the proper chain of command, but will report directly to me on occasion."

"I don't understand, sir," Arnav said.

"There are a few openings at the moment," Joshi went on in his new, expansive mode, "I want deserving candidates who can make crucial decisions based on experience and quick thinking. Mhatre says good things about you." Joshi beamed like an indulgent parent. "I have his recommendation on record."

"Yes, of course, sir." Mhatre nodded. "I wish Rajput all the best."

This was an opportunity Arnav couldn't have foreseen; reporting to Joshi would enable a close watch on his activities: who he met, who visited him, and why. On the other hand, this was totally outside of protocol.

"Rajput?" Joshi clearly expected a delighted, grateful acceptance.

"Yes, sir."

"Don't you have an answer?"

"It is all quite sudden, sir. My promotion isn't due for at least three years."

Seniority, not merit, was how Mumbai Police worked.

"Are you saying you don't wish to be promoted to senior inspector?"

"I'll think about it, sir."

"That's not what I've heard about you."

"Sorry, sir?"

"According to reports, you jump first and think later. We need a bit of that right now. The teams are ready. Take on a few cases. I could transfer you with the same designation and promote someone at that station, but I prefer you in charge."

Joshi's phone rang and he rose as he answered. "Right, sir," he said. "I'm leaving now."

He ended the call and made his excuses to Mhatre. The Home Minister had asked for an immediate meeting based on some intelligence. Twenty days between the most important Hindu festivals—on Dussehra, the god Ram had vanquished Ravan, and on Diwali he would return from exile. The countdown to the heightened alerts during Diwali had begun.

"See you soon, Rajput." Joshi stretched out his hand to shake.

He walked out, Mhatre behind him, leaving Arnav with a lot of questions and a difficult choice—miss an opportunity to keep tabs on the person responsible for injustice toward his sister, or let go of the Aksa and Versova cases.

CHAPTER NINETEEN

MUMBAI DRISHTIKON NEWS

Dance bars to be reopened in Mumbai, rules Supreme Court of India

2:30 PM IST 18 October, Mumbai.

In a ruling that has been controversial on social media as well as off-line, the country's top court ruled that dance bars in Mumbai will be allowed to renew their licenses. They imposed new regulations, however. Performers can be tipped, but guests may not shower them with cash. The dancers and the bar owners will sign formal contracts, the structure of which will be decided by them. An amount of payment can be agreed upon, but the bar owners are not liable to pay a salary, or install CCTV cameras inside the bars, citing privacy concerns.

A three-judge bench of Justices B K Bhatt, Asheesh Nehra and Amrit Solanki set aside Section 6 of the Maharashtra Prohibition of Obscene Dance in Hotels, Restaurants and Bar Rooms and Protection of Dignity of Women (Working therein) Act, which forbade the granting of licenses to discotheques. Hotel and restaurant owners, performers and others had challenged the Act in separate petitions to various courts.

With dance bars operational in Mumbai again after fourteen years, various sectors have reacted differently to the news. While it has naturally pleased bar owners and women seeking work in dance bars, several religious institutions and women's rights groups have condemned the move.

"We understand that many women who work at dance bars are the primary breadwinners," said Shikha Paranjpe, President of the Women's Association in Nerul, in response to the Supreme Court decision. "On the other hand, the government must restrict the trafficking of minor girls. Dance bars should reopen, but they need strict implementation of laws so that women are not exploited."

Bar patrons, on the other hand, are excited about the return of quality and variety to the Mumbai bar scene. A patron, who refused to disclose his name, said, "I'll be one of the first at the Blue Bar next week. Some of the bar girls from years ago are making a comeback, and a famous firecracker will be opening the show."

CHAPTER TWENTY

TARA

Fourteen years. Fourteen years was the term of a life imprisonment in India. It was the length of the exile into the forests for the god Ram. Tara made a face at the thought. It was quite the opposite for her: Mumbai was the exile and the prison. This time around, she would not let it become either. A week. That was all. Then she would leave again, for good.

Tara dragged her small suitcase and stepped out of the air-conditioned airport and into the heat and humidity of Mumbai. She scanned the crowd of drivers with placards, searching for her name. Her boss, Shetty, was supposed to have sent a ride.

She drew herself to her full height, calming the frisson of panic that crowds at travel hubs still brought her—she was at the Mumbai airport, not the Borivali railway station. The phone in her hand was her own, not given to her by Shetty. She could take all the time she liked. No three-minute deadline, nor the terror of the unknown if she missed it. Tara took a long, steadying breath.

Mumbai smelled different. Or was it her? Shetty had paid for her maiden flight. She understood the announcements in English now, and the snatches of conversation around her. Her new clothes were different, too. Gone, the shiny, too-tight *ghaghra-choli* she wore while dancing at the Blue Bar. Gone, too, she sighed in relief, the scratchy, blue-sequined saree she wore to the railway station. She sported a pair of dark jeans and a full-sleeved shirt: a woman on her way back from an office trip. No-nonsense walking shoes and hair tied in a severe ponytail completed her outfit. Tara had dressed for her new job. She was older, and at thirty-one, her body had rounded out despite the hours of chores and dancing she put in every day.

After a good minute, she found her name, a simple "Tara" written in crooked letters on a flimsy piece of paper. She walked over to the short, gray-haired driver. He led the way to the pickup spot and asked her to wait for him to bring the car around from the parking lot.

She'd once imagined her entire name, Noyontara Mondal, splashed on billboards and magazines. Tara straightened her shirt. She'd never act in movies, never be known beyond the few students she trained and their parents, the small neighborhood gigs she choreographed, and Zoya, who lived across the street and got by with babysitting and applying henna and beauty treatments to those who couldn't afford a salon.

Tara held her hennaed hand to her nose, breathing in the earthy, hay-like fragrance, and smiled.

"This is for luck. A smart, modern design," Zoya had said as she applied it. "Shetty won't mind. And you're not a mere dancer now. You're also a choreographer."

Shetty was not bad as far as bar owners went. Not lecherous or violent like the others. He'd made sure no one molested his girls. He sent auto-rickshaws to fetch them, paid off the security guards in the apartment block in order to keep them safe, and hired bouncers to throw out anyone who groped the girls without their permission. But he also worshipped money, and never let his bar girls forget that.

"What about the loss we caused him when we ran?"

"Stop worrying," Zoya had reassured her. "Shetty has known all this time exactly where we live. You don't think he would have acted sooner to extract his pound of flesh?"

"I don't know, Zoya. You keep saying it was your Rasool who protected us, but—"

"He has. What do you think our calls were about, huh?"

Zoya and her boyfriend, Rasool.

Rasool Mohsin had gone from being a potbellied underling of a mafia boss to becoming a don himself. Each morning Zoya used to return with bruises she did her best to hide—her throat, her breasts, her back, other places she wouldn't let Tara help patch up. He showed up each afternoon with perfumes and roses, then begged and sobbed outside the Mira Road apartment Tara and Zoya shared with six other girls. Rinse and repeat.

That stopped fourteen years ago when Zoya escaped Mumbai with Tara, along with bundles of black money stolen from Rasool. Rasool had every reason to have their throats slit, a routine affair in his profession. He hadn't, though.

Tara sighed. Only Zoya and Rasool understood their relationship, which had turned long-distance now with Zoya in Lucknow. He'd begged Zoya to accompany Tara to Mumbai, but only Tara was here now.

Around her, passengers jostled each other, clanged carts, and muttered apologies. Arguments broke out. No one glanced her way. This was a change, too. Sweat trickled at her temples and pooled in damp patches at her armpits before she noticed the driver making his slow crawl through the jumble of taxis, app cars, private vehicles.

Once in the air-conditioned car, she heaved a sigh of relief. More than a decade ago she'd run from Shetty like a wanted fugitive, and now he'd sent her a not-half-bad saloon car. Not shiny or new, and it reeked of tobacco, but still. It showed that Shetty had meant it when he'd assured Zoya that Tara could do her job in safety and comfort, take her payment, and leave. She needed money. He wanted a good lead dancer and choreographer who understood the job but wouldn't ask for the going rates in Mumbai. Seven nights of dancing at the revamped and relocated Blue Bar, and training a few girls. Easy.

The last thirteen years were about diapers, potty training, school-work, mealtime tantrums. Her Pia.

A reality divorced from the one she'd left behind in Mumbai.

She watched the huge billboards that flanked the road and stared at the latest crop of movie stars. She'd been naive—dreaming of the impossible. Her phone buzzed and she checked the message.

Pia, asking her if she'd landed yet. She dared not call Pia unless she was by herself—the less Shetty knew about her current life, the better. She tapped out a message, promising her daughter she'd call later. Tara exhaled, and closed her eyes. All this caution might prove pointless.

Zoya had argued that yes, their escape had hurt Shetty's business, but the bigger disaster was the banning of bars in Mumbai. Now that the government was approving licenses again, Shetty could make his money back, and more. Tara need focus only on Pia, and the new international school where she might get admission, if only Tara could put together the fees for the next few years until her daughter became eligible for scholarship.

Tara needed to cash in on her strengths while her body lasted, while she could swing double duty as both lead bar dancer and choreographer. By the time she hit forty, she'd have to fall back on choreography. That didn't pay much in a smaller city like Lucknow, and she didn't have enough connections to make it in a megapolis like Mumbai. Pia would be twenty-one by then—graduated from college. Ready for higher studies, and marriage, someday.

Zoya had asked her to call Arnav, tell him about Pia and ask for help—but what would she say? *I didn't tell you, but you have a teenage daughter? I missed you more than I imagined I would?* Where would she be today had she run to Arnav instead? No point in giving in to fantasies. Arnav must have married by now, fathered other children. An illegitimate daughter could not be on his wish list.

Tara opened her eyes when the car stopped, stuck in traffic. A *pao bhaji* stall sat on the opposite side of the road, and Tara recalled the spicy curry that used to set her tongue on fire. She slid open a window for a better look, but closed it soon after. Mumbai's fumes had grown stronger. Traffic smoke hazed her windows. In the rear seat of an old Maruti van ahead of her car, she spotted a huge white goat, its face as big as the window, its body barely fitting the width of the car, its eyes wide in terror. Tara turned away and made herself breathe till the car moved again.

An hour later, the driver turned into a swanky apartment complex. "We're here, madam."

She'd never seen where Shetty lived, but with his old scooter he rode to work, it couldn't have been in this gated condominium. The driver waved to the guard, who opened the high gates for the car. Fountains, a lush garden, small pathways—the walls had hidden away the secret garden, one untouched by the slums across the road. No open drains in this Mumbai, no squalling, half-naked children, no cows or goats, no stray dogs. The same city, but two countries, poles apart. Shetty seemed to have done well with all the other restaurants he used to boast about. Why was he even opening a dance bar again? The car pulled up in front of a glass-walled lobby, and Tara straightened her shirt before stepping out. Time to face her old boss.

Shetty's man led her to a lift and punched in the fifty-ninth floor.

Moments later, the lift dinged open into a living room, making Tara sway as it came to a stop. Tara recognized it as Shetty's apartment because of the gold-trimmed carpet, the chairs and tables on gold legs, and the gold-framed deities that covered the walls. The air was dense with incense and camphor burned over years.

It reminded her of Shetty's previous office, a small, windowless room tucked upstairs at the rear of the bar—fragrant with incense, sandalwood, and flowers from an altar brimming with gods attired in white and gold.

In those days, he never wore anything other than a white short-sleeve shirt and a white *mundu*. White ash marked his forehead in a vertical streak.

Tara took a step back when her boss, giving her the same old fatherly smile, parted heavy brocade curtains and emerged like a ghost from yesteryear. He had grayed at the temples and sideburns and walked with a slouch, but was otherwise much the same. The smear of ash at his forehead remained, and he still favored the same white outfit. The only change was the assortment of studded gold rings, gold bracelets, and chains that weighed him down.

He gestured her to a chair. That was new. She'd never sat in his presence.

Tara took in the expanse of sky visible from the balcony behind Shetty. The highest she had ever been, if she did not count the recent flight she'd taken.

With a faint clink of his bracelets, Shetty lowered himself into a chair, ornate enough to have been picked off the set of a historical movie. "You must be tired after your flight."

This was new, as well. *Tired, what tired,* Shetty said often, with his smile in place, his eyes stern. *Drink a glass of water and get back onstage.*

Zoya, who had trained her when she first came to the bar at thirteen, would warn her: *You dance well, but save it for the right clients who come in late at night, or you'll be too tired by then. The older men toss more money.* Tara had laughed. She didn't believe dancers were showered with money till she saw it for herself, peeking from behind the door that served as the makeup room for the fifteen girls who worked at the Blue Bar.

This was not the Blue Bar, but it didn't seem all that unfamiliar as Shetty inspected her like the grocer back in Lucknow watched the weighing scales. Assessing, measuring. "You are all grown up, but Zoya was right, you don't show your age."

Tara perched on the edge of a chair opposite him, the cushion unyielding under her butt. No reply was expected. Tara made none.

"You will open the show, followed by the other girls—Zoya tells me you've worked as a choreographer?"

How much had Zoya told this man? Tara wanted the money, but she also wished to keep Pia and her life back in Lucknow sealed away from the week she would spend here.

"Tara?"

"Yes."

"Teach the girls. Some of them are new. These days the audience expects more than they did in your time. Make sure they look good together."

In your time. Tara was in her thirties now. New girls, new world. She wasn't a bar girl all over again, but the teacher. Someone who told them what to do.

"Any questions?"

Years ago, Tara would have shaken her head. She stood up instead. "My advance?"

"Taken care of." Shetty motioned to his man who stood quietly by the door. He stepped forward and handed her a packet. "That's for the first two nights," Shetty said. "Do well, and you won't leave unhappy."

Tara slipped the packet in her purse, knowing she would count it as soon as she was alone.

CHAPTER TWENTY-ONE

BILAL

In his small one-room place, Bilal sank into a soft, much-used leather chair. This hideaway was not close to the boy's Andheri apartment, but not so far that he couldn't rush back if summoned. The boy had given him the third degree, and he'd stomached it: kept quiet through the verbal lashing and even a shove. Rasool *Bhai* was his contact. His role was to make sure that things meant to vanish didn't reappear. Now Mumbai Police had found three of the old burials, and this last one. Bilal put his face in his hands. He should have run when he had a chance.

His phone would ring any minute now. Bilal told himself not to sweat. He'd handled this for a while. Rasool wouldn't find out.

Rasool had waged a war with Vijayan and lost a huge chunk of his business to the don all of Mumbai knew as *Uhnna*, but he'd also made *Uhnna* retreat to Dubai. If he came to know that Vijayan's men had procured the bodies he buried, well, Bilal could picture a few repercussions. All equally unpleasant. Bilal had tried telling the boy, but the boy wouldn't listen.

Bilal's phone rang exactly at 4:00 p.m. He wished all of India would learn punctuality from the mob bosses.

"Thanks for talking to me, *Bhai*."

Bilal had a complaint, but after his last exchange with *Bhai*, he needed to play this carefully.

"You've called about the trouble with the package."

Rasool knew, and hadn't told him. They all called it a package, as if it were not human. It wasn't any longer, not after the boy was done with it.

"I wish you had let me know, *Bhai*. The *pandus* found three old ones."

A *pandu*, or an idiotic policeman. Except that the inspector who discovered the bodies held quite the opposite reputation.

"The old ones must have rotted by now. The new package will tell them nothing. The delivery van was unmarked. No one will find it. Don't worry."

Bilal wanted to slap the don till his ears rang. The unwritten contract said never bury them in Mumbai. How could Rasool's men have buried three bodies that close to one another? With the money Rasool had lapped up, Bilal could have bought an apartment or two in a film star neighborhood.

"The agreement was to make them disappear, *Bhai*."

Always be polite; never mention how much you paid, Bilal reminded himself.

"The boys panicked this time." A hint of dire menace entered his tone. "They are not on my team anymore."

After a beat or two of silence, Rasool continued, "We'll do it for free the next time."

"There won't be another time." If the boy messed up again, Bilal wouldn't hang around to clean it up. He'd taken measures.

"There will be a next time. What about the items my boys sent to you? Are they working?"

Bilal had forked out a huge sum for said items, but Rasool *Bhai* made it sound like a favor.

Bilal cut the call with more assurances from *Bhai*. Years ago, Bilal's contacts at the mosque had put the two in touch. *Bhai* didn't know Bilal's real name and address. Bilal wondered if that was still the case.

Would Rasool's men do what they were paid for—take the fall if they were arrested? They were not the professionals Rasool had led him to believe.

Bilal stood up. If the investigation heated up, he must disappear, no matter what he'd promised, or to whom. He needed a backup plan.

CHAPTER TWENTY-TWO

ARNAV

Despite the days spent mulling over it, Arnav was no closer to a decision on Joshi's promotion offer.

He needed to speak with his boss, but Mhatre hadn't returned to his office since that day—he was at a weeklong seminar.

Arnav stared at the board facing him, where he'd scrawled the cases in order.

Cold cases.

N M Joshi Marg Police Station: 2002
Woman's pelvic structure and the femur. No skull, hands, feet. Unsolved.
Investigating officer: retired, untraceable.

Dadar Police Station: 2003
Bones similar to above. Discolored sequins found during soil analysis.
Senior Inspector Bendre: died in a traffic accident.

Azad Nagar Station: 2008
Decomposed body, found in a sewer with no hands, head or feet.
Investigating officer: Inspector Gawde, transferred to Worli Local Arms
Division.

Arnav called Naik. She had left for the day—trouble with the fitting for her husband's artificial arm.

"Did you find out more on the death of Sub-Inspector Bendre?"

"Traffic accident, sir, but they never caught the culprits. Mhatre sir signed off on the file."

Arnav paused. So Tukaram had been right.

"No CCTV footage?"

"No cameras on that stretch of road back in 2003, sir. Nor any witnesses that late at night. The road was under repair. No identifiable tire tracks on the gravel. By the time they found his body, he'd been dead many hours."

"Right, Naik, thanks."

"I've emailed you the details." Naik paused. "Thank you for the reference, sir."

"Don't mention it."

Arnav cut the call and refreshed his email, tapping his feet as the slow connection tested his patience.

An official reference from Arnav amounted to a free consultation for Naik's husband—a small thing to do for a good officer. He often wished he could do more. His job references for her husband hadn't helped as much as the word with the doctor.

Arnav turned back to his board.

The other investigators had disappeared, but he could have a chat with Inspector Gawde.

Arnav checked his computer. He'd given an interview a few days ago for the Versova case. Several newspapers had picked it up. He'd mentioned the connection with Taneja's site, but not the bodies Meshram discovered, and he'd refrained from even a whisper of the cases at Dadar, Azad Nagar, and N M Joshi Marg. He couldn't afford to tip off the killer.

The snippet articles that stemmed from his interview might flush out information from someone in cahoots with the culprit or the disposal team. Many in Mumbai's underworld combed the crime section of newspapers looking to sell intel in exchange for a slice of the not insignificant budget the Mumbai Police maintained for their informal sources.

Arnav's gang of *khabri* scurried about in the alleyways of Mumbai like an infestation of rats. Not large rats, the ones the sanitation department employed an army of workers to kill, those intimidating bandicoots going about their business on Mumbai pavements with more conviction than some of its human inhabitants. His men were stealthier, but he hadn't heard a peep out of them yet. A group of rats was called a mischief, Arnav had learned in school. He chafed for them to be true to their name.

Ali hadn't managed to sneak into the garage for a picture of the black van. Nor had he sent in tips on that disposal contract. The small-time goon who had babbled about it had vanished. Rumor said he might not return. This fit in with Arnav's theory that Rasool had taken the contract. He'd snuff out a tattletale in a snap. Ali must receive another reminder, and an offer he couldn't refuse.

Arnav next checked the updates from Naik—two women missing from different zones of Mumbai, otherwise matching the victim's approximate description, ruled out. Neither had a birthmark under the breast.

Arnav took a snapshot of the board with his phone, so he could refer to it even when far from office. He then turned the board to face the wall. Before he left, he must finish his pending reports, and notes for testimonies due in court.

His phone beeped: a message from Dr. Meshram asking if he could call. He dialed Meshram's number.

"I need to apologize," Dr. Meshram said.

In all the cases he'd handled so far with Arnav, Dr. Meshram had never made an apology.

"What's the matter?"

"A new finding in the Versova case. It resembles an earring but with clamps on both sides. I'll email you a picture."

"Why didn't we spot it earlier?"

"My regular assistant was on leave on the postmortem date. His replacement hired a daily temp as his helper. This man stole it from the body."

"We were at the crime scene," Arnav said. "We would've spotted it."

"It was stuck under the body, the helper says, between the legs. He thought it was a fake stone, but it should be examined. Looks like a sapphire."

A sapphire? This was curious. Arnav recalled that the murdered woman's entire body was depilated. From his experience in other cases, this was a frequent practice in the porn and prostitution industry.

"How do we know it is from that particular body?"

"We hired that particular helper on that case alone. My temporary assistant saw the man with it today. You know how some of them are."

The helpers touched the bodies no one in the police force would. They ferried cadavers within and outside the morgue, to crematoriums and burials, and occasionally assisted with positioning the bodies or machines during postmortems. They were either high or drunk most of the time, and often red-eyed. He didn't blame them. To survive without training, and with minimal protection, the routine horrors of unclaimed bodies—decomposed, bombed, charred, run over—anyone would take to drink.

"Send me that picture," Arnav said.

"Right away. It has an *M* scratched on one surface. Or it could be a *W*, depending."

"Please make a note of that detail," Arnav said. "Dr. Meshram, I'll have to put this in my report to Senior Inspector Shinde."

"I was hoping . . ."

Arnav softened his voice. "I'll describe the details of the event, and make sure your temporary assistant and the helper are mentioned. I'll not mark you for negligence, but that's the best I can do."

If he wanted Dr. Meshram to go out of his way for him on cases again, Arnav had to cut him a break. Relationships ran the police world, just like any other.

"Is there anything else"—Arnav weighed his words—"from any of the cold cases we sent to you for review?"

"I was about to come to that. The bones from the Dadar case. They have chips or marks on the shinbones, the tibia and the fibula. These are at the lower end, where they meet the talus to form the ankle joint. The device used might have been a saw, based on the shape of the marks."

"This confirms that the foot was sawed off?"

"Yes." There was a sound of pages being turned. "This case was from 2003. Whoever is cutting up these bodies may have . . . made progress with experience, *kya*, like a medical student. This time the cut was clean, through the joint. I'll send you pictures."

A Ravan who had improved with practice. Arnav huffed a sigh. Seven women over the years. There could be more—many of them never found. This Ravan was unlikely to stop unless the police nabbed him. Neither Mhatre nor Joshi seemed to realize that this case could be much bigger than Raman Raghav, who had bludgeoned dozens of slum dwellers to death many decades ago. That arrest had earned the police officer involved a President's Medal and a promotion to the post of assistant commissioner of Mumbai Police.

More importantly, the killer might even now be stalking their next victim.

Arnav required a longer article, in bigger papers. An in-depth investigative feature about all the stalled investigations in an international newspaper could do the trick. A police corruption angle tied in, with Joshi in the crosshairs. He'd have to tell Shinde about the detailed feature, the jewelry, and most crucial—that Rasool probably owned the black van and had a contract with Taneja.

Joshi and Mhatre would look the other way due to Taneja's connections in high places. A tycoon like him could certainly afford a contract for the disposal of bodies, or sapphire jewelry.

Arnav's phone rang—the very man he wanted to speak with.

"Why have you spoken to the papers without telling me?" Shinde snapped, with no attempt at a greeting. Arnav paused before responding to his friend. Shinde needed to ease off on people and take his painkillers on the regular.

"You asked me to assist on the case—this is part of the process. If someone has a tip, they will come forward for the right reward."

"I'm taking you off the case."

"I may have useful information. It could lead to Rasool."

"Doesn't matter. You may already have warned Rasool off now. Return the case to the Versova station."

"Let me talk to you at home first, all right? Why are you—"

"No more interviews to the press, you hear?"

"Fine."

"You'll hand over the case as soon as I'm back at office."

Arnav must stall this till he knew more on the black getaway van, and the sapphire. Shinde would act reasonable once he noticed progress.

When his phone alerted next, Arnav clicked on the picture Dr. Meshram had sent him. He scrolled through the photos of the bones, noting the chips Meshram had remarked on. The jewelry, silver with blue stone teardrops, had no hoops or fasteners, only thick clamps at the ends that you could bend. He asked Dr. Meshram to send him the item. The good doctor may not have specified what it was, but Arnav had a good hunch about it.

CHAPTER TWENTY-THREE

BILAL

It was a risk for Bilal, deploying the items he'd bought from Rasool at the boy's apartment or the farmhouse. If the boy found them, Bilal would be the sole suspect—the only one who cleaned the bedroom and, occasionally, the study.

Not keeping track of the boy made him anxious, and with good reason. If caught unaware, he wouldn't know if and when to cut and run. Hunkered in his den, Bilal stared at the device he'd sneaked out from under the boy's bedside table. It could easily be mistaken for a screw in the furniture, and didn't come cheap. Long-lasting battery, the best microphone, large memory.

He downloaded the file, connected his headphones, and listened.

Much static, music. Voices. The boy's conversations, some of them with himself. It didn't amount to a lot. Some were on topics Bilal had zero interest in. Others, he already knew about. This was how he liked it.

One of the calls gave Bilal pause. The Home Minister had risen in the ranks with help from the boy, and the boy had decided to call in a favor. The poor policeman who had found the package would see a transfer, routine or otherwise. Bilal huffed in relief—once the investigation stalled, no one would come looking for Bilal. If things turned hairy, the boy wouldn't hesitate to make Bilal a scapegoat.

The next call was with *Uhnna*, the one man the boy addressed with respect. No more deliveries, *Uhnna* remained firm, even if the packages remained intact. Not to the farmhouse, and not even to the railway station.

"This case won't go any further." The boy's recorded voice remained steady. Bilal could picture him, sweating, dressed in khaki, having snorted a line of white from the table. The boy never sounded as measured as when he was high as a kite.

"My men did their job. I won't put them at risk. They cost good money."

The boy begged, promised favors. Swore it wouldn't happen again.

Bilal chuckled. In Mumbai, everyone performs for someone else. Everyone comes with a price tag. He scrubbed the device clean, ready to plant it again. All was safe, for now, as long as the boy succeeded in stalling the Versova investigation.

CHAPTER TWENTY-FOUR

ARNAV

The irony of the situation was not lost on Arnav. He wanted to meet Mhatre, but there he was instead, seated on a wooden bench at the dojo, waiting for his appointment with the actor his bosses had dumped on him.

His *sensei* had let him have the place this afternoon—the large, well-lit hall with its cement floor covered by exercise mats. The dojo sat hidden by entire rows of street shops selling everything from bright plastic Chinese toys to groceries and traditional cast-iron pans, flanked by the odd tailor shop, and a shop selling *ittar*, little bottles of perfume distilled from old herbs and dried flowers. The fragrance drifted in, a faint whiff of jasmine and lavender, the scent of Tara at her neck, her hairline, a mixture of her hair oil and talcum.

The actor was late. Ten more minutes, and that would be the end of that. Arnav dialed Naik, who he hadn't seen in two days because of their clashing shifts at work.

"Any progress on the Aksa case?"

"Not so far, sir; the sequins on those bodies were too old. I checked some of the evidence from the Versova case—the watch strap from the site is not an expensive brand, but it's not cheap, either. No serial number on the strap. The blue sequins are pricey, but quite common. Most bigger markets stock them. We're asking around about their use."

"And the other item?" Arnav didn't bother spelling out *nipple clamp*. He trusted Naik to know what he meant based on the internet links he'd sent her along with the pictures from Dr. Meshram. After the initial jokes, his team had researched all companies that offered online deliveries of sex toys in India. This particular design, like an unwieldy ear ornament with added clamps, was not included.

The blue sapphires, delicate teardrops encased in silver, were the genuine goods. Blue sequins and a blue adult toy—the killer might harbor a fascination for the color blue. And a relationship to the letter *M* or *W*.

Dr. Meshram had mentioned that the cuts showed surgical experience. A medical professional, maybe.

Arnav placed his odds on the clamp being custom-made, so he'd asked his team to check if it was sold in a shop locally, or bought outside the city. A constable had prepared a list of boutique shops in Mumbai.

"Any luck with the jewelry shop list?"

"We've eliminated quite a few, sir."

"Keep me updated. What's new on the CCTV footage?"

Ali still hadn't managed to photograph the hidden van, but had passed on the address of the garage. CCTV in the area might provide glimpses of that vehicle. Arnav hadn't yet spoken to Shinde, who had to go in for surgery on his arm.

"We may have some relevant footage, sir. We're working with video forensics."

Arnav asked for updates on other assignments he'd given the unflappable Naik, and cut the call. The conversation had taken fifteen minutes, and Rehaan hadn't come in.

Arnav started switching off the lights, preparing to hand over the keys to the guard, when Rehaan Virani walked in, leaving his shoes at the door. He seemed to overwhelm the low-ceilinged hall and the faint strains of zen music wafting in the air. A bright-blue cap held his long hair in place, and he wore dark glasses.

"Sorry to be late," Rehaan said as he extended his hand, "but very pleased to meet you again."

"I wish I could say the same." Arnav smiled to show he was joking. "But I'm here on official orders."

Rehaan raised his hands in a sheepish gesture of apology quite at odds with his wrestler's build. "I'd asked my agent to look you up, but my mother had already 'helped' me by then. She's a huge fan of using people for her own ends."

Arnav disliked the way Rehaan spoke of his mother, but having had a father married to the bottle, he felt a certain sympathy for a man who couldn't stand his parent. And Arnav himself was no different from Kittu Virani—teaching karate with ulterior motives. The *sensei* wouldn't have approved, had he known.

Arnav didn't want to train an actor on orders from his superiors, but he did want information on Taneja. This was as good a way as any.

"Why don't we sit?" He gestured to a shiny wooden bench, one of several lining the wall.

Rehaan took off his cap, placing it on a shelf near the door. "We'll begin with shooting the climax of the movie—that's why all this." He waved his massive hands around his beard and ponytail.

Arnav had read up on Rehaan before this meeting. Two of Rehaan's girlfriends had called the police—one because he was being abusive, and the other for wrecking her car. So much for his talk about Taneja's treatment of women. Rehaan had a reputation for his temper, despite being the brother of Karan Virani, the star known for his genteel calm. Tara worshipped the ground that sappy chocolate-boy walked on. Arnav caught his wandering thoughts and focused on Rehaan's spiel.

"I'm playing a Mumbai Police ACP in my next film. I have some martial arts training, of course, but my director wants me to work with a karate expert, because the character was a competitive champion before joining the police. You're an inspector—I could learn aspects of protocol in the police force as well."

"Sure. I'll do my best. When does your shoot begin?"

"In a week, but they won't require you right away when the shoot begins."

"What sort of preparation?"

"Depends on what you think I need. Some consultation during the shoot. The action director might request guidance on the set with Karan. Also, a little help with the body language and life at a police station. The struggles, the rewards."

"Karan Virani is part of this movie?"

Rehaan laughed, and Arnav realized why girls swooned over this man. Despite all the facial hair, his rich laughter turned him charismatic.

"Yes, he's the villain," Rehaan said. "His first-ever negative role, so there's a lot of excitement. I must get each nuance exactly right."

Tara used to drag him to Karan Virani's singsong movies, which were as balmy as the man himself. No one was sad. Everyone drove Ferraris. Their biggest problem seemed to involve not having the perfect outfit to wear to a party—typical cotton candy Bollywood nonsense. Arnav used to sit through the headache-inducing crap in order to watch Tara alternate between rapture and tears, an unspoken ambition and longing in her gaze.

"The action director had asked to join us today," Rehaan's voice broke in, "but I told him I should talk to you first."

"Let's try out a few stances." Arnav wanted to gauge the work that lay ahead. "Follow my lead. We can try sparring. *Kumite.*"

Rehaan nodded, left his sunglasses on the bench, and rose to take his place on one of the mats. Arnav switched on the lights and placed himself at the ready. Rehaan was the taller of the two and broader, but once they bowed to each other and began the *kumite* in earnest, Arnav noted Rehaan's slower responses. The way he carried his muscular bulk, and instances when the actor's crescent and roundhouse kicks lacked finesse. As Arnav moved from one stance to another, Rehaan faltered, but soon fell into the rhythm of the exchange. He was trained—although he moved with a certain flourish, like a dojo ballerina who'd never been in a real fight. Arnav was about to call a halt when he heard someone call Rehaan's name. A woman.

Rehaan took his eyes off the fight. A blow from Arnav that should have been parried landed on the movie star's chest. He staggered and fell. Arnav reached out to help him up, but couldn't stop staring at Kittu Virani. She approached in a tight-fitting dress that must have seen life as a shower curtain at some point.

"How long were we supposed to wait? You think we have nothing else to do?" Kittu swanned in on tall heels.

Before Rehaan could speak, Arnav said, "You need to take off your shoes before entering the dojo."

"And who made those rules?" Kittu turned the expressionless mask of her face toward Arnav.

"I'm sorry," Rehaan said to Arnav. "We'll leave now."

Kittu ignored Rehaan. "You are a police officer, with a job. Do what your boss tells you to do. Let others worry over rules."

"Like who, Ms. Virani? Does Mr. Taneja make the rules? You are a woman yourself. Aren't you curious why we found three dead, decomposing women on a site where your fiancé's company is running a project?"

"Do you have any idea who Rahul is? He employs men like you as security guards and pays them double what you earn in a month. That project is mine, too. And that's not protected land. Go check who contested it before you make wild accusations."

Vijayan. Land mafia. Naik's words came back to Arnav. Vijayan had grabbed the site, but the government had sold it to Taneja Estate Holdings.

"I'm sure you can tell me."

"Let's go, Mom." Rehaan ushered his mother out, and turned to mouth to Arnav, "I'm sorry. Call you later."

He reached to pick up his shoes and cap on the way out, and the dojo was silent again.

Arnav ignored his annoyance at the haughty socialite, and considered the facts. Taneja and Vijayan didn't see eye to eye. Vijayan and Rasool Mohsin's rivalry had fueled legends for decades. Rasool Mohsin might have taken a contract for disposing of the victim from the Versova site. Had he taken the contract for the bodies at Aksa, and deliberately buried them at a site Vijayan was associated with in order to get his rival in trouble?

Arnav asked the dojo's security guard to lock up, apologizing for the drama he had witnessed.

Walking to his old car, he looked up the road to find a large black Scorpio truck parked at the turn. Kittu sat inside, and Rehaan stood outside, pacifying her. Another man sat beside the driver, but the semi-tinted windows obscured his features. Rehaan spotted Arnav, waved to him, entered the Scorpio, and drove off.

From the articles Arnav had found during his research on Kittu and Rehaan Virani, one thing was clear. No matter how much Rehaan resented his mother, she dictated the decisions in his life—who he should date, the events he should attend. Not for the first time, Arnav felt relief at being unencumbered. Family could be a right millstone around the neck.

CHAPTER TWENTY-FIVE

TARA

Her first evening in Mumbai, Tara checked her phone once more time as she prepared to meet Shetty's new girls. No word from either Zoya or Pia, and neither had read her messages. Pia must be home from school by now. Tara walked out of the three-star hotel room where Shetty had put her up. Striding through an airless corridor with a ragged carpet, she stepped out onto the street.

She dialed Pia, but the phone was switched off. When she called Zoya, her friend's phone played a long caller tune, asking the world in casual Hindi to stay chilled out, to relax, to be carefree. Tara hated these squeaky tunes that sang into your ear in place of the regular telephone ring. Mouth dry, stomach uneasy, Tara held the device tighter to her ear. Waiting on phones unsettled her—a reminder of the times she held on for one to ring, which would propel her into a desperate sprint across the Borivali railway station. She recognized the first stirrings of a headache, the tingling at her neck that meant she'd suffer later. Someone in the neighborhood had lit sandalwood incense, and Tara tried to ignore it.

The scent brought back that room where she'd worked for four horrific years of her life, starting when she was thirteen. Pia's age. At seventeen, she'd hated the place for the way it sucked the life out of her, and loved it for letting her live at all—walls plastered over with posters of Bollywood heroes, the mirrors framed in bright plastic, red, pink, orange; the icons of various gods and goddesses smeared with sandalwood, red *kumkum*, and in some cases, soot from the incense; the rickety stools and chairs the girls sat on, the cot where the older women rested their feet, sore from hours of dancing. That day when her life changed, she'd seemed to see the entire room at once. Each object harsh, separate.

At 3:00 a.m. on her chair, surrounded by the chatter of the girls packing up and calling cheerful goodbyes laced with swear words, it was all Tara could do to keep her stomach calm. She could taste each individual smell—tobacco, weed, perfumes—and craved nothing more than to get away, but her limbs would not obey her brain, which was zinging back and forth between snippets of odd fancies.

"Let's go." Zoya had slapped her shoulder, making her flinch. "You can finish up your dreaming at home."

That was Zoya, hurting you even when she meant to be kind.

Back in the apartment, Tara had crashed on her bed.

"What's wrong?" Zoya said. "You never sleep without a bath."

"Let the others take their turn. I might throw up."

The next second, Tara had run to the toilet. She'd returned to find Zoya hovering, a glass of water in hand.

"Salt and sugar water."

Tara had taken a sip, felt nausea rise again.

"You've been looking tired the last few days," Zoya said. "Is this the first time you threw up?"

"No, been a few times already."

"You know that you must get a checkup?"

Tara had looked at Zoya, and understood. Zoya had explained that she must be careful. She'd been careful. So had Arnav. If this turned out as Zoya suspected, what would she do?

"Don't look so lost. I'll come with you if you want. If there's a thing, get rid of it."

Zoya had gone for six abortions in the four years Tara had known her. This was the only option for Tara, too. Her plans were too close to working out, and like Zoya said, a bar girl's kids were like rats, spreading filth, drawing hatred from this world.

When it was her turn to use the bathroom, Tara had stepped into the shower and, after reaching for the loofah, scrubbed her skin of the leering glances and greedy hands that had touched her all night. In her village, the luffa vine grew strong on the back fence, heavy with gourds each summer. Her mother peeled off the outer flesh of the gourds they did not eat, squeezed out the black seeds, and let the sponge harden in the sun. *Noyontara, your skin will shine once you clean yourself with this. Always be clean.*

She'd gazed at her still-flat stomach, stroked it, softly at first, then with increasing roughness, patted it, slapped it, harder, curling her hand into a fist, biting her lips against the pain until she'd collapsed on the floor.

That's where Zoya had found her an hour later, naked, curled into herself, one hand holding the loofah to her stomach, the other fisted under her chin.

"Stop crying." Zoya had hauled her up. "And don't even think about telling him. Come to bed now."

While Zoya had fussed over her, helping her get dressed, Tara imagined Arnav holding her like in the movies and taking her to a fancy clinic with shiny floors and high ceilings, more a hotel than a hospital. A police constable could afford that for once, couldn't he? He gave her girlfriend-type presents. He did not hit her. He was not much older, barely twenty-two, and not half-bad-looking. She could tell him.

He wouldn't marry her, never that—not even in a temple alone, with the bells ringing. It was an accident, and meant nothing.

Tara told herself she didn't long for those bells.

She had Pia now. That was enough. She gathered herself, waiting for the caller tune to exhaust itself and die, when Zoya said hello.

"Where are you? Why haven't you been checking your messages? Is everything fine? Is Pia doing well?"

"All OK, Tara. Breathe."

"Why didn't you reply to my messages?" Tara said.

"I left my phone at home."

"I've deposited the money to your account, so you can pay off some bills."

"Don't worry, we are OK . . ."

"Is that Ma?" Pia's voice sounded faint in the distance.

"I'll talk to you soon—focus on your work, all right?" Zoya said. "I'm taking care of Pia."

"Ma?" Pia was on the line.

"How are you doing?"

Pia switched to video, and Tara put on her wired earphones.

"How are you, doll?"

Tara touched the screen, outlining her daughter's face, which still held traces of the child she used to be, round-faced and soft. At thirteen, she grew taller each month and her face looked more like Arnav's. His broad forehead, straight nose. She had Tara's large eyes, though.

"Did you get any work done today, Ma?"

Tara couldn't look away, but she wanted to. She tried never to lie to her daughter, not unless it came to the question of her father.

"I start tomorrow."

That was partially true. She wouldn't work in an office, but her first appointment with the girls was in a few minutes.

"You're wearing your gym clothes."

"Yes, I will head there now. Keep sending me messages and pictures, OK, doll?"

"You didn't even notice."

Tara pulled a serious face and peered at her daughter's image on the screen. "You have a new hairdo."

"A french plait, Zoya *masi* made it for me, and tied it with my favorite scrunchie—look!" Pia turned, showing off her hair, intricately braided, and a red scrunchie. Tara bought red scrunchies by the dozen so her daughter could believe she'd never lost her favorite over the years.

"Smashing." Tara borrowed from Pia's vocabulary. She tried not to encourage Pia obsessing over her appearance, but with a gaggle of classmates who thought of little else, it was hard.

"I think so, too." Pia prattled on about how long it had taken, how she'd worn it to school and been the envy of her entire class, and how she'd aced her math test.

They exchanged kisses before Pia cut the call. The show Pia watched each evening was about to begin. Tara rushed back to her room, because she was already late for her class with her new students.

On her way out again, she dropped Zoya a message. "Call me when she's asleep."

CHAPTER TWENTY-SIX

ARNAV

Early in the morning, when Arnav reached the Worli Local Arms Division, it looked desolate. Before he stepped out of his car, he checked through the file—Naik had given him photocopies of documents necessary for Inspector Gawde, the lead investigator of the decapitated body found at Azad Nagar Police Station. His phone beeped. Nandini. He hadn't been in touch in the past few days. She'd messaged to ask him to go with her to the opening of a bar.

He was early for his appointment with Gawde, so he dialed her.

"You want me to come with you?"

"Hello, Avi. I'm fine, thank you." Nandini laughed.

"I know, I'm sorry. But you're good, right? What's this about a bar?" The name sounded familiar. The Blue Bar.

"I'm doing a feature on Mumbai's dance bars and the decision to reopen them. I can go alone, but it might be more useful to take you along. You were part of the operation that enforced the closure of dance bars."

Yes, he was a constable in those days, right in the thick of the action. He remembered the Blue Bar now. Tara. That was the dance bar where he'd seen her first, while on assignment. She was young under layers of makeup, her expression the same as his mother's when stirring a chutney, only Tara danced on a small stage in front of a large cave of a room full of whistling, catcalling men.

Flashing strobe lights alternately obscured and emphasized her breasts, doing some of the work for her. She held herself back, unlike the girls around her, swaying where others gyrated. He'd gone there to watch his target, Rasool Mohsin, who was watching yet another—Tara's tall, rather pudgy friend Zoya. The second, and the last, time he went to the Blue Bar was when Tara disappeared. Zoya had vanished as well, and their friends said they might have left together.

An evening at the Blue Bar would bring back painful memories. Arnav was tempted to refuse Nandini, but he'd ignored her, and owed her one.

"How long do you wish to be there?"

"I want to go in late. See if I can speak with any of the girls."

He didn't long for Nandini, though he wished he did. She was a journalist, not a bar dancer, and she cared for him. She was also present in his life. Hadn't disappeared without a trace, like a whisper in the night.

He shook his head—if you can't give your girlfriend the attention she craves, the next best thing is your time. Arnav said yes, and entered the police station.

He came upon Gawde trying to troubleshoot with his team. The door was open and Arnav could hear the discussion as he paced the main office area, waiting. The team was deputed on a train journey across state borders to escort an accused awaiting trial, and alleged that earlier travel expenses had not been paid. Gawde assured them he'd look into it, asked them to come up with an estimate on how much the trip under discussion would cost, told them he was fighting in their corner. A competent police officer. Yet he'd been shunted out on what Mhatre had called a punishment posting.

Once the team had dispersed, Gawde invited Arnav into his office.

"How can I help you, sir?" Gawde gestured Arnav to a seat and lowered his stocky frame into a chair. "We have a small team, as you can see. I don't think we have any undertrial from your station."

Arnav wondered if this was sarcasm, but Gawde's smile was friendly, open.

"It's about a case," Arnav began.

"For you to come all the way here, it must be quite important."

"I wanted to hear from you. You were the first officer on the scene." Arnav reminded Gawde of the Azad Nagar case, giving him a quick summary.

"That was quite a while ago. I left that station soon after. Why are you interested?"

"The case is still unsolved. We might reopen it."

Gawde said, "You've been transferred back to the Crime Branch?"

Arnav laughed. "You know I was at the Crime Branch?"

"You won a President's Gallantry Award a few years ago for that shoot-out case, right? I've kept track."

"I'm not moving back, no. I wondered about this case"—he handed over the photocopies—"because we came across a similar one last week." Arnav showed Gawde the details from the Versova file.

Gawde considered the papers on the table.

"All the information is already in the *panchnama*." He turned away. "It was so long ago."

"I understand. But you found the body on November 26, 2008, right?"

"The Municipal Corporation, BMC, called us early that morning. A main sewer pipe had developed a blockage. Upon investigating, they discovered the body. By afternoon, we had made the *panchnama* but before we could investigate further, the control room sent out an emergency call."

"You engaged in action against the terrorists?" Arnav asked the question, though he already knew the answer. He had read up on Gawde.

"Only as backup."

"What happened to the case?"

"For a few days, as you know, everything was up in the air."

"And later?"

"No one came forward with any information, and we couldn't identify the body. All we could conjecture was that it may actually have been dumped somewhere else."

"What makes you say that?"

"The body was covered in mud and cow dung. BMC confirmed no cow dung in the sewage. They said the body could have laid buried in an abandoned farm area farther along the length of the pipe, near the Sanjay Gandhi National Park. That pipe had broken a week or so earlier, and mud had fallen in. Maybe the body slipped into the pipe along with the mud, and was flushed farther into the drain."

Sanjay Gandhi National Park. That was less than an hour's drive from the body found near Versova.

Gawde turned to the door, as though wishing for someone to enter. "Then I was transferred."

"A routine reshuffle?"

Mumbai Police went through occasional reshuffles at the higher levels, commissioners and deputy commissioners, often influenced by political decisions. Some of that trickled down to the lower rungs of the hierarchy. Arnav wanted to confirm Mhatre's statement about the punishment posting.

"How is that related with the case?" Gawde looked annoyed now.

"The case went cold, so I'm gathering all the information possible. Did the press report on it?"

"Once you're transferred, you're transferred." Gawde stood up. "The press was busy reporting on more important matters at the time. Look,

I've given you all I can. You need to leave now. I'm scheduled to meet someone."

Arnav noted the lack of enthusiasm. He wouldn't get another word out of the inspector. Gawde shook hands and followed Arnav out of the police station.

Arnav paused on the way to his car to check his messages. Gawde stepped into his car, started it, and leaned out the window. "Leave that case alone. From one policeman to another—no good will come of it. And watch your back. Especially with your boss. Ravi Mhatre, right?"

Gawde drove off before Arnav could reply.

Once in his car, Arnav messaged Mhatre, asking for a few minutes with him. He knew what to say to his boss now.

CHAPTER TWENTY-SEVEN
—
TARA

Going by the frayed and discolored red carpet, a few decorations hanging on the walls, and the boxes and chairs piled up in various corners, Shetty had given Tara an old wedding reception hall for their practice.

The gaggle of women she'd met the day before stood chatting under bright-white lights. Various ages—a few teenagers in western clothes, others much older. They turned when Tara entered. Some of them smiled.

One of the older women called out, "So *you* are the teacher? The same Tara? You look as slim as ever."

Tara struggled to place the round-faced, curvy dancer who seemed to know her. She hadn't come in yesterday.

"Don't stare like we've never met." The woman broke into a grin, and memory slid into place. She was the sprightly girl Shetty had asked Tara to train more than a decade ago. Tara remembered her open, sleepy, warm smile that transformed her plain face into a remarkable one.

"Mithi?"

"Who else? You are a teacher now?"

"I teach, but I'll also perform for the opening week."

"You're still a bar girl?"

Mithi had lived in the apartment barely a month before Tara left Mumbai. She was from those days in the Mira Road apartment when

Tara woke up at 6:00 a.m. after going to bed at dawn, worked up a sweat with her calisthenics and yoga, slapped on a face pack, and read the newspaper to improve her English. Tara felt a pang of sadness for that foolish girl she once was. She had believed she could succeed if only she tried hard enough.

"We'll talk at lunchtime? You know how Shetty is."

"Yes, work, work, work."

"Let's get to it." Tara smiled, dropped her bag on a chair, and approached the women. "The opening is in two days, and Shetty wants a show to remember."

She spoke in her teacher voice. Pia, and even Zoya, listened to her when she used that tone. She arranged the women in a semicircle and asked Mithi to play the songs Shetty had sent. A crass Bollywood dance number burst from the speakers. She asked them to move to it. The results did not encourage her. Shetty had picked them for their looks, not talent. Each woman had ideas of her own—"sexy" steps, gestures likely to encourage the biggest shower of currency. In some ways, so little had changed.

As a child, she'd loved to dance. Her mother said, *Keep dancing like this, Noyon; always be happy,* but she wasn't Noyon anymore, nor Noyontara. She no longer moved to follow the rhythm the way she used to, uncaring of who watched her. For those four years in Mumbai, she'd danced in the smoky, flashing, colored light of the bar, twirled for the eyes of men, hungry eyes, rude eyes, eyes that clamored to take from her till she had nothing left to give, eyes of pride, of anger, of greed. Dirty eyes. She'd received a long reprieve in Lucknow—Pia had given her that—fourteen years of dancing without worrying if she'd dressed sexy enough to earn her keep. Now, she must again reach for that seasoned, seductive Tara. Teach these women a thing or two about being a bar dancer.

Tara introduced them to the concept of dancing together, to the beat. By the time Tara called for a break, she was on the point of collapse. She strolled out onto the street, and dialing Zoya, heard that Pia was out in the neighborhood with her friends. She cut the call and turned back.

"Did you just talk to Zoya on the phone?" Mithi stood behind her, wearing a big, guileless smile. Tara couldn't find it in herself to be upset. She nodded.

Mithi's eyes lit up. "So you and Zoya are all right."

"Why wouldn't we be?"

"Shetty went crazy on us after the two of you ran off. He looked scary, and I thought, *off kara diya.*"

Tara had heard that underworld slang, about getting someone murdered, whispered around the bar a lifetime ago. She waited for Mithi to continue.

"After we couldn't find you that night or the next day, Shetty talked to all of us. Yelled. The next week he asked us to line up and get our pictures taken. Nothing changed for a while, but then Gauri, you remember her, right?"

Tara nodded.

"Well, he gave Gauri some work."

"What?" Tara said, though she already knew.

"Whatever you used to do on the side. That's all she ever told me. One day, I saw her wearing a shawl and stepping into an auto. Strange it was to see her wrapped in that shawl in the afternoon. Last time I set eyes on her. She never returned."

This sent a chill through Tara, though they stood in the sun, across from a road with traffic, people. A shawl, as she had once worn.

"What did Shetty say?"

"He told us Gauri had gone to her village, like you two. Her things were gone. Soon after that, the bar shut down. So who knows, maybe Shetty was telling the truth. He was right about you guys."

Tara could not bring herself to speak. The terror she had escaped fourteen years ago clawed its way back in. Shetty, and his assignments to the railway station. And worse still, the temptation and dread of his "night work."

Tara had entered Shetty's office to return the saree and get her pay. The difference in Shetty's tone had put her on alert when he said, "Will you do night work?"

Night work meant selling her body. No shame in that, Zoya had said, as long as the woman was safe, and fine with the man she had to service. A woman owned her body. Zoya did it often enough, as did the other women. Tara knew the going rate: ₹5,000 a night. Full service—the client could get whatever he wanted, no questions. Tara had avoided it thus far. The thought of touching anyone other than Arnav made her gag.

"Safety guaranteed." Shetty's face was stern. "The pay will be sixty thousand. You'll have to do what you're told, but it will be a different kind of night work. No one will lay a hand on you. No touching at all."

Sixty thousand rupees for a night. She made that in six months of dancing, shaking her body from 7:00 p.m. to 3:00 a.m. six days a week, with only a few short breaks in between. She'd never seen ₹60,000 in one place.

Who paid that much for a private dance? And the client would not touch her? Even at the bar, men angled to grope or pinch her when they could. Logically, Shetty gave her a small cut of any money she received for the assignments, and pocketed the rest. Her head spun to think how much Shetty must have been paid for him to offer her ₹60,000.

That was money she'd needed for her career then, and money she must earn for her Pia now.

"I have children at home," Mithi said, "or I wouldn't be here."

Same here, Tara wanted to say. She tried to swallow the fear and bile in her throat, but after Mithi's story about another bar girl who had disappeared, it wouldn't go away. If not for Pia in her womb and Tara's escape in order to protect her, Tara might have vanished, too.

"Tara?" Mithi's eyes widened in concern.

Tara reached for her voice, but failed. She cleared her throat and nodded instead.

Mithi smiled. "Well, I'm happy you're back."

"I'm glad to see you, too," Tara found herself mumbling, though this wasn't true. She hated reminders of her earlier life in the city of broken dreams.

"I don't know any of the other girls. They are a little different, aren't they?"

They were. They seemed less harried, as if they'd decided to enjoy their sordid days and capture themselves on their phones. They spent a lot of time scrolling, typing, and smiling away. No one who looked at their pictures would get their torment.

Tara checked her watch—the break would end soon. She didn't tell Mithi she would leave after a week. Once was bad enough. Twice would be a betrayal.

CHAPTER TWENTY-EIGHT

Arnav

Arnav arrived at Nandini's building a little past 11:00 p.m., a tad late because his meeting with Mhatre had gone on for longer than expected. Leaning back in his seat, he considered their exchange.

"Take the promotion, Rajput," Mhatre had said. "That's your best option. Shinde asked me whether you could help, from one senior inspector to another, but when I said yes I didn't expect you to give an interview about the Versova case without consulting me or him. Joshi sir instructed you to lay off. Your serial killer theory sounds like reaching for what isn't there. Clear out your desk by Diwali and hand over your cases. Report to Joshi sir in Bandra."

This was Arnav's first proper conflict with Mhatre, who hadn't been his usual self of late—hitching a ride in Arnav's car when he could easily have used an app, and baldly denying facts. Any civilian who read a few crime novels could understand that targeting women of a similar height and age range, and killing them in the same way, indicated a serial killer.

Gawde had made a cryptic, puzzling statement about Mhatre. Arnav had looked up Gawde's station postings, and he had indeed worked with Mhatre for extended periods. Mhatre had also signed off on Bendre's suspicious traffic accident. A chat with Tukaram might help. Arnav was about to dial his gregarious friend when the car door opened.

Nandini entered in a faint cloud of her usual perfume. She wore a clingy black dress, her hair down, high heels. She leaned over to kiss his cheek, and they drove off.

"You should wear plain clothes more often," Nandini said.

"Women prefer a man in uniform." Arnav smiled at her as they took the road to Bandra West.

"I like you fine in uniform, just not on duty."

Arnav wanted to tell her that he was on duty twenty-four hours, that the calls never stopped unless he switched off his phones, but he was too tired to make conversation.

"I heard they're promoting you to senior inspector?"

He didn't need to ask her how she knew. Shinde.

"Not taking it up."

"What? You've been promoted to work under Commissioner Joshi."

Shinde could turn the screws with such ease. They were inspectors together for a while, but Shinde hailed from the Scheduled Caste. His promotions came in faster under the quota system protecting lower castes. Four years from inspector to senior inspector, while it took twelve years for someone like Arnav, from the general category.

"Told my boss I wasn't interested."

About ten days to leave his desk at the Malwani station. He didn't know what to do next, but that was another matter.

"You can do that? Refuse an order?"

"Technically, no. He's within his rights to transfer me without a promotion."

"Why *are* you refusing?" Nandini sounded intrigued. "This could be your chance to nail Joshi like you've wanted for years."

He'd once told Nandini all about his sister, and Joshi's role in the entire tragedy, after they'd finished a bottle of red wine between them.

"I don't want to leave behind the case I'm working on."

"You could tell them that. Accept the promotion after you solve the case in hand."

"Not that simple. Can't talk because it is an open case right now. Someday you could write an article on it."

With the stand Mhatre had taken, Arnav must bring the details to her sooner rather than later. Might as well give her an indication now.

"What do we know about Rahul Taneja?"

"Taneja Real Estate Holdings?"

Arnav nodded.

"The word is, he's into kinky stuff. No judgment there, but he's also a creep—probably groped all the women he's worked with."

"Yes, I saw the MeToo allegations. But what does your grapevine say?"

"He's joining the Virani family because that will solve a few of his headaches."

"Namely?"

"You didn't hear this from me—this is from a man who covers the real estate beat at work. Kind of has a crush on me, you see." She waggled her eyebrows in a good-natured, exaggeratedly saucy gesture.

"With good reason," Arnav laughed. "Anyone would crush on you the way you look tonight."

He had to make an effort, keep her happy so he could handle the evening ahead. This was a new Blue Bar, new bar girls, and Nandini the antidote to the ache of memories.

"Quit flirting." Nandini grinned back. "You already have me. But back to Taneja—he's been receiving death threats, though he doesn't talk about it. He has the police in his pocket, but marrying into Bollywood would give him additional protection. They all have deep connections."

"Kittu Virani?"

"She knows everyone."

"And what else?"

"Kittu's company has decorated the homes of most of Bollywood, and many others besides. She's a bigger social media influencer than her movie star sons, and she would work for him now—eliminating any competition for TEH's new interior design arm. She's not much to look at, but she's calling Taneja her *first real love*. Win-win for him. He can get his women anywhere."

"I see."

"Are you investigating him?"

"I can't confirm or deny that." He turned to glance at her face, alight with curiosity. That brightness, the questioning look reminded him of Tara—why was it Tara he kept returning to?

Traffic had thinned. The car sped till they hit a signal near a corner tobacco shop, casting a white light on its rows of *masala* packets and canned drinks. The portly owner stood surrounded by his customers, joking with them while handing out his wares, his hands a blur as he applied pastes or *supari*, folded the shiny green *paan* leaves and accepted payments, all at once. Arnav wished he could excel at this sort of mechanical, repetitive job. No complexities or politics.

"I've noticed a curious fact about your Joshi." Nandini broke the silence in the car.

"Yes?" Arnav had asked her to keep a lookout for any news about him.

"You know how I write articles on up-and-coming businesses?"

"Of course."

"In the last year, Moringa Consultants seems to have skyrocketed. I haven't figured out who the investors are."

That sometimes meant an influx of cash from the shady underworld—the Mumbai dons who kept up fronts while they ran their drug and arms cartels outside the country.

"Is Joshi mixed up in this?"

"His sister-in-law is one of the owners."

"Nothing else?"

"There's talk that Vijayan is using it as a laundry for his dirty money."

CHAPTER TWENTY-NINE

TARA

Tara had danced on stages often enough in her life, but never seen one quite like this. The lights, for starters. Cleverly concealed, they went on and off in time with the beats. Shetty had hired a lighting technician and a DJ and installed speakers that caught each note and projected it into the large cave-like space, with a stage, a bar, restaurant tables, sofas in draped alcoves, each space lit with chandeliers and mood lights that could be dimmed till they winked like starlight on the ceiling.

Shetty said that he had found such places on his Bangkok trips. An evening's entertainment at some of the restaurants included glamorous dancing girls who set the stage on fire. This looked less like a dance bar from Tara's younger days and more like a nightclub from a movie set. She'd tried asking Shetty to lower his expectations of her new troupe—they had barely started moving in coordination. This called for more practice sessions.

"I don't care what happens with the others. You must produce a night to remember," Shetty had said the evening before in his usual sedate yet make-it-worth-my-money tone.

The chat with Mithi had made Tara wary. She wanted to talk to Zoya about it, but Pia answered the phone without fail. Tara couldn't discuss Shetty within her daughter's hearing.

On a short break in her room after lunch, Tara dialed Zoya again, hoping Pia had left for school, but Pia picked up and switched it to a video call.

"How are you, doll? Did your English exam go well?"

"Of course, Ma." Pia rolled her eyes in a gesture that was so like her father's it made Tara's heart flip. "When are you back?"

"In a week, when I have tickets. Where's your Zoya *masi*?"

"Making dinner. Half-day at school today, Ma. It is Saturday."

A knock at her door. That must be a girl come to fetch her.

"I forgot, sorry. Talk to you later. Be good." Tara cut the call and rushed out.

That evening, wearing a skimpy gown for her performance, Tara sweated in the cold dressing room, getting her girls ready. She flitted from woman to woman, adjusting hair, makeup—an earring here or a pleat there, encouraging and reassuring them. If they followed the music and her instructions, they'd win the evening.

This was different from fourteen years ago, when this man or that from the audience showered ten-rupee notes on her as she sashayed down from the tiny stage and, avoiding groping paws, accepted money from the customers and poured them a drink. By law, bar dancers were not supposed to leave the stage, but everyone turned a blind eye because the currency tended to be much bigger if the girls strutted about and seductively drew the money out of grubby male hands.

She wondered if any of these girls standing before her would do the same today. They probably would. Women did what they had to.

When she reminded these new students to stay on the beat, they nodded, biddable for once, the music having cowed them. It made the walls throb, the dressing tables shake. It held their hearts in fists and twisted their guts, nameless yet overpowering. The DJ was doing his warm-ups, his test set. Tara had instructed her students in moves that ranged from traditional to fusion to outright western, from pirouettes to jerky hips and pushy, rhythmic thrusts.

The number moved to *Tu shayar hai*, a remix of the Bollywood number that said, *You are a poet, and I'm your poem.* In the movie, the svelte lead, Madhuri Dixit, seduced with her body and also her eyes, but it gave Tara flashbacks of being blindfolded, of suffocating in a burka, of the sneering man in the dark. She rushed to the DJ. This hadn't been in his lineup earlier.

"Mr. Shetty added it in," the DJ told her.

Breathless from having run and the fear that threatened to paralyze her, Tara couldn't find the right words. At one time, her performance to this number was the flavor of the month for the bar scene. Shetty expected old clients this evening—he would never agree if she asked for a change in music.

Did that mean he would appear—the jackal from whom she'd run? He loved *Tu shayar hai*. He'd made her dance to it each time. Tara sank into a chair and gulped harsh breaths, refusing to let old terrors take hold of her.

Shetty called the Blue Bar an orchestra bar, but it was still a dance bar. He could hire all the DJs in the world but, in the end, it was about the amount of money dropped. Tara and her girls were the target, the ones the audience tossed money at. The women must set the evening alight, worth getting sloshed over, for the money to come pouring in. Tara must deliver. The jackal wouldn't come in—and even if he did, so what? She would go out there and dance. For her contract. For Pia.

CHAPTER THIRTY

BILAL

Bilal flicked channels on the massive television in the boy's study, on mute. No one could know Bilal was watching TV, alone, because he was supposedly in meetings with the boy. The boy had gone walking, the way he did at least once a week.

It lets me breathe a little, Bilal.

Sometimes after a walk, the boy came back with a bundle of notebooks. Other times, cheap trinkets from roadside shops. Food, that Bilal gave away. Each time, the boy returned covered in dust. He took long baths afterward. He'd worn the khakis today, and carried a bag with clothes and supplies, sounding excited. That nervous energy boded grief for Bilal. He grew anxious. What if someone spotted the boy in a place he had no business in? The uniform or the Sikh turban wouldn't get him far. *That's the thrill, Bilal. You won't understand,* the boy had murmured when he protested. *No one will spare me a second glance or dare give me trouble.*

Bilal enjoyed these spells in the study, neatening up once the TV shows bored him, but he felt ants crawling over his skin today. He'd developed a finely tuned sense for the boy's episodes. Another was on its way. He deftly replaced the device hidden behind the table, placed new pens and notebooks at the boy's desk, sorted the stationery. He watered down the whiskey the boy kept in a back cabinet, because the boy's liver was hammered up with years of abuse. Opening a tiny drawer, Bilal checked the quality and amount of the white powder. The boy must not overdose by accident. His friends asked him what it was like to work for the boy. If only they knew.

He spent the rest of the time flicking the remote, and playing games on his phone. The boy liked games. After his father died, he'd introduced them to Bilal. In some ways, Bilal was his father. Telling him what to stay away from. Protecting him. Where was he now? Was he walking the roads, rubbing shoulders with those he held in contempt? Was he headed to the railway station? Was he arranging another delivery? Had *Uhnna* relented?

On Choti Diwali evening many years ago, the day before the festival of Diwali, Bilal had found them both, their clothes askew—the woman triumphant, the then fifteen-year-old boy shamed and trembling on the hotel grounds not far from the railway tracks. She had sauntered off, with a smile on her face that alarmed Bilal.

The boy often said, *I'm fair, Bilal. I don't tie up those women. They aren't alone. They have a choice. I never had one.*

The boy was upset with Bilal for botching the last cleanup. The master, the boy's dad, said often: if you don't change something, you choose it. *That's not true, sahab,* Bilal wanted to inform the ghost of that man. *You did the choosing, and now it is too late for me to make a change. Looks like it's also too late for your son.*

CHAPTER THIRTY-ONE

TARA

The DJ announced Tara and her attributes in a loud, accented, drawn-out warble, and as she stepped on the stage he spat out lyrics in a rap, following one phrase with another in a cascade. Tara had practiced her entrance several times, and yet the spotlight managed to blind her.

She let her body take control, but that momentary blindness took her to the terror and regret of that first night-work assignment when she'd sat blindfolded for who knew how long, wearing a burka, in the rear of a car, flanked by two men.

A tinny Malayali song. The reek of stale tobacco and booze. The window sliding down. The click of a lighter. Cigarette smoke and damp outside air. A splash of water as a vehicle passed by. The growl of the car. The rosewater smell of Zoya's burka she'd stolen. The bristle of the sequined saree at her waist. The lure of ₹60,000 for a night.

You're here.

The first time she'd heard the jackal growl from the shadowy gloom.

The frenetic dance in the dark before an invisible, silent, menace-filled audience of one.

Once again, she was under the light, being watched from the dark. Only this time she was not alone. Poised to step out, her girls stood in the wings. She followed the advice she'd given them—letting her limbs ride the music, taking in her surroundings through half-closed eyes. Tara didn't see joy in dance—that was for those who could afford it—but this came close. She lost track of time as her solo progressed, but right on cue, her new students joined her onstage in ones and twos, their movements a counterpoint to hers.

She skipped from the stage onto the ramp leading toward the bar and let the barman help her up. There, with a swish of her cream skirts, she twirled between clients who were supposed to throw currency at her. Instead, notes blanketed the counter and flew off as she dipped and swung in tight circles. From the audience on the barstools touched by her billowing skirts came yells, piercing whistles.

Amid the charged air, an eerie stillness descended on her. She felt eyes on her skin, a knowing gaze within the whirl of motion and noise. Could the jackal be here?

Walk to the bed.

Where are you, saab?

His disembodied voice from the past echoed, splitting her in two—the body thrusting and swaying to the music, the mind lost in remembered dread.

Sweat trickled at her armpits and beaded above her lips. She gulped when she heard polished Hindi. *I was told you will do as I say. Don't call me saab.*

Ji, saab. Hungry gaze on her face, her throat. Lower. The prickle of alarm at her neck.

Already with the saab?

No. I mean, yes. I mean, Ji.

Zoya's words from earlier. *You're still a child. Just seventeen. You have no idea.*

Dark room, shadows, invisible man. Sixty thousand rupees.

Take off your burka and sit on the bed.

The rustle of the burka to the ground. The cold of the air-conditioning on her exposed waist.

Sit.

139

Silken, slippery bedsheet. Cold like the horror pooling in her gut.

The scratch of the blue-shimmering saree.

Goose bumps on her bare arms.

Cologne, one she'd never smelled before, like pricey alcohol on old wood and cinnamon.

Charas, the air heavy with its drugged stupor.

You dance well, I'm told.

The strains of *Tu shayar hai.*

Dance, then.

The mockery and malice of the jackal of her nightmares, with the snarl of a creature far more lethal.

What's wrong? Expressionless, but furious. *Oh, you can't dance unless you're being showered with notes.*

Dead insect wings on her eyelids. Petals, dried rose petals.

Get on the bed and dance. Let me see you.

A whir of limbs and little else.

Now that's more like it.

A whir of limbs, then, as now. She focused on her retreat along the length of the bar, the slope of the ramp, the wings of the stage. The girls would carry on, solos for those with skills and pairs for the others. Tara struggled to collect the pieces of herself—the shivering girl of yore, and the frenzied yet defiant woman now. She hit the greenroom for her next change, where an assistant stood, dress in hand.

Tara had ignored her glass of wine earlier. She downed it at a gulp while the girl unzipped her gown. The DJ turned up the music even louder. She heard it inside her body, right next to the beat of her heart, like the jackal's deadpan, echoing laugh. Unease mounted. The next track would begin in a few seconds. She sucked in her breath as her assistant zipped her up. Mind in a tumult, she hurried to the stage, and paused for her cue.

This second time she remained onstage, along with a few of the girls. It was a slower number, and her eyes had adjusted enough to spot the uniformed waiters in the dim light beyond the stage, weaving between the sofas and the tables, serving drinks. The buzz of guests. The girls dancing in formation in the cue for her to take over again. She scanned the crowd as she pivoted and spun, certain she'd missed a pair of eyes that shouldn't be there.

Adrenaline fueled her through the rest of the evening. She went through the motions, gyrating her hips and breasts, slow, slow, soft, then harder, faster, the changes, the flutter of paper in air—fake notes bought with real currency—perfume and sweat as the girls kept pace with the music. The evening ended with her final, most arduous solo number, back at the bar table. She dived into the rhythm—her moves seductive, reckless—but a part of her on high alert.

That's when she saw him, at a back table, dressed in black, his gaze fixed on her. Over his left hand, the hand of a woman whose face remained in darkness, but Tara caught glimpses of long, blow-dried hair, smooth arms and legs.

Holding a drink, he stared at Tara. Arnav Singh Rajput.

CHAPTER THIRTY-TWO

On most nights, pacing his seaside apartment balcony relaxed him enough to go to sleep, but he'd returned past 3:00 a.m. from a remarkable event. It still glittered in his memory—a vision of peril and longing.

His assistant Bilal wasn't good at many jobs, but at others, he excelled without trying. Or even knowing what he'd done. In the same newspaper that had brought the pictures and descriptions of the last package, that had driven a bit of alarm into both of them, he'd spotted a different feature—about the reopening of bars. An old firecracker would be the opening number, it said. The one he'd wanted so badly, several years ago, because she was a dead ringer for the Item Number in her heyday. He'd stolen a few pieces of the Item Number's jewelry for her, but she'd slipped away at the last minute.

It was an adventure—going out again to a dance bar after all these years. Those left after the ban had gone to ruin, the women too cheap and miserable. He'd lounged at the hot new bar this evening, taking in the scenery while hidden in the dark.

He chuckled and took a long breath of the salt-laden breeze. He couldn't see the horizon, but a few stars twinkled in the distance, along with lights from a sleepy boat or two anchored offshore. From the deck of those boats Mumbai must look beautiful even now, its curved necklace bright, all the lighted buildings rising from the dark, disembodied, floating in air.

A car screamed on the road by the bay. Some fool had decided to race another at 4:00 a.m., like their cars couldn't skid off, hit the sea wall or a road divider, and snuff out their insignificant lives. Just like that.

He'd promised Bilal, so he wouldn't take it too far, but this was a sign. No matter how often *Uhnna* refused, he would get the man to arrange one private performance. Her body was all curves now, no longer a girl. When she danced, even the most subtle of movements was an invitation, as was her smile, and those eyes that searched the darkness every once in a while. It was like Item Number come to life in her old avatar.

Her hotel was less than twenty minutes' drive. He'd tailed their group. It would be easy to find out which room. That thought jolted him back to his senses.

He couldn't talk to the fat Malayali himself, and with good reason.

It was too early in Dubai right now. He would make that call in a few hours. Money, multiples of what he'd offered so far, was the answer. *Uhnna*'s men came at a price. She was worth it all, though—the other women faded in the shadows to her light.

He ambled to his study and reached into the cubbyhole of his desk, thumbing through the trinkets he'd put there, the small bits and pieces he stored in velvet bags—each one a face, a scent, an echo. Where were the little blue darlings, the Item Number's sapphires? One day, he would place her diamonds there. The Item Number wore diamonds on her earlobes, twinkles of taunting lights. They'd wink out.

He'd played with the sapphires on others, but he'd had them crafted for this one, who shimmered like the Item Number herself. He rang the bell to wake his man Friday. If Bilal had lost them, he'd have to pay.

CHAPTER THIRTY-THREE

Arnav

Over the last fourteen years, Arnav had imagined meeting Tara a hundred times. Not once in any of those scenarios had she appeared as calm as this.

She lounged at her usual corner of his sunken-down sofa, like she'd never left. He stood, restless, on edge. She didn't spare him a glance, taking in his living room instead.

"Want some tea?" Arnav said in Hindi. *Chai chalega?* Literally, Will tea do for you?

Why was he being nice to her? He'd dropped Nandini home, but couldn't haul himself back to the station. Instead, he'd ended up outside the new Blue Bar, followed the car that had dropped her at her hotel, and now here she was, at his house after 3:00 a.m.

When she had first stepped on the stage, brassy smile in place, he'd nearly sprung from his seat in shock. Imagining he was making a mistake, he'd scrutinized her face. He hadn't seen this seductive version before, but underneath all the glitter and sass, it was her— remote and somehow untouchable, the quality that had entranced him still intact.

He'd meant to bring her in, ask her a few questions, but by remaining silent in the car she'd gained the upper hand. Number one rule of interrogation, make the suspect you're questioning sweat even before you've spoken a word. He was the one sweating. All for this girl.

Only she wasn't a girl anymore. She'd said she was nineteen when he'd first met her. In the time she'd been away, she'd grown up. She wore different clothes now, instead of *salwar-kameez*, and the way she carried off the jeans and the collared T-shirt told him she wore them often. Her hips had grown heavier, and it wasn't just her hips—it was her entire personality. Despite her jaded air, the Tara he remembered had a certain impudence about her, a sense of expectation and restlessness. This Tara knew her place in the world, had made peace with it. She glanced about, her gaze on the threadbare curtains, the faded paintings his mother had put up decades ago, but did not respond.

"I asked you a question," he said.

"You kidnap me," she said as she turned from her inspection of the sitting room, "and then offer me tea?"

"I don't remember forcing you into the car."

"So I may leave?"

"After you've answered my questions," he said.

"Why haven't you moved?" She tucked her hair back behind her ear, a gesture he knew so well.

"I'll get you the tea." Arnav escaped to the kitchen.

When he returned, she was looking through some of the medals he'd shoved in the old corner cabinet. They lay in a heap, gathering dust. He walked up to her as she picked up a tissue and wiped a medal, holding it gently by its now fraying ribbon.

"You still like cleaning up," he said. It struck him that he had never brought Nandini here. That in his mind, his home had remained Tara's domain. He'd never changed a thing about this aging bungalow. Not due to sloth, but because it had felt like an act of erasure. He realized how shabby the place must look to her, bare and empty.

"You won quite a few medals." Tara kept at her task, not turning toward him.

"That's all they do, give you a medal to shut you up." Arnav put the cups down. No biscuits because there weren't any. Why was he worrying about biscuits when she'd dumped him and run?

"Come sit here."

She brought the medal with her, picking up a tissue on the way to the sofa.

When he handed her the teacup, her fingers trembled a little. So she was putting her acting skills to effective use. It was strange, now that he considered it, that he'd known her for less than two years. It seemed much longer.

He sat next to her and noticed her feet, toes curled. He remembered her cold toes in bed, on Sunday mornings when he rubbed her feet after she landed at his place, exhausted from hours of dancing on a Saturday night.

She sipped her tea. "You've become good at this."

"I can find my way around the kitchen."

"No wife to make tea for you?"

She wanted him to say the words. No one entering this barren space would mistake it for a married household. His mother was the homemaker—most of her efforts at upkeep had fallen victim to his benign neglect.

"I'm the one asking questions. No husband?"

She put the cup down and glared at him. "If you've brought me here to make fun of me . . ."

"Were you poking fun at me when you asked me if I was married?"

"Who would marry me?" And in a flash, she was the young girl he'd met in another lifetime.

He stared at her. "Anyone. You're . . ." He paused, realizing what he was about to say. He needed to be clearheaded about this: get some answers and take her back to her hotel. Never see her again.

"Why did you leave?"

This. This was the question he'd asked her in his head, again and again, year after year. He'd thought they were close enough for her to give him a chance to stop her, or at least say a proper goodbye.

She reached for her cup and took a sip. "Why do you care?"

"You were all right the week before. Then you vanished. The girls said you and Zoya had taken off."

He had watched the place for weeks afterward, asked his nascent group of *khabri* at the time, offered to pay them. It did seem like Tara had disappeared without telling him. He'd given up—why should he search for her when she didn't even bother to say goodbye?

"You went to look for me?"

"Your phone was switched off. What did you expect?"

"You believed them and left it at that. Why ask now?"

"Because you're here." He leaned toward her.

"Who was the woman at your table this evening?" So Tara wished to learn about Nandini. As a young girl, she'd listened to him, open-mouthed. This woman was entirely different.

"Answer me first," Arnav said.

"If I do, will you tell me?"

"Quit hedging, Tara. Why did you go away?"

"Why does any bar girl leave? I'd had enough of it. Zoya was in trouble, and she wanted to quit."

"You didn't tell me."

"Would it have mattered?"

"What if I'd gone away like that?"

"Look, Avi . . . I mean, Arnav, you made it clear we had an arrangement. I wasn't your girlfriend. Did your friends know about me? I was a bar girl, a nobody. So I behaved like one."

You were never just a bar girl. Did I not tell you that? He longed to shake her, make her lose her cool. From the corner of his eye, Arnav caught a glimpse of her toes. Yes, still curled into themselves, even tighter. She was holding her own, but she was also holding herself back, though the tilt of her chin would convince anyone she didn't give a damn.

"You're not telling me everything."

"You're going to go *policewala* on me. You're no longer a constable."

"How is that related? You ran away to follow Zoya? Because you were tired of bar work? And now you're back?"

"Bars are getting licenses again, and Shetty needed dancers." A faint stutter when she said that. Still lying. When did Tara get so good at it? Or maybe she'd been that way, and he'd never noticed.

The smaller orchestra bars had stayed open, but they didn't earn as much as the erstwhile mega dance bars. That's why Shetty had jumped back into the game by renovating the Blue Bar. He could earn sacksful, and maybe even help launder some underworld money on the sly. The bars would create their own ecosystem again—waiters, cloth and cosmetic suppliers, and the bar girls themselves—but owners like Shetty would gobble up most of the pie, not Tara and her peers. Tara was older now. Shetty wouldn't pay her much.

"Why are you here, really?"

She paused for a while. The earlier Tara wouldn't have met his eyes, but this one didn't hesitate.

"Why do bar girls dance? Not for art." She stood up. "Which reminds me, I have to return to the hotel."

"This early in the morning?" Arnav checked the wall clock.

Nonplussed for a second, she stood straighter. "I'm the choreographer. I need to be fresh and early."

"You're a teacher? Why with Shetty? You can work with anyone. Many openings in the industry these days."

With her obvious talent, she would flourish away from the bar scene. Times had changed in the past decade, with several dance competitions on TV and internet platforms. According to Nandini, a lot of them lacked good choreographers.

"Drop me back, please." Tara made for the door.

Arnav touched her elbow. "I'm talking to you."

"And I'll listen. In the car." She looked implacable, as if a headmistress had taken up residence inside her.

"You've changed."

"It's been years." She removed his hand from her elbow. "What did you expect?"

She copied his earlier words and smiled, and that grin was all younger Tara—mischievous, warm, who fed him while they lounged in his bed, who teased him about his mustache.

"Must all policemen have mustaches?" She'd run her thumb over his lips, making him yearn to bite it.

"Most do. Not a rule, but I like it. Makes you look like a real man."

"A real man is more than his mustache." She'd grinned at him. "I can kiss you so much better without it."

He wanted her to kiss him now. Would her lips yield against his, as before? He found himself leaning forward, and pulled back.

"Yes, it's been years," he said.

He lightly punched the air under her chin, in a gesture that his body remembered. His knuckles grazed her, and he drew them lightly across her soft skin. "I'll take you to the hotel now, but I'm picking you up tomorrow after the show. No argument."

No argument—another phrase from long ago. Tara had stilled under his gaze, and when he led her out with his hand on the small of her back, she didn't protest.

Once in the car, they were silent again. He rolled down the windows because Tara had once complained that air-conditioning suffocated her. Riding the dawn breeze came the smell of flowers or rubbish or snacks frying in oil, depending on what road they drove on; the calls of men beginning to push off for the day on cycles, scooters, and carts. The sky loomed blue-gray, with scattered ribbons of clouds. Pigeons wheeled, landed, and took to the skies again. He liked how they didn't discriminate and uniformly spattered the world beneath them with their droppings—the traffic islands, the forlorn statues and shrubbery, and the hoardings of the municipal corporation.

He parked right where he'd picked her up earlier. He reached for her phone, dialed his private number, and returned it to her.

"That's me." He held her hand for a moment before letting it go. "I'll pick you up."

She nodded and left.

After he'd watched her walk in through the hotel entrance, Arnav considered what he'd seen. A picture on Tara's screen saver that was the spitting image of his sister as a teen. It wasn't Asha, though. This was a digital, color photograph. The girl wore a T-shirt and grinned. Asha had never smiled for the camera.

One more question Tara must answer.

Arnav turned his old car and drove off, right as his phone flashed with Shinde's number. Shinde was adamant about having Arnav transfer the charge of the Versova case to one of his other inspectors. Arnav took a deep breath before beginning the long and patient call—to explain yet again that the inspector at Versova who could have competently handled the case was still on leave. Arnav would hand over any intelligence or credit for developments related to Rasool Mohsin. Shinde was like a cranky grandfather when in a hospital bed. Arnav kept him appeased, dead set on nailing the culprit who had tortured and killed so many women with impunity.

CHAPTER THIRTY-FOUR

TARA

The last time she had done this, Tara was seventeen. She felt too old to sprint on heels, but race she would if that meant she might earn more out of this trip. She wouldn't return to Mumbai again, not even for Pia and her school fees.

The air-conditioning in Shetty's car gave off more sound than air, and she wilted in the heat of the shawl she'd wrapped about herself. All she'd longed to do after she returned this morning was lie in bed and dream about Arnav, about what he'd said, the way he'd acted, the questions he'd asked—but instead, she had trained the girls harder, correcting their mistakes from the night before, moving right alongside them. Now, after a hurried snack way past lunchtime, she was headed out to Borivali Station once more.

Last night, after the performance ended, Shetty had spoken to her.

"Well done, Tara. You brought the house down tonight. I'm adding a bonus to your payment."

Never good news when Shetty gave you a bonus. This time, he'd offered extra work.

She'd considered it. The blue saree. The silver blouse and heels. The shawl. Mithi and her story about Gauri. Maybe they went to the station, too, wearing the same blue saree she wore right now. Maybe they didn't have a choice. A lot of her friends at the Mira Road apartment used to send money home to support their families, their children.

She understood that compulsion. She was here because she hadn't been able to argue with the money—money that would help support Pia, give her the opportunities she deserved. The fat Malayali bastard had offered Tara a bunch of it, and paid her an advance.

Cash. She would take what she could get. Over the decade and more of raising Pia, Tara had found little faith in Ma Kaali, the goddess her mother worshipped. She'd have to look out for herself, as she'd always done, and this was her chance.

Here she was, despite all her misgivings, her heart beating hard.

Leaving the car behind, with instructions on when and where to return for her, Tara headed up the stairs. The railway platform was cleaner, the shops shinier. The train announcer sounded less sleepy. Even during afternoon hours, passengers milled about. Better-dressed people than fourteen years ago, and everyone on a mobile phone. The beggars remained, but they'd been pushed to the street corners outside. She strode down the stairs to the platform number she'd been given this time, and realized it was a different one. Perhaps because there were tall buildings surrounding the place now.

Someone was watching her, whether from within the station or without—that jackal-voiced man in the dark. She'd mulled over it again this morning, and it had to be him—the one paying Shetty, and asking him to send out women in blue-sequined sarees. No longer as young or reckless, she would never take up night work should Shetty offer it. She'd agreed to come here only because this was a public space, safer than that bungalow she'd gone to, clad in a *burka* and the same blue and silver outfit.

The strings that held up the tiny blouse bit into her back, and the sequined saree chafed her waist. She could not wait to take them off after she left the station. A three-minute limit. Why not less or more? What if she failed?

She peered at the faces of the men who walked by, sat hunched behind newspapers, or spoke on their cell phones. He could be anywhere. Anyone. And he wasn't far. That sent dread coursing through her, like in those days when she sweated in a car, escorted by Shetty's thugs.

On one of her blindfolded visits, she'd spotted a policeman's khaki cap with a gold-embroidered black band. From the brief glimpse, it had belonged to a highly placed officer. It wasn't like the one Arnav wore as a constable, simple, soft. She remembered assuming that the jackal was a police officer with too much black money, who couldn't be seen openly visiting a dance bar. That the men escorting her might not be policemen, but they wouldn't hurt her if they secretly reported to a police officer. A part of her wanted to laugh at seventeen-year-old Tara, who'd felt so invincible—lying to Arnav about her age, thinking nothing of going on mysterious, terrifying assignments, telling herself the jackal wouldn't touch her.

She knew better this time. If he was a senior officer then, he might be placed much higher now. She shuddered.

Pia had no father: she hadn't met Arnav and never would. Tara had responsibilities beyond herself.

Striding along the platform, she weighed the risks. The stairs looked a long way off, and quite steep. The distance was longer than before—this platform lay farther away from the new entrance. She set a three-minute timer on her phone, to start at a click. She needed proof to show Shetty, just in case: not that he would take it into account—it was her word against the client's. Her stomach churned, same as her last assignment more than ten years ago.

Arnav has a right to know, a voice had chanted inside her, making her nausea worse. Right when she had thought she might vomit, the car had jerked to a halt.

"Talk." Someone held a phone to her left ear.

"The client changed his mind," Shetty had said, his voice deeper than usual.

"So I'll go back?"

"No." Shetty had paused. "They want you to decide on an offer."

Tara hadn't replied.

"They're willing to pay a lot more. Five lakhs. Five lakhs, and you must obey all instructions."

Obey all instructions. Zoya had warned her against any situation where she could not say no. Five lakhs. Double the amount she'd earned for all her night-work assignments combined. Almost enough for her to quit bar dancing. She'd rested her hand on her belly. She'd need to make up her mind soon, the doctor had warned, or it would be too late.

"Tara?"

"Too late," Tara had blurted out.

"You will do it? Should I confirm?"

Five lakhs. Which meant Shetty would draw at least ten. Why would the jackal who ogled her from the dark agree to spend fifteen lakhs on her, a commonplace bar girl? He wouldn't. She wanted the money, but not when she didn't know the risks to herself and the new life growing within her. Her father may not have been a father, but her mother had striven to protect her.

"Can you hear me? Tara?"

"Yes," Tara said. "I mean, no. Ask them to take me back."

"Think it over. You may not get another chance like this one."

"I want to go back."

"Will it help if they raise the price? Six lakhs."

Tara's breath caught, and her nausea returned. Shetty had added a lakh. Like it meant nothing. If the jackal was indeed a policeman, as that cap seemed to show, he was worse than a *Bhai*. He could make her vanish and ensure no one ever looked for her.

"No," she'd said, her voice firm. "Take me back."

She had relaxed her fingers, her hands, her arms, like Zoya had taught her to do right before a difficult routine. She, Noyontara Mondal, would succeed where her mother had failed: she would make a new person who needn't know lack, who wouldn't be sold off, who could aim high without fear.

Calling up that old resolve, Tara touched her midsection once more. She'd left Mumbai for Pia's sake, and she would do this for Pia, too, despite her fears. She added a deliberate spring in her step. This was an enactment in broad daylight—she refused to back away or reveal her terror. She would show him the finger and take his money. She had escaped earlier. She would do it again.

When the phone rang, she was ready. She let go of her shawl. Standing at the end of the platform, keeping her expression neutral, she did not let her body tremble. It was all very well to feign confidence, but she felt stripped. Exposed. She imagined that whiff of old wood and cinnamon, and steeled herself not to turn around. The jackal wouldn't venture close.

After endless minutes, when the phone squealed a second time, she clicked the timer on, grabbed her shawl, and dashed off. She flew up the stairs, her fingers skimming the railing for balance so she wouldn't crash on the high heels. Her years of dancing had not been without injuries. She collided with others in her mad gallop across the main bridge, and though her chest burned and her legs threatened to collapse, she pushed on.

She'd nearly cleared the outer stairs when she ended up darting two steps down instead of one. Her weight landed on her right ankle. A jolt of agony shot up when she righted herself, and each step made her bite back screams. She didn't pause, but when she stumbled out of the station, the timer had gone beyond three minutes. The jackal had watched her fail. She would soon discover the consequences.

CHAPTER THIRTY-FIVE

TARA

A few final touches to her hair and makeup, and Tara was ready to go onstage. Her phone beeped, but she ignored it. Was that Shetty, doling out the consequences for missing the three-minute deadline? Or worse, the jackal himself, from an unknown number? In either case, her hands were tied—no one would believe her if she told them she'd done such a strange thing at a railway station, and if they did, they would point fingers at her greed. Other girls had disappeared after such assignments. Could she tell Arnav? No. Especially not him, because she didn't need him digging around her life and finding out about Pia.

She made herself take a peek at her messages, and sagged when she saw the name. Arnav. In her relief, she forgot to hesitate, typing out a yes to seeing him once again that night.

\If yesterday was anything to go by, she'd finish by 2:00 a.m. Too late to call Zoya and Pia. After meeting Arnav, she'd been longing all day for her daughter's voice. Arnav had taken her phone to key in his number—had he noticed the screen saver with Pia on it? He wouldn't know who it was, but he might be curious. At the corridor behind the greenroom, she pulled up two chairs, sat on one, and put her feet up on the other. The ankle hadn't been sprained during her adventure this afternoon, and icing it had helped. She must dance on elastic-bandaged feet, so she'd worn the *ghaghra* skirt lower.

Huffing as her feet relaxed, she changed her screen saver, and called Zoya in Lucknow, who picked up on the first ring. Pia was asleep.

Tara checked her watch. Ten thirty. Of course her daughter was in bed. Disappointment weighed her down.

Zoya said the admission forms for the private school for Pia had arrived. The fees were steep, as they had known.

"We should have more money by tomorrow," Tara said.

"How? You've banked the advance."

"I asked him for more."

Tara couldn't tell Zoya about the railway station saga, so she spoke of Shetty's impossible demands of her as a choreographer, the costumes that didn't fit, and her trouble with training the inept dancers. All of it true, but given time to dwell on it, Zoya would never believe Shetty paying her extra. To distract her friend, Tara told her about Mithi, and the disappearance of the other girl, Gauri.

"She's making up stories," Zoya said. "We all went out with who we liked. When Shetty made the introduction, he took a cut. What bar owner didn't? I'm sure he still sends girls to clients. He never forced me to go. Nor you, right?"

Tara didn't care to answer. It would take the conversation into dangerous waters again. The railway station assignments. The dance in the dark in that mysterious house.

"I met Arnav today," Tara blurted out, regretting the words as soon as she said them.

"What? Where? What did he say? Are you seeing him?"

Before she could answer, the assistant came looking for her. The DJ had changed the music. Thankful for the interruption,

Tara said bye, cut the call, and rushed off, handing the assistant her phone.

When she stepped on the stage, swaying to one Bollywood remix after another, Tara let her feet do the talking while her mind wandered to Arnav. She scanned the crowd for him, but he wasn't there.

CHAPTER THIRTY-SIX

TARA

By the time the night ended, Tara's mind was like one of Pia's old windup toys, high on the energy of the evening, ready for more. Her body struggled, about to shut down. She'd been working nonstop for sixteen hours, a whole lot of them spent dancing. Her ankle thrummed when she loosened the elastic bandage to accommodate the swelling.

Once Arnav opened the car door for her, she leaned against the old seat and shut her eyes. She woke up when they reached his place, realizing he'd buckled her in. She leaned on the wall while he unlocked the door, staggering at the threshold. Why was she here? She had a lot to lose if he found out about Pia. He wasn't married, nor interested in children, but he might decide Pia would be better off with him in a big city like Mumbai. Unable to continue that line of thought, Tara collapsed on the sofa. She put her feet up. Arnav locked the door, switched on a lamp behind her, and said, "Give me a minute."

A noise woke her. To her consternation, she'd dozed off, her head lolling on a cushion.

A steaming bucket stood next to the sofa.

Years ago, on Saturday nights, after endless hours of dancing at the bar, she came straight to his home, crashing on this very sofa, like today, resting against the cushions. At seventeen, the dance bar routine had been punishing, but today it had felt even harder, especially with her hurting ankle.

"Get up and dip your feet," Arnav said.

She said, "Too warm," just as she used to.

"Don't argue. Dip in your toes first. I'll fetch the salt."

The exact words from before, like dialogue from a play they'd rehearsed. From the look in his eyes, he remembered. She could not bear to return his gaze, so she gave in and rolled up her loose jeans to her knees.

"You twisted your ankle? And you were still dancing?" He shoved her hand aside and unrolled the bandage. "It looks painful. How are you even staying upright on this? When did it happen?"

Tara watched the steam rising from the bucket—she didn't wish to relive the desperate sprint at the railway station. Instead, she dipped her toes till the warmth became bearable, then soothing.

"You can take a job somewhere else. Shetty might have upgraded his bar, but he treats his employees no better."

Tara let her head fall back. She closed her eyes, and moved her toes in the warm water.

"You're not talking to me now?"

"Shetty paid me an advance."

"How much is he paying you?"

"Enough."

She heard him huff in frustration and stalk off. No help for that.

He returned, a bottle in hand. Two glasses with ice. He poured her a small measure of gin and a large one for himself. She took a sip and let the liquid warm her.

"You still watch movies?" Arnav said.

That made her smile. She had dragged him to so many. These days she was lucky if she caught a late-night show on TV. Between raising Pia and keeping the household going, there simply wasn't time.

"No," she said. "You?"

He hated movies. She'd meant it as a taunt, but his belly laugh caught her by surprise. He'd rarely laughed when they were together, but she remembered the rare times he did—the way he crinkled his eyes and threw back his head. That hadn't changed, either.

"You don't give up, do you? I'm training a movie . . ." He stopped and rose to refill his glass.

"What?"

"Nothing. I've watched a few Rehaan Virani movies."

"Your . . ." She bit her tongue. *Your daughter likes Rehaan Virani, too.* Exhaustion and alcohol were not a good mix.

"My what?" He refilled her glass and his own.

"Your place still looks the same."

"That wasn't what you were about to say." He rose and left the room.

Those were his habitual words, too, from long ago when she used to trip up while trying not to talk about the money she was making off Shetty's assignments. She'd wanted to tell him she could finally save up for acting classes and gym memberships—but was afraid he might interfere.

She had never spoken about herself, not even when he asked. Sundays used to be the one untroubled portion of her life in Mumbai— she had no desire to complicate them. It was dangerous to let people get close to you. It gave them power and Arnav already held all the power in the relationship. She could not hope to scale the many rungs on the social ladder between a policeman and a bar dancer.

She'd spent most of their time together either cleaning up Arnav's home, tinkering in the kitchen, or in his bed, luxuriating in the way he massaged her shoulders, her sore legs and feet. He didn't pay her to spend time with him, buying her random gifts instead: clothes and perfume, costume jewelry, magazines. As a bar girl she was supposed to have pushed him for more. She had not.

She remembered preening under his attention, his hands across her stomach as she hovered over him.

"You're working out?" he'd asked.

He understood muscles, abs, knew the work they took. She'd returned the gesture on his washboard stomach, tickling him into a wide grin, thinking he'd have made a good movie hero. His chin and nose were too sharp, but his gentle smile and square jawline balanced them out. The director would have asked him to shave off his mustache.

"You should try acting." The words had burst out of her before she could stop them. "You have a nice body."

He chuckled. "Really?" He'd tweaked her nose. *"Pagli."*

She liked these nicknames he gave her. Being called a nerd was better than the other names, like Queen Bee and Honey Baby, that the middle-aged patrons of the Blue Bar yelled at her.

"Come here, *Pagli.*" The words yanked her out of the past and made her wary. They had way too much history, and he hadn't forgotten any of it.

He held a steaming towel. She reached for it, but he didn't hand it over. Laying the towel flat on the sofa, he gestured for her to place her feet on it. When she did, he draped them with the hot towel and massaged them. She bit back a moan. For years, the only person Tara had touched, and been touched by, was Pia. She tried to withdraw, but Arnav held her feet over his thighs and used his thumbs to draw the soreness away. Like a lifetime ago. She let the quietness wash over her. Maybe he cared, maybe he didn't, but right now, she felt all right. She wouldn't fight it. He soothed her legs, careful around her swollen ankle, and she did not protest, closing her eyes once more.

"I could help you get out of this. I should have said it a long time ago—but I was a foolish boy then, and didn't know any better."

"I'm OK. I promise." She gazed at his face, but his focus remained on her injured ankle.

"You don't seem fine to me. Or maybe you're OK and will vanish again."

Yes, she would, but it won't help to share that with him. He had worked to lessen her pain, even if for one night. That was the important thing.

"Let's not worry about yesterday or tomorrow, Avi. We can just be here."

"Why did you come with me today?"

"I keep asking myself the same question."

He let go of her feet and put cushions under them. "Have you eaten?"

"You're going to cook for me?" She chuckled. Arnav had many talents, but cooking was not one of them.

"I can make instant noodles."

"Is that what you usually eat?"

"I dine out, or eat at Shinde's. Sometimes at the dojo. You rest for a while."

Shinde. So the sleaze was still Arnav's friend.

"Tara?"

She considered refusing, but saw no point. She said yes. She was safe, and he was offering her noodles. She watched him lope off, return wearing a sweatshirt and gym pants, and enter the kitchen.

She limped into the bedroom to look for body oil. The woman he'd been with at the bar, did he bring her here?

On a shelf, she found an old bottle of moisturizer and smoothed it onto her legs. Relaxed, she leant against the pillows and decided to lie back for a few minutes, till he called her to eat.

He gently shook her awake.

"Here." He passed her a bowl, and the scent of years long gone wafted up to her: the flavor of those days at Mira Road. The bar girls cooked instant noodles when they were too wrung out to make anything else. She'd not eaten them since. When grocery shopping, she avoided glancing at the noodle packets. Now, as she twisted a fork around the strands and popped them into her mouth, she did not mind. When she dropped a strand on herself, Arnav took over, feeding her and himself. He set the empty bowl aside and kissed her cheek when they'd finished. She didn't turn away. He kissed her other cheek, her nose, and then her lips. *Here he is and here I am. What harm in pretending nothing else exists but this room?*

She sat up with a start in the light of early morning, alone. Arnav must have stepped out for his run. She recognized each corner of the room. He hadn't changed any of it. Neat enough, but bare. The curtains hung limp, the bedsheets clean but faded. She went to the toilet, freshened up, and took a bath. Her shower at the hotel before Arnav picked her up had been brief. She peered into his closet and was tempted to borrow a shirt.

Seeing her in a man's shirt might prove too much for Shetty's thugs, so she wore her own. She contented herself with sniffing Arnav's clothes and spraying on his cologne. After a while, she went looking for him, but he hadn't returned. He never jogged this late. Maybe he'd left for work. This was probably his way of saying goodbye without so many words. Tara felt the sting of tears, but didn't let them fall.

Last night, she'd let herself go. It had seemed real enough. He'd been a generous lover in the past, still was, but he'd also cradled her as if he needed her in more than his bed. As if he'd missed her. Well, she'd missed him, but did she want to tie herself down?

She gathered her bag and was about to leave when the door opened. Arnav stumbled in, laden with plastic packets.

"What are you doing?" He glanced at the handbag on her shoulder. "I bought us breakfast."

"I thought you'd gone to work."

"In a bit." He dropped a kiss on her head on the way to the kitchen, as if he did it every day. "It is early yet. Let's eat first. I'll drop you back."

She left her handbag on the table and followed him, her step light.

Arnav unwrapped all the packages: *vada pao, samosa, pakoras, aloo-poori*. Tara grinned at the spread—all her favorite street snacks, fresh-made. He'd remembered. She hadn't eaten *vada pao* in all these years—the softness of the bread and the spice of the filling satisfied a craving she'd been unaware of. He wiped the grease off the crisp *pakoras* with a napkin, the way she used to do in her attempt to cultivate an actress's body. They fed each other, laughing at the spills, surrounded by the mouthwatering smells of tamarind and green coriander chutney. Like lovers. He kissed the sauces off her lips and chin.

Once they'd eaten, Arnav went off to shower and change, and with nothing else to keep her hands busy, Tara cleaned up. Her body felt heavy—with memories, and longing. This could have been her everyday life had she not danced at a bar. Not been poorly educated. Not been Tara, in short.

Pia had been conceived in this house. She had a right to this home, to know who she was, who her father was. To flip through the albums of family photographs Arnav kept hidden in his cabinets, to touch all the medals he'd won, be proud of them. Tara paused. Was she being unfair to Pia by not telling Arnav? She arranged the medals in the showcase, the ones she'd cleaned yesterday. A thorough polish would do them good, but they already looked a lot better.

Arnav hugged her from behind, smelling of shampoo, cologne. She twisted away, laughing, and Arnav said, "Have you forgotten?"

"How to escape if someone grabs you from behind?"

He had taught her, worried about her returning late at night in the hired auto-rickshaw—*Karate and dance are similar, pagli, you need to be aware of your body and how you move it. Spin. Duck. Aim for the ribs or stomach, and run.*

She'd practiced it with him dozens of times. She spun, ducked, mock-hit him. He backed off, mock-flinching.

He could teach this to Pia. She turned away to hide her expression.

"You know what this means, don't you?"

He was tuned to her moods. His voice had lost all trace of their joking horseplay.

"What?"

"You can break it off with Shetty. When you plan to run this time, tell me."

"What makes you think—"

"I'm older. I'm a policeman. You're staying at a hotel—not telling me stuff." He nuzzled her neck. "If you change your mind, I'm here."

She nodded, not sure what else to do.

They remained silent again during the drive back. A part of her didn't wish them to reach her hotel.

Right before parting, he caught her hand in his. "Remember. If you get into trouble, you'll come to me this time."

She felt her face lose color, but couldn't think of a reply. She stepped out of the car. Waving to her, he drove off.

At the hotel entrance, she met Shetty's man. "Sir wants to see you."

She nodded. "I'll be down soon," she replied, and strode to the lift. The man had expected her return. Shetty knew she hadn't slept in her room last night.

Inside the lift, she opened her handbag to check on the piece of tissue she'd squirreled away in a small compartment. Not thinking it through, she'd torn off a few sequins from the electric-blue saree before returning it to Shetty's man last evening.

CHAPTER THIRTY-SEVEN

ARNAV

At the daily briefing, Arnav listened as a sub-inspector droned on about the routine trivia of the Malwani station—calls in response to domestic violence, reports on robberies, internet scams—but his thoughts kept flitting back to the woman in his bed last night, and that child's face on the phone screen. He'd been tempted to check Tara's phone, but watching her sleep, open-mouthed, a trickle of drool on the pillow, stayed his hand. He'd blamed her for so long for what she'd done that he'd let slip his initial misgivings. Was she in trouble when she left? She'd been a little evasive during the weeks before her disappearance, not staying on Sunday evenings. Was the picture on the screen the cause? He didn't dare let himself give words to it.

Had he led Tara to think he wouldn't care? He was an angry fool in those days, less than ten years after his sister's suicide, and quite soon after his parents' death. He fished out his wallet and stared at Asha's snapshot. She was fresh out of school when that photo was taken. The resemblance to the girl on Tara's phone was uncanny. He wished he could call Tara and ask.

His phone buzzed and he snatched it up, hoping to see a text from her. It was Rehaan's agent—fixing an appointment for the next training session, and this time Karan Virani would join them. He'd turned into a schoolboy—why would Tara call him in the middle of the day?

He looked up from his phone to find Naik staring at him. Her puzzled expression warned him he'd been dreaming again.

"Sir, what do you think?" Naik said. The others had left the meeting room.

"An important message. Sorry, Naik. What were we talking about?"

They rose and walked toward his office.

"The Aksa beach case, sir. Where we found the three buried bodies. Dr. Meshram says we have all we need. We can release the construction site back to TEH."

Taneja would be happy. Arnav's only hope of solving the cases at Aksa was to investigate the dead body dumped at Versova.

Shinde would be released from the hospital tomorrow. He would start asking questions.

"Did we check the call records for the Versova case?"

Naik nodded. "I checked the phone numbers present in the area at the time against a list of owners of the black van model. No hits so far, but two of the phones don't belong to Maharashtra, sir. Both are switched off. One address is based in Lucknow, the other in Bihar."

"Fake phone numbers?"

Government regulations demanded identification before a sim card was issued, but criminals devised ways around this.

"Possible, sir. We're trying our best."

"The CCTV footage?"

"Video forensics has detected two likely matches for that van model from the area you had information on—the Andheri-Kurla Road. We can't see the number plates clearly."

The garage Ali had described was located in that area. Now that Shinde had made so much noise, Arnav must get a photo of the van for verification before raiding the garage. His friend wanted to be the one to nab Rasool.

"Anything further on the sequins?"

"I had them checked by some experts in the market. They say that nylon thread is often used in sequin embroidery. These sequins are expensive. They could have been torn from a designer purse or dress. Lower-end clothes don't use imported sequins."

"I see."

"We're also still working our way through the jewelry shop list."

A custom-made nipple clamp, with real sapphires. Depilation of her entire body. Sequins that could have belonged to a luxury garment or bag. This woman might not have been picked off the street. Why had no one reported her missing? Dr. Meshram had sent the viscera for examination. Arnav dialed the forensic officer.

"Did they send the reports back from Kalina?"

"I was about to call you." The doctor's voice sounded pleased and genial, in contrast to the subject of the conversation: liver, kidneys, stomach from a dead body. Arnav waited.

"She was drugged. They found traces of vecuronium bromide."

"What does it do?"

"It is a neuromuscular blocking agent used in operating theaters to keep a patient immobile during surgery by relaxing all their muscles, alongside support for respiration and anesthesia. Needs to be administered by an experienced clinician."

"You mean the killer is a doctor?"

"Not necessarily. They may have administered the dose to paralyze the victim before making the cuts we've seen. Without clinical assistance, the victim would have been paralyzed, aware of any pain inflicted, and eventually choked to death."

CHAPTER THIRTY-EIGHT

TARA

Tara valued smartness above all, and she did not feel smart at the moment. Even as she dressed for the meeting with Shetty, she missed Arnav's touch all over her—her face, her back, her legs. She'd ruled herself beyond the need for men. She knew better now.

Shetty had left by the time she was ready to meet him the day before—and Tara was glad. He'd sent a message again today, though. Perhaps he wanted to ask her where she'd been last night. She couldn't tell him about Arnav.

Nor could she go to Arnav for help. She could not talk to him about Shetty, the assignment at the train station, or that sinister client, who was possibly a policeman. She didn't care to go on another assignment, ever, but what if her refusal made an enemy of Shetty? Could she count on Arnav?

A recklessness seized her. What harm would it do to pretend for a while that a strong man, a Mumbai police inspector, no less, might come if she called? She longed to call him, like those sniffly girls in the movies falling in love. She was not in love with Arnav. Only rich, respectable folk could afford such emotions, not a bar girl, not even one masquerading as a choreographer.

No point in fancy dreams. Choreography didn't earn her the money—it was the wolf whistles when she appeared under the lights. When she glanced at a guest at the Blue Bar, she convinced him it was business with everyone else, but not with him. She was, after all, a *barwali*.

Was she not also Tara, though? The one whose name Arnav called with such huskiness in his voice?

Yes, she was Tara, but only for a while. She was Ma first, the name her daughter called her. *Calm down. It is Pia you're supposed to think of. Not yourself.*

At her mirror, Tara piled on the gunk, deepening her eyes, reddening her lips, covering up the faint wrinkles that showed she was no longer in her twenties. Picking up her handbag, she left the room.

Shetty's new office, right above the bar where they performed, was a far cry from the old one. This one boasted plush gold-trimmed sofas and cushions, a marble table, and a swanky office chair. Deities presided over a golden temple in one entire corner of the office, complete with lamps, garlands, and burning incense. Shetty glared at her as she walked in.

"Here's your pay for the last assignment." He slid an envelope across the table.

"Thank you."

"Before you thank me, let me tell you it's only half the amount we agreed on. You missed the three-minute deadline."

She released a long breath, but didn't let herself sag with relief, instead preparing to argue. She'd missed it, but only by a few seconds. About to open her mouth, she stopped herself. She needed the entire pay for her remaining performances. Antagonizing Shetty might backfire. In her world, men held all the power. Her lot wasn't as bad as that of the prostitutes who couldn't choose who used their bodies—or perhaps it was. Maybe it was better to have sex with a stranger and be beaten up, than live in fear of not returning to your daughter.

"I'll get to work," Tara said.

"I know you're strapped for cash."

Tara didn't see a way to respond, so she kept quiet.

"You used to visit for private dances. The same client wants you to do it one more time."

Tara shivered. The jackal. So the consequence wasn't merely a pay cut—that was clear after her chat with Mithi. Gauri had vanished. Tara kept her expression blank.

"He's ready to pay. For one hour, you'll make more than all of this week."

Tara studied the dizzying patterns on the carpet. The image of a trip in the dark toward the voice of her nightmares made her stomach churn. Her terror aside, if she went and didn't return, her daughter wouldn't stand a chance.

"Don't say no out of hand. You're doing well. If you like, I can make arrangements for you to stay on. Your daughter can go to a school here."

She met his eyes. How did Shetty learn about Pia? She hadn't told anyone, not even Mithi.

"I make it my business to keep tabs on those who work for me," Shetty said, his manner placid, as if he'd carried out an obligation, not invaded her privacy.

It must be her phone. Her assistant. She'd made calls, messaged Zoya about Pia. Tara lowered her gaze. It wouldn't do to show her anger.

"Take your time to consider the offer." Shetty grew paternal. "It would be foolish to lose such an opportunity. I guarantee your safety—you know you can trust me."

Shetty had uttered much the same words on the night she'd cut and run from Mumbai. Tara was now thirty-one, and a mother. She didn't want to take her time.

"I'm sorry," she said, keeping her tone polite. "I'd just like to finish my contract."

CHAPTER THIRTY-NINE

ARNAV

Arnav sparred often with Shinde, but at the dojo. This was different.

"Two women at the same time?" Shinde gaped at him. They sat in Arnav's car at the hospital parking lot. "That's why you didn't visit me—why you've been phoning in and emailing your reports?"

His right arm trussed up and a ratty sweatshirt draped over his shoulders, Shinde looked nothing like his usual ebullient self. For as long as Arnav had known him, Shinde had been a terrible patient. Each time he was injured in the line of duty, staying in the hospital for extended periods, he made life difficult for his entire team, for his family, and Arnav.

"Well?" Shinde said, as though interrogating a culprit.

Arnav shouldn't have mentioned Tara. He'd hoped talking about her would make it more real. It still felt like a dream, Tara coming back.

"I'm here today first thing in the morning," Arnav said, "and I'm taking you home. *Vaeeni* visited you every day. You didn't have a serious—"

"A deathbed wouldn't be serious enough for you."

Arnav ignored Shinde's grumbling. Driving out of the hospital, he eased the car onto the back roads that would take him to his friend's apartment, and stopped at a slow traffic light.

His phone buzzed. Rehaan's agent wanted to cancel the training appointment—the movie star had to be elsewhere. They needed him to visit the set instead. Arnav dashed off a reply confirming he'd stop by on the new date but couldn't stay long.

"Why did I not know about her?" Shinde wouldn't give up. "You never told me a thing about this Tara."

"Did you tell me about all your women?"

"Does Nandini know you've taken this bar girl home?"

Arnav held his tongue. He did need to tell Nandini. Break it off with her. He'd tried hard to pretend it didn't matter what he had going with Tara, but it did. Nandini deserved better.

While one road gave way to another, from tree-lined avenues to highways running through slums, the silence between them hardened, grim and brittle.

"You don't have the balls to answer me," Shinde said after a while, shattering the quiet.

Arnav fixed his gaze on the road ahead. "Let me look after my life, you worry about yours. I'll stop by your office tomorrow morning to hand over the case."

"Not a moment too soon," Shinde said. "You're refusing a promotion for no reason, you've been ignoring my calls about the case, and now you're carrying on with a bar girl."

This was one thing Arnav couldn't stand about Shinde—his tendency to twist matters to suit his narrative. Arnav had answered each one of his calls. At work, the man was his senior, not a friend. Besides, the term "bar girl" rankled Arnav. Tara was a choreographer now.

"I'm waiting for an update on the Versova case today." Arnav sped up on the narrow road near Shinde's place. "If I hear a word, you'll be the first to know."

"I never receive updates these days. Not about work, not about your women."

"I told you about the forensic conclusions: the drug used on the victim. I also have a lead that might help us find the van," Arnav said.

If they found evidence, Arnav aimed to be the one to conduct a raid. For all his bluster, Shinde was still recovering from his operation. The doctor had recommended taking it easy for two weeks before he started physiotherapy.

"You're a fine one. Arguing with me over a *dhandewali.*"

Dhandewali. A woman who sold her body. Arnav stopped the car, thankful they had reached Shinde's apartment building.

He helped Shinde out of the vehicle, and noticed his children waiting in the lobby.

"We can talk when you're ready to speak about Tara with respect." Arnav greeted the children, then left without looking back.

Having spent time with Tara, he'd been forced to accept two facts. She brought him joy, and he should have pursued her when she left.

He drove slowly, giving himself time to calm down. A dozen traffic horns blared when he cut onto the main road during rush hour. Bristling at no one in particular, Arnav collected himself. Logically, Shinde was right. Tara had abandoned him once and was likely to leave again. She hadn't told him about her life outside Mumbai. What he wanted, though, was to keep seeing her.

Nandini took care of him, had stood by him. It *was* strange that it was Tara, who'd dumped him years ago without ceremony, that made him come undone. He'd never staked out the place where Nandini lived, never worried if she was doing OK, or chased her till she gave in.

Arnav slowed down near a turn. A bent old man stuffed a huge cart with flower garlands and stalks. A stray calf stood next to him, chewing away at the leaves he discarded. Arnav beeped the horn and waited for the man to make way.

His phone rang.

"This is about the black van, sir," Naik said.

"Yes?"

"The constable who chased it at Versova has taken a look at the photo you sent me. He's sure it's the one, sir."

Ali had come through again.

"Make a record of the reason to search the premises," Arnav said. "Send it to the magistrate's office. We'll enter the garage on a good-faith basis. Text me the coordinates."

"Right, sir."

"Pick a team. I'll join you there. Alert the control room—we might need forensics."

Arnav turned onto a back road, hoping to avoid traffic before he caught the Western Express Highway that led to the garage. Flanked by tall trees and dense scrub jungle on both sides, this stretch had broken into potholes, and avoiding them took all his attention.

He dialed Shinde, but clicked off. Maybe he should give his friend some time to cool off. In any case, the man couldn't come for the raid. He left Shinde a voice message instead, giving him the details, keeping one eye on the road.

He must bring Tara out on empty roads like this one—maybe on Sunday, when the Blue Bar was closed. He could take her with him to Rehaan's movie set at Filmistaan—she'd enjoy that. From there, he'd drive outside Mumbai, on a road surrounded by lush forests. A farmhouse restaurant near Lonavala, perhaps. He couldn't remember the last time he'd driven a car for fun—maybe once with Shinde and his family, years ago, when Shinde's son had thrown up all over him. During their trip, Tara might insist he play old Hindi movie songs. It would annoy him, and he'd grumble, but he'd play them all the same. He pictured that little girl, Asha's lookalike, in the back seat.

Arnav recalled the face on Tara's phone screen. Couldn't be younger than ten or eleven, but definitely not older than fifteen. Tara had stayed away fourteen years. All of it pointed to one answer. To his surprise, instead of running from it, he hungered to learn more. He wasn't great at family or commitment. With Tara, though, neither seemed like a bad idea.

He could easily imagine Tara had never left, that it was routine to hold her in his arms. He'd stroked her hair last night as she slept, and it had felt like being home for the first time in years. The last two nights had made his current life recede into a mirage, a distant thing. Tara alone was real.

By the time he noticed the black truck speeding up right behind his car, it was too late. He scrambled to brace for impact as his car hurtled off the road toward a tree in slow motion. After a few seconds of excruciating pain in his shoulders, the universe went dark.

CHAPTER FORTY

TARA

The day before, Tara had tried and failed to contain her joy. In her mind, she'd pictured one of her mother's *rutis*—the pale, air-filled sphere, a marvel of perfection before it deflated into a thin, soft flatbread. Mother made them fresh, and Tara tore into each steaming *ruti*, heat singeing her chubby fingers. Happiness hurt. It didn't last.

For a while, she'd had both Arnav and Pia, wondered if she should bring them together. Now she stood in a hospital lobby, unsure if Arnav would wake up. The hospital wore the air of a fancy hotel: spick-and-span floors, potted plants, framed pictures, room freshener, hushed voices. The pharmacy was a supermarket shop, its medicines stocked in neat rows, sanitary and dental supplies, hairbands, flowers, greeting cards. A different universe from the government hospital where she took Pia.

Tara sought to quiet the churn in her stomach and stop pacing, but her body did its own thing. It didn't seem real that Arnav lay unconscious a few paces away—his left shoulder bandaged, beeping machines, pouches filled with blood and saline hanging about his bed. She'd kissed his laughing face that morning. Her mother would have prayed to Ma Kaali, but if goddesses were real and cared to protect those you loved, Arnav wouldn't be in an accident.

"I knew I'd find you here."

Tara turned. Nandini, two paper cups in hand. The woman who'd held Arnav's hand that first night at the Blue Bar.

"I brought you tea." Nandini handed a cup to Tara.

Tara thanked her and took a sip. It was a funny black tea, not the sort she was used to. She tried to like it. From the name printed on the cup, she knew it had cost more than ten cups of her usual. Nandini lived in a world of teas like this one, of long English sentences spoken too fast, of expensive restaurants. Closer to Arnav's world than hers. And yet this woman had been kind to her.

"It's not nice?"

"No, no, it's good, thanks." Tara feigned a smile.

"You're welcome."

"Thank you for telling me . . . when I rang."

She'd dialed Arnav, but the phone went on ringing. After she'd called several times, Nandini had picked up and told her about Arnav's accident. Tara had rushed here, half out of her mind. It had brought home to her that she could pretend all she liked, but she'd dropped everything to be by his side. Only Nandini was already there.

"Hey, are you OK?"

Nandini's question startled her into taking a bigger sip of tea than she'd intended. It scalded her lips.

"Yes. Yes. Sorry."

Earlier, she hadn't dared stay too long with Nandini in Arnav's room. It would've been difficult for Arnav to wake up and find them both there.

Nandini had gone quiet. She put down her cup and said, her voice low, "Why are you saying sorry? You have every right to be here."

"Nandini . . ."

"You've said this a few times. You've been a lot of trouble, you only wish to make sure Arnav is OK. You'll soon return to Lucknow. I heard. Do you know what he wants?"

"How can you be this calm? You're with him, right?"

"I am. Was. Two years. Don't know if he was with me. Busy with his work most of the time, which suited me fine. I was busy, too. He never made any promises. I never asked."

"You were with him that evening." Tara lowered her head. "You saw me . . ."

"I'd gone there for work and took him along. I'm drafting a report on the reopening of dance bars. I'm good at my job, you at yours."

"You're different."

"My parents say *Do whatever you want, but do it well.* My mother's a scientist, my father a businessman."

"You live alone?"

"They live in the US." She met Tara's eyes, her long hair an artful mess she kept flicking away. "Why are we talking about me?"

Because we can't talk about me.

"You lead an interesting life." Tara rose. "I need to call into work. Give me a minute?"

Nandini was a nice woman, the one who should rightfully be seen with Arnav. Not a bar girl.

Tara was running late—she'd asked Shetty to excuse her from practice. Mithi could handle them for a few hours, but Tara must rush back for the afternoon makeup and hairdo sessions. She wanted to stay as long as possible, to hear from Arnav's doctor. *If you're in any trouble, come to me,* Arnav had said to her. He was in trouble here. She wouldn't desert him.

More than that—if he were to—she couldn't even say the word to herself. He'd never know he had a daughter. Pia deserved to meet him, and he to know her. Tara was in the way.

She passed by the room where Arnav lay, aching to look in. Nandini's gaze prickled her back. She didn't stop. Once in a different hospital wing, she paused and called Shetty. She sent up a prayer of thanks when he didn't pick up. Maybe Ma Kaali was listening, after all. Tara could wait a little longer for her Avi to open his eyes. It was OK to call him that, to herself.

CHAPTER FORTY-ONE

—

ARNAV

Someone dropped a steel tray, followed by a muffled curse in Marathi. Beeps, mechanical, at regular intervals. A high-pitched tinny whining like a giant mosquito that wouldn't stop. Arnav strained to cover his ears, but his hands felt heavy when he strove to lift them, his arms heavier. In the air, a smell of air freshener, a chemical pine scent of Indian five-star hotels. He didn't want to open his eyes, but he must, because this dream had gone on for too long, chasing dark wraiths in squelchy alleyways, Tara walking away in the gloom of an afternoon, his gun turning to dust in his hands.

Through a sliver of light he saw hazy white shapes. They resolved themselves into women in uniform. Nurses. He struggled to call to them, but managed only a groan. They turned. The older and bulkier of the two asked the other to run and fetch the doctor, then approached the bed.

Arnav remembered now—he'd been in an accident. Only it couldn't have been an accident—that truck had targeted him, driven him off the road into the slope and blinding agony.

"Can you hear me?" The nurse took his pulse.

He couldn't form a word in response. A woman in a white coat opened the door and rushed in. He was at a hospital, a private room with blinds and a painting on the wall. The police department paid only for government hospitals. Who had brought him here? He tried to ask the doctor, but his throat remained clogged. The nurse injected him with medication, and the world dropped away again.

When he woke next, the room was dark. He strained to sit up.

"Avi." Nandini rose from the shadows and walked to his bed. "I'll call the nurse."

"How long have I been here?"

"A few hours." Nandini looked pale and haggard, dark circles under her eyes. "The doctor says you're lucky to escape with no lasting injuries."

After a nurse checked him and left, Nandini told him that passersby had called the police and driven him to the nearest hospital. Shinde had visited, along with some of the other inspectors and sub-inspectors.

Did Tara know? Arnav wanted his phone. If she didn't hear from him, she might worry.

"You gave us quite the fright." Nandini reached out to stroke his hair. "Shinde should return soon."

The man in question turned the handle and entered, but Nandini didn't move away. Arnav waited out the discussion between the two about medications, doctor's reports, and handovers.

"Ring this bell if you need anything." Nandini put a switch within reach of Arnav's right hand. "It will alert the nurses."

Nandini had never made any public display of affection, but this time she bent to kiss his forehead. Arnav expected a few swear words from Shinde the minute Nandini walked out of the room, but his friend didn't speak.

"*Abbay narangi pandu*, why that face?" Arnav asked, provoking his friend. "Aren't you happy I have broken bones, too?"

Instead of a return volley for being called a drunk policeman, Arnav received silence. Pain clawed through his left shoulder and all the way down his arm. Typical of Shinde. Wouldn't shut up when Arnav willed him to, but now that he craved answers, distraction, maybe even an argument, Shinde turned away to the window without offering a word.

"What's with you?" Arnav let his annoyance show.

"Avi." Shinde stared outside. "I need a promise."

Shinde looked even worse than this morning—the sweatshirt draped over his shoulders was askew, his jeans stained.

"Are your painkillers making you high?" The throb at Arnav's shoulder picked up as he spoke. He itched to fling a tray at Shinde and hear a satisfying crash.

"You love my children, right?" Shinde's voice was pitched so low, Arnav barely heard him.

"This morning you were barking all over the place. I'm not dead, you know. Of course I love them."

"You'll hear me out for their sake?"

The pounding agony now extended to his neck and head. Arnav pressed the switch to call the nurse for more painkillers.

"You don't make any sense," he gasped.

Shinde started, checked his phone. His entire stance hardened, and he wheeled around to meet Arnav's eyes. "I must take this call. I'll be back."

CHAPTER FORTY-TWO

He sat up and looked out the window. Dad had inherited this place and a fair bit of money. He spent most of it on the Item Number, but left this farmhouse bungalow to him. The one good deed in his entire cursed life.

An hour's drive from downtown Mumbai, the farmhouse was an eerie place at night. The sounds of the mangrove jungle filtered up to him: the chirping of crickets, the hoot of owls, the howling of hungry stray dogs. The bungalow held all his memories, the best and the worst. On some evenings, he didn't know one from the other.

Wandering over to his study, he locked the door and pulled open his cabinet. His diaries. Who was Bilal to ask him to end it all? He'd paid that man lakhs of rupees in salary over the years. He spotted Bilal's name in a diary entry.

Today Bilal isn't around, and I don't know why Dad's home early. On his good days, Dad and I play cricket in the overgrown backyard, but sometimes the air changes. When I hear the swish of his belt, I try my best to hide. I often succeed, like today, curling up in the basement under a large table where we butcher the meat Dad brings in after a hunt. Wild boar. Deer. One side of the basement opens up to skylight windows that show the green outside. We rarely open those unless the place gets stinky after a night of chopping meat and Bilal ends up using too much bleach.

He's left them open today, and while I write these words, I want to curl up and disappear, or fly out of those windows and never return.

He flung the notebook across the room, and picked another.

I don't like Dad's green camouflage fatigues, but he made me wear one today. I hid my laugh—we were wearing the uniform of the protectors while going on a hunting safari.

I'll wear a uniform someday. Maybe the khaki—good camouflage, more power. We'll see. When I told Dad about choosing the khaki uniform of a policeman, he called me a fattu, *a pussy. I'm not man enough.*

I didn't say it, but I'm not the pussy in this household, the one who can't control his wife.

He doesn't notice that even when I stay away, when I act like I have a headache and stay in bed, she brings me soup. She touches my forehead to check for fever, then my throat and chest, and lower and lower, stroking me all over, all the while crooning straightforward advice, like I should eat well. I'm growing too weak, she says, I should go for workouts. I'm fifteen. She's twenty-three. Dad is forty-seven. Who should know better?

CHAPTER FORTY-THREE

ARNAV

Hospitals were not new for Arnav. As a boy, he'd waited for the release of his sister's body into his family's custody. A few years later, he'd sat by his father's bedside as the man wasted away with liver cirrhosis. Then his mother, through her chemotherapies. In his experience, he was the only member of his family to have returned home from a hospital bed.

The doctor said Arnav had a fractured but nondisplaced left shoulder, bruised ribs, and some concussion. Given proper rest and care, he should recover. Arnav grimaced once he was alone. He didn't need the injuries on top of the pile already on his plate—the Aksa cases, the transfer he aimed to fight, and whatever it was he had brewing with Tara. Not to mention someone wanted him dead.

He heard the door open. Footsteps. This wasn't Shinde's brisk, confident footfall. Had they found him here? He peered through his lashes. A woman.

"Tara?"

She rushed up to him. "Nandini said you'd woken up, so I came in."

"Nandini?"

Tara was here, and had met his girlfriend. Why hadn't he broken up with Nandini yet?

"I kept calling your phone and she picked up."

Her shirt was crumpled, hair a mess, her eyes swollen. Had she been crying?

"When did you come here? Isn't it time for your performance soon?"

"I was worried. I thought . . ."

Arnav moved to rise, but his shoulder hurt too much. A nurse walked in, and Tara shut up while the woman in uniform checked the machines, the drip, and scribbled notes on his chart.

"I'm fine," Arnav said.

"Sure." She smiled, but it looked wobbly. "You look like someone gave you a sound beating."

Arnav reached out with his good hand, and she held it.

"I'm so glad you'll be fine. I need to tell you—should have told you long ago, but—"

Before she could finish, Shinde strode in.

"This is Tara," Arnav said, his pain receding. His thoughts regained clarity. He turned to Tara. "This is Hemant Shinde."

"What's she doing here?" Shinde said.

Tara drew herself up to her full height. She was a lot shorter than Shinde, but her posture, rigid and straight, made her appear taller than she was. "You're Shetty's man, aren't you? Did he ask you to check on me?"

Arnav stared at the two of them. This was his day of mysteries and adventure. Tara and Shinde knew each other, and weren't on good terms. He addressed her, the saner of the two, and the one likely to give proper answers.

"Tara?"

"Well, ask him." Tara's voice was low, but heavy with accusation.

Shinde glanced away. Arnav's left arm had turned into a mass of aches. He must corner Shinde, figure out what was going on.

"Give us a few minutes, Tara." He put the sum of his feelings into his gaze. "Don't go far."

When she nodded, looking unsure, he added, "This won't take long. Please."

When Tara had closed the door behind her, he scowled at Shinde. "You'd better explain."

CHAPTER FORTY-FOUR

Bilal had gone missing. Not for a few hours, which was normal, not the entire day, which was unusual but acceptable, but for two days. He might actually have left for good, like he said.

He tried Bilal's number for the hundredth time. The rings tapered off into a voice message. *"Hello. I'll call you back."*

Last week, seeing no point in keeping it to himself, he'd mentioned in passing to Bilal that he'd received a delivery at the railway station.

"If you revert to your old ways, I'm leaving." Bilal looked up from loading his bag into the car. "I've handpicked and trained the staff. You can choose a housekeeper from among them."

"She'll come to the farmhouse. For a dance. I promised you—nothing else."

"You've made promises before." Bilal had stormed off.

That day was packed with meetings, so he hadn't taken Bilal at his word. In his free moments, he'd pictured only the one who flew away, the dead ringer for Item Number. He wanted to watch her tremble in a blue-sequined saree, sobbing and terrified, yet gyrating to each item song he remembered.

Uhnna had been difficult. At first, he'd remained set on his earlier stance of no deliveries. A while later, he relented, but insisted on guarantees. No spillage, no damage. As if *Uhnna* cared about the woman. To add to the insult, he'd demanded five times the previously agreed amount and extra favors, which didn't bear thinking about.

He'd given in. A firm yes to each of the conditions. He dreamed of making the Item Number dance to his tune, but this woman would do for now. She'd earn him a good night's sleep—a respite from his nightmares of the Item Number in blue.

Once, someone had caught him, and had to be fixed. He'd kept a low profile for a few weeks and gone about his duties as usual. What a bother, but also, if he was being honest, a satisfaction.

The silk sheets on his bed irked him—he punched the pillows. He hankered to brush shoulders, melt into a crowd, lose himself till he heard news of the new delivery. He craved a break from all the shit in his life, the nemesis who refused to die despite a well-executed traffic accident, the home falling into chaos in the absence of a diligent house-keeper. If only he could wear the uniform, not at work, but to thrill in the escape from discovery. He longed to prowl the streets to drain his restless energy. How to run away without Bilal, though? Once more the call to Bilal's number, and the message, *"Hello. I'll—"*

Before Bilal's recorded voice could finish, he tossed the phone.

He strode to his dressing table and tossed on his clothes. He'd burned half of his treasure—his notebooks, his collection—and for what? He didn't need Bilal's care or his warnings to be discreet—better if the man wasn't there. With no one to clean up afterward, he wouldn't forget himself. He'd stored enough pictures, the remaining diaries, and memories. He'd survive, ditch the uniform, go for a walk in his own backyard garden.

CHAPTER FORTY-FIVE

ARNAV

At thirteen years old, Arnav had smashed the windows of one of his neighbors' cars because the man had called his recently dead sister an ugly name. When the car owner caught him, a few local boys gathered to watch the spectacle. The owner, a towering goon, grabbed Arnav by the throat, murder in his eyes. Arnav threw out his gangly arms to block the punches about to rain down on him. They never came because a strapping young man intervened.

He calmed the goon down, made him release Arnav. As Arnav gaped and blabbered, the youth promised that Arnav and his family would pay the damages. The young man, whose mustache had made him look far older than his nineteen years, hustled Arnav off before the owner could change his mind. That was Arnav's first meeting with Hemant Shinde, which started a friendship spanning more than two decades.

Arnav let the silence in the hospital room stretch out. Shinde stood with his face turned away from him, staring at the floor.

"I used to have an arrangement with Tara's boss at the Blue Bar. Shetty. He sent women out to clients from time to time. You remember how hushed it was since the government ban on dance bars—he could only retain licenses on the smaller bars. I made sure no one looked into it."

"*Hafta?*"

Hafta, the innocuous Hindi word that simply meant "a week," was Mumbai's term for weekly protection payments extorted by mob bosses, and often the police. Sometimes a stall owner paid *hafta* to both the police and the mob, so neither would bother him. The money was collected from various businesses, aggregated, then distributed per a fixed ratio starting from the ministers, to the top cops, all the way down to the constable. Arnav had stayed out of the system. He'd assumed so had Shinde.

He would've laughed at his own naivete had his shoulders hurt less. Those you loved either didn't stay in your life, or didn't stay the same. Trust no one. Arnav had lost sight of these important lessons.

"I'm not proud of it." Shinde rubbed at his unshaven cheek.

"Was that why you railed against Tara earlier? You didn't want me to find out she knew you?"

"I had no idea who Tara was. I just didn't think a bar girl was better than Nandini."

"Really?"

"I'd only seen her a few times long ago while chasing Shetty for his payments at the bar. I didn't know her name."

Payments. Shinde spoke like it was owed him. Who was this man?

"What did you want to tell me earlier?"

"I . . ." Shinde lowered his gaze. "Remember that day I went with you to the morgue?"

Arnav sensed he wouldn't want to hear his friend's confession.

"The dead woman was Neha Chaubey. I recognized the birthmark on the underside of her breast." Shinde cleared his throat. "I couldn't tell you. Not without admitting how I knew her. She's . . . was one of Shetty's dancers from another, much smaller bar."

"How long has this been going on?"

No way Shinde could have seen the mark under normal circumstances. Neha was Shinde's woman.

His poor wife. Cooking, keeping house, raising the children, while her husband spent time with Shetty's bar girls.

"I was wrong, but what could I do? A man has needs. After work at the station, I need relief and Sujata is too tired or asleep by the time I'm home. You're not married, and have no clue. Girls throw themselves at you."

"Even if I let that slide," Arnav said as he addressed the wall instead of Shinde, "you're still a senior inspector who obstructed a murder investigation. Now I get why you've been acting strange, ordering me to turn the lead over."

Arnav bit down a groan as his shoulder throbbed and his mind grappled with the enormity of what Shinde had done—taken bribes to help Shetty, concealed evidence, and cheated on his wife. If this came out, at the very least, Shinde would face an enquiry. He could be fired, and his wife might leave with his children. No wonder he'd tried his best to remove Arnav from the case. The only upside to this entire *locha*, this messy shit show, was the discovery of the victim's identity.

"I wasn't sure how you'd react. I never imagined it would lead to this."

"This?"

"We both know this was an attempt on your life." Shinde gestured at Arnav's injuries.

"What's the connection?"

"When you stayed on the Versova case, I spoke to Shetty about Neha Chaubey."

"Shetty ordered this hit on me?"

Arnav strained to sit up, but the room turned into a blur. His right arm spasmed. Knowing it wasn't broken, Arnav pushed his hand into the bed in order to rise.

"I won't let anyone harm you." Shinde rushed to the bed and helped Arnav. "I promised your mother on her deathbed, Avi. I may be a jerk, but I keep my word."

"I see."

Arnav didn't see, not at all—not how he'd been stupid enough not to recognize his friend's true nature. Nor how he'd feel any loyalty or affection for Shinde ever again.

"Hear me out, please. The thing with . . . Neha was part of the . . . payment. I had no clue what had happened to her till I saw . . . her on that table." He sank down on a chair beside the bed. "She'd told me she was going back to her village. She wasn't a good dancer. The bar was not for her."

"Is Shetty behind this, or not?" Arnav pointed at his own bandaged shoulder. "And the women?"

"He said he'd get the Neha Chaubey situation fixed. A while later you received a promotion offer, and I was relieved. You, being an ass, didn't take it. You even gave interviews to the press."

"I like that you're calling me names. You understand I must report you, right?" Arnav said.

"I cannot stop you. I've known Shetty for years—didn't expect him to do this."

"I've known you, too." Arnav let that statement hang in the air.

"You should take the promotion." Shinde met Arnav's eyes, shamed but defiant. "Once you're away, you'll be left alone. Whoever is behind these murders will not sit quietly while you drag them into newspapers."

Arnav recalled the earlier cases, in various police jurisdictions. The investigating officers who were either transferred or died under suspicious circumstances. The women's bodies merging into soil over the years.

"Did you orchestrate my promotion? What about Mhatre and his warnings?"

"No. But if you report me, Mhatre will be aware you're still investigating Aksa and the other cases."

"You haven't talked to him?"

Mhatre had been cagey and odd all last week—unwilling to acknowledge that the cases could be related. He'd backed Commissioner Joshi on not investigating Taneja Estate Holdings and on Arnav's promotion out of the Malwani station.

"I'm telling you I haven't," Shinde said. "Someone with higher connections is pulling the strings—not Mhatre. He's only a senior inspector."

How could Arnav be sure Shinde wasn't lying? Arnav felt like he'd stumbled into quicksand. Taneja, Joshi, Mhatre, and now Shetty and Shinde.

"Avi, this is serious. I put my wife on a flight to Delhi this afternoon along with our children. I won't have a job with Mumbai Police after this, and if you go public, no one will hire me at a security firm. I've posted plainclothes guards in the corridor. If someone wants you eliminated from this case, it will happen, one way or another. Are you willing to risk your life?"

"What sort of man is Shetty?"

"I've worked with him for seventeen years. He's a regular bar owner, and he doesn't force the girls. My role included locking up any clients who acted smart or hurt the girls during private performances."

"You didn't know the clients?" Arnav said.

"In most cases, no. He had men escort the girls to the locations and bring them back. Not all clients demanded sex. Some asked the women to sing or dance. One even insisted a girl should act like his wife, cook for him, and keep his house clean."

"What aren't you telling me?"

"I can't say right now who—"

Nandini knocked and walked into the room. "Tara is leaving." She stared at Shinde.

"Where is she?" Arnav said. He couldn't let Tara go back to Shetty.

Tara strode in. "I'm going to work. I'll see you in the morning."

"Wait, you can't—"

"I have to, Avi. I'm already late." Tara looked anxious. "I'd taken leave only for the afternoon."

Her use of "Avi" didn't go unnoticed by the others, but neither commented on it.

"No," Arnav said. "Come here."

"I have a contract with him." She glanced at her phone. "He's calling."

"Shetty can't be trusted," Shinde said to Tara and Nandini. "Talk to Arnav." To Arnav he said, "I'll go make a few calls, and tell Naik you're awake."

"How can I trust you?"

"I have a lot to atone for." Shinde stepped out, leaving Arnav faced with the two women.

A month ago, if someone had suggested to him Nandini and Tara would ever stand in the same room, he'd have laughed. Yet there they were.

Nandini was chatting with the nurse who'd come in. He watched Tara. She looked beaten, a different woman from the one he'd dropped off that morning.

"Did Shetty know about me?" he asked Tara, his voice low. He felt like an ass, speaking of it in Nandini's presence, but Tara was in danger and he had no choice.

"I'm not sure. Why can't I go to work?"

"It isn't safe. Switch off your phone."

"I can't." She was agitated, her eyes wide with fear.

"You must. For anyone else who needs it," Arnav said, "pass them another number. I'll give you an extra phone."

"If I don't go," Tara said, "he'll send men to look for me."

"You won't stay at the hotel tonight. Switch it off. Now." He watched as she did it with unsteady hands.

"She's coming with me." Nandini had finished talking to the nurse and stood at the foot of his bed. "My building has security."

Tara said, "I'll wait here."

"I never make an offer I do not mean. You'll be safer at my condominium." Nandini smiled, all matter-of-fact, and turned to him. "It is time for your dinner and medication. I'll take care of the formalities at reception, and drive to the lobby to pick her up."

Nandini made it sound normal, but it couldn't have been easy. She waved at him and left before he could thank her.

CHAPTER FORTY-SIX

TARA

Tara sat beside Arnav's bed. Dark circles under his eyes, bruises on his forehead, neck, and arms. His left shoulder was in a cast, and his chest was bandaged. Why had he asked her to not go to work? What had Shinde told him about Shetty? She didn't wish to upset Arnav, but disappearing from work wouldn't bode well for her contract. She couldn't afford to forget why she needed the money. Pia.

This could be the only time she'd be alone with him. Once he knew the truth, he wouldn't stand in her way.

"I'm going to break it off with Nandini." Arnav's voice startled her.

"What?"

"I nearly died—"

She raised a hand to stop those words, but he caught it in his own. "I know what I want," he said. "I can't be with her."

She considered asking him who he longed to be with instead, but she wasn't ready. She wasn't certain she'd ever be. She went on the offense instead. "And I'm supposed to stay with her?"

"Only until I leave the hospital."

"That's taking advantage of her."

"No one could take advantage of Nandini if they tried. She offered. Like she said, she means it."

"I need to finish the contract with Shetty. What did your friend tell you?"

"I understand you wish to keep working, but tell me about Shetty, Tara. Both our lives may depend on it. Start from when you first met him."

What could she say to that? Fear and shame battled within her. Fear won, and she started speaking, keeping her gaze on their joined hands.

She recounted the strange assignments at the railway station. The high-paid, creepy appointments to dance for a client who stayed in the dark. Mithi's suspicions. Her latest trip to the Borivali railway station. Shetty's offer for a private dance performance. Her refusal. She expected Arnav to react, but he merely said, "Tell me what you recall about the drives at night to this client's place."

"I was in a *burka*. They used to take me to a car and blindfold me. We drove for a while, and changed cars."

"When you arrived, was it a bungalow or an apartment?" Arnav said.

In her mind, Tara heard the creak of a gate. A calloused hand steered her by the elbow, and she was relieved to find paved ground beneath her feet.

The air smelled of jasmine, and other flowers she didn't recognize. Breeze rustled through trees as she stumbled, then righted herself. Someone held up her left hand and placed it against a wall. A harsh male voice—*Keep your hand on the wall and walk straight.* She tiptoed on, mouth dry, breath short. A door slammed behind her and a bolt fell in place. That sound, its finality, and the sticky darkness sent a chill through her even after all this time.

"A bungalow, I think. No lift. They dropped me outside a long corridor. I could hear the rustling of leaves."

"What else?" Arnav said. "Close your eyes and try to remember."

She described the birdcalls she heard sometimes, the lack of traffic noises when she arrived. They drove through empty roads. The men smoked and listened to Malayali songs. She spoke of the mysterious client she'd never seen.

"What did he sound like? Young, middle-aged, old?"

"He wasn't old."

"Would you be able to identify his voice if you heard it again?"

I was told you will do as I say.

The jackal didn't speak her language, the streetwise *tapori* slang of most of the customers who frequented the Blue Bar.

"I . . . think so. His voice had a smile in it, as if he knew a lot I didn't, and I'd be sorry one way or the other. Educated man. Spoke like rich people do, who use Hindi only when they must. It was years ago, though."

"What did he talk about?"

"He asked me to dance on a bed."

"A bed?"

"Yes, but quite firm. There were silk sheets. My feet slipped on them sometimes."

She described the dark room, and as she spoke about the showers of dried rose petals, the light, sickly sweet scent came back to her.

"Did he ever touch or threaten you?" Arnav's tone was flat when he said it, but she noticed his bruised hand tremble on hers.

"He kept his distance, but the way he spoke, asking if I was tired, or thirsty, as if he was laughing at me—was scary. Like a jackal. That's what I call him in my head. The jackal."

"What about the men? Do you recall any of them? Were they the same each time?"

"I don't know. The man who came to pick me up and drove the car to the halfway point, I saw his face. He blindfolded me."

"Describe the smells. What did the car smell like? The corridor? The room?"

"The car reeked of cigarettes, and sometimes of alcohol. I could smell perfumes in the corridor. The room, I'm not sure. Roses. A strong cologne. And *charas*."

"You're certain?"

"Some of the girls in my apartment smoked it. I remember the smell."

"How much money did Shetty pay you?"

If her mother had been around, she would have said, *Is this what I taught you?* She had seen only a piece of luck, a painless way to get out of the hole she was in, to reach for her dreams. It sounded so shameful and foolish now. She'd gone, despite the risk, because of the money. As she spoke, she imagined Arnav's gaze that she didn't meet. The pity in it. Maybe anger. Disgust.

A sob escaped her.

Arnav placed his hand on her shoulder. "You grabbed an opportunity. It took guts. Nothing to be ashamed of."

"They gave me sixty thousand rupees for each night." Best to reduce it to numbers.

Her ignominy was complete—Arnav was trying to make her feel better.

She'd lied to him about her age, adding two years. She'd been seventeen, four years older than Pia was now. A baby. No wonder Zoya had called her naive.

Tara described her last evening in Mumbai, when she'd run like a thief in the night, despite the cash offered.

"Come here," Arnav said, his voice low and deep.

For a while, she let him hold her. *Tell him now,* the voice within her screamed. *Tell him you carried his daughter with you.*

They sat close, Arnav stroking her hair, kissing her temple, her forehead. When the nurse came in, Tara sprang away and made to rush out.

"Wait, Tara."

She paused, and walked to the window overlooking another part of the hospital, gray walls of concrete within which fervent hopes and much prayer waged war against illness and death. She'd seldom prayed, but now she sent up an appeal to whoever was in charge, maybe her mother's Ma Kaali: *Give me the courage to tell him about Pia.*

The nurse gave Arnav an injection, checked the drips, and left. Tara went back and stood beside his bed, her face flaming. She'd been weak just now. She'd never wanted anyone to see her like that, especially not Arnav.

"Tara . . ." Arnav said.

"I can't talk about this anymore."

"I know. Do you remember anything else at all?"

She mentioned the police cap she'd seen, and watched as her words registered.

"Could the jackal be a police officer?" he said.

"He sounded commanding. Like he owned half of Mumbai, and expected to be obeyed."

Arnav clenched his jaw, and seemed to go far away in his mind. After a while, he turned to her again and, scrolling through his phone, showed her pictures of police caps.

"Any of these?"

Tara pointed to a peaked khaki cap with a gold-embroidered black band. "Like this one, but I can't be sure. It was dark." All of the caps—the khaki, the gold embroidery, the brown bands and black—blurred the faded image in her memory.

Arnav paused before asking the next question.

"What train station was this?" he said. "Did you go to different ones each time?"

"No. It was Borivali, earlier, and now. And I wore the same set of clothes."

"Same clothes?"

"Yes. Shetty gave them to me, and I returned them, along with the phone."

"What sort of clothes?"

Silver blouse and the blue-sequined saree, the silver heels. She wished she had never set eyes on them.

Arnav dragged himself up. "A blue saree with sequins?"

"Yes."

"Would you recognize the saree or the sequins?"

Tara remembered the brush of the saree's silk lining on her skin. The scratch of sequins when they touched her arms.

When she said yes, Arnav opened his phone and showed her photos. Blue sequins in a small plastic bag.

She'd done one thing right in all her career with Shetty. Wordlessly, she stood up and headed to her handbag on the table. Returning to Arnav, she placed the tissue with the blue sequins on his bandaged palm.

CHAPTER FORTY-SEVEN

ARNAV

A police officer, Tara had said. That terrified Arnav. A senior officer, if Tara was right. He could have moved up the ranks by now. His cap may have changed.

Trust no one.

Blue sequins. Tara's sequins matched the photos on his screen. Maybe it was the same saree over decades, maybe not, but a police officer as the culprit made sense. A senior police officer would know how to evade notice and stall investigations.

From his own experience, Mumbai police officers didn't cut a heroic figure. Joshi hadn't investigated Asha's rape. Mhatre had ordered him to ignore what was clearly shaping up as a serial killing, because of Taneja's clout. Shinde collected *haftas* like a mob goon, went out with bar girls despite being married, and had not disclosed recognizing a murder victim.

Shinde didn't return, nor did he pick up Arnav's calls. Amid the agony that was his shoulder, worrying whether Tara would go back to Shetty, and mulling over what Shinde had told him, Arnav wished Naik would show up soon. He could get her to sort Shetty out.

And name the devil, he murmured to himself, because Naik knocked and came in.

Anyone else would have started off with asking how he was, and whether they could help. Not Naik.

"Good to see you awake, sir. There's an update on the black van."

He liked her ability to come straight to the point.

"Located it?"

"Yes, sir. Our constable has identified it. Forensics are processing it now. The van was washed, but the team says they've detected traces of blood under the floor mat in the back."

"I'll make a call and hurry them up," Arnav said. "Any arrests?"

"We've rounded up a few suspects for questioning. We don't know who was driving the van yet. The constable who chased it says one of the suspects is a match. Similar height and build to the man who dumped the suitcase. Walks with a stoop."

"What about this suspect's call records?"

"We're looking them up. We've also confiscated his phone."

While Naik gave her account, Arnav mulled over ways to keep Shinde and Tara out of this, at least for the moment. To protect Tara, he must tell Naik about her role as a victim and witness. He would hold on to Shinde's misdeeds for a while—at least until he'd had a more detailed chat, discovered the extent of his transgressions.

"I have an informer who says we need to look at Shetty," he finally said, "the owner of the Blue Bar."

"Should I set a tail on him, sir?"

"Bring him in."

"We have nothing to link him to this case."

"We know the victim was Neha Chaubey. The informer says she was a dancer at another of Shetty's bars. Check the missing persons records for her name. He's still sending out women in blue sarees." He handed over the sequins to Naik.

"We have a witness?"

"Yes, I'll get her to testify." He hoped Tara would agree.

Naik made notes as Arnav told her about Tara's accounts of her assignments, and that she was staying with Nandini.

"Interrogate Shetty. You can take Tara's statement tomorrow. Don't tell him we have Tara, though. And nothing about the blue sarees."

"I understand, sir." Naik glanced about the room. "Should I place a request to move you to a government hospital?"

The department would pay for his expenses at a government hospital, but that would also make him far more accessible to anyone aiming to finish the job.

"No, thank you, Naik. The doctor says I should be discharged soon."

"Right, sir."

"Show Shetty Neha Chaubey's body. Keep him talking all night." That would ensure Tara's safety for now. "And send some women constables to speak to a girl who works there. Mithi. Ask her and the other women if any of their colleagues disappeared, or returned to their villages."

"Sure, sir."

Naik seemed happy to follow orders, even though she must know Arnav had been asked to step back from the cases. He told her he hadn't accepted Joshi's offer of promotion.

"You might yet be rid of me," Arnav added. "Mhatre sir may not give me a choice and make me move to Bandra."

"Congratulations, sir," Naik said with a forced grin. She looked crestfallen for a second, which puzzled Arnav.

"You don't seem to mean it."

"No, no, sir," Naik said. "It is sudden, and I was surprised—that's all."

"I'll understand if you'd like to back off from the Aksa beach case, given what I've told you. And the Versova case wasn't ours to begin with—I was assisting Senior Inspector Shinde."

"I owe you, sir." This time her smile was genuine. "Besides, I'd like to solve the Aksa case—the killer won't stop unless we catch them. Other women might fall prey."

"For now, keep the case low profile."

"Mhatre sir has left for the day. Shinde sir has requested everyone to support you, so we should have few problems."

So Shinde had been active. He used to be at Malwani Police Station before his transfer with promotion to Versova. He'd helped most of the Malwani staff at one time or the other—with a delayed application for leave or a home remedy for a cough.

Naik finally asked the question she seemed to have held back all along: "How did your accident occur, sir?"

Arnav filled her in on the truck that had deliberately hit him, speeding out of nowhere, despite his attempt to avoid it. Naik asked more questions in order to file a case against an unidentified culprit. Her face remained calm, but the way she clutched her pen spoke otherwise.

"This case might get quite dangerous. You have your family to think of," Arnav said.

"I'll be fine, sir."

"Has your husband applied for other jobs?"

Naik was the family breadwinner after the amputation of her husband's arm.

"He's looking, sir. He should find an opening soon."

"You don't owe me anything, Naik. You must do what's best for your career."

"We'll catch this killer, sir. And whoever is trying to obstruct this investigation."

Arnav could only hope his assistant was right. Shinde still hadn't been in touch.

CHAPTER FORTY-EIGHT

TARA

Tara paced the lobby of the hospital wing, waiting for Nandini. Arnav had said similar blue sequins were part of a murder investigation. If Shetty had given her the blue-sequined saree, she couldn't trust him. But she didn't care to stay with Nandini, either.

Nandini's car glided in, large, sleek, and shiny black. She smiled and nodded for Tara to step in.

"We need to talk," Tara said as she opened the car door.

"Sure, we can speak on the way."

"I don't think it's a great idea to stay at your place."

"Why not?"

"I shouldn't drag you into my mess. Arnav says my boss is a dangerous man."

"All the more reason to avoid hotels," Nandini said.

"I'll be safe enough outside his room."

"If Arnav said your boss poses danger, you can be sure they'll keep him busy tonight. You look like you need some rest—my place is better than the hospital."

"But—"

"The police will also have someone watching Arnav."

Tara couldn't insist on staying at the hospital without sounding like she wished to lay claim to Arnav. She gave in. "Only for tonight."

Nandini drove off, handling her car with an ease that irked Tara. Nandini was intelligent, confident, more suited to Arnav than Tara could ever be. Tara now owed her a favor she could never hope to repay. To top it all off, Nandini didn't know Arnav intended to break up with her. Tara itched to hug this woman, and hurt her.

"Why do you want to help me?"

"What if I told you I'm doing all of this for my job?"

Nandini focused on the traffic, not looking at Tara.

"Your job?"

"I've been thinking about it—your life, everything you've been through, and Shetty. It would make a fantastic addition to the feature I'm doing on the reopening of bars. I'm a journalist, Tara."

Tara tried to picture how she appeared to Nandini. Her unkempt clothes, her cheap perfume. The seedy world of Shetty and the Blue Bar. The car radio played Bollywood tunes that echoed in Shetty's bars, bringing back flashes of her dancing, her reckless stupidity in accepting his assignments.

Tara shook herself out of the memory, thankful the songs had paused for the news, which Nandini listened to, her expression keen.

Arnav's girlfriend wore little makeup, the fine lines under her eyes visible. Her square jaw, her bright, kind eyes, the capable hands on the steering wheel showed Tara what she could've become if she had an education. Practical, useful, successful, a woman who knew what she desired and went for it. This was the sort of woman Tara aspired for Pia to become.

She turned away and watched the filth and glitter of Mumbai pass by through blurry eyes. With Diwali fast approaching, many homes had put up lights on their gates and balconies. The festival of joy, which celebrated the king and hero who had vanquished the demon Ravan on Dussehra, didn't echo in her heart this time. Each year, she spent it decorating her home, filling her kitchen with sweets. On the evening of the darkest night in the Hindu calendar, she helped Pia light lamps, sparklers, firecrackers. This Diwali, she didn't know what the future held for her or, more importantly, for Pia.

Tara sucked in a calming breath. It was rude not to respond to Nandini, but she needed to get ahold of herself. She could burst into tears any moment.

"Look, Tara. I won't pretend it doesn't hurt . . . about you and Avi. The thing is, he's encouraged me to see other people if I wished. I didn't because what I had with Arnav was convenient. Both he and I deserve more than that."

"I'm returning to Lucknow soon." Tara kept her voice even, her gaze trained on the traffic stop: the streetlights, the office workers scurrying home, the slum dwellers on the streets.

"That's easy then, right? You can stay with me until then. You'll be safe. I'll gain the material for a story. We'll call it even."

CHAPTER FORTY-NINE

Arnav

Arnav limped into his office, jolts of pain at each step. He'd made the doctors discharge him that morning, against medical advice. Good thing Tara remained at Nandini's place, because he couldn't imagine either of them letting him get away without a fight.

The constables greeted him and cleared out of his way. When one of them scrambled to offer a hand, Arnav waved him off. His left arm was bandaged and in a sling to support the broken shoulder, but he could use his right hand on a wall for support if he stumbled. His legs were bruised, not broken. He could walk, and he would bloody well do it without help, even if it killed him.

"Get Naik," he barked to the constable, "and join the meeting."

When the constable reached the door, Arnav called out his thanks after the man, and lowered himself slowly into his chair. No point in being a boor to those who sought to help. The world didn't need more nastiness. He sat back and scrolled through his phone, trying not to smash the darn thing. Tara had gone to the railway station wearing a blue-sequined saree two days ago. She could have ended up like . . . Arnav longed to barge in and interrogate Shetty right away, ask him what he knew about Tara and the mysterious client, but that wouldn't help, not without a briefing from his team.

Naik entered a few minutes later, and behind her, a constable carrying a tray with a steaming drink and porridge.

"What's all this?"

"Shinde sir stopped by," Naik said. "He said he'll come in soon. I can update you while you finish your breakfast, sir."

Arnav wasn't hungry, and the last thing he needed to do was suck on porridge in front of his direct reports. "Give me the updates first."

"Please eat, sir," Naik said. "He briefed us. We're here to help."

"What do you mean?"

Had Shinde spoken about his own involvement with Neha Chaubey?

Naik cleared her throat. "Shinde sir asked us to make sure you take your medicines. And Mhatre sir will join us soon."

Arnav liked this woman's guts. She was threatening her own boss with a visit from his. He picked up the drink and took a sip.

"You've got Shetty?"

"He's been here all night, sir. After we showed him the evidence from the Neha Chaubey case, he clammed up for a while, but we've kept up the interrogation."

"He admitted he knew Neha Chaubey?"

They had located a missing persons complaint for Neha.

After not hearing from Neha in two weeks, her younger brother and mother had come to Mumbai the day before and registered a complaint. Neha's mother had identified her body last night. Her brother had confirmed she used to work for Shetty, and showed them Neha's picture taken at one of Shetty's other bars. Shetty could no longer deny recognizing her, but he claimed Neha had told him she was returning home to her village.

While Naik spoke, hunger compelled Arnav to set about the painful and awkward process of feeding himself using his injured hand.

"What has he said so far?"

"Shetty says he doesn't know about the jewelry with sapphires or the blue sequins. We've showed the item to jewelers, sir. They say it is custom-made, by hand. The *W* or *M* could be a mark of the person who was assigned the task if it was forged in a traditional Indian jewelry shop. We're canvassing those. The bigger jewelers wouldn't do special orders."

"What about the black van?" Arnav said.

"Sir, given the circumstances," Naik replied as she met his eyes, "I sent a special request to Dr. Meshram to expedite the van's forensic examination."

How much had Shinde told them? Arnav hadn't reported Shinde yet. He must speak to the man first.

The blood type detected under the plastic carpet in the van was a match to Neha Chaubey's, and Naik was following up on the DNA tests.

Right after Arnav's team left, Mhatre came in.

Arnav wished his looming boss a good morning and rose to offer his chair as per protocol, but Mhatre gestured at him to stay put.

"I heard the doctor wouldn't discharge you for a while, yet here you are. I received a call from Commissioner Joshi this morning." Mhatre sank into a seat opposite Arnav. "He said you will be transferred—though it's up to you whether you take the promotion. You will report to him."

Arnav couldn't disobey a direct order, but saw no harm in pushing a little to figure out how loyal his boss was to Joshi.

"We discussed the possibility that this is a serial killer, sir. A previous case was under a zone headed by Joshi sir. I'm in charge of the Versova and Aksa cases, and I'm being transferred."

The whirring of the small computer fan remained the only sound in the room for a while.

"I spotted that piece speculating about serial killings, even after I warned you about the first article. Watch what you say, Rajput. I let you assist with the Versova case because Shinde asked for it. Hand it over to him now he's returned." Mhatre frowned, leaning back in his chair. "And do you have any evidence proving a solid relationship between the unsolved cases and transfers or deaths of the investigating officers?"

Arnav paused. He could point out again that all the bodies were decapitated and dismembered, that blue sequins were found on or near them. He could also tell Mhatre about Shetty's dubious activities. Shinde and Neha Chaubey. His own accident, which wasn't one. Joshi's sister-in-law's company, Moringa Consultants. About Tara, her blue saree, and her jackal with a police cap. All of it pointed to a killer who had escaped notice over decades because of connections on both sides of the law. There could be a connection between Joshi, Shetty, and Taneja. The mystery client could be Taneja, but it could just as easily be Joshi.

"No, sir, but I'm sure I'll find the required proof if I pursue the existing leads."

"You're hinting at a big accusation here, against a decorated senior officer, with no solid evidence." Mhatre looked angrier still. "You've been harassing Taneja with calls despite Joshi sir and myself telling you not to, and for that alone you could be suspended for insubordination."

He had called Taneja once, and definitely had not "harassed" him. As a police officer, that would be unproductive as well as unprofessional. A few days ago, Arnav would have taken the gamble of pushing further, but now he had Tara to think of. If he revealed he'd begun connecting the dots, that could endanger Tara. Whoever ordered those private dances was connected to the murders. His boss could alert the wrong people.

Mhatre stood up and paced in the small space between the door and the chair. His tall frame crowded the office.

"Follow orders, Rajput. Report to Commissioner Joshi as soon as possible. I'm going on leave starting today until after Diwali. I don't expect to see you when I return."

"May I apply for one as well, sir?"

Taking leave would help him sort out the situation with Shinde and coordinate the response to the Versova case with Naik. Arnav watched for a reaction from Mhatre.

"Medical leave?" Mhatre's face remained blank.

"I'm injured."

"One week. After that, if you come to work, it will be at Bandra station with Commissioner Joshi."

"Yes, sir."

"If I were you, I'd be careful, Rajput. No heroics. Better to be a *fattu* than get in trouble."

Arnav wanted to ask Mhatre if he was calling himself a spineless pussy or Arnav, but Mhatre turned and left the room.

CHAPTER FIFTY

She made me tie my feet together again today. She says I look better this way, my socks on, my school tie a small snake around my feet. You look like a proper little man, she says. That's what I want to look like, a proper man.

He wanted the Item Number to disappear, and with her that gnawing urge to destroy her, again and again, the way she'd destroyed him. Not all women were like that, Bilal said. Women could be nice and generous. But Bilal said many things. The Item Number was a greedy slut. After Dad died, he would have been on the streets if not for Bilal. Bilal and his stupid, stupid faith in women.

He picked another diary at random and flipped through the sepia pages, his handwriting now faded, but not the images they carried.

Today was Choti Diwali, or Bhoot Chaturdashi, the evening of ghosts and demons. The evening before the grand lights of Diwali night.

We'll have the fireworks tomorrow for Diwali, she said, but Choti Diwali, the small Diwali, is right for our perfect little celebration, just you and me.

The Item Number took me to the railway track near the hotel.

It's different on the tracks, she said. Come lie down here on this blanket. You won't feel a thing, not the stones, not the track. Tie your feet. Here, let me do your hands for you. You can keep your clothes on, I can unzip you when I need to. With her hovering above, I heard the first murmur, the faintest of rumbles. There's a train coming, I said. She said it was only a goods train and everyone knew they crawled, it would take at least three minutes to reach us, so even a child could get away, lie back and take in the trembling of the earth, but I felt the lightest of shakings within the tracks like black snakes that would bring the train hurtling down on me and I struggled, trying to throw her off, but her thighs were strong on my throat. Come on, she said, come on.

He shut the journal and sprawled in his nest of sheets and pillows.

The Item Number's shadow had failed the three-minute test, hadn't she? Anyone who failed the test must pay. He was generous—he merely cut half their pay the first time. She'd escaped fourteen years ago by refusing the six lakhs. Few women could resist that kind of money, their greedy little hearts beat too hard. They came to dance for him one last time, their eyes shining with avarice. They never left. Bilal would have said he had no business summoning this woman, but Bilal was gone.

Besides, he didn't force any of them. They came on their own. Their greed was their downfall. Women just couldn't help it. This one wouldn't, either.

What if she was different and refused, though?

He rose from the bed. In the bathroom, he switched on a small light. He selected a new razor, and sank into the marble bathtub. No Bilal to patch him up, so he'd have to go easy. He made shallow cuts, and cursed when some of his tears fell on his thigh, stinging. He remained a *fattu*, easily hurt. No uniform could hide that. Wiping his face with his forearm, he reached out to the corner for the stash in a hidden drawer. Bilal replenished it each week. The right dose, no more. All the equipment polished and clean, damn the man.

He could find replacements for Bilal, but he couldn't trust them. The one man he'd taken for granted had betrayed him.

He shook out the straw, and with practiced ease laid out a thin white line on the cold black marble. The phone rang. He picked up the call and listened to *Uhnna*.

She had refused, blast her.

"Whatever it takes," he chewed out the words. "Get her to agree."

"We can pick her up tonight, if you like."

"No. She must decide on her own."

"Is it?" *Uhnna* said. "You have funny ideas about how women make up their mind."

"Take care of it."

"It will cost you. And if you damage any more packages, we're done."

"No damage. And I'll throw in extras. Whatever you like."

Funneling information, kissing babies in front of cameras, OK'ing projects he wouldn't otherwise look at twice, all for a bit of fun he wasn't even allowed to touch. He could handle it by himself, though. He would show Bilal.

Yes, it was dangerous, a disaster, having his man Friday escape. Bilal knew all his secrets, could tell the world who he was underneath.

Uhnna could deal with Bilal, but there would be questions. Already, people had asked after his elderly assistant. Bilal was on leave, he told them. If someone filed a missing persons complaint about Bilal, fingers would be pointed at the boss. Him. He couldn't afford that, not now, after the task he'd given *Uhnna*. Foolhardy to try to flush his housekeeper out—the man had dealt with Rasool for many years. Rasool could prove a match for *Uhnna*. The feud between Rasool and Vijayan had once set the city on fire.

He used the straw, holding it over the line of white powder. The inside of his nose burned as he inhaled and sighed. Blessed escape.

CHAPTER FIFTY-ONE

Arnav

The minute his boss left, Arnav dialed Shinde. He wanted to question his disgraced friend before stepping in for Shetty's interrogation.

"I need to speak with you," he said, once Shinde picked up.

"You walked out of the hospital—is everyone taking care of you at the station?"

Arnav let the silence hang between them.

"I'm headed your way." Shinde cut the call.

Arnav spent the next hour handing over his cases and generally making it look like he had no immediate care other than going on his break.

Having spoken to the women at the Blue Bar, Naik returned with a list of names Mithi had given her. Girls from Shetty's other bars had confirmed at least three other women missing. All three had said they were leaving town. Some had left behind their personal effects. Gauri, Hamida, and Preeti had disappeared near the end of different years. No one had heard from them since.

"Did you search the missing persons records for those names?" Arnav said.

"No matches so far, sir. I have tried to find their home addresses. We'll be making calls."

"I'll go on leave starting today. Shinde has—"

Naik must have read his expression. She said, "I'll help."

"Are you sure? It will mean extra hours, and this could get dangerous."

"I don't mind, sir." Naik wore a rare, small smile on her face. "If this case is solved, it'll work in our favor. Besides, with both you and Mhatre sir on a break, I'll have more responsibilities."

"Eyeing my chair already, are you?" Arnav returned her smile.

"There has been an attempt on your life, sir." Naik's round, fair face turned somber. "Your team will do its best. In any case, when we die on duty, all they give our families is a medal and a little money."

"That's true," Arnav admitted.

"I have another update, sir," Naik said. "On Neha Chaubey's murder. After you called forensics to insist, they rushed the results. The blood in the van is Neha Chaubey's."

"Pick up the garage owner."

"Sir, we interrogated the men, and one of them confessed that the owner isn't their leader. The garage is a front for Rasool."

Arnav drained a glass of water after Naik left.

He pulled out a notebook and copied all the details from the board. It was no longer safe, even with abbreviations. He scribbled in his conclusions. He had dug up information on Moringa Consultants with the help of his friends from the Crime Branch. They suspected Vijayan was making payments to Moringa through various layers of shell companies, making it difficult to bring litigation or collect taxes.

Rasool
Possibly owned the black van used to dump Neha Chaubey's body.
May have taken a contract for body disposal, as per Ali.

Taneja
Three decomposed bodies found at his construction site.
Seemed to have sway with Joshi and Mhatre.

Had MeToo allegations against him.

Joshi
Ordered a transfer and promotion which would pause the investigation into the bodies.
Tara mentioned a police officer cap at the mystery client's place.

Mhatre
Supported Joshi, and denied obvious indications of serial killing.
Signed off on the traffic accident that killed Bendre, inspector in Dadar case.
Gawde warned against him.

Shinde
Concealed Neha Chaubey's identity.
Took bribes from Shetty. Is Shetty delivering the bar girls to Taneja?
What else has he not disclosed?

Vijayan
Has dealings with Moringa Consultants, a business connected to Commissioner Joshi.
Grabbed the land sold off to Taneja.

Shetty
Sent Tara to mystery client with blue-sequined saree.
Had underworld connections. Vijayan? Malayalis tend to stick together.

So far, two dons had emerged. One Hindu, the other Muslim, known to be at loggerheads with each other for decades. The policemen and the businessmen. He must find the common link between all the names.

Traffic noises filtered in from outside the police station, forming a muted but annoying cacophony. The painkillers turned him woozy and dull. His shoulder made itself known, but he ignored it. Pain would keep him alert.

At a knock on the door, he said, "Come in."

Couldn't be Shinde because he never knocked. It was Tukaram, in civilian clothes, wearing a perfume he might have borrowed from his wife.

"You?"

"What? You were expecting your girlfriend? Word has it you have one, even if you think me unworthy of sharing the secret. She kick your butt and land you in bandages, huh?"

Tukaram gave Arnav an exaggerated lecherous grin, but Arnav sensed the concern in his friend's eyes.

"Is that what you've come all the way to ask me?" Arnav gestured Tukaram to a chair. "On a working day?"

"Shinde told me about your accident, said you were in the hospital. Should have known you'd be here already. I'm finishing off the leave owed me. Preparing to retire, don't you know?"

"A lot of years in you yet, young man." Arnav fell into the easy banter between them.

"What does your boss say about all this *lafda*?"

"He's gone on a break. Till after Diwali."

"Strange he is, to do that when one of his inspectors was recently hospitalized. Not been right in the head ever since his wife ran away with his driver."

"Really?" This was news to Arnav.

"Long time ago. Not many people talk about it, see. He never married again."

"His family?"

"Father, dead. He lives alone. Takes women to his place in Bandra sometimes, I hear. Mhatre's brother is in politics, in another state, you know. His father wished him to be a professional. Sent him to the best boarding schools in India. But no luck, see? Mhatre failed his final year as a medical student, and appeared for MPSC to join Mumbai Police."

"Where did you find all this info?"

"My wife's brother works in security at his father's bungalow. An officer of some sort. Such an illustrious political family—the very highest in society, from Malabar Hills. Old money."

Arnav loved listening to the frail Tukaram recount details, his eyes wide, his gestures expansive. Most Mumbaikars harbored a huge fascination for a larger-than-life existence. Arnav didn't see the charm—more you owned, more you stood to lose.

Arnav's bruises hurt and Tukaram's perfume gave him a headache, but he had time till Shinde came in, and he saw no harm in indulging the chatty sub-inspector. Tukaram spoke on, excitement higher than ever at having found a ready, attentive listener.

"You should see their bungalow here in Madh Island—abandoned now, but they held such rave parties at one time."

Arnav sat up. "He owns one here on Madh Island?"

Aksa beach was on Madh Island.

"Ask one of your constables to take you there one day. They shot movies there, decades ago. Nobody goes there anymore. They say it is haunted."

Arnav made a note under Mhatre's name in his notebook. Rows of "shooting bungalows" around Dana Pani beach served as filming locations for Bollywood and Hindi TV serials. This was part of what kept the rest of Mumbai, especially Bollywood, connected to Madh. Fascinating that Mhatre's family owned a bungalow there.

As Tukaram rambled on, now waxing eloquent over the women he'd met on movie sets, Arnav read the notes on his boss. He had been a senior police officer for a while. Mhatre had a lineage and history he kept hidden from others. His wife had left him. Arnav had witnessed his discomfort around female colleagues. He had once been a medical student—and might possess enough experience with dissections and human anatomy to carry out the carnage Arnav had seen on the victims' bodies. The cramp in Arnav's shoulder ramped up, but a part of him seemed detached, quite separate from the agony and Tukaram's relentless spiel.

He added more notes under his boss's name.

Naik rushed in after a knock, startling him.

"I'm sorry to interrupt, sir, but Shetty is being a nuisance. We'll have to either arrest him or let him go. Would you like to speak to him now? Here's the analysis of his public records that you'd asked for."

Arnav debated the wisdom of confronting Shetty. What if it backfired on Tara?

But Tara would never go back to that life. He couldn't predict the future, but he'd make sure Tara didn't have to worry. He scanned the paper Naik had given him, and spotted the name Taneja Estate Holdings. He would speak with Shetty. This interview would be his last action at the station in case he never got to return.

"I'll be right with you," Arnav said.

"Sure, sir." Naik walked out.

"Shinde will be here soon," Arnav said to Tukaram. "Let's have tea before you leave. Arnav turned and strode toward the interrogation room. He wished he could have spoken to Shinde before meeting the bar owner, but better to fly blind than risk losing him.

He remembered Tara's tear-soaked face by his hospital bed. Shetty must answer a few tough questions.

CHAPTER FIFTY-TWO

TARA

Nandini's rooftop apartment on the thirty-seventh floor was the tallest place Tara had ever stayed in—toy cars crawled on the roads down below and toy houses sat in neat rows. The distant hum of the city beneath, the glass reflections from skyscrapers, and the imagined stench rising from the surrounding slums kept her from stepping onto the balcony. She paced the cane mat in Nandini's living room for a while, meandered into the neat kitchen, retreated to the bed, but sprang up soon after and headed out to the living room again.

She'd spent the entire morning describing her time as a bar girl to Arnav's journalist girlfriend. Nandini had stepped out a while ago, which was a relief and a bother at the same time. Tara didn't need to answer questions for a spell, but that conversation had been a good distraction from her worries about Arnav and Pia. She'd spoken to Pia early this morning using Nandini's phone while her own remained switched off, and she'd given Zoya Nandini's landline number. She'd tried calling Arnav, but he didn't pick up.

Tara flicked on the news, picturing the life of a broadcaster—or a journalist like Nandini. Some of the broadcasters on the screen dressed like Bollywood actresses. She snuggled into the sofa and tried watching a movie, failed, settling instead on a video channel with Rehaan Virani, the main man in Bollywood these days, dancing with his brother, Karan, and a string of new actresses, derisively termed "nubile nymphets." Tara only had eyes for Karan, the eternal lover boy—a stark contrast to the bad-boy Rehaan, who danced as if chased by demons.

Zoya was a fan of both. Tara and Pia teased her about it. She missed Zoya, the one person to whom she could vent, who stood by her no matter what.

She was dozing off, her body reclaiming the rest that had eluded her during her time in Mumbai, when the landline rang.

Tara picked up the notebook and pen Nandini had left her in case she needed to take down a message, and said hello.

"Tara, thank Allah I found you." It was Zoya, her voice trembling.

"What's wrong? Is Pia OK?"

"She's fine, but we had a scare today. I think someone has been following me."

"You're imagining things."

"The same dark-blue Maruti has stalked me the last two days. A few minutes ago, at Pia's school, two tall men stepped up right behind me in the crowd of parents."

"And?"

"They strode by me in a hurry and melted away onto a side street."

"And Pia? Was she scared?"

"She wasn't with me. I'd gone to pay her fees, leaving her with the neighbors."

"You must be mistaken."

Trust Zoya to be afraid of shadows. Lucknow was a small city. Crimes occurred, but not like in Mumbai.

"I've been a don's girlfriend, Tara. These men were not local. You're with your policeman now, correct? Pia's father?"

"No, he's in the hospital. He had an accident."

"Tell him about Pia. Come back as soon as you get your money. I don't have a good feeling about this."

CHAPTER FIFTY-THREE

ARNAV

Arnav walked into the corner room, where Shetty sat at a table under a bright overhead light. This was not a hard-interrogation room that stank of blood, urine, and fear. Here, a ceiling fan whirred overhead, and a jug of water sweated on the table in front of Shetty. The man looked beaten, but no one had touched him. So far. His white clothes could use a wash, and the smear of holy ash on his forehead was smudged.

"You're saying you have nothing to do with Neha's murder?" Arnav stepped into the room, Naik behind him.

It was best to cut to the chase with men like Shetty. His interrogation had lasted all night, and if he wanted to walk out, he could. Shetty must have realized he'd lost Shinde, because Shinde had stopped taking his calls. Arnav didn't have enough evidence to charge Shetty with murder, but enmity with the police would cost his business in the long run. This knowledge kept the man docile and cooperative.

"I told them already." Shetty used a white handkerchief to wipe his face, spreading the ash markings even farther. "I'm a businessman. How can I run my business if I get involved in a crime? This is my busiest week at work, right before Diwali. Your men keep badgering me with the same questions. They don't believe me."

"What sort of business is that? You send bar dancers to clients."

"I own lawful businesses—restaurants, grocery shops, licensed orchestra bars. The girls go where they please, sir. I give them a place to stay. They do their job well, I don't bother them and they don't bother me."

Arnav did his best not to flinch with pain when he sat down to hear more of the bar owner's whining. It gave him a better look at Shetty's face, while hiding the fact that his legs were not holding up. This man might have been the instigator of his accident, having alerted the killer that Neha's body had been found.

Arnav let silence work for him.

Rogues like Shetty meshed lies with truth. Shetty did own legitimate businesses, no doubt, and they made money. Most bars might have shut down in Mumbai because the government stopped renewing licenses—but some of Shetty's bars still held valid permits. With restrictions, it was true, but Shinde had helped with those. Shinde looked the other way when Shetty's bars stayed open beyond the permitted hours, when his dancers walked through the audience instead of remaining onstage, when they prostituted themselves to customers. Shetty profited from all of it. He didn't look pleased he'd been caught.

"Why did you deny recognizing Neha Chaubey's body in the pictures?" Arnav straightened more. With medication in his system and mounting fatigue, the room swayed before his eyes. He longed for a glass of water.

"The body didn't have a face. How did you figure out it was her? I thought she'd gone back to her village. I cleared her final payment."

"She's from your bar. We have witnesses. Your bar dancers will testify in court that you send them out on assignments. You'll be charged."

Arnav reached out for the papers, and Naik handed them to him. "Or you can write your statement here and sign it. Give me the name and number of the client who asked for Neha."

"No one can say I sent them anywhere, because I didn't."

"Not even Tara?"

At the mention of Tara's name, Shetty sat up straighter. "Tara, sir? We can't find Tara."

"Can't find her?"

"No, sir, she's not answering my calls. How do you know about her?"

Shetty might already have an inkling about Arnav and Tara, but his face showed nothing but sincere curiosity.

"We have our ways," Arnav said.

"The other girls filled in for her at the bar. Your police madam here has been asking me questions and making me wait. I haven't slept all night, sir. Please have pity on me."

"What about Gauri?"

If Mithi was to be believed, Shetty had done away with Gauri.

"Who is—"

"Think before you speak, Mr. Shetty. I have witnesses saying Gauri worked for you. We'll investigate further. We know which town she came from and will get in touch with police there."

Shetty wore gold rings on all fingers, each set with a precious colored stone. He twisted the rings around for a while. Arnav let the silence stretch again, trying to ignore his throbbing shoulder.

"Gauri used to work at one of my bars, but I haven't seen her in years now. She left after the permit for that bar ran out."

"You decide what's best for you," Arnav said. "I don't have the luxury of waiting for your answer. The doctors say I need to go lie down. Frankly, I'm wasting my time here."

Arnav addressed Naik, who stood behind Shetty. "You have his call records?"

"Yes, sir."

"Call each number, verifying who they are."

"No, sir, please." Shetty's voice rose this time. "I can't have police calling all my contacts. I have a reputation in the market."

"You should have thought of that before," Arnav said to Naik. "Start calling. Make sure to tell them you have Mr. Shetty here for questioning."

"You're going too far with this, sir." Shetty looked desperate, his eyes red.

"I am? What will you do, then?"

"I'm not helpless. Just because I've been polite . . ."

"We're only asking you to make it easy for yourself, Mr. Shetty," Naik said. "You know us. If you don't tell us, we have other means of finding out. None will be pleasant."

"Shinde told me about your arrangement," Arnav said. Naik would hear soon enough, anyway. She didn't show any other reaction, but her eyes widened.

Shetty lowered his head, and seemed to come to a decision.

"That bar wasn't making enough money. Some of the clients asked me to organize private visits. The commission was OK, and the girls were happy."

"I hope you remember that the license for your new bar can be canceled in no time."

"Please!"

"You can keep it open if you answer our questions."

"I've told you the truth. I have no idea who most of my clients are. Some of them have weird requests, but as long as my girls are safe and we're earning money, who am I to complain?"

"You didn't know Neha was missing?"

"Only after Shinde sir told me."

"What were these weird assignments?"

Shetty gave them descriptions that would have made most women flinch, but Naik held her ground, her face blank, as if she were listening to a weather report. She perked up when Shetty said, "One even sent me the clothes the girls had to wear."

"What kind of clothes?"

"A saree, with blue sequins all over. A silver blouse, silver slippers, blue petticoat."

"You said you didn't recognize the blue sequins we showed you?" Naik said.

Shetty didn't answer.

"Where did you send the women?" Arnav said.

"Sometimes to Borivali Station. They went by themselves, and they were given a phone. When that number rang, they had three minutes to leave the station."

"Did any of the women fail to exit in three minutes?"

"Gauri, sir."

"Anyone else? We need names."

Shetty named four other women, and Naik wrote them down. The names included Hamida and Preeti, both mentioned by Tara's friend Mithi. Arnav exchanged a glance with Naik.

"Were they paid if they failed to rush out in three minutes?"

"They were paid half the first time. Not at all the next time."

"What phone numbers did you receive calls from?"

"Various numbers. You couldn't ring them back. Different people called each time. Told me what they wanted, when, and how much they were willing to pay."

Arnav considered mentioning Vijayan's name, but held back. Tailing Shetty might yield better results. Besides, if Vijayan and Joshi were involved, it didn't make sense to alert them. He could ask about Taneja, though—he held papers that proved a connection between the business magnate and Shetty.

"Was anyone from Taneja Estate Holdings one of your clients?"

"No, sir. Why do you say that?"

"You tell me why you have calls with Rahul Taneja himself."

"He is not my client; I am his. I bought an apartment in a project he built."

"That still doesn't explain why you spoke with him and not one of his team."

"He requested me to give the contract for the interior decoration to his fiancée's company."

"I'm expected to believe that?"

"Whether you believe it or not is up to you, sir. I have the transaction records to prove it. She did all the interiors of my apartment—she created gold accents in all the furnishings."

He would need to verify the legitimacy of the transactions. It would be quite easy to use interior decoration as a front for another, less legal business.

"OK, let's say I believe you. What about your clients? They must have transferred money to your bank account, too?"

"They paid in cash."

Of course. Black money. He glanced at Naik, who remained in position behind Shetty, a recorder peeking out of her pocket. The information might not be used as evidence, but it was important to save all of it.

"I kept half the fee. The other half went to the girls. I was honest—gave them their share without fail."

Honest. Arnav wanted to laugh. Shetty seemed convinced of his own goodness.

Naik took over and fired off questions about the bar girls who'd been sent to this client. How many times for assignments at night. Dates. Payments. Shetty took out his phone, flipped to his notes, and began to read out loud.

CHAPTER FIFTY-FOUR

BILAL

Bilal paced the muddy path that led to the old, sprawling farmhouse from the jungle. The thought of returning gave him jitters, but he couldn't leave the boy alone. The papers spoke of the Versova case. A brief article, but it would create problems if the twenty-four-hour television news channels picked it up. Sooner or later, Bilal would have a target painted on his back, no matter where he escaped to. Either the boy or the police would get him. Meanwhile, his dead master's soul would haunt his nightmares, as it had done the past days he'd spent trying to leave Mumbai.

Protect him, the master had said on his deathbed.

Given the master's disdain for his son, Bilal couldn't understand his last request to protect his boy at all costs. Bilal had promised. Had the master not picked him up, he would have been scrounging in rubbish bins for breakfast or turning into a pickpocket on crowded Mumbai trains.

The master hadn't suffered a day of illness in his life. The sturdy forest officer's sudden heart attack seemed suspicious, but Bilal never talked to the boy about it. What would have been the point?

Bilal would never know why the master chose to marry that little piece of ass in his middle age. He could have enjoyed her without the marriage trap. He had a boy already, so it couldn't have been because he craved a son. He died before he could enjoy being a father to the younger son, anyway.

Unlike the master, Bilal hadn't been fool enough to get married or have children. The boy. As close to a child as he'd ever have. What kind of parent would escape at the first hint of menace? They'd evaded capture all these years, he and the boy. Maybe they still could.

Bilal kicked at a stone, smacked the newspaper roll on the trunk of a burly *semal* tree. He glanced up at the farmhouse—his home since he was ten, when the master rescued him. Put food in his stomach. Taught him to read.

Left on his own, the boy would destroy himself and others. Yes, that woman in her fancy blue-sequined saree had been a monster. But someone had to stop the boy. Bilal unfurled the paper in his hand and checked the article once again. He'd messed up the cleaning job—up to him to contain the spill.

CHAPTER FIFTY-FIVE

ARNAV

Arnav watched Shetty and Naik—Shetty was giving them all the information he could in a desperate bid to have his legal and not-so-legal businesses left alone. Arnav stepped into the corridor, took aside a constable, and asked him to highlight all the calls between Shetty and Taneja Estate Holdings.

His phone rang. Tara. He asked her to hold on so he could get himself somewhere more private.

On his way out, he heard a drunken man in the temporary lockup break into a Bollywood song, *"Har pal yahan jee bhar jiyo, Phir kya pata, kal ho na ho."* The drunkard was a regular, so the constables let him be. He sang in a soulful, broken voice, and caused no harm. They locked him up whenever he chased pedestrians, insisting they listen to him. This was Mumbai—too many artists, not enough art lovers.

Arnav paused a moment to take in the truth of the clichéd words sung over and over again—*"Live each moment down to its marrow, who knows if there is a tomorrow"*—thanked the constable who appeared with a glass of orange juice, and sipped it as he limped out of the station and into the muggy air.

"I'm in an interview," he said to Tara, pleased she'd called him. "What's my *pagli* up to?"

The station's gates opened on the main road, with its onset of evening traffic rush, the cacophony and headlights. Beside the police station, garlands of Diwali lights festooned the balconies of an apartment building, blinking in the growing dark.

"I know you left the hospital," Tara said, "Did you eat lunch? What about your medicines?"

"My constables are behaving like a bunch of nannies."

"We must talk. It's important."

Tara went on but cars honked and braked on the road behind him. He could not hear her. Searching for a quieter spot, he turned left from the gate and walked along the open-air corridor that led into the station's backyard.

"Zoya called. I need your help. Come to Nandini's once you're done?" She sounded upset.

"Are you fine? I'll—" but he was cut off by raised voices, and bursts of sound like the backfiring of a car. He recognized them for what they were.

Gunfire. A deafening fusillade from two directions near the road.

He'd pivoted and half sprinted as best he could toward the gate, his 9 mm out and firing back, instinct and muscle memory taking hold, making time both speed up and slow down. It was only when the recoil made his arm flinch and the pistol fly up that he noticed his right hand was so bruised it hurt to grip the gun. Unable to raise his left hand, he was shooting one-handed. He adjusted his stance for one-armed shooting—hunched forward on his right leg instead of the left, angling his elbow inward, bracing, keeping the Glock upright. A hoarse shout floated up when one of his shots found its mark amid his rallying cry for reinforcements. Adrenaline coursed through him amid the noise and flash of each shot he returned, his clear sight of the shooter from the open truck turning to a blur of vapor and dust from the wall to his left as bullets tore into brick and plaster.

He paced his shots, listening for the answering cries from his colleagues inside the station, until his gun clicked empty. Any moment now, a bullet would find him.

In his peripheral vision, others rushed up to provide covering fire as a shot plowed into the wall beside his ear, deafening him. With a harsh cry of "Avi!" a body barreled into him from behind, sending arrows of pain shooting through his shoulders, arms, and chest, rolling and twisting with the impact, making him land on his broken shoulder. Through the blinding haze of pain, he pushed off the weight. He'd recognized that cry. On his clothes a wet warmth. Blood. He hauled himself up as fast as he could, and turned to find Shinde, whose normally bright eyes looked glassy. Blood frothed at his mouth and from his uniformed chest. Arnav used all his remaining strength to press his hand to Shinde's wound, using the fabric from his own sling that had come off in the melee. Shinde coughed like a stuck carburetor, splattering Arnav's face with warm liquid.

". . . dojo . . ." the rest of it lost in the choke and rattle of him trying to draw a breath, his eyelids fluttering closed.

"Stay with me, *abbay narangi pandu saley*, keep your eyes open." It sounded like someone else.

Blood gushed through Arnav's fingers, sticky-warm and dark in the half-light of the descending evening. He pressed harder, ignoring the nauseating copper smell from the spatter on his face. He straddled Shinde in an attempt to hold him still, and use his own body weight to keep the wound staunched.

Seconds later, many footfalls and voices, familiar and not. Hands strove to draw him away. He refused to release his grip on the wound. First aid basics came back to him: *Apply pressure; don't release until help arrives.* Besides, if he moved, he'd have to let go of Shinde. He couldn't do that.

Sirens. Shrieking phones. Barked orders. Curses. Tukaram's reedy voice, *Are you hurt . . . the ambulance is five minutes away.* Fodder for his nightmares for years to come—the uneven rattle as Shinde struggled to breathe, punctuated by Arnav's own curses, flinging back all the swear words he'd taken from Shinde over decades, during those brief moments that felt like years, lifetimes, alternately threatening and begging him to please open his fucking eyes. Shinde didn't oblige, stubborn and contrary to the end.

As medics claimed Shinde, the drunk freshly released from the lockup burst into his pent-up song on loop, *"Phir kya pata, kal ho na ho."* Someone shushed him, and he halted in the middle of the next phrase, *"Har ghadi badal rahi hai roop zindagi."*

Firm hands drew Arnav away and into another waiting ambulance. On the blank canvas of Arnav's mind, the words registered: *From moment to moment life changes its face.*

CHAPTER FIFTY-SIX

ARNAV

Arnav floated on the cloud of tranquilizers the doctor had dosed him with while resetting his shoulder and bandaging it all over again. Even at 4:00 a.m., the government hospital sounded like a marketplace, with policemen scrambling about near the mortuary.

He'd wanted to ask the doctors if they'd made a mistake about Shinde. It was quite possible that bastard was faking it, his whole life a huge pretend, his fakery only pausing for a second when he'd flung himself in the path of a bullet intended for Arnav, and gushed blood. So much of it. The doctors had fought a losing battle. Arnav had rushed into the room, the floor splashed with red, the debris of their battle scattered everywhere. Been rooted at the sight of Shinde's ashen face still uncovered on the operating table, lips pulled back in a grimace. Arnav's knees threatened to give way—but he held himself like he would at a parade. A man and a Mumbai police officer couldn't afford a public display of grief. He must deal with that when he was alone.

The entire Malwani station had gone on high alert. Naik and other officers grilled the injured gunman who'd been captured. In the years before Arnav joined the force, shoot-outs with the police were common. Terrorist attacks had occurred in the last two decades, but not many gun battles like this one. Someone had paid a lot of money to silence him, and they wouldn't be happy.

Others might conclude Shinde was the target, given his reputation as an encounter specialist and his assignment to arrest Rasool, but Arnav knew better. His head carried a price tag. A few weeks ago, this would have pleased him, brought him a rush of adrenaline. Now, he merely aimed to find the threat and eliminate it.

Arnav dialed Ali, who picked up immediately.

"What have you heard about a *supari* on me?" Arnav said.

Arnav had learned the term *supari* before he joined the police force, thanks to Bollywood movies. To a layman, it was a betel nut; to the denizens of the underworld, a contract to kill.

"Sorry about the *locha* at your station, *saab*. Not from my *Bhai*."

"Tell your contacts—this will mean a big reward."

"It is a little strange, *saab*. If you are the target, why attack the station? So much harder."

Arnav wondered about that, too. "Find out all you can."

He cut the call. He couldn't bring Shinde back, but he could ensure Shinde's family received closure. Shinde's corruption was not *Vaeeni's* fault, nor that of the two children.

Despite protests from the team, he booked a car and strode out. Shinde dealt with men like Shetty. He must have kept a dossier of information that would bring others down. An insurance of sorts.

Once *Vaeeni* returned home, it would be rude and unnatural to focus on Shinde's papers rather than support her to organize Shinde's last rites, but if he moved now, he could use Shinde's spare key. If Shinde's papers threw up any names, he'd call Ali and get him to dig further.

At Shinde's place, he felt like a robber, rifling through a bereaved family's drawers, tables, and closets, but he persisted. The longer he took to chase the culprits down, the harder it would be to nab them. He'd set his team to track down leads from the shoot-out at the station, but only he could carry out this search. His arm and shoulder throbbed as he bent and straightened, looking through the house as unobtrusively as possible. His mind spun. He would never see Shinde again. Was he cursed to lose the people he loved? Asha had committed suicide, Tara had left, and Shinde had taken a bullet meant for him. Or maybe he himself was a curse to those he loved, the harbinger of misfortune.

His exhausted brain played those final minutes with Shinde over and over, but it became increasingly blurred, like a scrambled video with scratchy sound.

Asha's last words were *Get me a sevpuri and a pao bhaji? Extra tamarind chutney.* He couldn't recall what Shinde said to him. All he remembered was the warm spatter of Shinde's blood on his face, its raw, metallic smell, the way his fingers had slipped over the hot, gaping wound. What were his parting words to Shinde?

A litany of curses. He recalled their heat and heft inside his mouth as he spat them out. Shinde was family, but he'd betrayed both Arnav and the Mumbai Police Force. Before Arnav could sort out the work situation with Shinde and hammer out his personal sense of betrayal, Shinde had flown beyond the pale of questions and answers. Death. Familiar yet remote. Shinde's gurgled words came back to him, *Avi, dojo.*

By the time Arnav arrived at the dojo, the morning karate classes had begun. His tall and wiry *sensei* had the face of an ascetic, and despite being well into his sixties, his body retained the limber movements of youth. When Arnav took him aside and told him about Shinde, he looked stricken.

"Stay the week, until this blows over." The *sensei* gestured him toward a chair. "You live alone. I worry about you. Students often take up the dojo rooms upstairs."

"No reason to worry. I'll be fine."

"No harm in being careful, either. Your accident, and now Shinde gone. I taught him since he was eleven years old, years before this dojo was built. He brought you here. Stay with me for a while. For me, if not for yourself."

Arnav choked down the emotion in his throat. A staff member brought him a warm drink. Arnav could taste the ginger and turmeric. He wasn't a fan but, with the *sensei* watching, he downed it all.

"Come back here after you're done for the day."

Arnav nodded. "Can I bring a guest? A woman. She's a witness on a case."

"Yes." The *sensei* smiled. "Just a witness?"

"For the moment." Arnav rose.

"Ah, yes, your friend Rehaan left these here," the *sensei* said. "He wasn't here for very long, I heard. I didn't remember I'd picked them up."

He handed over a pair of sunglasses in a paper bag.

"I'll need your help," Arnav said. "I don't know if I can train him, with my injury. Will you come with me?"

Arnav didn't want to miss the opportunity to speak with Rehaan, or Kittu if she showed up. Taneja and Kittu were out of town, but they were to return soon.

"All right," the *sensei* said. "Why don't you rest upstairs for a while?"

"Somewhere I need to be." Arnav pocketed the paper bag, thanked his *sensei*, and headed to the lockers.

When he heard a step behind him, he thought the *sensei* had followed him there, only to find Naik and a constable on her team.

"Sorry, sir, but we couldn't let you leave alone," Naik said, her brows creased. "Your teacher said we'd find you here."

Arnav felt too exhausted to ask them to buzz off, but he gave them a look, hoping they would understand his need for privacy.

"We'll wait for you at the entrance, sir," Naik nodded and left, and Arnav sighed at the task that lay ahead.

Arnav and Shinde kept each other's duplicate keys. Arnav had never used Shinde's because he never carried anything for his friend. Shinde dropped boxes off in Arnav's locker when their work schedules clashed. *Vaeeni* sent him snacks, and occasionally a small gift on his birthday. Arnav swallowed. At the dojo, Shinde's locker was the place to search.

Shinde had stuck an old print from the movie *Sholay* on his locker door. Arnav traced his finger over the square-jawed Veeru riding a bike and the lanky Jai in the sidecar, both their arms spread out, smiles wide, swearing eternal friendship.

Jai saw no problem with sabotaging Veeru's relationships, but in the end sacrificed his life to save his pal. Shinde had played the role to the hilt.

Arnav laid his hand on the cold metal door and made himself open it with a quick twist of the key. A backpack sat inside, a file and a diary visible from the top. Arnav flipped open the diary and found records of transactions in Shinde's neat hand. One name jumped out at him: Moringa Consultants. The company that Nandini said was possibly being employed to launder money for Vijayan.

CHAPTER FIFTY-SEVEN

At the farmhouse terrace, he sank back into the swing, pressing a cushion over his face, and didn't breathe. This cleared his head, filling it with a pleasant darkness, not unlike the times when he tore apart a new saree with blue sequins, shiny midnight blue, turning darker still with blood.

He smiled and let go of his breath. Bilal was back. Thank all that's good and holy. Bilal didn't know the plans for the coming weekend, but he'd be OK with them—only music and dance, even though she had failed. *Uhnna* said he had run into delays, but he would deliver the package, using whatever leverage possible.

Of the two targets, one had died. The other, with the lives of a cat, had survived again. No matter. Soon, he would either move to Bandra station or be out of a job. Maybe he was scared. He sure had good reason.

Bilal wouldn't be happy with the amount spent on this one weekend. The man looked the very picture of disapproval ever since his return. Bilal wanted him away from this farmhouse, from Mumbai.

But he loved these spread-out acres, the backyard stretching into wilderness, and the cherished rose garden, his best revenge, the one only Bilal knew about. He also adored this terrace where he could lie back, swing a little, watch the stars twinkle on, one after the other. His mother had assured him that all loved ones turned into stars.

He drew in a deep breath of the tepid air steeped in a million insect songs. Each insect a voice, a life. Some days he wished he were one of them, an anonymous little creature with a life brief enough to have no past, nor future. Only the now, singing in the darkness, a call to another.

Bilal was back, but he was no more than one of those insects. Easily squashed, his annoying song stopped forever. He was back because he was stupid. He'd never leave again.

CHAPTER FIFTY-EIGHT

ARNAV

Morning sun filtered in through the curtains at Nandini's apartment and lit up the tastefully furnished living room. Arnav sat on the sofa, Shinde's diary in hand, gathering the courage to look inside once again. When he opened it this time, there was no going back.

"I still can't believe it. Shinde dined with us just the other day," Nandini said from the balcony. She was arranging earthen lamps for Choti Diwali two days later. Arnav had clean forgotten.

"Are you doing all right?"

Arnav nodded.

Tara had remained in the guest bathroom for the half hour he'd spent in the other one, freshening up the best he could with one arm. When stressed out, she often lingered in a shower for hours, cleaning each square inch. She'd sounded worried yesterday; had asked to talk. He must speak with her at the first opportunity—ask if Shetty had made any attempts to contact her.

He'd ordered Naik and the constable to go home so they could change and get a meal, but Naik had sent in replacements in plain clothes, who awaited instructions right outside Nandini's condominium.

"We can't take risks, sir," Naik had said. "This was a brazen attack on a police station."

Arnav could set the men to work only after he looked at the papers. He half expected Shinde to enter the apartment, swear words at the ready—challenging him, asking how Arnav dared steal the documents from the locker. Arnav rubbed his unshaven cheek, letting the pain in his arm distract him.

In Shinde's diary, a lot of the writing was shortened names, numbers, and dates. Sums added up. Bribes: *hafta*. This was his best friend's other life, one Arnav had known nothing about. Arnav took pictures of the pages and uploaded them to a private cloud backup as he worked. This was unstable dynamite that called for delicate handling, a record with the potential to bring down the whole racket.

Arnav flipped open the bulky file. Pictures and newspaper cuttings. As he clicked snapshots on his phone, he recognized some of the faces from police photographs, others from the news.

"Interesting pictures." Nandini peered over his shoulder.

"We need to talk."

"Sure." Nandini sat down.

"I have no words to thank you. I've already made a transfer to your account for the hospital bills." Arnav raised his hand in a pleading gesture at Nandini, who looked like she was about to protest. "Please don't decline it."

"All right."

Arnav turned to glance at the closed door of the guest room. "And you didn't need to do this. I could have arranged a safe house for her."

Nandini smiled. "I didn't do it for you."

"I'm so sorry. I should have told you earlier."

"I'm not thrilled. But I don't blame you, either. You've been calling her name in your sleep for years."

He'd called Tara in his sleep? Arnav filed that away for later and focused on the right words for Nandini.

"You deserve a better man. Not me."

"I agree." She smiled, a rueful grin. He'd only ever taken from her, giving back little in return. Why was she so good to him? Arnav had never claimed to fathom women, but even so, Nandini was far beyond his understanding.

"I'll be around to help, but . . ." He gripped Nandini's hand, like a friend would. He meant it.

"I'm counting on it." She withdrew her hand after a while. "Do better for her, all right?"

He nodded. Silence lingered between them, but he could find no words to break it.

"What are those pictures? I seem to recognize some of them."

She was giving him an out. He took it.

He told her about Shinde's involvement with Neha Chaubey, and how he'd tracked down the file and the diary.

"Shinde. Our Shinde?" Nandini looked as devastated as he felt.

Shinde was Arnav's friend, but he and his family had become Nandini's friends, too, over the years of shared meals and festivals.

"This can't be easy for you," Nandini said after a pause.

"You are thinking about what's easy for me right now? Only you."

Any man would be fortunate to have Nandini in his life. She did deserve someone miles better.

"I knew him," Nandini said, "or thought I did. You can talk to me about him if it will help."

Arnav didn't want to go there, release the mixture of rage and grief, of disappointment and devastation. It was one thing to lose your friend, quite another to have him give his life for you, and more complicated still when you found out you didn't know him at all, despite more than two decades of friendship. He picked up Shinde's diary.

"This mentions Moringa Consultants." He pointed to a page. "You said Joshi's sister-in-law owns it. Any updates on the firm?"

Given his situation, he couldn't dig too closely around Joshi's relatives.

"Not so far, but I've found sources I'm trying to persuade." She examined the pictures as he spoke. "This is Rehaan Virani, and his family—Shinde had this?"

"Yes. And that's—"

"Vijayan," she said. "And Home Minister Namit Gokhale. And isn't this Commissioner Joshi?"

It was. Rehaan and his family, with Vijayan, all dressed in Sunday casual. Maharashtra State Home Minister Namit Gokhale with them, in a pair of blue shorts and a white T-shirt, standing with his arm around Joshi's shoulder. The pictures seemed to be from a poolside party, taken surreptitiously from a distance.

"The Viranis campaigned for the Ektawadi party during last year's elections," Nandini said. "Remember their family video with Namit Gokhale? It went viral, helped Gokhale win his seat and become a minister."

Mumbai Police reported to the state of Maharashtra's Home Minister, to Gokhale. He held the power to fire or transfer anyone in Mumbai Police, regardless of designation.

"Rehaan's mother is related to Namit Gokhale's wife. Cousins." Nandini checked her phone as she spoke. "The two are said to be close. Mrs. Gokhale turns up for all of Kittu Virani's events."

Kittu Virani. Arnav remembered Taneja's fiancée's visit to the dojo, when she'd warned him to stay in his lane and let others worry about making the rules. Here was the connection he'd been looking for. Taneja's fiancée knew all of these people.

"What do you know about Rehaan Virani?" Arnav said. Rehaan wasn't happy with his family. More information on him could help Arnav dig up dirt on Kittu and Taneja.

"Blue is his favorite color. I was watching his interviews." They both turned at Tara's voice.

Arnav caught a whiff of her jasmine fragrance, and yearned to rise and hug her.

"He gave a blue car to his latest girlfriend," Tara said. "Kittu was upset about it, I think. She's quite controlling—even shows up on his sets."

Nandini shifted, making space for Tara. Freshly scrubbed, Tara seemed a girl playing dress-up in Nandini's *kurta*, its neckline too wide for her slender neck, the sleeves hiding her wrists. Arnav made a mental note to arrange for proper clothes for her.

"I'll try to get this analyzed later," Arnav said as he handed the diary to Nandini, "but in the meanwhile, could you take a look? It mentions payments from Taneja Estate Holdings and Moringa Consultants to this Fat Beauty Company."

"Fat Beauty creates designs for plus-size women," Tara piped up. "It is a brand by Rehaan and Karan Virani. I watched their ramp walk videos yesterday."

"That's the kind of information we need more of," Arnav said.

"If we can verify all this, it might establish proof of transactions between Vijayan, the Virani family, and Taneja." Nandini took the files and began flipping the pages. "This could be a scoop."

"Make a copy of all the papers," he said to Nandini. "Don't keep the originals with you."

"Where, then?" She looked up from the file. "I'll need these for my story."

"In a safety-deposit box. Don't publish any stories unless I tell you it's OK."

"All right," Nandini said. "There's a note about a thumb drive—did you find one in the bag?"

Arnav reached for the bag, but tendrils of pain crept up his arm. Tara picked it up, turning it upside down. A tiny steel casing fell out. Nandini dragged her laptop across the table and plugged it in, but the thumb drive was password protected.

"I'll figure this one out," Nandini said. "I know someone who can help."

"Be careful who you speak to," Arnav said.

"I'll get tea." Tara rose and left, despite Nandini offering to make it instead.

"I'll stay at the dojo for the next few days," Arnav said. "The police station is right next door. I'll take Tara with me."

"With Joshi in these pictures, can you trust the police?"

The police. Joshi, who schmoozed with the underworld. Mhatre, on leave and a no-show even after a shoot-out at his own station. Considering all that Tukaram had told him, Mhatre could easily be a suspect.

"No. I'm leaving the thumb drive with you. Duplicate it and put the original in the safety-deposit box along with the papers. I'll be OK with the *sensei* and the other students around me."

Arnav sent the plainclothes constables back to Naik at the station. He could trust Naik, but he didn't want extra pairs of watching eyes, not when Tara was with him.

Pulling out his notebook, he added notes.

Joshi
Ordered a transfer and promotion which would pause the investigation into the bodies.
Tara mentioned a police officer cap at the mystery client's place.
Friends with Taneja, but also Namit Gokhale, Rehaan Virani, Vijayan

Shinde
Concealed Neha Chaubey's identity.
Took bribes from Shetty. Is Shetty delivering the bar girls to Taneja?
What else has he not disclosed?
Connected with Vijayan, Joshi. Possible money laundering connection.

If Joshi was transferring Arnav out due to the Versova case, it could be to cover up for any one of those men.

For years, Shinde had known about Joshi's connection to Vijayan—he had made detailed notes of the amounts Joshi received in cash via Vijayan's shell companies. He'd never mentioned it to Arnav, despite intimate knowledge of Arnav's desperation to bring Joshi to justice. What else had Shinde hidden? That was a thought for later. For now, he must tie together all the open threads in the case.

Or maybe there were more connections to uncover.

Nandini held a picture of Mhatre, with Joshi and Taneja. Twinkle-eyed Shinde, lounging at the bar. Joshi stood in the middle, with the looming Mhatre and the urbane Taneja flanking him, champagne glasses in their hands.

CHAPTER FIFTY-NINE

TARA

Tara didn't want to admit it, but her heart felt lighter after she left Nandini's apartment with Arnav. The discussions between Nandini and Arnav about Shinde's papers, and Nandini's kindness, had overwhelmed her.

The *sensei* had welcomed them to the dojo this morning and assigned them two small rooms facing each other on the upper floor. The rooms were bare, a single bed and dresser in each, but she was moved to see clothes her size in her dresser. Arnav had remembered that her suitcase was at the hotel, to which she couldn't go back. She wished they were going to his home, where she could take better care of him. Arnav was adamant—this was safer.

He'd been on the phone nonstop and encouraged her to get changed into more comfortable clothes while he finished his calls and met with his assistant. She'd not been alone with him even once, and it gnawed at her. She must tell him about Pia, and the men Zoya had seen.

Worrying about Arnav after the shoot-out and anxiety over money had kept her up most of last night. How would she pay for Pia's school? She'd spoken to Zoya—Shetty had called Zoya, asking for Tara's whereabouts.

Tara hoped Arnav would go easy on her when he realized he had a daughter. And, now that she wasn't earning money, why was she still in

Mumbai? She could book a flight back and spend Diwali with Pia. Who knew if they'd get another chance? She cursed her absurd foreboding. *Don't give up—find a different way to fund Pia's education.* She would return as soon as Shetty gave up asking about her and Arnav said it was safe for her to leave.

She was about to dial Zoya when her friend's name flashed on the screen.

"Hello! Aren't you supposed to be dropping Pia to school?"

"Where are you?" Zoya sounded hoarse. "Why won't you . . . pick up?"

"Did you catch a cold? Why are you breathing so hard?"

"Tara!" Zoya's voice rose.

"What's wrong?"

"They took Pia."

"What are you saying? Who?"

"I'm near Pia's school . . . stepped out of the auto . . . paying them when a car stopped and it was so fast . . . and by the time . . ."

Tara heard her sob. Her mind went blank. Pia.

"I'm sorry, I should never have . . . I told you," Zoya babbled and gasped on the phone.

"Get ahold of yourself." Tara spoke with feigned calm. "Tell me what happened."

As she pieced together Zoya's account, Tara sank down on the bed, phone in hand. Zoya had ferried Pia to school a little later than usual. While she was paying off the auto-rickshaw, she'd spotted the same blue car as before. Three large men had rushed up to them and, before Zoya could react, grabbed Pia. While Zoya screamed, two of them held Pia and the third put a cloth over her mouth. The car had raced off.

Zoya had given chase in the auto and noted down the number, but she wasn't sure she got it right.

"How long ago was this?"

"I've been trying to reach you for the last fifteen minutes."

All that time Tara had spent dreaming about spending time with her daughter, someone had taken her.

"What should we do?" Zoya said. "I'm sending you the digits on the number plate. What next?"

Tara didn't know. Had the men mistaken Pia for someone else? Similar incidents had occurred in other parts of Lucknow, but the victims belonged to rich families. She'd read about them in the papers. Ransom calls. Police raids. Why would anyone want Pia?

"Tara, are you there?" Zoya's words startled her. "Should I call the police? When will you be here?"

The police. Arnav. He'd know what to do.

"I'll call you back." Tara's voice shook. "Go to a friend's place. Keep your phone switched on."

CHAPTER SIXTY

ARNAV

On a wall of the cramped room the *sensei* had given him, Arnav re-created the board from his office. He jotted down a mind map of the serial murders and the suspects, using his notes and phone snapshots. The details from Shinde's papers went up on the board one by one.

Naik's team was interrogating the shooters who had attacked the Malwani station. Working out the connections between the suspects was the only way Arnav could help Naik.

Arnav looked up at a noise from the door. Tara stood at the threshold, her hair rumpled, her eyes wild.

"Avi."

The helpless terror on her face yanked Arnav to his feet.

"They took Pia, Avi. Zoya said . . ."

He heard her words, but his brain refused to understand. Tara's voice carried a broken, desperate note. Pia could only be . . . that girl on the screen. He'd imagined what it might mean. It had now turned real.

"I should've told you much earlier. I meant to tell you at the hospital. Last evening. This morning. I swear to you. Zoya had told me she was being followed. I should have talked to you."

Zoya was the friend Tara had escaped with. The other girls said Zoya had taken care of Tara since she was first brought to the Blue Bar.

Arnav hugged her. "Tell me exactly what Zoya said."

He brought her to sit on the bed, and stroked her hand while she talked, as much for himself as for her. The room seemed to spin a little. Pia was his. Tara had run away not in order to abandon him, but because she'd assumed he wouldn't support her. He had a daughter, his flesh and blood. He kissed Tara's hair, let her sob as she spoke incoherent words, trying to take it all in and order his chaotic thoughts. A daughter. This was why pregnancy took nine months—to get you used to the idea of being a parent. That could wait. He had to find Pia first.

"What did you tell your friend? Has she made a police report?"

"No. I was coming to you when she rang again. Someone called her. They asked for my number so I gave Zoya this new one. If she tells anyone, makes a report, they said they would, they would . . ."

"Harm Pia." Arnav finished the sentence. The first time he'd spoken his daughter's name. It felt strange, yet right—the weight of the word, its syllables.

"You must find her, Avi. She's thirteen. Tell your colleagues. Zoya noted the number on the car." She handed him a slip of paper. "The police can help, right?"

The police can help, right? The exact words he'd said to his father after Asha was attacked.

The plate number was probably fake. Before he acted, he needed more information.

"Avi?" Tara's gaze burned into him. "We must get her back."

We. Us. A few days ago, there was no such thing.

"Zoya had asked me to return." Tara covered her face. "Why am I even here?"

Because of me. You're here because of me. He sighed. *There you go, Arnav, all about yourself.*

With his uninjured arm, he held her as she shivered and did not speak.

Pia was why Tara worked for Shetty. Arnav poured Tara a glass of water. She may have hidden his daughter from him, but like she'd said earlier, she hadn't stopped him from searching for her. If he'd traced Tara, she wouldn't have had to raise their child alone.

Maybe he was lying to himself. Hand on his heart, fourteen years ago, would he have wanted this? Probably not. Tara took a sip of the water, and putting down the glass, curled into him. He placed his unhurt arm about her and strove to forget that he'd failed his sister, his parents.

Moments later, he leaned away from Tara, studied her face, the sheen of tears. He had failed then. Not this time. Setting emotions aside, he must fight for Pia and Tara, his new family, use cold reason to do what he excelled at: police work. Who would kidnap Pia and why?

"How long ago was this?"

"Less than half an hour."

"Talk to Zoya. Ask her if she can remember anything else at all. When they warned her not to inform the police, did they make any demands? She must tell you each word she heard. The smallest detail might help."

Tara picked up her phone.

"Maybe wash your face first? You need to be calm for this to work."

He knew she would take a bath—the one thing that steadied her.

Tara was a teenager when she fell pregnant, practically a child herself, and she'd not only given birth and raised a child, she'd made an entire life in a new place. She was here, trying to build their child's future. And he'd thought of *her* as selfish and irresponsible. Another thought struck him just as she stood up.

"Who else knows about Pia?"

"Zoya, obviously." Tara paused. "And Shetty. He mentioned he could arrange for her education if I went on the private dance assignment."

Shetty. He shared all his information with the police. Did he know Pia was Arnav's daughter?

"What's wrong? Do you think Shetty took her? Is this because I refused?"

"It sounds like a planned attempt—they were following Zoya for several days." He stroked her back. "We'll find our daughter. I promise. You and Pia will never be on your own again. You have me."

He must get in touch with the two people he could trust in Mumbai Police—Tukaram and Naik. And his star informer, Ali.

CHAPTER SIXTY-ONE

A knock at the door leading up from the stairs, and Bilal stood in front of him, his pants as sharply creased, his smile confident, like he'd never run away. Bilal always walked into his presence carrying a tray with a meal or a drink or a snack, as if to keep a demon appeased with offerings.

Bilal set the tray down and settled himself on a stool. No one else ever dared sit without permission.

He picked up the whiskey—Bilal's offering—and leaned back on the swing, kicking gently on the terrace floor to set it in motion. The old man knew how to pour the whiskey right, with a large round ice cube, the size of a ping-pong ball.

"*Bhai* called. The police raided one of his garages," Bilal said.

There it was. No small talk. He liked that about Bilal, but it also annoyed him. Others would take time to introduce a crucial topic because they were suitably respectful. Bilal had never been taken down a peg or two. If he had been, it wasn't often enough.

"It won't matter." He let his body slide back farther. "They'll close the case soon."

"They found the van," Bilal said.

"The van?"

That moron Rasool had fucked up again.

"The delivery van. He says they took it away. He's trying to find out who the zero dial around him was." Zero dial—a man who made a living ratting out his friends. The people the Mumbai Police called the *khabri*.

"What did you say to him?"

"It was the fault of his men. It had better not lead anywhere."

"Did they have the van cleaned?"

"They washed it." Bilal looked down, not meeting his eyes. "But they thought it would never be traced."

That presented a problem.

"Rasool will handle it," Bilal said. "I'll never have to clean up another one, right?"

He wanted to say no.

"If you need to punish women, punish the real one. The one who is responsible. Why play dress-up with others?"

The Item Number. This was why Bilal was dangerous. He knew it all, and wasn't shy about bringing it up.

"You know why."

"No, I don't," Bilal said. "The other reasons aren't true anymore."

"They are, and will remain."

"You're afraid. Why don't you admit it? You're scared of *her*."

He would have struck Bilal, but he was used to masking his emotions.

"Yes, I was." He chuckled and turned his gaze to the twinkling stars. "Maybe I shouldn't be. OK, check on her schedule. Let's make her an offer she won't refuse."

Bilal left.

Dad used to say *Go big, or go home*. Maybe that was the way out of it all. Time for her star to twinkle out. And Bilal. If he could silence Bilal forever, Item Number would remain obscure, as would the other secret that had stayed his hand so long. Time to make plans.

He chose a spare phone and used one of the SIM cards he'd been given. After a while, the don himself came on the line.

"I would have called you today."

"We think alike, *Uhnna*."

"No, we don't. We need to handle your *pandu*. He got away again—and he has the package you want."

This was bad. "He kidnapped her? How did he know she's the one?"

"He doesn't. She's his girl, I'm told. He'll be there when we call her."

He was going to get the Item Number, but he also wanted the replacement. She was a double of the Item Number, and she'd failed the three-minute deadline. The least she could do was dance for him. The Item Number couldn't dance anymore. And even if she could, he wouldn't bother to watch her. But that could wait.

"Use your leverage to make them stop investigating the case instead."

"Are you sure?" *Uhnna's* voice held a note of curiosity. "What about the girl?"

Once the investigation stopped, she would be easier to nab because unlike him, the *pandu* would soon lose interest in her.

Of course he wanted this woman, but he needed the bodies back in the ground even more. Along with nightmares of the Item Number, those women had chased him the past few nights. Silent, headless specters, flying at him as he ran.

"I'm sure."

"As you wish, but I'm not returning any payments."

He let that pass—no don ever returned money. He asked instead, "Will your shooters squeal?"

"Not my men, guns-for-hire we picked up. One is dead; the other is in their hands."

"And?"

"Don't worry, I've taken measures."

He lay back. *Uhnna*'s "measures" would damage the Item Number's prospects, hit her where it hurt. She'd be more eager than ever when Bilal approached her. Sipping his whiskey, he smiled. His dad wouldn't call him a foolish *fattu* if he saw him now.

CHAPTER SIXTY-TWO
TARA

Tara splashed her face with water, but her tears wouldn't stop.

Walking into the shower, she wet her hair. *Take a bath, Noyontara,* her mother had advised Tara each time Tara's father left home, having kicked and punched the two of them. *It doesn't just clean your body. It cleanses your soul, makes you ready for good things to come.*

No time for that now. Tara wrapped her drenched hair in a towel and went to Arnav's room.

He made space for her among the files and papers strewn on his bed, and rose to lock the door. She dialed Zoya's number, switching on the speaker. Zoya picked up at the first ring.

"Did you tell Arnav?"

"Yes, he's right here. I've put you on speaker."

"Is it all right if I ask you a few questions?" Arnav said.

"Sure." Zoya's voice was husky with tears.

"When they called you, did they make any demands?"

"No. They said they'll call Tara."

"They know she's Pia's mother, then."

"Yes. They said, *Tell Tara we'll call her.*"

"Can you describe the men?"

"They were well built. Tall. Wore jeans and T-shirts. They seemed to be from South India. One of them said, *Polam, Manu, polam.*"

"You're sure about the exact words?"

"Yes, they were not locals. One wore ash on his forehead."

Tara had seen men with ash on their foreheads. Shetty and his men. Shetty knew about Pia.

"If they call again," Arnav said to Zoya, "tell them they need to return Pia. Keep them talking."

Call done, Arnav rose to unlatch the door. Tara stopped him.

"Shetty. The men sound like his thugs."

"I'll follow that up."

"What can I do now?"

"You need to record the calls you receive. I'll explain how. Put all unknown numbers on speakerphone so I can listen in. Teach Zoya to record any calls, too."

After her return to Mumbai, Tara had striven to keep away from Arnav. Even when she was in his bed, she'd kept her heart apart, with room only for one. Pia. Or so she thought.

Arnav's words returned to her: *You won't be alone anymore.* Did she want that, though?

She'd been her own provider, even before her father sold her for a few bottles of drink. Tears leaked and she wiped at them.

She startled when Arnav held her, lightly. "Stop this. We need to be strong for her."

"Without Pia . . ." Tara sobbed, and though she didn't wish to give in, she found herself hugging him. She couldn't breathe past the weight on her chest. Her tears were not only for Pia, but for Arnav, who'd been abandoned again and again. For herself, who couldn't hold on to what she treasured most.

"Does Pia know about me?" Arnav spoke into her hair, his voice trembling above her.

Tara moved out of his arms. He looked as if he'd left home and wasn't sure of a welcome upon his return. Could a policeman and a bar girl make a home together? Impossible. No one would accept it.

"Unwed mothers carry a stigma, especially in smaller cities, so I said I was a widow. We've stuck with that story."

"You told her I'm . . . ?"

It wasn't easy, but he deserved the truth.

"I never imagined we'd meet. Or that you'd want her."

In the distance a train whistled as it hurtled toward a faraway destination. The dojo shared the neighborhood with a local station.

"Did she ever ask about her father?"

"After she started going to school. She knows you were . . . are a policeman. She's seen pictures of you."

"She'll know who I am?"

That look of hope in his eyes he tried hard to hide. Tara ached to hold him, but knew better. She contented herself with a nod.

"We men are strange beasts. Love us and we run from you. Leave us, and you're never far from our thoughts."

Tara had never known a man who stayed. It didn't matter if he was loved or not.

"Promise me you won't do anything foolish." He kissed her head, and the faint smell of his aftershave calmed her.

"Yes." Maybe she could count on him, after all.

Tara practiced recording the way Arnav had shown her, while he made a flurry of calls. The brutal part was not being able to help Pia. Would they molest her? Tara pushed away her terror. She stared at the phone for a long while, willing it to ring. When it didn't, she returned to her refuge, the shower, and let the water pummel her. Arnav had massaged her feet the other night. It had felt good to be taken care of.

Had Pia taken a bath? She closed her eyes and pictured her smiling little girl, who liked to snack on roasted peanuts, drew henna on Zoya's hands, and had to be told to turn down the music.

Tara thought she heard a distant ring. Her phone—she'd left it in the room. Cursing, she wrapped a towel around herself and rushed out. By the time she reached it, it had stopped ringing. A call from an unknown number.

She threw on new clothes from the dresser, checked the phone once again, and dialed Zoya. No answer. She was about to drop it on the bed when it rang. Another anonymous call. She put it on speaker and hit the record button.

"Want to see your daughter?" A male voice she did not recognize. A faint southern accent to his Hindi.

"Who is speaking?" Tara said. "Hello, where is Pia?"

"If you want her, you must do as I say."

Arnav had coached her to ask to speak to Pia first, but Tara's head went blank. "Yes. Anything."

"Are you alone?"

"Yes."

"Get your lover to lay off the case."

"What case? How is Pia? Can I speak to her?"

"Don't act smart." The line went dead.

Tara turned at a noise behind her, startled. Arnav stood at the door, and he had heard it all.

CHAPTER SIXTY-THREE

ARNAV

In his sparse dojo room, Arnav sat with Shinde's diary—his head spinning. He hadn't slept much since he'd discharged himself from the hospital. He felt keyed up, raring to go, but his body ached after an entire day of pacing and calls. The painkillers slowed him down. He copied out some of the codes and numbers on his board, and stared at them.

His mind drifted to Tara as he wrote. She'd asked him about the case the kidnappers had mentioned, and he'd told her—blue sequins—making her blame herself all over again for coming to Mumbai, meeting Shetty, not telling him about Pia early enough.

He'd begged the *sensei* to keep her engaged, so the *sensei* had recruited her to help at the dojo kitchen.

Arnav resisted the urge to check on her. The kidnappers hadn't called again since the afternoon, and that had put them both on edge.

Logically, whoever had blocked the earlier investigations was behind this—and wanted him off the Aksa and Versova cases. The suspect behind the serial murders, Tara's mysterious client, had attempted to get him transferred, then killed, and now had taken his daughter.

Conclusion: that person knew about him, Tara, and Pia. That couldn't be Taneja. Only Shetty had that information, had mentioned it to Tara. Arnav had sent the words *Polam, Manu, polam* to a Malayali constable on his staff. The words meant "Let's go," and *Manu* was possibly a name. Vijayan was famous for using men exclusively from his community. There were no non-Malayalis on his payroll.

Arnav had asked Naik to stop by, keeping his voice casual. He couldn't go to the office or log in from his devices to investigate Pia's kidnapping, not while on leave, given the sticky situation with Mhatre and Joshi. Tukaram couldn't handle the database very well, which left Naik.

He was hoping Naik would show up now, before Tara returned to her room. He had covered the picture-covered board with a sheet of paper so as not to alert Naik before he had a chance to speak to her. A knock on the door made him turn.

"Good evening, sir." Naik looked quite rested despite all the stress at work. Arnav was sure he appeared as run-down as he felt in his casual clothes. Arnav dragged in a chair for her from the corridor, but she didn't sit. Greetings done, she was her usual brisk self.

"The shooter has finally begun to speak, sir. He said he came from his village two weeks ago and trained to use a gun for a week. If he had succeeded, he would have been paid one lakh rupees."

"Did he say who the target was?"

"You, sir. Between him and his friend who died, they were to receive two lakhs."

"Who ordered the hit?"

"The suspect has named history-sheeters, sir. No luck flushing them out so far."

History-sheeters. Those with long criminal records, who had spent a lot of time in jail. How safe was Tara at the dojo if hit men came after her? Good thing the rooms featured single, high windows, with sturdy metal grilles.

"Keep pushing. Anything else we've missed?"

"We've tailed Shetty. He has met with a man with past connections to Vijayan."

"Stay on that tail. And continue with the shooter's interrogation."

Arnav scribbled in his notebook. Shinde told Shetty about Neha Chaubey's body being identified, and if Shetty was connected to Vijayan, was Vijayan the don who arranged the *supari*, the target painted on Arnav's back?

"Yes, sir," Naik said. "Please be careful."

Arnav detected a strange note in Naik's voice. She seemed distressed. Not like an assistant anxious about her boss or a case, or even a grateful colleague who owed a favor.

Shinde used to tease him about her carrying a torch for him. *Have you noticed how she looks at you? As if the sun rises and sets from your ass.* Arnav dismissed it. Shinde's outlook on women was not worth dwelling upon—he must stop letting his friend's voice echo in his ears.

"Thank you, Naik."

"I heard you have the witness with you here. Should I interview Tara?"

Tara. Tara had locked herself in the bathroom after she finished with the kitchen chores. She'd not emerged for more than an hour.

"Sir, are you OK? Is there anything I can help with?"

He'd called Naik to ask for help, and her concern seemed genuine, but he had trusted before and lost. He struggled to get the words out—Pia, kidnapping, Tara. From downstairs the voice of a dozen karate students floated up, united in an exhale during a routine. Maybe he needed a few more minutes.

"Yes, fine," Arnav said. "Any updates on the other investigations?"

"In the Versova case, we found several men's DNA in the black Maruti van. A set matches the suspect our constable identified as the man who dumped Neha Chaubey's body. He has a previous record for drug peddling."

"What does he say? Is he connected to the shooter?"

"We haven't been able to make the man talk so far, sir, but a number he's called is listed to Kittu Virani."

"Are you sure?"

Kittu Virani. The name kept popping up. Was she the one behind all of this—hiding a dead body to protect her fiancé or even getting them for him? The marriage would mean a huge gain for her. Shinde's pictures showed she knew Vijayan, and Vijayan might be using Shetty to procure girls for reclusive clients. His men might have nabbed Pia.

"Yes, sir. We think she might have scored drugs from this man because she throws big Bollywood parties. We also have the app on his phone that shows a few locations as favorites, and one of them is her main residence."

Arnav paced the room. "I see. Give me a minute to think this through."

He heard a rustle behind him and turned, only to see the paper covering his board fall off, revealing the pictures he'd tacked up. As he bent to retrieve the paper, he saw Naik stiffen, her gaze riveted on the board and the pictures. Under the unforgiving glare of the white tube-light, the details stood out.

The Viranis. Joshi. Shinde. Taneja. Mhatre. Namit Gokhale. Vijayan. An intriguing set of characters.

"Sir?"

That single word asked many questions. Arnav was relieved to have the decision taken out of his hands. If Naik was to help find Pia, he had to share all he knew. Anyone on his team would face as much danger as he was in.

"Sit down, Naik. This will take a while."

Arnav filled Naik in about Shinde and Neha Chaubey. Shinde's diary with the details of *hafta*. The photographs. His own conjectures about who the mystery client could be—the cap of the senior police officer Tara had spotted. And Pia.

Naik's face blanched. He let her process it all while he updated the board. When he turned to Naik, she was still absorbed, her gaze trained on the names and photographs.

"Now you know the entire picture, do you still wish to get involved? I called you here to request your assistance, but I'd understand if you refuse. I know your situation at home."

"Yes, sir. This was why I joined the force."

Not for the first time, Arnav sent up a thought of gratitude for this assistant.

"Thank you very much, Naik. We're not filing a missing persons report on Pia, so that part of the investigation will be unofficial."

"Understood, sir. How do we proceed? Should we arrest Shetty?"

"Tail him for now."

"After the attack at the station," Naik paused to clear her throat, "Joshi sir has combined the investigations. We're now investigating Neha Chaubey's murder, as well as the attack on our station. He says you may have stepped too close to the culprit, and the cases are connected."

Arnav sensed Joshi behind the scenes, already at work. Was he the jackal, or Mhatre?

"And Mhatre sir? Has he showed up?"

Mhatre was the unknown quantity. Malwani Police Station was under his jurisdiction. If he was involved, both Arnav and Naik might be in a world of danger.

"He's still on leave, sir. Personal reasons."

"We'll analyze everything. All of Shinde's information."

He remembered another item in his possession and pulled from his backpack the paper bag the *sensei* had given him. "And this. These are Rehaan Virani's. Get them checked for DNA, and match the findings against the forensic evidence detected in the van." Arnav sat down on his chair. "If Kittu Virani's name has come up, we must eliminate all possibilities."

Naik gaped at him, with the same expression as Shinde had when Arnav contrived to promote a pawn into a queen. In normal times, he would have cracked a joke at Naik's expression.

"I'm training him in karate," he said. "He left them here."

A memory prickled at the edge of his consciousness. It would come to him after he slept, but sleep proved elusive. He'd closed his eyes a few times. Shinde appeared, gasping, slick with blood.

"Sure, sir." Naik rose to leave.

"Thanks," Arnav said. "And Naik?"

"Yes, sir?"

"Watch your back at all times."

Arnav turned away from the neat figure of his assistant walking down the dark corridor, and hoped he'd done the right thing.

The *sensei* walked into the room a while later. "Call for you," he said. "Send the phone down once you're done."

Arnav had given Naik and Nandini the *sensei*'s number and asked them to use different phones when calling him.

Arnav nodded his thanks. Nandini was on the line.

"I have information, but we can't talk now." Nandini didn't bother with greetings.

"I can come down."

"Sent a friend down with the info. She will be there soon."

There was a pause. Nandini lowered her voice further. "This is not good."

Being afraid was unlike Nandini—her job tended to ruffle feathers. She sounded terrified.

Downstairs, Arnav found a girl waiting for him. He accepted the sealed envelope, and she left without a word. Back upstairs, he opened the envelope to find notes in Nandini's handwriting, and a thumb drive. Over the next few minutes, he found what he'd looked for all his life. Evidence that nailed Commissioner Neelesh Joshi.

On the thumb drive were calls recorded between Joshi and Shinde, Joshi and Shetty, Joshi and Taneja, Shetty and Vijayan—undeniable proof that Joshi had bent the law, accepted bribes, and risen in the ranks through support from his connections in high places.

Arnav had helped arrange Shinde's wedding, been with Shinde outside maternity wards as his children were born. Shinde had listened to Arnav rant about his father, about the spineless judicial system. Helped carry the body of Arnav's father to the funeral pyre. Sat beside his mother's hospital bed when Arnav worked two jobs. Fed Arnav when he was hungry.

He was also the one who'd kept Arnav from fighting for justice for his sister. Arnav wanted to drag Shinde back from the dead to ask him a few questions.

CHAPTER SIXTY-FOUR

Three minutes. You can't even keep it up for three minutes? It was a goods train, for heaven's sake! Want me to talk to your father, tell him you stole my earrings and sold them for pocket money?

He woke up with a start, a vicious cackle in his ears. Flinging aside clammy sheets, he padded across the plush carpet to the dark bathroom. At the basin he splashed water, cooling his heated face.

When they had come back from the railway tracks, she told his father. It was the truth, for once. Dad hadn't said a word. A week later, when they returned to the farmhouse, Dad had tied him to a tree in the backyard, stripped off his pants, and used his belt. *That will teach you to steal.* He hadn't been able to sit down for days afterward. He'd bitten into the pillow as Bilal tended to his wounds, gnashing his teeth to keep from making a noise in case she was listening.

He'd never failed her three-minute deadline again. She'd made it into her private little game. Three minutes to get her tea without spilling a drop, three minutes to finish his bath, three minutes to make her come.

Let's see how good you are. Three minutes.

The words still taunted him, years after she'd spoken them. He would fix this. He brought one of his diaries to bed, a talisman. When he wrote or read an entry before bed, he slept better. Reading a little might help him. He switched on a light, flipped the journal open.

This one is gone, but I'll make her last a while. One year, two years. Pictures last.

It is a shame I suffer and not the Item Number. That she gets on with her life—trips to the salon, girlie lunches—and here I am in this den, waiting for her to go away, because I can't make her. I want her gone gone gone, and to stay gone. Disappear. To not have come to our childhood home, never smiled her siren smile.

I was better this time. I took away who she was for a while. Severed the hands that touched me, the feet that carried her to my room, that hateful face. I've robbed her of her power, and she won't return. I can sleep for a few months. Who knows, maybe I fixed it for good.

Instead of emptiness today, my heart is full. I'm pure again, not dirty. I can be who I fancy, inside of me, because no matter how much I playact on the outside, it is the inside that matters, where the devil lurks, ready to strike with her red-lipped smile.

She moved her hands while she danced—each finger spoke in air the way they sang on my skin. No one is quite like the Item Number. And this is the agony and the humiliation. She disgusts me, but I seek her flyaway curls, her lithe body, her tinkling laughter, in each one of them.

This last one did well, she said what I wanted her to, did as I asked. Greed at first, then intrigue. Later, dare I say, love? Of course, love. I'm truly lovable when I choose, everyone knows that. Deep inside, I'm the boy I was before she came. But love does not last long. It must be replaced by fear. Three minutes.

That's what would help, to instill fear into a woman. If he looked hard, he could see shadows moving about in the mangroves, like his memories, with a malicious sense of purpose. Those shadows would pause, at least for a spell, when the new one came. Maybe on *Bhoot Chaturdashi* again this year. Soon, now.

CHAPTER SIXTY-FIVE

TARA

Tara watched Arnav pace the small empty space in his room like a caged animal. Late-morning sun filtered through the cloudy window panes. He spoke Marathi into his phone too fast for her to catch, with someone called Tukaram. She waited for a lull, but when he didn't pause, she walked up and placed her hand on his forearm. He clicked off the phone.

"Did they call again?" He looked wired and drained, dark circles under his eyes, his face shaven unevenly, his hair rumpled.

"You've told your office to stop? The next time they call, I'll tell them you stopped, and they will—"

"I'm on leave. As far as anyone is concerned, I'm off the case already. To bring Pia home, we have to either solve the case, or find the kidnappers. Both will lead us back to the same culprit."

"Pia's safety depends on you dropping the case." She put steel in her voice. A warning and a plea.

"How do you know? Are you sure they'll keep their word? We have experience with such situations, Tara."

He was mistaken if he thought she'd back down. She had given up all her dreams for her daughter. She wasn't about to lose Pia to Arnav's stubbornness.

"They'll kill her. They nearly did you in with that accident. They shot Shinde. She's a little girl. They won't think twice."

"They'll lose all leverage if they do."

"Pia is a bargaining chip now?"

"I didn't say that. You don't understand."

"No, *you* don't understand. You didn't rush her to the hospital each time she was ill, or to school when she was late. You don't care. About her, or me. This is all a mistake."

She should never have met Arnav again, let him bring her to his place. She was to blame for this. She lifted one of his files and hurled it at the wall. Papers flew out, fluttering in the air like the notes clients tossed to her at the Blue Bar. A bar girl couldn't ever count on a man.

"Tara!"

Tara stormed out of Arnav's room, and when he followed, she slammed her door in his face and locked it.

She took herself to the window. A lone *neem* tree swayed in the breeze in front of a garage. Yellow orioles screeched and fought, pecking on the bunches of bitter fruit, like in her childhood home in West Bengal.

Reflexively, Tara stared at her phone lying on the table. As a mother, she had one job—to protect Pia. She sat down on the bed, considering her options. The only other people she knew in Mumbai were Nandini and Shetty. Arnav called her name, knocking on the door. She ignored him.

The phone rang, scaring her, but it was the voice she wanted to hear.

"Have they called again?" Zoya said.

"No. They demanded that Arnav back off his cases."

"Will he do it?"

Tara couldn't lie to Zoya, so she spoke what truth she could.

"He's promised Pia will be safe."

"I'm going to Rasool."

"Rasool *Bhai*?"

The thug who had turned into a big don, one of Mumbai's most infamous.

"Yes. Well, I don't have his number, but I know someone who does."

"Are you mad? Why would he help you?"

"He predicted I'd return to him one day, of my own free will. He was right."

Zoya couldn't go back to that life, those bruises.

"No. Let me talk to Arnav first."

"You do your thing; I'll do mine. Rasool has connections. He'll sort it out, in exchange for me."

"Don't say that, Zoya."

"Pia is thirteen. Pretty. She's your daughter, but also mine. Don't stop me." The line went dead.

CHAPTER SIXTY-SIX

I hate sequins. Rubbed against you, they can scratch you raw till you bleed.

Each time I've seen a counselor Bilal has arranged for me, they have asked me questions. Write down the answers, they said, even if you can't speak about it. Write them down for your own eyes. It will help you at school. Express yourself.

So that's what I'll do now.

Let's start from the first occasion she entered my room one afternoon Dad wasn't at home.

I loathed her smirk.

That's not true. At my so-called elite boarding school, the only time someone touched me was with their fist or feet, or a rare pat on the shoulder. How many days can a human go without being touched with affection? What does it cost to stay away from all touch, good or bad? Dad's belts caressed me more than his hands. Slaps, punches. Bilal nursed me each time. So when she stroked me at first, it was on my hair, my forehead, and I liked it. Then I didn't. Then I did, so much. I didn't hate it. Later, I was scared because she told me she would tell Dad.

He can't keep up with me, she'd say, but you can. Come here, she'd flick her finger, and I'd go. How do you touch someone you ache to strangle and kiss at the same moment? I burned to kiss her, no denying it. All over. She let me when she was in the mood. Her game. Her rules, her timing. That Diwali evening in the study when Dad was in the shower, when she had returned from a party in her sequined saree. Gagging and suffocating between her legs, my face scratched by the blue sequins, terrified for my life. I can't stand Diwali now. Makes me want to set the world on fire.

CHAPTER SIXTY-SEVEN

ARNAV

In the afternoon buzz, Arnav moved through his warm-up stances. Each movement sent tendrils of pain coursing through his broken shoulder and injured arm, but he needed to assure himself that he could still his mind; and his legs were in working order. In the days ahead, he would need both. A week ago, Tara wasn't a part of his life, but now she'd become the epicenter of a slow earthquake, his days on the brink of collapse.

She'd tried to steal away last night to go beg Shetty for help. It had taken all of *sensei*'s persuasive skills and Arnav's pleas to stop her. She'd finally fallen asleep at dawn. It was as if her mind had decided to shut her down.

Afterward, he'd stayed up, leaning against her bed—terrified she might run again. He'd had little to no sleep, but it didn't matter. He'd coped with worse.

To add to the mess, Rasool might now be tracking Pia, thanks to Zoya. If Vijayan was the one behind Pia's kidnapping, with or without Shetty's involvement, the whole situation didn't bear thinking about. Little Pia would be at the center of a tug-of-war between Rasool and Vijayan. She was now missing for more than twenty-four hours, and her father, a policeman, couldn't file a complaint or use the formidable resources of Mumbai Police to locate her. Would Arnav fail her just as his father, Constable Rajput, had failed Asha?

His stance went wrong, landing his foot on the ground too hard, jarring his shoulder. He sank down with a grunt and breathed through the cramping agony. Slumping on the floor, he reached out to check his phone. No message from either Ali or Naik.

Arnav entered the kitchen to find Tara clearing up after a late lunch, wiping a plate as if her life depended on it. He eased the dishrag from her hand.

"Why can't you ask your team to step down?" Tara's lips trembled, her hair wild. "Get them to search for Pia, instead."

"They're keeping a low profile, and I've given every appearance of backing off. Tukaram will be here soon—we are working on getting Pia back."

If Arnav made the search official, that would only increase her peril. Tara wanted him to be a father, but Pia needed him to analyze and weigh risks like a police officer.

Tell her how you feel. About her, about Pia. He could do that to set Tara at ease, without compromising Pia's safety.

"I was trying," he began, "to recall what my last words to Shinde were."

She touched his jaw, her gaze turning soft. "You were with him when he died."

"Yes. All day, I'd been pissed at him. Raving mad. About everything he'd done. And he was gone. One moment to another. I didn't get to speak with him before . . . so I'm telling you, in case I don't come back when—"

"Shut up." Tara's words were flat, but her eyes blazed. She cupped his face in her hands. She wasn't as uncaring as she liked him to believe.

"I've spent so many years being upset with you for leaving out of the blue but, truth is, it was my fault. I failed to remember you were a girl yourself. I'm so sorry. I can't say this without sounding like some dumb Bollywood movie, but I couldn't see beyond you then, Tara. Still can't. I wanted you to know."

Her eyes were red and swollen. Similar to his in the mirror a while ago. He watched the fire of emotions in Tara's eyes, but before she could reply, his phone rang, flashing an unknown number. Maybe Ali had traced Pia.

"Good evening, sir."

It was Naik, not Ali. Arnav returned the greeting and waited.

"We have new information on the shoot-out, sir. Upon further questioning, one of the history-sheeters has given us a name."

"Shetty?"

"No, sir. They had heard the name Rahul Taneja."

CHAPTER SIXTY-EIGHT

Blood washes away all thought: watching blood flow, first with a gush and then a trickle and a drip. It needs to leave the body, wash out all its sins, the memories it has carried in arteries and veins. The body remembers all assaults, big and small, and blood keeps it moving, from joint to joint, organ to organ. Before they go, they must be cleansed so their filth doesn't touch anyone.

Last night I dreamed of bathing in a bathtub of blood, and it was warm and thick. Nourishing. Not unpleasant. The good thing about blood is that everyone's is the same, mine and theirs. Smell and taste and look— all the same. Each cut I make, blood wells up on my skin, and theirs. No difference.

I'm told I need help, but I don't. I've helped myself. I'm sovereign. No one can hold my arm and twist it, no one can pull my head down against my will, to lick and suck and fuck what I don't want to. I'm not a boy anymore. I don't have to shower anyone with rose petals. If she insists on a shower of petals, she'll get one. Dried petals, rough and crawling, like insects.

The roses in my garden would put a flower contest to shame. They bloom on a diet of blood and faces and hair. They make the ugly, beautiful. When I walk amid them, I step on all that is rancid and dark, but my soul is filled with colors and a muted fragrance.

CHAPTER SIXTY-NINE

ARNAV

Arnav's world had turned into a cacophony of squealing phones. He anticipated and dreaded each in equal measure.

Ali had called back. Someone had recruited one of his Mumbai contacts to pick up a girl being driven down from Lucknow. He didn't know the child's age, but she was a young girl. This gave Arnav hope. Pia's abductors would use a car, and hire a new crew when entering Mumbai.

He stared once more at the board taped up with pictures and scribbled all over with names and arrows, and began jotting down his conclusions in his notebook.

Rasool
Owned the black van used to dump Neha Chaubey's body—his man identified as suspect of dumping body—suspect's DNA in van.
May have taken a contract for body disposal, as per Ali.

Kittu Virani
Taneja's fiancée—phone number in the contact list of Rasool's men.
Knows Vijayan, as per Shinde's pictures.
Her son Rehaan Virani (sunglasses sent for DNA)
or

Taneja, her fiancé, might be suspects—she could be helping them hide their crimes.

Taneja

Three decomposed bodies found at his construction site.
Seemed to have sway with Joshi and Mhatre.
Had MeToo allegations against him.
Kittu Virani's fiancé.
History-sheeter said he ordered the Malwani station shooting.

Joshi

Ordered a transfer and promotion which would pause the investigation into the bodies.
Tara mentioned a police officer cap at the mystery client's place.
Friends with Taneja, but also Namit Gokhale, Rehaan Virani, Vijayan, Kittu Virani—long-term money laundering transactions with Vijayan.
Has the connections to procure girls and get rid of the bodies through Vijayan.
Has know-how to evade detection.

Mhatre

Supported Joshi, and denied obvious indications of serial killing.
Signed off on the traffic accident that killed Bendre, inspector in Dadar case.
Gawde warned against him.
Has problems with women, wife ran away.
Has connections to procure girls and get rid of the bodies.
Has know-how to evade detection.
Tara had seen a police officer cap at the mystery client's place.

Shinde

Concealed Neha Chaubey's identity.

Took bribes from Shetty. Is Shetty delivering the bar girls to Taneja? Connected with Vijayan, Joshi. Possible money laundering connection with both.

Vijayan
Has dealings with Owns Moringa Consultants by proxy, a business connected to Commissioner Joshi. Money laundering through Joshi. Connected to Shetty.
Grabbed the land that was later sold off to Taneja for a spa—what's the relationship between them?
May be carrying out Taneja's orders behind Pia's kidnapping and the Malwani station shoot-out.
No phone records between Taneja and Vijayan.

Shetty
Sent Tara to mystery client with blue-sequined saree.
Had underworld Connected to Vijayan. Malayalis tend to stick together.
May have informed Vijayan about Pia being my daughter.

Arnav couldn't question Taneja without Joshi's approval. An impossible roadblock. With Mhatre still on leave, Joshi had taken over the station, instead of handing it over to an ACP.

Joshi had ordered Naik to focus on another case last evening. As a result, she hadn't been able to sneak out to the jewelry shop her constable had identified as a source of the nipple clamp found on Neha Chaubey's body. Naik was supposed to call Arnav once she'd checked the CCTV footage and spoken to the shop owner.

Arnav's phone rang again, and he grabbed it, hoping it was Naik, but it was Rehaan Virani's agent reminding him of his appointment on the film set in a few hours.

"I've been in an accident. Broken shoulder, bruised ribs, and a leg injury. I'll come with my *sensei*."

The agent had heard of the *sensei*, and agreed.

When he cut the call, the dojo assistant stood at his door, phone in hand.

"Call for you. The *sensei* will lead a class," the man said as he handed Arnav the cell phone. "He's asked you to keep it."

"Hello, sir." Naik's voice floated in from the other end of the line. "We seized footage of the customer who the jeweler says ordered the clamps. The customer gave them a pair of sapphire earrings and requested them to be modified with clamps. I'm sending you the CCTV screen grabs, sir."

Arnav paced the room—this could be a solid lead.

"Do we have enough for identification?"

"Not sure, sir."

"Anything else?"

"Your call to Dr. Meshram about pushing the DNA tests helped once again. The DNA on Rehaan Virani's sunglasses matches traces inside the van."

Arnav sank onto the bed in his room. "Are you certain?"

"Yes, sir. I double-checked."

Rehaan Virani was in the van with Neha Chaubey's body. There had to be an explanation.

"The CCTV screen grabs don't show the face, but the height and build match Rehaan Virani. The man was wearing a blue cap."

Arnav remembered the cap Rehaan had worn for his practice session. "I'm going to meet him this evening."

"Sir?"

"Not on an official basis. His agent called me—they need me on the movie set today."

Arnav had sent in the sunglasses expecting Rehaan to be ruled out. The movie star was friendly, approachable. Violent toward women, but too high profile to risk being involved in murder or kidnapping. He remembered Rehaan's picture with Vijayan, though. Sometimes the best-looking, most innocent faces hid criminals. Kittu Virani might be covering up her son's ghoulish activities, not Taneja's.

"You're not well, sir."

"Thanks for the reminder," Arnav said. "The *sensei* will go with me."

"I could come along, sir."

"Would the bosses approve?"

"We now have proof, sir."

"Which we can't use yet. The *sensei* is a karate expert. We have the perfect excuse to go on set, and enough protection."

If Rehaan Virani was the mystery client, he would recognize Tara, and Arnav wanted to catch his reaction. And as he pictured Rehaan Virani at the dojo with Kittu Virani, that elusive memory his medicated brain had been trying to grasp slid into place. The truck that had run him off the road was a black Scorpio, like the one Rehaan had stood beside, talking to his mother.

On his board, Arnav circled three of the abbreviated names as Tara's possible mystery client—Joshi, Mhatre, Taneja—and added Rehaan Virani.

CHAPTER SEVENTY

TARA

Pia nestled in the crook of Tara's arm, a squirming bundle of towels that made the quietest of sighs as she stirred in her sleep. Tara breathed as lightly as possible so as not to move and awaken this tiny thing, all heartbeat and impossibly soft skin. A mess of wavy hair underneath the cap the size of a fist, finer than silk, nestled against her heavy, aching breasts, the smell of baby powder on her clothes. Tinkling bells in the distance. The bells grew louder, turning into the keening siren of an ambulance. They'd come to take Pia away—Tara startled, to find herself resting against Arnav's chest. She'd fallen asleep in a moving van, headed to the Filmistaan Studios.

Silent air-conditioner, muted music, plush seats, bottled water, and magazines, a far cry from the transport Shetty had sent her. This ride sent for Arnav, that cut across evening rush hour traffic, was exactly how a movie star would enter the sets. In another life, Tara might have burst for joy. She had dragged Arnav to the Filmistaan grounds more than once.

Arnav's *sensei* sat on the front seat, seeming restless, quite unlike his normal calm. Arnav spoke on the Bluetooth with his assistant, Naik, in whispered tones: the entire police department was gathering the next day for Shinde's funeral. The body would be handed over after postmortem. With the erupting crisis, she hadn't bothered to think about what Arnav had gone through—two attempts on his life, his best friend, however sleazy, shot down—and now, a daughter he hadn't met, kidnapped.

Tara sought to cool her anger at Arnav. He *was* Pia's father. Not a mythical figure in the one photograph Tara had showed Pia over the years, but a father who had promised to bring her back safe. Who would keep searching for her—because that's what fathers did, protected their children. Didn't sell them to the nearest predator, like Tara's father had. She hoped she wasn't wrong about Arnav.

Filmistaan had changed: more security, or maybe it was this particular set. It loomed against the growing dark, a ghost object made out of bamboo and cloth, tarpaulin and plastic sheets. Once they'd parked outside, they were issued guest identity cards, and went through a round of checks.

"Both Karan and Rehaan Virani will be on set today," the woman who issued their identity tags said. "The director is busy. Please wear your tags at all times. Keep your phones in the car. They are not allowed on the set—security instructions."

The idea of being separated from her phone sent Tara's stomach into free fall. What if the thugs who held Pia called, and she couldn't receive it?

"It won't take long." Arnav held her hand.

The security person in charge led them through a gloomy, cold space lit by distant yellow lamps—the temporary ceiling made of canvas and asbestos several stories high. Tara had no idea sets could be that big, or that chilly. Everyone, including the security men, wore jackets. She heard a hum rise from the lighted space at the center, the "shooting area," as their guide called it. Arnav took her aside, making sure no one heard them.

"Remember how you told me you thought the jackal was at the Blue Bar at its opening? I'll watch you, and will know if you sense anything amiss."

According to Arnav, the man who haunted her nightmares was behind Pia's kidnapping, one way or another. He'd murdered women in blue-sequined sarees over decades, and now that he was about to be caught, he wanted the investigation derailed. Arnav had reason to believe the jackal would visit the set.

"If he's here, he might spot me first."

Tara felt a shiver go through her. She remembered her dread at Borivali Station—peering into faces to figure out who was watching her. Arnav wouldn't tell her who he suspected because he didn't want to influence her—but he squeezed her arm, his eyes on her a caress and a reassurance.

"I'm counting on it. You have nothing to fear as long as you're within my sight."

Tara steeled herself. Her daughter was missing. Fear wasn't an option. She would do it for Pia. Turn into bait.

"All right. Let's go."

She followed Arnav's lead through the cables thick as wrists that snaked all over the floor. Men and women carried tables, flowers, cameras, bags. The set was a bungalow sliced neatly in half, with a winding staircase on one side. A large camera, bigger than her old television, moved on the rails placed around it. The action director greeted them—a tall, limber man with an open smile. They spoke, and Tara tuned out. Arnav introduced the *sensei*, his gaze darting around, as if he expected threats from shadowy corners.

Tara hugged herself in the cool air. Arnav took off his jacket and wrapped it around her. She would have protested—he needed it more than she, with all his injuries—but he seemed on edge. He seated her against a darkened partition, right behind the director's chair, tucked away from the hustle.

"Stay alert," he said.

Arnav picked his way to the director and a group of assistants deep in conversation, avoiding tripping over the cables, tripods, rails. She liked that he didn't limp anymore.

"Rehaan is on his way," the action director said to Arnav. "We'll finish the close-up shots while we wait. We only need you for his first shot. No one wants to work during these Diwali days, but what to do?"

They walked off and their voices faded, becoming one with the buzz on set. Tomorrow was Choti Diwali. A day when she prepared sweets with her daughter, who liked adding sugar and kneading the dough. Pia probably cowered right now in a dingy room or van, blindfolded.

Tara cleared her mind of the image, drew in a steadying breath, and focused on her surroundings. She had to remain watchful.

The neat staged area in front of the camera emerged like an island of calm amid the surrounding buzz and clutter. Karan Virani, the man she'd watched on-screen for more than a decade, stood talking to the *sensei*, laughing out loud. He wore makeup—bruises, dust, and blood— his clothes were torn and disheveled, his white-streaked beard matted with mud, but his stance said he owned the place and loved sharing it with everyone else. He put his hand on the *sensei's* shoulder, and the *sensei* patted his back—like old friends.

For a moment, Tara imagined working opposite a famous star she'd admired for so long, in this beehive of assistants and technicians who moved at random but carried a purpose. Would she have had Pia, though?

What if Pia's kidnappers had already called?

Tara didn't own a watch. She checked the time on her phone. Without it, the minutes seemed endless. The star repeated the same snippet of dialogue, *This is not what I expected from you*, for the fifth time with different light settings, voice modulations, and camera angles. Arnav shot glances her way, checking on her often. She tried to catch his eye long enough to signal to him they should leave. She hadn't felt the jackal's scrutiny—no hint of menace, only a bunch of people busier than waiters at the Blue Bar at midnight.

Despite Arnav's jacket, the freezing air-conditioning seemed to seep into her bones. She stood up and stretched her legs. No one noticed her. The *sensei* and Arnav seemed busy with the action director. If she sneaked out now to get a look at her phone—the kidnappers may have called—Arnav wouldn't notice. Her window of time was short.

She stepped off. She would race to her phone and return before Arnav missed her.

Behind a partition on the site, she heard male voices. Not raised, but the intensity of the conflict unmistakable. She paused for a moment to get her bearings, unsure of the way out.

"You're marrying my mother, but that doesn't give you the right to order me about."

"I'm not telling you what to do. It is common sense—this project will benefit us all, but especially her."

"You're going to tell me what to do for my mother?"

Unable to contain her curiosity, Tara peered through a gap in the partition: Rehaan Virani wrapped a bandage on his hand while speaking to a man in a business suit, a corporate honcho. She recognized the type—a few had frequented the Blue Bar in the past week. Shetty had pointed them out.

The argument went on, Rehaan getting angrier, the other remaining mild, when a third man joined them.

Karan Virani stepped between the suit and Rehaan, and told them to break it up.

"You can argue about this at home." He put a gentle hand on Rehaan's shoulder.

"I don't want him anywhere near my home," Rehaan said, petulant.

"Tough," the suit said. "Your mother will be living with me starting next year."

"This is not the place. An assistant will walk in any minute. The shot is ready." Karan's voice was gentle, reassuring. "Mr. Taneja, we'll see you later."

That was when she smelled it, the fragrance of old wood and cinnamon soaked in alcohol from long ago. A soft menace in the air. The men left, and she was about to enter the partition and follow them, when someone grabbed her elbow.

She knew Arnav's touch, but it still spooked her.

"I told you not to leave my sight." Arnav drew her away and out into open air.

"I think he's here."

"You saw him? Who is it?"

"Not sure." Her heartbeat had changed, as if she'd been inside one of her nightmares of the jackal.

"You didn't get a good look?"

"One of the men in that room. I don't know which."

She told him the names, and it made his expression go taut—jaw clenched, a tightening around his eyes. It had to be that businessman. Taneja.

"We need to find out. I'll try and get you close to each of them, separately, all right?"

Tara nodded, but she wasn't sure how she'd do it. She didn't recognize the jackal, but he knew her. Night had fallen by the time they walked out, Filmistaan reduced to a few lights on the main roads connecting sets hidden by surrounding trees.

Arnav walked her to their vehicle to check her phone, but there were no calls. While returning to the set, they sensed a hubbub within. They navigated the dark, twisted partitions of the structure and met the *sensei*, who was stalking out.

"We'll leave now."

"What's wrong?" Arnav said.

"Most unprofessional. Rehaan Virani flew into one of his rages, destroyed some of the set pieces, and stormed out. Karan Virani followed him, so he doesn't drive in this state."

"And Taneja?"

"Who is that? We're leaving. What a waste of time. The director has canceled the shoot for tonight."

As their car left, Tara shifted closer to Arnav, and held his bruised hand. When he asked her what was wrong, she smiled and shook her head. She sought comfort, unable to shake off the feeling of being watched by hungry, unflinching eyes.

CHAPTER SEVENTY-ONE

MUMBAI DRISHTIKON NEWS

Filmi Bytes

Kittu Virani to throw a lavish Diwali party with her new fiancé

9:30 PM IST 28 October, Mumbai.

The who's who of Bollywood, the business world, and top cricketers are to attend the annual Diwali bash at socialite, interior designer, and star-mom Kittu Virani's residence.

This is where the ageless Kittu, who has recently returned from a quick Bali getaway with her handsome businessman fiancé, is expected to introduce him to her Bollywood friends. Fans are eagerly waiting, not just for the Diwali party starlet selfies with Karan and Rehaan Virani that are sure to flood social media, but a date for the glam wedding as well.

Sources close to the family say this might be a good thing for Taneja, who has been in the news recently for all the wrong reasons. There was police activity at the Aksa beach site following a few gruesome discoveries, which sent the gossip mills churning.

Interestingly, Taneja's name has come up in another investigation regarding a recent dramatic shooting incident at Malwani Police Station, which left one officer dead and another severely hurt, along with injuries to passersby.

We only hope this marriage is as bright and happy for Kittu as her vacay snapshots from Bali (see below the sun-kissed pics from the infinity pool). She'll be wearing two different designer ensembles for the Diwali Pooja and the party afterward, reportedly costing several lakhs each (a gift from guess who?), and along with her legions of fans, we just can't keep calm.

CHAPTER SEVENTY-TWO

He was furious. Women. Putting their hands where they didn't belong. This chit of a woman thought she was so smart—as if she'd pin him down after all this time.

He picked up his buzzing phone. *Uhnna,* as expected.

"My men will stop by tonight with the bunch of sparklers you ordered. You'll have to guide them."

He looked out the window at the farmhouse. He must celebrate it before it vanished, a big Diwali. A grand film with a large cast, and soon it would be gone, like the movie set it used to be, where Dad had first met the Item Number on a film shoot.

"Are you paying attention?" *Uhnna* sounded like a testy old grump.

"Sorry—I thought someone was at the door."

You've got to keep the big man calm, he told himself. *A lot hangs on him getting things perfect.*

"Is everything ready?"

"Yes. I'm alone. I'll tell them what to do, no problem."

The don asked him to hold on for a minute, and his mind drifted to the sparklers. Explosives Bilal would know nothing about, for the climax of the movie.

Item Number would be the difficult part of the cast to procure, but Bilal would swing it. Tell her stories. She'd wonder why it had to be here. Fearing. Rightly so. Bilal would be useful one last time. When a rocket crosses the upper reaches of the atmosphere, the boosters detach one by one before the astronaut can go into space.

"The Malayali is being questioned again."

He loved how *Uhnna* called Shetty the Malayali, as if he himself wasn't one.

"He isn't much use anymore," he said. "If things get worse, he takes the fall."

"That wasn't the original plan. You wanted someone else pinned."

"We both did. No help for it now. You have time to change things around."

The Home Minister had agreed this was the best option. The investigation was in the papers, and the inspector might not shut up. Pin it on Shetty and deal with that pesky inspector later. The commissioner would do his bit, the way he'd done all these years.

"I don't like this, but all right." Maybe *Uhnna* liked Shetty, after all. "You make sure the girl comes in."

"Why can't my men lure her out?" *Uhnna* said. "Far less trouble."

"She has to decide, make up her own mind."

The Item Number had never given him a choice—not at the railway tracks, nor in his bed. He wasn't a monster like her. He let women choose.

"Your money, your rules. She hasn't reported her daughter missing yet, but that could change. We must be careful. They'll send her a little gift today then, as incentive."

"Don't make it gory. There's an election coming soon."

The sooner this mess disappeared, the better. The Home Minister would not like him if the "little gift" turned into a blood-soaked sensation, ammunition in the hands of the opposition party in the state, and the media. That *fattu* had spoken to the papers more than once.

"My men are on the job. You'll get your girl. Unless that boyfriend of hers pokes his nose where it doesn't belong."

"Then he'll add one more to the count. Take your time. You and I both know how this will end."

Choti Diwali tonight. Once Bilal was taken care of, time enough for fun before everything came apart. Proper Diwali the day after. He'd destroy all the journals. The basement workshop would go after he'd used it for the final time—Bilal was already removing the extra equipment, and should be done by evening.

His collection in the cubbyhole remained. Letting that go would be painful. Cleansing hurt.

He pulled them all out, laid them out in their individual ziplock bags. Beads from a necklace, a hook from a bra, a nose ring. Maybe he'd keep them for today. The finale was not for some time yet.

He'd made plans, paid for them. Now he must wait. When in a hurry, slow down, Dad often said.

He put the bags back, but his gaze caught at a piece of paper sticking out. This was before the copies, the diary notes. He slid out the black-and-white photograph, careful not to tear it. It had been stuck in there for a while. Dad and Ma. Him between them, grinning with all his teeth.

He crumpled the photo, preparing to toss it into the trash, but no. He was cleaning things up. Must do it right. He scrabbled around in his drawer, snatched up a lighter, and gloated over the burning photo. He held it till it singed his fingers. He would do the same to the Item Number, after he'd made her pay. He knew what she was afraid of.

Diwali, the night of victory of good over evil. Of light over darkness. Oh, there would be light. So much light.

CHAPTER SEVENTY-THREE

TARA

Back at the dojo, Tara snatched up her phone, catching it mid-ring. An unknown number. Heart beating hard, Tara put the call on speaker, switched on the recorder, only to hear a familiar voice ask, "Tara?"

"Zoya! Where have you been? I've called you a hundred times since morning."

Tara turned to find Arnav standing right behind her. There was a pause on the line. "Mumbai."

"You're here? Have you heard about—?"

"Can't talk long. They are bringing Pia here."

"What? How do you—"

"I'll call you when I know more. Keep the phone with you."

The line dropped. Tara tried dialing back but was told the number didn't exist. How did Zoya know where Pia was? Was she already with Rasool?

Arnav reached out to hold her with his good arm, and she buried her face in his shirt.

"If she rings again," Arnav said, "tell her to get Rasool to hold back."

"Why?"

"Trust me on this. Ask her to share the location, but leave the rest to us."

If Rasool's men found Pia, they would clash with Vijayan's gang. No one wanted that.

The phone rang once more, and Tara went through swift motions—switching on the recorder, the speaker.

"Zoya? Where are you?"

"Do you want your daughter or not?" A gruff male voice answered.

"Yes . . . yes." Tara struggled to keep her voice steady. "Is Pia with you? Is she all right?"

"We're sending you proof. It should be at your door."

"Let me talk to her."

Tara said hello a few times but the phone had gone silent. Arnav rushed out, and Tara followed. A dojo staff was coming up the stairs.

"Someone sent this box for you." He handed a parcel wrapped in newspaper to Tara.

"Did *you* receive it? Who gave it to you?"

"A street child from the neighborhood. Didn't recognize him. He said, *Give it to Tara*, and left."

Tara was about to tear it open, but Arnav gently pried it from her hands. "Let me check first."

He weighed the package in his hand, examined it from all sides, and, after taking it into the dojo kitchen, wedged a kitchen knife into one of its corners. Inside was a large, twisted hank of hair, tied with Pia's favorite red scrunchie. Tara felt the air leave the room as she strained to breathe in big, harsh gulps.

Her phone rang moments later.

"You must come alone if you want her alive."

"Is she fine? Is she—"

"We'll be in touch." The man hung up.

"Hello?"

Arnav was on his phone, asking if the call could be traced.

"They didn't speak about your case." Tara looked into Arnav's haunted eyes when he cut the call. "It's me they want now."

CHAPTER SEVENTY-FOUR

BILAL

Bilal didn't like it one bit. It frightened him, all this spying, but yesterday, one of those men had turned up and asked for the boy. Said he had a phone.

That call was crucial. The boy had dismissed Bilal and stayed at the farmhouse the whole evening. Never a good sign.

Bilal had escaped with the device hidden under dirty clothes. His hand trembled as he plugged it in and, slipping on his headphones, settled in his chair.

First came the boy's screams. Bilal's own voice, soothing him, taking him a cup of chocolate. Their chat about Bilal's assignment to bring in the Item Number, his report on the progress, with a request to take it easy, that ended in an explosion from the boy—*Stop telling me what to do.*

The morning noises, rustles of newspaper, windows opened and shut. Bilal, announcing *Uhnna's* man, and the boy, moments later, on the phone.

"I'm supposed to call you, *Uhnna*, not the other way around," the boy grumbled into the phone.

Bilal flinched. The boy was growing reckless. You did not use such words with a man who ran a multibillion-dollar business, spoke to chief ministers and national leaders every day, and could get people shot from thousands of miles away with a word. Bilal ought to warn the boy but wasn't sure how.

The boy's recorded voice spoke into Bilal's headphones.

"He is loyal to me. Don't worry about it. He will bring her." The boy was speaking of Bilal. Couldn't be anyone else. And there could be only one *her*.

"She'll be missed, which is why we will do it on Choti Diwali. No one else knows where I am—I've taken leave from work."

Each year during the Diwali week, the boy held his parties for one. Some wrapped up with a shower of dried rose petals. Most ended in blood.

"Yes. All of it. Ask your men to come prepared."

Bilal took off his earphones, but the words echoed. He sat with his head in his hands. Later, he walked out of his den. He shouldn't have returned.

Now that he had, he would trust the boy on principle, and protect him till the end. But not without preparations of his own. He scrolled down his phone to look for Rasool's number.

CHAPTER SEVENTY-FIVE

ARNAV

Arnav didn't know so many things—a refined kind of torture, not knowing.

Arnav knew of Shinde's end, and the sort of desolation he'd witnessed with his parents when Asha committed suicide.

On this Choti Diwali afternoon, he felt as if he stood at the edge of another abyss. The evening ahead might define the rest of his life—a new beginning, or a devastating finale.

That hair sent to Tara was indeed Pia's. Tara had confirmed it. So they had to assume Pia was in Mumbai. The demands had changed between the first call and the next—from making him back off from the case to demanding that Tara go alone to meet them.

The abductors hadn't called since last night, nor had Ali's friend been given charge of Pia. Arnav couldn't put his finger on what was wrong, but he required a plan and a team in place.

On the chair across from him sat Tukaram, his skin dusty, unshaven, a sight unusual enough that Arnav hadn't recognized him at first. With Arnav's broken shoulder, he needed someone to drive him in case of a confrontation with the kidnappers. He could think of no one better than the thin old sub-inspector, the star of dozens of police chases. Tukaram looked stern, different from his usual jovial manner—he'd come straight from Shinde's funeral.

Naik stood beside Tukaram, looking a little less worn out, but only a little. From downstairs came the gong announcing the start of yet another karate class.

"You have quite the setup here," Tukaram said.

"Safety in numbers. If either of you opt to back out at any moment, I'll understand. Why don't you sit down, too, Naik?" Arnav pointed to the extra chair he'd brought in from Tara's room.

"You said you have undeniable proof against Commissioner Joshi," Tukaram said.

Arnav passed them the printouts Nandini had sent. "These are the accounts Senior Inspector Shinde maintained over the years."

When Arnav had finished explaining the connections between Commissioner Joshi, the don Vijayan, Shetty, and Shinde, both of them looked up from the papers.

"We haven't found further evidence to implicate Shetty for Neha Chaubey's murder," Naik said, "but Joshi sir says that murder was Shetty's doing, as well as the shoot-out, and your accident. Shetty needs to confess to it. We'll be arresting him soon."

"Commissioner Joshi wants to bury Shetty so he himself remains unscathed," Arnav said, and went on to lay out all the evidence on his board. The murders over the decades, the attempts to cover them up, the sequins, Tara, Pia, the van, the jewelry store screenshots. The pictures of the don, the politician, the Bollywood family including Taneja, the police officers. The conversation Tara witnessed between Taneja and Rehaan Virani, and her suspicions.

Tukaram said, "All of this is circumstantial. Suspicious, but none of it will stand up in court. You're talking about a mafia don, a senior Mumbai police officer, a Bollywood star, a businessman, and now the Home Minister, in the same breath. These families can afford the most expensive lawyers in India."

"The Home Minister alone can ask a commissioner for transfers within the department. These documents show a clear conflict of interest, and at the very least, the Anti-Corruption Bureau would investigate."

For the ACB, a high-ranking police officer with a money trail leading to a don and a Home Minister was cause for concern.

"Shinde also recorded phone calls. I have them copied here."

"We have a case for corruption against Joshi for sure." Tukaram leaned back in his chair after he had heard a few calls. "Maybe even Mhatre. In fact, the tall man in this jewelry shop screenshot could easily be Mhatre in disguise. You could make sure by showing pictures to the witnesses."

"I don't think Mhatre sir is involved," Naik said.

The vehemence in Naik's voice surprised Arnav, though he had to admit he found it hard to imagine Mhatre would get Pia kidnapped. Then again, he hadn't caught on to Shinde's double life, either.

Before Arnav could speak, Tukaram challenged Naik, "And why do you think not?"

"Posing for some pictures with Joshi sir and Shinde sir doesn't make him a culprit."

"He has the means, the opportunity, and most importantly, motive. He hates women," Tukaram said.

Tara knocked on the door and entered. She held a laden tray. "I hope everyone likes *roti-sabji*, because the *sensei's* kitchen cooks simple fare."

Tara had clung to that hank of Pia's hair for a long while, until Arnav explained she could help by making Tukaram and Naik feel welcome. Arnav had nothing to offer them in return for the favor he would ask.

Arnav made introductions. At this moment, scrubbed clean of all makeup, wearing a pair of jeans and one of his shirts, Tara was a beleaguered mother, but not defeated. Tukaram seemed to warm up to her.

"The culprit is secondary," Tukaram began the discussion. "Our priority is to bring your daughter back. We have to tell the constables we're going to rescue a little girl."

Naik agreed. Over the early dinner, Naik, Tukaram, and Arnav picked men for the evening's operation to storm Pia's abductors, once Arnav received confirmed intel. Zoya had promised to call with more information, and so had Ali.

They couldn't recruit too many constables without alerting Commissioner Joshi—not at such short notice, for an unauthorized raid.

"If all else fails, I must go to wherever they call me. It is"—Tara glanced across the room at him—"our daughter."

"You may not need to," Arnav said. "We'll receive Pia's location soon."

For the first time since he'd woken up in the hospital bed, he saw Tara smile. It was wan, faded, but it was real. He pictured this smile on Tara as their daughter laughed between them. Mentally, he crossed his fingers for Ali to come through once again, with Pia's whereabouts this time.

As they finished dinner, Tara's phone chimed its musical notes. Everyone sat up straighter. An unknown number. Arnav set up the recorder, and Tara snatched up the phone, putting it on speaker.

"They're taking Pia to a warehouse in Andheri." Zoya's whisper sounded hoarse and disembodied. "They'll wait for further instructions. They'll be there soon, Rasool says. I'll send you the info now. Hurry."

CHAPTER SEVENTY-SIX

TARA

Tara fretted in the rear seat of the car, Arnav by her side. The thin old Sub-Inspector Tukaram had driven like he was in one of those loud races in small cars, then melted into the night to join Naik. They were parked close to the Andheri address Zoya had given them, and from the conversations she heard on Arnav's phone, Naik's constables had the place surrounded.

The car stank of stale food and petrol. Its air-conditioning whirred but did not work, making the interior sultry. Tara sweated inside the saree blouse chosen at the last minute. The blouse hung loose where it was supposed to be tight, and bit at her armpits. It was already soaked through. Arnav had told her they wouldn't need it, but she'd disagreed; what if they did? What if Pia wasn't at the location? Tara couldn't wear a pair of jeans. The jackal had a thing for women in sarees.

She wiped her leaking eyes. Pia loved her hair. Cutting it that short, along with her scrunchie, they would have yanked at her head . . . Tara stamped that thought down. Pia was all right. Safe. It was hair.

Tara stared at Arnav's profile—his bruised jaw, his bandaged shoulder, all stiff, the veins on his forearm, and his grip on her hand as he spoke into the Bluetooth—he hadn't let go of her for a moment all the while they'd been in the car. She'd been angry with him, but he might have been right, after all.

The kidnappers had not mentioned Arnav's investigation this time. Why the change of plans? Who was behind it all? Was it Taneja? Had he noticed her at the movie set and changed his mind?

"You should have stayed at the dojo," Arnav said. "I could have gone with them—only Naik and Tukaram have guns. We have no police radio."

I could go with you, Tara wanted to say, but knew his answer. She was not a trained officer like Naik. Arnav had been nothing but kind to her, and in his gaze she'd seen a mixture of accusation, guilt, and suffering each time she'd insisted on preparing to meet the abductors. He didn't understand—for her, Pia was her very breath. Not just her daughter, but her savior from another time. She wouldn't hesitate for a second if she could save Pia's life by giving up her own. Pia had another parent now.

Tara let her glance linger on Arnav—the shadows under his eyes, the sling and cast on his arm. Beyond him, the alley stretched dark. Distant Diwali lights twinkled on balconies, but she could only see Pia in her mind's eye—the entire day it had taken to deliver her, how she was torn apart when Pia came, holding that tiny squirming body in her arms, counting the minute little fingers and toes, at her breast, suckling, how she'd laughed when her sleeping daughter had smacked her lips, like an old woman after a hearty meal.

She held on to Arnav's firm hand on hers, trying to fight off her panic. What if they couldn't get Pia?

The phone buzzing on her lap made her start. It was again an unknown number. Arnav pushed the phone into her hands.

"Lower the volume and put it on speaker," Arnav said, so she did.

"Tara?" a woman's voice, barely a whisper.

"Zoya?"

"The place I told you. Don't let anyone in there. It is a decoy, rigged with bombs."

CHAPTER SEVENTY-SEVEN

He dressed with care for Choti Diwali. He would celebrate with the Item Number tonight.

The right clothes put you in the mind space you wished to be in. In his white shirt paired with dark jeans, and his favorite blue cap, he was the king of calm. Of control. He wasn't scared, because he had prepared well. Bilal was on his way, and so was she, all agog for those papers. He pictured the Item Number, sitting in her car, phone in hand, scrolling through rubbish.

Things hadn't all gone as planned. That *pandu* was still around, but not for much longer. *Uhnna* suspected that his plans had leaked—he was taking a detour via Andheri. If the *pandu* didn't fall for it, he would follow the little girl and her mother right into the trap here—pay for all the trouble he'd caused.

With *Uhnna*'s men guarding the farmhouse and the fireworks arranged for tomorrow, his soul was ready for its cleansing. It had better be worth it because it had taken all his savings. Gone. To *Uhnna*. He didn't mind—everything had a price, and he was willing to pay. This far, *Uhnna* had proven himself as good as his word, unlike that other don, Bilal's man. He scoffed to himself, setting his cap at a jaunty angle. *Happy Diwali to you and your family,* he crooned.

Bhoot Chaturdashi was here. Time to welcome the Item Number.

His phone tinkled, a merry, merry sound he'd set as his ringtone today on his special phone, and he called out a cheery hello. The man at the other end would never know him, but would obey.

"The kid is being brought in. Where do you want her?"

"Below the theater room. Make sure she can't move or speak."

"She won't last long."

A twinge: he had no quarrel with the child. Maybe he did? She would grow up into a woman, wouldn't she? Best she disappeared, along with her mother.

Her mother.

He would take his time with that one, after the Item Number was gone. She didn't know how much she resembled the Item Number. Could have been her body double. Well, she was, at that. Not even a shadow of the Item Number could be allowed to remain in this world, especially not one who thought she was smart enough to catch him.

Tomorrow. She would be the last one, the one to bring him freedom, on Diwali night proper, the festival ending in flames and those sparklers *Uhnna* had sent him.

CHAPTER SEVENTY-EIGHT

ARNAV

Arnav punched his seat, forgetting himself in his frustration. Pain coursed through his shoulder, but he didn't care.

"Can we call the bomb squad?" He spoke into his Bluetooth.

What if Pia was in there and Zoya was wrong? If she was right, though, he would be risking lives. Arnav made rapid decisions at work, but he'd never been in operations involving family.

"Not without alerting certain people." Naik meant Joshi.

"What now?" Tara tugged her hand from Arnav's grip. "If she isn't here . . ."

Arnav waited for Tukaram to return to the driver's seat. The abductors had prepared the warehouse; they were watching it. Now they knew Tara wasn't alone.

Tukaram returned to the car. Tara's ringtone sang, the sound Arnav dreaded and anticipated. Tara switched the call to speaker, and Arnav pinged Naik to locate the caller.

"Come to Borivali Station. Ten p.m."

"Where's Pia?"

"Don't be late."

"What exit? Where?"

"The Indraprastha Shopping Center Gate. Come alone or you won't see her." The line beeped.

Naik wasn't able to trace their location. They had chosen the sprawling Borivali Station again, with its multiple exits. That meeting point would be jam-packed with commuters and last-minute Diwali shoppers.

"We don't have time," Tara said. "You've given me the watch. You can follow me."

The watch contained a GPS tracker, but it was no guarantee for Tara's safety.

"She's right." Tukaram started the car. "If we don't leave now, we won't make it to Borivali Station by ten p.m."

"OK." Arnav made up his mind, dialing Ali.

"Ji, saab."

"Where's your friend now?"

"Outside main Mumbai. Got cut off before he could say where. They have the girl."

"We need to know where she is. Now."

"Give me a few minutes, *saab*. I'll call you. I'll forward his live location if he manages to send it."

Arnav checked his watch. It showed 9:43 p.m. Seventeen minutes to Tara's appointment with the abductors.

"You have ten."

Tukaram revved the car. His face grim, gray mustache drooping over pursed lips, Arnav's old friend steered the vehicle through impossibly small gaps. Arnav tried to calm Tara, who alternately whispered, closed her eyes, and urged them to go faster—couldn't they see it was already late? She could not, would not be late.

Arnav had forever been enchanted by Tara's eyes, large, long-lashed, hiding nothing. When he'd first seen her so many years ago, she was on a raised stage—the most graceful of the bunch of women in gaudy clothes under flashing strobe lights. He'd been drawn to her gaze, which was so far removed from the lewd gestures her hips and breasts made. Eyes that had seen suffering, that called for help, but knew none would come.

He glanced into those eyes now as often as he could in the half-light of the car racing through the by-lanes of Borivali, weaving around stray firecrackers and children playing with lit sparklers.

Stuck behind an open truck filled with Diwali revelers and a tangle of bicycles at a crossing that would lead them to the main road, Tukaram stepped out to clear the way.

"If anything goes wrong," Tara whispered, "promise me you'll take care of Pia."

"We'll know where Pia is. My informer will call any minute."

"Promise me."

"Nothing will go wrong." He had to believe it.

He'd hugged his sister all those years ago and told her he would grow up and protect her, make sure she was never hurt again. He'd found her body hanging from the ceiling less than an hour later.

His entire life, he'd fought for victims. Terrified of another loss, he'd run from attachments, the merest whiff of family. He strained to get the words past his choked throat but failed. Arnav kissed Tara instead, holding on to the one still moment amid the din of the crackling radio and his desperation. In that kiss, his touch on her cheek wet with tears, all was said, and he knew she understood.

Tukaram jogged back, and they took off. Arnav checked the GPS on the sub-inspector's phone stuck to the dashboard—they would arrive in three minutes. It was 9:48 p.m.

Ali was supposed to call by 9:53 p.m. If he had the information, Tara wouldn't leave the car.

He confirmed with Naik—she and her men had followed in unmarked cars, two minutes away.

Tara's phone rang. He hoped it was Zoya, with Pia's location.

Tara was about to accept the call when Arnav grasped her hand. "If it is them, ask to speak to her."

He swiped the screen and put the call on speaker.

"Come alone." The disembodied words from the phone filled the vehicle, the tone steeped in menace. Arnav longed to throttle the owner of that voice, but all he did was squeeze Tara's trembling hand, and mouth the word "Ask."

"How do I know you have her?" Tara's voice wavered, but she managed to say the words. Silence followed her question.

"Ma! Let me go . . . Ma!" A shrill voice rang out before it was silenced. His daughter. The very first time he'd heard her.

"Don't be late. Indraprastha Entrance." The line went dead.

9:50 p.m.

They definitely had Pia with them. If Ali sent in Pia's live location in the next three minutes, they had a chance—Naik was stationed nearby.

"Hold on," Arnav said. "We'll get her position."

"They have her." Tara's voice was steady. "They want me. I'll go to them."

And what of me, he yearned to ask her. *Do you not need both Pia and me? You'll walk away once again, but what do you want me to do without you?*

He merely said, "How do you know they will let Pia go? What if they take both of you?"

According to Ali, Pia was outside Mumbai, not here at Borivali Station.

"That's our daughter." Tara grabbed the door handle and fought to open it.

"It is 9:52. Give it two more minutes." Arnav willed Ali to call but his screen remained dark. Borivali Station near the Indraprastha Entrance was a rapid deluge of people, especially on Choti Diwali night. Naik had a man monitoring the CCTV cameras at all entries and exits, but it was small comfort to Arnav. He double-checked the tracker watch and its connected app on his phone.

"It will take me time to walk to the entrance." Tara yanked at the handle, but Tukaram had locked the rear doors.

"Please, Tara. Wait." Arnav gripped her arm, pain in his broken shoulder dizzying him for a moment.

"We'll lose her." Tara sobbed once, swallowed, pled with her eyes.

9:54 p.m. No message from Ali. If Tara left any later, she wouldn't reach the gate by 10:00.

"Naik is asking what we should do," Tukaram said. "Her men are spaced between here and Indraprastha. Do you have Pia's location?"

"Unlock the door," Arnav said to Tukaram. "Tell Naik."

Tara would be lost within seconds—the only way to navigate the crowd here without being trampled was to slide into the general direction you wanted to go and let the momentum of crushing bodies propel you forward.

He turned to her. "Watch and listen. Try to remember. The men's faces. Voices. Notice everything. When you're afraid, breathe."

He struggled to tell her how he felt. No words came. A tremulous smile and a teary glance from her, and she stepped out. The noisy commuters and shoppers formed a fast-moving river, and she was soon swallowed up.

He gave the tracker app to Tukaram so they could both watch it.

Less than five minutes later, Naik admitted on the speaker, "My men lost her. We should have brought more constables."

A hundred constables wouldn't have made a difference in that massive surge of rushing humans.

"They're moving now." Tukaram honked to clear his way. "They must have grabbed her before she reached the entrance to be able to leave this fast."

Arnav should have held on to her the last time she ran, tracked her, found her, and kept her safe. Kept Pia safe. The terror-stricken cry for her mother, right before it was smothered, rang through him.

His phone pinged with a message. Ali had sent his friend's live location. Madh Island. But it was three minutes too late.

CHAPTER SEVENTY-NINE

BILAL

Bilal wished the boy didn't want the policeman's girlfriend brought in. The boy's moods had changed lately. Bilal had tried but failed to reason with him about that poor girl, and her mother. Granted, the boy had not specifically asked for the little girl. It was Vijayan. But now it was done, Bilal couldn't bring himself to think any further. The boy had asked him to remove most of the instruments. The table remained. And the saw.

The boy's silences were not friendly, his lips curled in a sneer when he thought no one was watching. Bilal watched all the time, though. He was glad he'd spoken to Rasool.

Rasool's gunmen arrived with the movers shifting furniture to the boy's Bandra apartment. The others left, but Rasool's men stayed back—hiding in Bilal's room. Five of them, scraggly but polite, drinking tea, biding their time, the sixth acting as Bilal's assistant.

Bilal couldn't take his assistant into the workshop without making the boy paranoid, but the crook helped carry the implements out as Bilal placed them in the backyard—knives, saws, drills, spades—not disposing of the items as per the boy's instructions, but storing them on the property where the boy would never find them. Bilal would serve the boy till the end, but only as the boy deserved.

The day's chores done, Bilal led in the Item Number, under no illusion about her fate. He had known this irate, evil woman, draped in a blue shimmery saree, for years.

For so long, he'd cleaned up after the fact—in answer to an incoherent call for help from the boy. This was the first he knew of, beforehand, but he didn't regret it. He had told the boy he would escort her to the living room. No farther. He had left a sturdy wheelchair for the boy to move the Item Number down to his workshop.

Even now, on this evening that could end it all, Bilal would do what he knew best. Hide.

CHAPTER EIGHTY

—————

ARNAV

Arnav watched the tiny dot move on his phone screen. The trackers were innocuous, useful things, bought online. He handed them out to his informers, to be worn when on assignments for him. At least two drug addicts owed their lives to the trackers, leading Arnav to them before they could come to harm, but the devices were not reliable, and tended to stop working if banged about. He hadn't dared use anything more sophisticated, fearing discovery.

Naik had received Tara's location and tracked it as well. "Not sure exactly which car or van she's in, sir."

Arnav compared notes. Naik was closer to Tara's vehicle on the highway.

"You follow her. Keep your distance. I'll head to the other target. They've taken Pia to Madh Island."

He was torn. Logically, the abductors should take both mother and daughter to the same destination if they aimed to hand Pia over to Tara. But the highway didn't lead to Madh Island.

"Madh Island," Tukaram said. "I told you it was Mhatre. He has his family home there."

"It simply isn't true. I have confirmed information he's not on Madh Island at the moment," Naik said over the speaker. "I can't tell you right now how I know, sir."

"Where is Mhatre's bungalow?" Arnav turned to Tukaram. "You said you've been there?"

"Close to the Dana Pani beach."

"Pia is located beyond the Atharva Tech Park." Arnav pointed at the live location Ali's contact had sent. "Here, at the edge of the densest portion of the Dharmapala mangroves."

"Isn't this near the site of the Versova case, sir?" Naik said.

"It is not far, but it lies across Versova Creek," Arnav said. "The map shows a building. A bungalow or a farmhouse."

"Not Mhatre's. His is on the west side." Tukaram adjusted his rear-view mirror as he stepped on the accelerator. "Dharmapala is on the east side of Madh Island. On the way there, we'll pass close to Malwani Police Station."

Under normal circumstances, Arnav could have rallied officers from the Malwani Police Station. They would reach the farmhouse much faster. Whoever had grabbed Tara had at least one or even two men in his car. If Arnav's suspicion of the abductors' underworld connections was correct, they would all be armed. And not too shabbily.

Naik was the only armed sub-inspector in the other team. Junior constables didn't carry guns. The five men with her, two of her constables and three from Tukaram, would only be useful when making arrests. Not before.

Arnav's phone rang, bringing their conversation to a halt. He placed it on speaker so everyone could hear.

"*Saab*, I just heard from one of my team that *Bhai* has sent men to guard someone near Dharmapala."

Ali's *Bhai*. Rasool Mohsin.

"Where, exactly? And how many?"

"Six, *saab*. Can't ask questions without making them suspicious."

Ali was right. If he was found out, he wouldn't last too long.

"How many men with your friend?"

"Four, I think." Ali's voice took on an oddly flat note. "Other than my friend. *Saab*, for his help I'll need to pay him five times what he's getting from the other side."

"Don't worry about payment. For him, or you. I need updates."

Rasool Mohsin had posted six men somewhere in Dharmapala—it could easily be at the location where they held Pia. Four men were with Ali's friend, guarding Pia, and they had a connection with Vijayan. He had to assume a gang war could break out any moment. Even if half those men packed guns, he and Tukaram would be outnumbered.

"We'll need more men, sir," Naik broke in, echoing his thoughts.

"I could make a call," Tukaram said, "but it would be faster to get men from Malwani Police Station. Even a few senior constables and sub-inspectors would do. We'll require permission from Mhatre, though."

"We should call Mhatre sir," Naik said. "Please believe me on this. He is not involved."

Maybe not with the kidnapping, but what about everything else? Arnav recalled the photographs among Shinde's papers—the picture of Mhatre, Joshi, and Taneja, champagne glasses in hand.

"He'll alert Joshi," Arnav said.

"Trust me, he won't, sir."

Trust. A word Arnav did his best to stay away from.

"I can't explain for now, but I'm certain about him, sir."

His head buzzing with painkillers, Arnav gritted his teeth against the shards of agony moving down his arm. The road ahead was a scattershot of nighttime headlights.

Mind desperate for answers, Arnav considered his options. To have faith in his assistant. And his boss, contrary to his better judgment. Or risk losing Tara and Pia.

He'd trusted his sister and she'd committed suicide on his watch. Shinde had betrayed him every step of the way. Tara had gone away. But it had been worth it to love and trust—Asha, Shinde, Tara. Asha was in too much pain. Shinde saved his life. Tara had a good reason to leave.

Tara and his unknown daughter—worth fighting for, risking his trust again, now and later.

"Go ahead," he said to Naik, hoping he hadn't put his family in further jeopardy while trying to rescue them, "but stay on Tara's trail."

"Yes, sir."

"Find out who the bungalow belongs to. It doesn't seem to have a name or address on the map."

In the heavy silence that followed, Arnav watched as Tukaram navigated the congested Diwali traffic.

"Naik must be right." Tukaram glanced at Arnav before focusing back on the road.

"I sure hope so."

"You're in this because of your girlfriend and daughter. I'll retire next month with nothing to lose. But this will cost her if she's wrong. Naik is sticking her neck out."

Arnav had considered it before—but only about the risk to Naik, and his appreciation for her help. Tukaram had framed it well: his assistant wouldn't call Mhatre unless she knew certain facts he didn't.

His turmoil calmed, Arnav focused on the job ahead. He inspected his Glock—he might have to use it soon. Small enough to carry and big enough to fight with, but even with its lower recoil, it would still be the very devil for his broken shoulder. The shoot-out with Shinde returned to him in technicolor, how he'd flinched and missed, the blood and ringing silence amid the noise. Arnav took a steadying breath. One-armed, he had to shoot slower, keep extra-steady on the trigger. No flinches no matter how much it hurt. He'd come prepared, though, and packed reloads. This felt like the early days of his career, when shoot-outs were commonplace in certain zones of Mumbai. This time, his world was at stake. Arnav felt the twist of dread in his stomach.

"We'll get them," Tukaram answered his unvoiced thoughts.

"We must."

"This Tara . . . you love her, right?"

Arnav shocked himself by snorting with laughter at the old man's question. He'd never taken Tukaram for a romantic. In view of what was about to go down in the coming hour, he saw no sense in lying to Tukaram. Or himself.

"Yes." That one word settled inside him, fitting like a bullet within a chamber.

When you close yourself off from people because they might end up hurting you, you shut out not only the hurt, but life itself. You have no control over what will happen to you, but you can choose whether to risk it all, or retreat. Given a chance, he would take a gamble at love again, make a start this Diwali. He could only hope he wouldn't lose.

Naik called. He put her on speaker.

"We might all be headed in the same direction, sir," Naik said. "They turned left toward Madh Island. We'll arrive ahead of you."

They were moving Tara to the farmhouse Pia was at. Tukaram smiled, a fierce grin, without taking his eyes off the road.

Arnav's other phone flashed with a message from Ali: *Friend still there. Girl is thrashing about.*

Pia's desperate cry over the phone echoed in his mind. At thirteen, he'd been a child, terrified and clueless when Asha ended her life. It must be so much worse for his daughter—to be snatched, gagged, and have her hair shorn off.

"Arrange a doctor on standby," he requested Naik over the speaker.

Arnav crossed his fingers—*Let Pia be OK. Let me reunite her with Tara.* He heard Naik pass on the message to one of her constables.

"Did we pin down the bungalow owner?"

"Seems old." Naik paused. "A constable is searching the records."

"Naik?"

"I spoke to him, sir." She sounded hesitant. She meant Mhatre.

"And?"

"We'll have reinforcements soon. I assured him we have evidence for further action. He'll keep this to himself. The station is not under his direct command at the moment, so he can't talk to the inspectors on the phone. He's heading there."

If Mhatre was helping them, that took him off the suspect pool. The jackal was someone else.

The car would soon turn onto Madh-Marve, the tree-lined road reputedly haunted by a ghost-woman in bridal finery. The images of the disintegrating body at Aksa and the decapitated woman stuffed in the black faux leather suitcase flashed before his eyes.

Tara. He had to reach her. He stared at the map and blinked. He couldn't spot her signal.

He asked Tukaram to dial Naik. Her voice shook as she said hello.

"I don't see her, Naik. You?"

"They turned toward the Versova jetty, sir. We lost her signal."

CHAPTER EIGHTY-ONE

TARA

The stench brought her around.

Tara had calmly walked between the two men who had escorted her into a large gray van, permitted them to search her and take away her phone, but when they didn't respond to her questions about Pia, she'd asked them to let her speak with her daughter or stop the vehicle.

When she'd tried the door handle, one of the thugs had bound her hands behind her, silent and businesslike. Seconds later, the other smothered her with a rough, sweet-smelling cloth. She gasped at a pin-prick at her shoulder. The last thought as she struggled with numbing drowsiness was Arnav. Was he still tracking her?

And now, over her dry mouth, a gag that tasted chemical, grassy. Nausea roiled within, and the seat moved in a way no car should.

Based on the noise of the motor and the metal bottom digging into her back, she was in a small boat. The stink came from the water around her. She didn't want to alert the men who chatted on their phones in anxious bursts of quiet Malayalam. She resisted the urge to struggle. Her hands, still tied, had gone numb. Worse, she couldn't feel Arnav's watch at her wrist.

Tamping down rising hysteria, she strove to figure out where she was.

When you're afraid, breathe. Notice everything.

Were they taking her to Pia, or away? Where was the jackal?

Once, long years ago, she'd boarded the ferry from Versova jetty to Madh with Arnav. His bike was allowed on the ferry, and it was barely five minutes before they'd hit the other side and ridden off to catch the shooting of a movie in a Madh Island bungalow.

A dull light shone from the front. She'd been left near the back, like a sack of goods. They were traveling along, not across, a canal. Ghostly trees on both sides reached their arms over the gloomy waters. The night was alive with the call of mating bullfrogs, a noise she knew from the mangrove marshes near her village in West Bengal.

A few minutes passed, Tara now shivering despite the sultry air. Whatever they had drugged her with had worn off, leaving behind nausea, headache, and the quaking.

The boat's engine died. It glided onto the bank. The men stepped off. They lifted her, but stumbled and dropped her back into the boat with a thud. She let out a muffled cry.

"Get up and walk." The tallest of the three dragged her up. With her hands trussed, she lost her balance and crashed again. Her legs hurt with the fall.

The men consulted between themselves in Malayalam, and one of them reached out to untie her hands. He dragged her out of the boat.

"Walk." The man shoved her, and Tara blundered forward, about to upchuck her guts, her head heavy.

In the dark, she grabbled for her watch but couldn't find it. She silently called to Ma Kaali. *Protect Pia. Lead me to her. Bring us help.* She staggered and nearly fell again. When a man hauled her up, she sagged against him, taking him by surprise, landing on top as he sank into the mud beside the narrow, scanty track. The others rushed in, pulling them up, cursing.

They trudged toward dim lights that outlined a large building beyond the trees.

In her other life, Tara had often lightened her drunken clients' pockets. *Part of the trade,* Zoya had told her. Tara hadn't planned on applying that long-forgotten skill, but she wasn't one to lose an opportunity. Using the pretext of fixing her mud-spattered clothes, which had come undone, she tucked the item she'd filched into the waist of her saree. She'd managed to switch it off, and hoped the thug wouldn't notice his phone missing anytime soon.

CHAPTER EIGHTY-TWO

He smiled to himself. The Item Number was here—not knowing she wouldn't leave. She used to be a sensation in her time, the queen of item numbers, thrusting her breasts at Bollywood male stars far older than her at one point, and eventually with younger newcomers, till she lost the right shape for sexy dance videos.

He sized her up from behind the curtains, where Bilal had left the wheelchair. It would come in handy later.

She'd worn the blue saree like he'd specified, and stood in the room that was once his father's study, drumming her ringed fingers on the mantelpiece, scrolling through her phone. Her body had bloated in places, shrunk in others, despite all the surgical procedures she didn't tell the world about. The outfit looked ridiculous on her—the blouse too small, the saree lying oddly because of her thickened waist. Why had she terrified him all this while? She had but one bargaining chip. He should have devised a way around it a long time ago.

She assumed he was giving away this place so she could build a resort here, in exchange for a nondisclosure agreement. She trusted Bilal because he'd been nice to her, ever respectful. She had come alone—her first mistake. Bilal had driven her.

"You're here."

"Let's get this over with." She didn't look up from her phone. "I need to do a million things for Diwali. Make sure you're on time."

Always giving orders. That would stop soon.

"Why all this drama? Wear this, go there. You could've signed it and brought it along tomorrow," she said.

"You don't remember this saree?"

"You've gone totally nuts, I can see. You sent it to me with Bilal. Why would I remember it?"

Either you don't remember or you're pretending. Either way it will be fun to remind you.

Bilal had done an excellent job this time, even though he refused to be part of it any further. Pity he had to go.

He took himself to his father's old seat. "Not before we reach an understanding."

"We have. You sign the dotted line. I'll never open my mouth about the one thing you care about—it is all written there. This place should have been mine to begin with."

He liked it when she was like this—worked up, but trying to cover it with her superior air.

"Sit down."

"Don't you dare take that tone with me."

"The papers are here." He gestured to them on the table. "If you want them signed, you can sit down."

She did, and it was her second mistake. Never give up power.

He rose. "A drink?"

"I'm not here to sit and drink to the old times with you."

"The old times?" He poured the whiskey into two glasses. "You mean the day you first walked in here?"

He needed to take her face off, the lips that had grazed his stomach, the hands that had grabbed his butt at his fifteenth birthday party, the feet she squeezed his throat with as she came. He wanted them severed. She was the original Item Number. She would convulse through each second of losing her hands and feet. He would waltz on the floor slippery with her blood.

"The world thinks you're such a nice man. Now look at you."

"You don't need to look at me." He stood behind her. "Here. You know your single malt."

He clinked glasses, and watched her down her drink. Once he'd stuck in the injection *Uhnna* kept him supplied with, and taken away her treasured phone, she'd come truly awake. Fun times could begin.

CHAPTER EIGHTY-THREE

ARNAV

Arnav secured the sling on his shoulder tighter, till it hurt. Damn the woman—he'd asked her to hold on a minute longer. Now he'd lost the dot on the screen that showed him where she was. Arnav paused. He could damn himself, but not Tara. He'd abandoned her. Been unable to rescue Pia. Put Tara in danger.

Time to fix his mistakes. If the men had taken her to Versova, he could only assume they'd brought her across the waters onto Madh.

"We're quite close now," Tukaram said, peering at the map on the phone with Pia's location. He lowered the window. The noise of crickets, and air laden with the stink of rotten vegetation floated in.

Their headlights sliced the darkness, showing an unpaved, tree-flanked road. Tara's signal on the screen remained dark.

"Stop here. Kill the light."

Arnav listened for vehicle noises ahead, but all was quiet. By his watch, they'd driven for about an hour.

The twisting road led to a dead end, and the map showed a building between the trees. Behind the building, more vegetation and the Malad creek. Pia was in there. And, he hoped with all his being, Tara.

His phone buzzed with an unknown number. He answered, but instead of Ali, it was Mhatre. He was taking precautions.

"Our men are ready to move out. Tell me about the location."

Arnav briefed his boss. The possibility of a back exit into the Malad creek, and that both Rasool's and Vijayan's men could be about. He knew of ten, but it wouldn't shock him if there were more.

"You're sure you have the evidence?" Mhatre's voice sounded faint but firm. "You're risking your career because of your personal connection, but if this turns out to be false . . ."

"The evidence is in a safe place. We'll have leverage."

"Those you are accusing are not ordinary men."

"I'm aware, sir."

He'd spoken to Nandini. If things went south, she had all the material for an exposé to pitch to the appropriate outlet. Once the party in power at the center got wind of it, it would be game over for the state government.

"Don't move until we get there."

"Right, sir."

He exited the car and walked. Tukaram followed him. "Are they coming?"

Arnav turned. "Wait for Naik. I'll scout around. Mhatre sir will know to place constables to cover all the exits. Park the car away from the road. Can't alert anyone who drives out."

"You can barely walk."

"We can't dawdle. Won't be long before Joshi finds out. I'm fine."

Arnav did feel fine. All his pain had vanished. The familiar rush of the chase alleviated the gnawing worry in his stomach. He had to find Tara. At the least, he could cause a distraction or delay, making time for Mhatre's and Naik's teams to surround the place.

His 9 mm in hand, Arnav stumbled, letting his eyes adjust to the dark. His only advantage was the element of surprise. Light trickled in through the foliage. A sprawling farmhouse lay ahead. A car started up, and Arnav dragged himself behind a tree, his boots squelching in the mud. A hooting bird flapped past and alighted on the tree, startling him, but he stayed hidden, crouched, ignoring sore legs. Some of the pain pushed through the medication and adrenaline. He rooted through his pockets for the painkillers he'd stowed away, swallowed two.

Headlights approached. A lone man drove a van out. Black and large, but it resembled the van from Rasool's rental company. Ali was right—his *Bhai* had sent men here. He couldn't get it straight: Shetty and Shinde had been in touch with Vijayan. The shooter was Vijayan's man. What were both Vijayan's and Rasool's goons doing here? Impossible that they had joined hands across a fault line of communal differences and assassinations.

An animal cried in the distance, then stopped all of a sudden, mid-scream. A fox? He'd walked close enough he could see the farmhouse gates. Large and wide open, lit with white halogen lamps. No direct approach to the entrance without being spotted from the windows. He typed a message to Mhatre. As he sent it, a piercing shriek floated up from the farmhouse. A female voice. He dropped the phone in his pocket and sprinted forward.

CHAPTER EIGHTY-FOUR

TARA

The men pushed branches aside and entered an overgrown backyard, Tara hoping each minute a denizen of the jungle would bite or sting one of them. Back home, the mangrove was alive with spiders and snakes. This forest seemed to be ailing. Plastic packets wreathed the tree roots.

Watch everything. Remember.

She feigned a bout of dizziness that slowed her down, and made note of the number of doors and windows at the back of the sprawling farmhouse: three entrances leading up from the grass, eight windows on each floor—if she was able to use the phone she'd stolen, she'd tell Arnav.

They entered, leaving the insect noises behind, the door opened by a bald old man with the straight posture and crisp clothes of a waiter at a good hotel. She collapsed to the ground, so they'd think she was still drugged. She took in a wide courtyard, open to the sky, with some kind of garden, before they hauled her down a flight of stairs into a room, dumped her on the floor, and locked her in. She had glimpsed two long pillared corridors on both sides with several doors. The room next to hers was guarded, and she heard sobbing. Pia? If that was her daughter, she would risk it all to reach her.

She recalled hearing the word "inspector." They were posting watch.

She was grateful they didn't think of tying her up. She struggled to her feet and untied the rough cloth from across her mouth. Her legs hurt from the fall earlier, but she was otherwise in good shape. Her room was empty, with light from one bare, dim bulb. A framed photo far above her on the wall. A high, grilled window. Shadows of tall grass. Ground level. She was in a basement, then. She would do her best to break out and get Pia, but she must talk to Arnav first. Tara reached for the phone tucked at her waist, switched it on and turned it to silent. With trembling hands, she dialed his number.

CHAPTER EIGHTY-FIVE

BILAL

Bilal's unease increased as the evening wore on. Vijayan's men lounged about, seven of them, ostensibly because the boy wanted them to remove the package this time. *Your Rasool failed me,* the boy had said, *and this is the real Item Number. Can't make mistakes.*

Their job was to wait till it was late enough for them to carry the package out and sanitize the workshop.

You deserve a break. Take an early night, but stay here in case I need anything later.

The boy was fiendish in his cunning, but Bilal wondered how he hoped to hide the carnage in the workshop from Vijayan, escape blackmail from his *Uhnna.*

He asked no questions of the boy because he knew he wouldn't receive answers.

The boy had been all smiles today, making no secret of his glee in anticipation of the Item Number. He thought Bilal suspected nothing, but anticipating threats was practically Bilal's job description. Fill a need before it was voiced. Prevent a disaster before it occurred. That was how he'd survived with the master, and now the master's son. Bilal made himself useful, serving dinner to Vijayan's team, unasked, doing a job before he was bidden.

He'd accepted the delivery of the woman, and invited the three Malayali crooks who brought her in to have a bite with their colleagues in the upstairs dining hall. He sent his assistant with water for the little girl, and asked him to stay on watch, while Bilal kept the plates of Vijayan's men filled.

Instinct told him to run, but in some ways, he was like the boy. The boy was afraid of the Item Number, but he couldn't bring himself to hurt her. Bilal cursed himself. He was scared of the boy now, but he couldn't abandon the child he'd raised into a man.

Vijayan's crew thought he didn't speak Malayalam. Pity. They didn't know Bilal Musliyar was born a Malayali. He'd forgotten most of it in his master's service, but not so much he didn't understand when someone spoke of killing him while he brought them chicken curry and rice. They planned to get him in his sleep. He had half a mind to drug them all, but that would get him on the don's hit list.

Heart in his mouth, Bilal sneaked back to his room to tell Rasool's men to be ready to escort him out. He found his semi-dark room a haze of cigarette smoke, and a fierce, whispered discussion in progress.

"You didn't tell us you had Vijayan's men here," the leader's tone was accusing. Taller than the others, he had the air of a don-in-the-making.

"My boss got them. I didn't know."

"Our boy here," the leader said, pointing to Bilal's scruffy pretend-assistant, "tells us there's a little girl in the room in the other corridor. We've been following her, but she was spirited away."

"Yes."

"And a woman next door to her?"

"Yes, why?"

"*Bhai* would like to talk to you. Wait."

After the tall leader sent a message, a hush descended as if the group awaited word from Allah. When the phone vibrated, the man picked up, said a respectful *haan Bhai*, and passed the phone to Bilal.

"I want that girl and her mother," Rasool Mohsin's high voice, crisp and businesslike.

"*Bhai*, there are—"

"I know the place is crawling with Vijayan's men. We'll discuss that some other day. You'll help my men get the girl and the woman."

What the hell did Rasool Mohsin want with them? The two were heavily guarded. Wouldn't be easy to bring them out.

"I'll not charge you for the service this time. All you have to do is make it easy for my men."

Not bad at all. Bilal wouldn't mind the boy's frustration when he found the two gone, and no one left to take care of him when he called for Bilal in his demented, helpless state.

"They are important to you?"

"They're important to someone who is."

In the quiet background of the don's call, Bilal heard a woman sobbing, and a shushing sound from the don. Bilal could have sworn Rasool sounded human. A woman had stirred him, too, but unlike the boy's Item Number, this one saved lives. Bilal could get behind that.

"As long as they keep me safe, I'll do whatever you need, *Bhai*."

Bilal walked out, his assistant in tow.

A saloon car at the gate. No visitors ever came to the farmhouse. Not family or friends. The car pulled up and the tall, smooth-talking businessman Bilal had met a few times with the boy stepped out.

CHAPTER EIGHTY-SIX

ARNAV

To avoid the lights at the gate, Arnav approached the farmhouse via the cover of the trees to his right, losing crucial seconds. If that scream was Tara, she didn't have long. The gate appeared to recede from him the faster he ran toward it. He cursed when his phone vibrated at his hip, but hoping it was Ali, he tapped on his Bluetooth.

"Avi."

"Tara?" Arnav sagged with relief.

"I'm at the rear of this building. Near the water. It's like a basement."

She spoke in gasps, as if she'd been running.

"Are you OK?"

"For now. They sent men toward the front courtyard. Use the back entrance."

He listened, falling in love all over again. He'd ask her later how she'd snagged a phone. For the moment, he plotted his way into the farmhouse even as she spoke. Tara said he'd have to watch out for an ambush. The goons expected police to show up. He typed in staccato messages to Naik as he listened over the Bluetooth.

"I'm going to get her."

"Listen to me, Tara. Sit tight."

"If I don't make it, she has you. Don't call back." She sounded calm, determined, and cut the call before Arnav could reply.

His heart sinking, Arnav was about to break into another sprint when a twig snapped behind him. He turned on his heel, pointing his gun.

Tukaram. He lowered his arm. His gaunt friend was too old to be here.

"Tukaram, I thought I said—"

"You're not going in alone."

Arnav considered Sub-Inspector Tukaram, strapped in a ridiculous waist pack and carrying a Glock. The belt bag was large and strung with a mini flashlight and flex-cuffs. "I came prepared," Tukaram said, patting the pack. Extra rounds.

"Let's go." Arnav jogged off, ignoring the soreness in his legs. "They expect police, but not a full-scale raid."

"Naik is five minutes out."

They stayed away from the halogen lights, melting into the shadows.

Arnav glanced at his watch as they neared the corner. Bending down, he picked up a stone and flung it at the trees opposite him, toward the boundary of the property, and ducked back as a shot tore a chunk off that wall, sending pieces of brick and cement flying. They had set a lookout.

Before he could grab Tukaram, the old man dived, rolling and weaving, and found cover behind a pile of cement. While Tukaram fired a few shots, Arnav took a quick peek. He spotted movement in an upper-story window. Letting his eyes adjust, he modified his stance to shoot with one arm. Deep breath. Aim. Fire. The shadow in the window jerked and staggered. A flash in the corner of his eye made him duck back moments before three shots tore large pieces of plaster from the wall. He counted down with his fingers and pointed to Tukaram. His friend unleashed a barrage of lead at the other shooter's window. Using the distraction, Arnav sprinted through the shadows.

A hand on his shoulder stopped him cold out in the open. Arnav twisted and bent, striking back with his elbow into the goon's solar plexus, feeling the man's huff of exhale against his own throat. With his left arm out of action in a sling, he continued the motion, not letting go of the gun, raising and slamming his right forearm against the man's neck to haul him forward and ducking at the same time to use his body as a shield against the flurry of shots from above. The goon sagged with a moan. Arnav shot blindly from under the man's heavy arm. Tukaram came to his aid with covering fire. Arnav's luck held. A yell from the window, his barrage in the dark finding its mark.

Arnav let the dying man drop, hopped over his form, and raced on, Tukaram now close at his heels. A door ahead slammed open. Two men darted out. Arnav fired twice without slowing. One man screamed and clutched his ruined hand to his chest. The other crumpled, holding his leg. Tukaram popped up from behind Arnav and tasered the goon who was still upright, sending him down, twitching and grimacing. Arnav checked his gun as Tukaram restrained both men. Once his friend was in control, he moved on.

Using his uninjured shoulder to push against the heavy door the men had exited, he found its weight had latched it shut from the inside. In the background, gunfire. Shouts. The Malwani Police Station teams had arrived.

The building plunged into darkness, power turned off as part of the raid. Somewhere, a generator kicked on. Lights flickered on in a window or two. Smoke—in the periphery of his consciousness he registered the presence of fire. Tara, Pia! How close were they to it?

Arnav raced toward the rear of the farmhouse. An overgrown yard surrounded by mangroves. He paused to reload his gun and catch his breath, shrugging to wipe off the sweat dripping from his face with his unhurt forearm. No pain—as if his shoulder had healed and was whole again—his mind centered, his punished body dissociated, far away, in a flood of adrenaline. The stench of burning grew stronger. Three doors, all closed. A low cry from a fourth, hidden by trees and shrubs. A woman. Was it Tara? She'd said she was in a basement room.

The entrance was locked from inside, but Arnav could see the keyhole. He took a shot at the latch, ready to face return fire, but none came. The door swung open, revealing a ramp downward into a basement. A door to the right. Choking sounds. He padded swiftly in, keeping the entryway in his sight, finger on trigger. The ground shook once beneath his feet, and again. Bombs? He hoped Naik and Mhatre would call in the bomb squad—he had no time to warn them.

The low, choked moans kept him moving. In the dim light he wasn't sure of his bearings. Chains hung from hooks on the wall. Translucent cobalt plastic curtains. A tall, shadowy figure wearing a blue cap, facing away from him. A metal table with something on it. A glimpse of shimmering azure under a lone bulb. The guy hadn't heard him because he wore large headphones. In his gloved hand, a whirring device that sounded like a drill. Arnav recognized it when it paused, and dark liquid dripped from it. Like Dr. Meshram's autopsy saw.

A stump. Clamped leg. Shiny blue saree. Tara? How could it be? Had he dragged her here in the minutes it had taken Arnav to arrive?

Beyond the curtains, the man turned, his face obscured by the blue cap, a mask, and a transparent shield. The beard and mane of Rehaan Virani. Another table stood between the curtains and Arnav. Smoke began to trickle into the room from the door behind the killer Arnav had chased for so long.

"Drop that." Arnav's finger hovered on the trigger. "Raise your hands."

CHAPTER EIGHTY-SEVEN

TARA

In the dim light of the bulb, Tara estimated the jump; she would have to propel herself high enough that she could move the large old framed photo and bring it down without a crash. A noise would alert the men guarding her room.

She was glad her legs felt strong enough despite the hurt from the fall and the lingering effects of the drug used to knock her out. This was the first time dance would bring her more than money. The strength developed through dancing would help her save Pia.

Stripping off her saree, she ensured her petticoat was secured well enough not to fall off and ripped the saree into long thin ribbons. At the third jump, she displaced and caught the frame on the way down. She sat up, swiftly removed the glass and the back, tossing away the faded photo. Padding her hand with the strips of her saree, she took the glass and shattered it as quietly as she could. She picked up the frame and, stepping on one of its sides, splintered it.

With a palm-sized glass shard and a pointy broken frame piece on standby, she secured the bandage on her right hand and rolled up her underskirt for ease of movement. She then crashed the back of the frame with as loud a noise as possible, hoping to attract attention. Snatching up her improvised glass dagger in her padded right hand

and the sharp frame piece in the other, she crouched behind the door, steeling herself. She must slash first, without hesitation.

As she'd predicted, moments after the noise, a thug unlocked the door and rushed in. Men never expected a woman to strike first. Adapting the moves she'd practiced with Arnav long ago, she sprang out and slashed with the glass shard, catching the henchman in the underarm, feeling the glass squelch in. She kicked him behind the knees as he yelled, and locked the guy inside before he could turn toward her. Her luck ran out as two thugs rushed at her down the basement corridor, their gazes straying over her blouse, petticoat, and bare midriff. She ran to slide past them, yelling for Pia.

The thugs grabbed at her as she struck out with the piece of broken picture frame, terrified she wouldn't reach her daughter. She cried out in agony as one of the men caught her arm and twisted it, expecting to be hit and dragged back. The next blow didn't come, because from down the corridor, other men ran at them, and her attacker loosened his grip in surprise. Tara didn't understand what was going on, but she took advantage of that moment of distraction to throw herself toward the door where she'd heard sobbing, while pulling away the padding on her hand.

Behind her, pandemonium broke out. Swear words. Punches, kicks. Gunshots. Pia's muffled cries floated out from the room. Tara made herself as small as she could, pulled a pin from her hair and worked on the lock—thanking Zoya for another useful skill.

She tumbled into the room to see Pia slumped against the wall, her hands tied, the gag on her mouth loosened, bruises on her face. She must have struggled once they cut away her hair, and they had subdued her. Before Tara could shut the door, someone barged in, sending her heart pounding. The bald man who looked like a waiter.

"Hurry up," he said, and extended his hand.

She gaped at him in disbelief, even as she worked to untie Pia.

"We must hurry. Rasool *Bhai*'s men can't hold them for long."

Rasool Mohsin, the don. Zoya's boyfriend. Tara managed to untie Pia. With no time to hold her close, Tara dragged her incoherent daughter out of the room and into the melee.

The bald waiter did his best to shove the guys aside and make a brisk, unseen escape, but as they cleared the scuffle, she heard a holler in Malayalam, and shots rang out. Two of the thugs broke away and came for them, guns raised, warning them to stop. Ahead, the bald man descended stairs going down yet another level. Tara shoved Pia at him, making him stumble. She turned to face the attackers, ready to do whatever it took to stop them, but a gunman raised his arm and fired. Pain jackhammered through her, spinning her around. A hot agony skewered her neck, and she was gone.

CHAPTER EIGHTY-EIGHT

ARNAV

A choked gasp from the table distracted Arnav, and now Rehaan held a gun pointed at him. Arnav caught a glimpse of messy beard before he ducked under the table and aimed at Rehaan's leg. He missed as Rehaan broke into a run. Fired again and scored a hit this time. Rehaan hunched over and his gun clattered to the floor. Arnav stood and called out a warning to Rehaan's back, telling him to raise his hands, but Rehaan swung his arm as he rose and a sharp, heavy object rammed into Arnav's injured shoulder, making him drop his gun. A trowel.

Rehaan leaped for his own gun, but Arnav, desperate with pain and fearing Rehaan would shoot him given a chance, tackled the other man with his unhurt right shoulder, pain ricocheting through his injuries. Smoke filled the room. It clogged his lungs as he struggled to hold the large man down, his mind flying back to the blood on the saw, and whose it was. Tara. They grappled in a tangle of plastic curtains. Rehaan headbutted Arnav's left shoulder, blinding him with agony, forcing him to let go.

As Rehaan scrambled to his feet, Arnav forced himself to rise and throw a kick at Rehaan's bleeding shin. It landed with a crunch. Arnav angled his injured shoulder away and used quick parries to keep Rehaan's fists away from him, wondering at the change in the fighting style: at the dojo, Rehaan had gone for the showy roundhouse kicks from the movies instead of sharp punches from the streets. Arnav weaved, avoiding Rehaan's workmanlike flurry of punches obscured by the sooty air and torn curtains, and kicked again at the movie star's leg, using his own arms only for balance.

A strangled cough issued from behind him. She was stuck on the table, bleeding out. In that moment of blank, mindless fear for Tara, Arnav lost track of Rehaan. He heard the man stagger up the ramp and out of the basement, but he had to tend to her first.

Calling Tara's name, telling her he was here, he unbuckled one leg, and made himself free the other despite the grisly injury. Heartbroken, he bent to tackle the restraints on her hands, and turned to her face.

Not Tara. Thank heaven.

Kittu Virani.

With relief came dismay—Rehaan Virani had done this to his own mother? He freed Kittu's hands, but when he tried to move her, she seemed inert. Like her body had seized up. She let out a stifled cry, her gaze frozen in horror. Where was Tara? He couldn't move Kittu with his one good arm—not without assistance. The smoke made breathing difficult. Flames peeked in from the backyard door through which he had entered.

"Rajput sir?" Naik's voice cut through the smoke, and Arnav responded with a hoarse shout. "Here."

Naik rushed in through a door that led in from the farmhouse, three constables in tow.

"Take charge here. Get her the help she needs." Arnav gestured to the table, and the constables headed there. Kittu Virani must bear witness to her son's atrocities.

"Did you locate Tara?" Arnav asked, clipping on the radio set Naik gave him, his heart in his mouth.

"No, sir."

"Secure the scene. Get the ambulance guys in here. Don't let this room burn if you can help it." Arnav grabbed one from a stack of blue towels and wrapped it around his face, asking the others to do the same. He asked a constable to follow him.

He radioed firefighters' assistance, urging them to hurry.

"Why have we not completed the rescue?" he asked the constable jogging along beside him—they had taken the door Naik had used, landing them in a first-floor corridor. He strained to catch the constable's muffled account amid the yells and gunfire.

"Two bombs have gone off, sir. The other side of the building has collapsed. There might be more. The Bomb Disposal Squad is trying to request a Quick Response Team."

"Why the delay?" Arnav cleared his throat.

"We can't find the additional commissioners, or Joshi sir."

Of course they couldn't find Joshi. Joshi would do his best to keep the elite team of highly trained commandos away from here. Tara and Pia's rescue was up to him and the Malwani police team.

Adrenaline rallied him, his lungs clearing as he ran in the open air of the corridor. Tara had mentioned entering the farmhouse from the back. How close were Tara and Pia to the flames, and the staccato firing of multiple guns? The courtyard was surrounded by pillared corridors on three sides.

Dense smoke obscured the entire right-side corridor where they crouched. Arnav sprinted, taking cover behind the pillars, waiting a few seconds at each, knowing a stray bullet could find him.

Flames leaped out of the doors. Pia or Tara might be on the other side of any of them. He stood, suspended in indecision, when his radio crackled to life.

"Avi, I don't see you. Naik said you're trying to get inside."

"Where are you?" Arnav asked Tukaram.

"The gate," Tukaram said. "I'm helping arrest those running out. Mhatre sir is with me. Did you find Tara?"

"No."

Mhatre's voice floated in. "Inspectors are taking the left corridor now."

Arnav faced the flames lapping out of the open doorways, the constable at his rear. He attempted to get into one room after another, the towel tied over his mouth. He saw no signs of life till he ran down two flights of basement stairs. Someone moved in the first room he entered, and he pointed his gun at the man, shouting a warning. The constable shone his flashlight, catching the bloodied human figure.

An elderly bald guy seated on the floor looked up with a bundle in his arms. "Take her. She hit her head."

Arnav's instinct was to rush in and check, but he kept his gun trained at the suspect.

"Show us her face."

"She needs help . . ."

Arnav cocked the gun. "Her face. Now."

The constable pointed the flashlight at the pale face.

It was Pia. This was not how he'd imagined meeting his own child for the first time. She had a bruise on her forehead. At a gesture from Arnav, the constable took her from the bald man's arms and confirmed she was breathing.

Arnav's relief was short-lived. Beside the man lay Tara, her face pale, her body soaked in blood—clad only in a blouse and petticoat. What had she risked to rescue Pia? Terror choked his throat as he switched on the radio, but he took a shaky breath and requested aid in a calm, measured voice. He checked the bald man for weapons but found none.

He ached to pick Tara up and hold her, but she lay in a pool of her own blood—he might injure her further. His hands trembled as he searched for the source of Tara's bleeding and held his fingers to her throat. A faint pulse. She was here, but barely.

His family—battered and bleeding. He hadn't been able to prevent them getting hurt after all. He caught that thought and smothered it. Tara would be well.

Around them the firing had paused.

As a horde of men led by Mhatre barreled in, surrounding Tara, Arnav reached for his unconscious teenage daughter, stroking the hair away from her forehead, checking for other wounds. He was never going to be parted from her, or her mother, again.

CHAPTER EIGHTY-NINE

TARA

This was not the family reunion Tara had pictured. Pia. Arnav. She woke with their names on her lips.

Based on the hum-swoosh of machines and the regular beeps, she wasn't doing too well. When she was not able to rise, or move her hands, her fears were confirmed. But she had no time for that. She asked the nurses hovering about her bed for Pia. They called her attendant, and there he was. Arnav, bleary-eyed, bruised.

"Pia?"

"They're stabilizing her with fluids—she inhaled a lot of smoke and bumped her head. She'll be fine."

"Can I talk to her?"

"They have sedated her. You must rest."

"What are you not telling me?"

"Pia is all right, I promise. You'll be OK soon, too. I'm here. Sleep."

"Who was it? The jackal?"

"Sleep now. I'll be here when you wake up."

Arnav resembled a beaten-up thug, not a police inspector. Fresh dressings on his arm, his face, his throat. He looked different, but her addled brain couldn't place it.

"Did you get shot again?"

"Don't worry. Get better, please?"

"Your mustache?"

He had shaved it off. The change made him look shorn, vulnerable, like a soul in need of comforting. She struggled to reach out, but her arms did not cooperate.

"You noticed?"

"Why did you . . . ?" she said.

"Someone once said it makes me look handsome. I could even act in the movies, you know. There's more to a man than a mustache."

A lazy Sunday in bed years ago came floating back, like a dream long forgotten.

"Yes," she said. "It is easier to kiss you now."

Arnav leaned over, but she felt as if he were kissing her with a mask on. The caress of his lips, the light scratch of his dressings on her chin seemed far away, receding. Arnav rushed out, as if possessed. Didn't stop when she called him. What was he hiding from her?

CHAPTER NINETY

Arnav

Arnav wanted to go to sleep and never wake up. If he slept, in his dreams Tara would laugh her soft laughter, run her fingers through his hair. He could feed her, laugh at her moans, nuzzle her neck. He didn't know whether he'd be able to do those things again.

Since last night, he'd alternated between Tara in intensive care and the room where they tended to Pia—rushing the medications the nurses needed, waiting for doctors' updates. Pia hadn't opened her eyes. Maybe she wished to remain asleep, like him.

The doctor's words rang in his ears. *The bullet we extracted from Tara's neck has paralyzed her, Inspector Rajput. We'll understand the extent of the damage in the next few days. I'm sorry.*

Under his exhaustion and wish to retreat from life, burned a larger, endless fire, a hunger for revenge. Naik's periodic updates from the station frustrated him no end. After all this havoc, they didn't have the accused in custody. Guilt and shame swallowed him up—he'd allowed this to happen to them, let Tara be injured in rescuing her daughter. He'd also let the suspect escape. When the *sensei*'s assistant came to the hospital waiting room to give him a break, he headed for the dojo to catch a shower and some answers.

His phone buzzed. Mhatre wished to meet him, outside the police station. Arnav invited him to the dojo.

After his bath, he heard all the expected words from the *sensei* over a simple lunch—Tara getting shot in the crossfire wasn't his fault, he should stay strong for Pia, and so on. Arnav let the *sensei* speak while he dug into the meal, not tasting it, remembering the last time he'd fed Tara. A change of subject was in order. He could use information on the Viranis.

"On the set, Karan Virani appeared to be friends with you," Arnav said. "Did you work with him before?"

The *sensei* turned away.

"Karan and I go back a long way. I was his schoolmate. We were never close."

"We have called Rehaan Virani in for questioning this afternoon."

Rehaan wouldn't return home if Arnav had anything to do with it.

"You suspect him of kidnapping Pia?"

"I didn't believe it at first, but I witnessed him . . . hurting his mother." Arnav recalled the ghastly scene obscured by smoke. "He escaped before I could arrest him. Now his lawyers are saying he has an alibi. Unfortunately, Ms. Virani died."

That was another mystery. Kittu Virani should have survived the smoke inhalation and loss of blood.

The *sensei* rose and stared out of the window.

"This sounds terrible," he said, his voice low, "but her death doesn't make me sad."

"Kittu Virani?"

Kittu Virani might not have been a star, but she was an influencer. Arnav had watched the hospital TV running in the background. The ticker tape on the news said that hordes of Kittu's adoring social media fans were inconsolable.

They speculated about the death of her fiancé in the fire. Firefighters had discovered his charred remains, and identified him by his expensive watch, which had lasted through the flames.

"Karan helped me when I lacked funds for this dojo. I'll tell you this: talk to him about Rehaan and Kittu, and speak with his assistant, Bilal."

"Bilal saved Pia."

Even as he said it, the question that had lurked at the back of Arnav's mind surfaced. What was Bilal doing at the farmhouse? He was Karan's assistant, not Rehaan's. And Karan was away at the time, at an intimate pre-Diwali party at Home Minister Namit Gokhale's place.

"I'll see you at the hospital," the *sensei* said.

Arnav longed to return to the hospital, but he couldn't muster the courage to face Tara and her questions.

The dojo receptionist walked in to announce that Mhatre waited for him.

Mhatre was the reason Tara was still alive. Naik hadn't managed to find a doctor willing to hop on a police jeep on Diwali at midnight. It was Mhatre's quick thinking and training as a former medical student that had kept Tara stable till the ambulance arrived.

"Thank you for last night, sir." Arnav shook his boss's hand. In the darkness, trauma, and anxiety of the night before, he hadn't noticed Mhatre. The week of his leave seemed to have hollowed him out, deep shadows underneath his eyes.

"I know what you're looking at," Mhatre said, as Arnav turned quickly away to pull over a chair. "I hope no one else figured it out in the dark last evening. This was my first round of chemotherapy. They would force me to retire."

So this was what Naik knew, why she trusted Mhatre.

"Are you OK, sir?"

"You mean, will I live? It is prostate cancer, early stage. I should recover. I'll need to take leave for each chemo session. I came in to examine your evidence against Joshi for myself. I want to be ready for the enquiries."

As they went through all the call recordings and Shinde's papers, Arnav cursed himself yet again for not arresting Rehaan on the scene. All the evidence might not be sufficient to put Rehaan Virani away.

Arnav had asked to interview the movie star. His leg would show the wound where Arnav had shot him.

"Joshi sir says we can only arrest Rehaan if we have evidence," Mhatre said. "Based on these papers, I understand why Joshi sir might be aiding a cover-up. But the truth is, Rajput, the bearded man you saw could have been anyone."

CHAPTER NINETY-ONE

Arnav

Arnav took a cab to his office on Diwali afternoon. Pain had become his constant friend—it distracted him from the crater in his life. How was it possible he had found Tara again less than ten days ago, and already stood to lose her?

Naik's knock broke into his endless fretting.

"We've arrested eleven men from the grounds, one of whom claims he knows your informer. Ali."

"Yes, he had sent me his location, which helped us track Pia's kidnappers."

"He's asked to talk only to you, sir."

"Let's go." Arnav paused. "Thank you, Naik. Calling Mhatre was a good decision."

"I noticed his prescriptions by accident, sir. Someone in my family has cancer, so I knew."

"You saved my life."

Naik grinned. A rare, bright smile that made her look years younger.

"Anything for you, sir," she said, her eyes glinting.

Arnav was puzzled at this display of emotion, and let it show.

"I mean . . . it was my job, sir. Shall we go?"

The room they walked into was poorly lit, but Arnav recognized the goon. Ali had texted him a picture. He tried to ignore the bruises on the man's neck and arms. Naik's constables had not gone easy on him. A part of him winced in sympathetic pain; his own body was sore.

This gray area continued to discomfit Arnav. Most informers were small-time criminals, protected because they led the police to bigger fish. Naik stood beside him, calm, as if she didn't see the suspect's injuries.

"*Saab.*" One of his eyes was swollen.

"You were supposed to protect the girl."

"I did my best, but the others had instructions to hand her over when we reached the farmhouse. Manu got the girl from somewhere. He hired me and my friends only to make the delivery."

"To whom?"

"To the man in charge there. Bilal."

This was news. Arnav fixed his gaze on Ali's friend. "Are you sure?"

"He locked her up in the room, and made the payment. Please let me go. I didn't even have a gun. I helped; I sent the location to Ali . . ."

"Did you say your boss's name was Manu?"

"Yes, sir."

Zoya had heard a kidnapper call the name Manu when Pia was taken.

They went back to his office, and he asked Naik about Bilal.

"We caught him trying to skip town, sir. He has handed over his phone, and requested to be a witness. We're downloading the photos from his phone, sir."

"What about Rehaan?"

"At his apartment. There's a crowd of media outside his home, sir."

"They know we want Rehaan for questioning?"

"They have asked for a press conference about last night's events."

Arnav checked the list of those arrested at the farmhouse, and circled Manu's name.

"Lean on this one." He pointed at the board. "Find out who he is working for."

"Sure, sir. When Pia is better, she might be able to identify some of them."

"Print out all the info we have on Rehaan and leave it on my table."

"He has a solid alibi, sir."

"Meaning?"

"He was with an entire crew at an outdoor filming location, all of Choti Diwali, until this morning."

"His DNA in the black van?"

"He says the van was rented by his stepbrother. He'd borrowed it for a short while to run an errand."

Rehaan Virani seemed to have an answer for all questions, but how did he intend to explain away the gunshot injury on his leg?

Arnav flipped open the file with the forensic photographs of the basement of the farmhouse. The steel table. The saw. The chains hanging from the wall. The bathtub. If necessary, he would send some of them to Nandini, breaking all the rules, in order to build pressure on the police via the media. They might trace the leak to him, and he could lose his job. But the world would know what went on in that farmhouse. He craved justice for Tara. She would not walk again, use her hands or arms. She had taken care of herself all her life. How would she cope with being fed and cleaned like an infant?

He called the hospital to ask for an update. Tara was sedated now, and Pia hadn't yet woken up. He would not be ungrateful, though, not on Diwali. She was still around. She had smiled. Tara. Images of her claimed him at odd times, and since last night, he'd come to a resolve. Throw himself at her mercy, ask her if she would make him a permanent fixture. Pray like hell she wouldn't refuse.

CHAPTER NINETY-TWO

BILAL

Bilal scratched his beard. He craved a shower, clothes, a meal—and a stool on which to rest his legs in their casts—but he must play this right in order to leave this windowless, stinking room alive. They had shut him up for hours now, in only his underwear. Mumbai Police were crooks. When he begged them to let him go, they'd offered to remove his underpants as well. He wished he could tell this Inspector Rajput they didn't need such measures.

Bilal wanted to talk, make a clean breast of it. He'd carried it around long enough. The boy must have broken. No one could put the pieces back together this time. Bilal knew the names of the people who were sheltering the boy now, and could lead the police to him.

Inspector Arnav Singh Rajput walked in. Bilal took a good look at the inspector the boy had tried and failed to take out over the past few weeks. Rajput had his left arm in a sling. His face was bruised and swollen, eyes bloodshot.

"Bilal Musliyar," he said, "You were instructed not to leave town."

Bilal said, "I was afraid for my life."

"You could have talked to us."

"*Saab*, when a loyal servant talks about his master, he needs protection. You have seen my phone."

Pictures taken over decades, as insurance against a day like this one. Pictures of the boy in one of his funks with a woman's body, blood draining from it. Dissociated, the doctor pronounced the boy, when Bilal brought him to the clinic. The doctor had no clue just how bad. The pictures showed the bodies Bilal had handed over. The heads and hands and feet he'd buried. He'd known the boy's day of reckoning would come. Bilal had prepared for a ticket out of it.

"I know you've not been bought, *saab*. There are others, higher up, who have been. Those pictures have copies, in different places."

The inspector sat down. "We're getting your phone and the photographs examined. We'll determine if they're fake. Even if they're genuine, the fact remains you helped him remove the dead bodies."

"I've often stayed awake at nights, gathering courage. I wasn't present any of the times he did those things. All the photos are of cleaning up—he called me later. Each time he promised it would be the last. I was scared of him, *saab*. He could have me put away without a trace. He tried this time."

"Why should I believe you?"

"I won't lie to you on Diwali evening."

The inspector laughed. "You don't even celebrate it, Mr. Musliyar."

"I can lead you to the missing parts of all the dead women."

That gave the inspector pause.

"What about this?" The inspector held up a ziplock bag. The damned blue things the boy had given Bilal so much grief about.

The police had found what the boy called his "little blue darlings."

"He had more of them made, *saab*. The earrings belonged to Kittu madam. He stole them, and snickered when she fired one of her maids. Check the pictures on my phone. I occasionally found them on the women's bodies—I missed these. He spent a few days with each of those poor women before . . . putting them out of their misery. I have more. I can tell you the shops where he had them modified with clamps. He went himself. It gave him a thrill, not being recognized."

"You got Pia kidnapped." The inspector spoke in a quiet tone, with the rage underneath controlled but evident.

So Bilal told him what he'd learned from snooping on the boy.

Of the boy's arrangement with Vijayan, who supplied him the girls through Shetty. Of Vijayan asking Manu to pick up Pia, as leverage on the inspector and his woman, Tara.

Of himself—how his relative had first given him Rasool's contact. How, over the years, Rasool had helped dump each of the bodies. How he himself had suspected that the boy was planning to get rid of him, along with Kittu madam, leading him to hire Rasool's men for his own protection. How Vijayan's henchmen and Rasool's had fought over the mother and her child. The accidental explosion and fire. How Taneja had showed up on Kittu madam's invitation.

With each word that poured out of him, Bilal felt terrified, but also lighter.

"Taneja was fool enough to try marrying Kittu madam—he thought he could use her connections and make himself untouchable. He had no idea what my boy was capable of. The boy contracted an entire shoot-out at the police station, and asked for the shooters to name Taneja." Bilal paused and drew a long breath, then continued.

"Taneja drove up that night, quite drunk from some fancy party, because Kittu madam had asked him to meet her at the farmhouse. She had good news to share. The boy had promised to sign over the farmhouse to her. It is a big place, and Madh Island needs new resorts. Taneja would have made a killing by turning it into a fancy hotel. I made him wait in the living room—what else could I do? She was in the basement with my boy."

"Rehaan Virani."

"No, *saab*. That was not Rehaan you met. They are the same height, and both have grown their beards for their latest movie. My boy would never let Rehaan know any of it. Rehaan is not who you think he is."

"I saw Rehaan."

"You don't understand, *saab*. I gave my word on Mr. Virani's deathbed, to protect his boys. I've been bound by that promise—because without Mr. Virani I would've died on the streets. I didn't tell him the truth because it would have killed him sooner."

"What truth?" The inspector leaned forward.

"It has destroyed my boy, my Karan, all his life. Not being able to talk about it to anyone. About what Kittu madam did to him."

"Karan Virani?"

The inspector stood up abruptly, staggering, his face carefully blank. So the police hadn't suspected the boy at all.

Bilal asked for some clothes and a stool to prop up his legs. Once he had both, he spoke further, describing what he knew of Kittu madam. How much the boy feared her and, strangely enough, loved her.

"If Karan Virani murdered so many, he could easily have taken care of one lone woman."

"He couldn't, *saab*. When he first met her, he was fifteen, and afraid of her. I couldn't protect him. We were terrified of the lies she'd tell his father. My master would have murdered him. Later, my boy couldn't let Rehaan grow up without a mother. All these years, Karan couldn't screw up the courage to kill the mother of his son. No one knows this, *saab*, not even Rehaan himself. Rehaan is not Karan's stepbrother, but his son. He was born when Karan was sixteen years old."

CHAPTER NINETY-THREE

The Item Number is no more, but her shadow still remains. I can tell you this: I shouldn't have idled this long. Her shadow will live on, live her own life, raise a daughter—that does not bother me.

The end I pined for will now never be mine. Item Number's blood. My own blood. All of it mixed together. And all for what? My son won't take my calls.

Now the Item Number is gone, now she reappears, taunting me with her rancid breath, her cackling laughter. I should have found another way, but it is too late. The police will find Bilal, or he will find them. It is all done now, all of it, and here I am without a phone, at the mercy of people who fawn over me, and ask me to get myself together. My leg hurts from the gunshot, but they won't call a doctor—too risky, they say. They have taken away my phone so I can call no one.

I can have crayons and paper, but who knows for how long. No sleep, that's for sure, because each time I close my eyes, she's back with her dark smile. Her lips are charred and black, and her touch, a living, crawling thing.

CHAPTER NINETY-FOUR

TARA

Long ago, in another life, Tara had lain in Arnav's arms as they watched a movie in his bedroom. *Akhiyon ke jharokhon se.* He'd changed channels before the movie neared its ending. *This doesn't end well. Let's watch another.*

She'd never looked it up in the intervening years, but the evening before she'd left for Mumbai, it had played on TV and she'd watched it with Pia, convinced Arnav had been confused about the unhappy ending. The movie could only end in happiness for the two married lovers, Lily and Arun.

But Lily had died in Arun's arms.

Caught in the half sleep brought on by medication, she'd asked the doctor what was wrong with her. The doctor had given her answers Arnav hadn't. The bullet had lodged at her neck. Tara wanted to rage at Arnav for not telling her. Instead, all she could feel was the need to console him. She couldn't move her arms, not even her finger, and might not hold him again. Nor Pia.

When she uttered Pia's name, she heard hushed voices, beeping equipment. She was never sure of when she was awake and what was part of her fevered dreams.

She called Pia again. And this time she opened her eyes.

"She'll be here soon." Arnav sat beside her.

"Have you spoken to her?"

She wished for them to get along, to recognize each other in their lives.

"She's been sedated so far," Arnav said.

"Have you heard from Zoya?"

"She rang once to ask about you. I told her you're with me. She's OK."

Arnav drew the pale-blue curtains that circled her bed. "I need to talk to you."

"Yes." She watched his unshaven face. The worry and suffering in his eyes, the exhaustion and hope.

"Will you marry me, Tara?"

"What?" She hadn't heard that right. Had not. Could not have.

"Marry me, Tara. Please."

From his face, he was not joking. At all. If he was serious, why now? When she wasn't even able to feel his hand holding hers? Tara closed her eyes. She willed him to go away. She prayed to Ma Kaali he wouldn't.

"Why?" she said.

Silence hovered amid the curtains, broken only by the low purr of machines. When he spoke, his voice was gruff and low.

"Because I'd like to belong to you. I've wasted so many years. When Asha left us, I was thirteen. She was my older sister. She would have loved you, you know, told me how lucky I was. She liked girls with spirit. She was a fighter, too. She gave up too soon."

Tara met his eyes. He didn't look away. He narrated Asha's history, from decades ago. The rape, the injustice, her suicide.

"Here she is." Arnav took out a faded photograph from his wallet. "I've carried her with me. After losing her and my parents, I thought I didn't deserve a family. I want one with you now. I can't make up for all the years, but would you let me try?"

Tara felt tears trickle down her cheek, and Arnav reached up to wipe them.

"Look who's here." A nurse spoke in a half whisper, peeking her head through the curtains, and parting them.

Tara watched as a second nurse brought in a wheelchair. Her Pia. Frail Pia in a hospital gown, her hair shorn, a bandage on her forehead. Even if she never rose from her bed again, she had achieved this. Her Pia. Safe.

"Ma." Pia's eyes lit up and she made to stand, but the nurse stopped her. "I'll help you." Both nurses lifted her into the bed, laying her right beside Tara. "Be careful," they said to Pia.

Pia burrowed her nose into Tara's arm and broke into quiet sobs. Arnav used his one good arm to cover Pia with the sheet.

For long minutes, the sobs were the only sound in the room.

Tara couldn't touch her daughter, and it gutted her. Arnav could, though, and he was here. She hadn't missed the note of desperation in his voice when he'd asked her—despite the fact that she might never walk or touch him again. He needed his daughter, and his daughter certainly needed him.

Tara had never seen beauty in marriage. This was, after all, a man, but watching Arnav's bruised fingers soothe their daughter, she could find no objection. If this was her fate, she would take her chances.

"Yes," she said quietly, and looked up to watch his eyes fill with emotion, true to his name. Arnav. The ocean.

She would be Noyontara now, like her mother used to call her. His Noyontara. Star of his eyes.

CHAPTER NINETY-FIVE

MUMBAI DRISHTIKON NEWS

Filmi Bytes

A tragic Diwali for the Viranis

10:00 PM IST 1 November, Mumbai.

Diwali is a festival of lights, but recent news from Bollywood has been filled with darkness, especially for the Virani family. Kittu Virani, famous socialite, social media influencer, and designer, died along with her real estate magnate fiancé Rahul Taneja, in a fire at her stepson Karan Virani's Madh Island farmhouse yesterday, on Choti Diwali night. The police have yet to clarify whether the incident occurred due to arson or by accident. There have also been isolated reports of gunfire at the scene.

Mumbai Police Joint Commissioner of Crime Neelesh Joshi has requested the media to act responsibly, but Kittu Virani's fans are questioning the police already, following a few leaked papers that seem to show Commissioner Joshi and Home Minister Namit Gokhale himself might have been involved in corruption. The authenticity of these records is yet to be verified.

Meanwhile, film star Rehaan Virani, the deceased Kittu Virani's son, was questioned by the police regarding the incident, while his older stepbrother, veteran actor Karan Virani, has been taken into custody under IPC section 84, and sent in for psychiatric evaluation. Several television channels are reporting that Karan Virani had been assaulting his stepmother when he escaped arrest. Shocking photographs of a severed foot have been leaked, purportedly from the crime scene at the isolated farmhouse, and are making the rounds on social media.

Maharashtra's Home Minister has dismissed such claims, calling them a cheap attempt to politicize a tragedy. In support of their allegations, opposition parties have cited police investigations: decomposed bodies of women found at Aksa Beach have been connected to a series of Mumbai's dance bars. The Leader of the Opposition in Maharashtra's State Assembly questioned the reopening of dance bars and vowed to close them if they were voted to power.

Kittu Virani's funeral is expected to be held a week from now after her body is released from postmortem, and is likely to be attended by a majority of the Bollywood fraternity, who have taken to social media to pay tribute to her and express solidarity with her grieving family.

CHAPTER NINETY-SIX

—

TARA

One year later

Six months after she was discharged from the hospital, Tara lounged at the Alibaug beach, gazing at her husband with longing, wanting to join him as he zigzagged on the sand, his loose pants rolled up, his T-shirt billowing in the wind, followed by a gaggle of children—Shinde's son and daughter, Tukaram's grandsons, Nandini's niece. And Pia.

Tara still could not feed herself, and on some days she railed at Arnav, asking him why he married her, why not leave her at the hospital where she had languished for six months, with the army of nurses to carry her useless body around. Not today, though.

Today, Arnav had promised Pia a beach picnic, and they'd decided to make a day of it with all the people who kept them going. Nandini and her clearly besotted colleague, who both ferried Pia to school when Arnav was hung up with his new duties as the senior police inspector at Bandra station; Shinde's wife and children, who entertained Pia when Tara labored through her endless physiotherapy sessions; Mr. and Mrs. Tukaram, who had added Pia as the granddaughter to their roster of three grandsons.

Tara wished Zoya were here, making snide comments about everyone, asking Tara to quit whining—but she was far away. Tara imagined her on another coast in Thailand or the Philippines, sipping a cocktail in the afternoon as she'd dreamed about so often. Zoya was not unloved—for her sake, Rasool had risked his men to help Pia and Tara.

The adults played a musical game around her, each carrying a Bollywood tune with varying degrees of success and a lot of laughter, sharing plates of *pao bhaji*, handing out ice creams. Tara joined in when it was her turn, singing a tune she used to dance to, one of her beloved Madhuri Dixit numbers. Madhuri, the graceful Bollywood diva. Tara had danced for nineteen out of her own thirty-two years, resenting it most of the time.

Now, she strove each day to get back on her feet. She would return to dancing, if only to show her daughter that in life it does not matter how hard you fall, but how promptly you try to rise again. She'd raised her child alone for thirteen years, protected her when it mattered. She would take a hail of bullets for Pia if she had to do it all over.

Waves danced upon the shore, ceaseless in their steps to and fro. The water must be cool to the touch, but she was too far away. Her sigh of longing ended on a shriek of embarrassed delight as Arnav snatched her up from her wheelchair.

To wolf whistles from the men of their party and clapping from the women, which was taken up by others at the beach unused to such public displays of affection, her husband carried her to the chair he'd already set where the waves could tease her feet, wetting the edges of her skirt.

A while later, they all piled into their vehicles. Tara leaned back in her seat as Arnav drove their spacious new car down the highway to a different beach at Alibaug to watch Ravan Dahan, Pia vibrating with excitement, singing along with Shinde's children and their mother to a raucous Hindi number more appropriate to a dance bar than a family trip. For once, Tara didn't care. She lowered the windows, let the sea air in, and, closing her eyes, pictured herself dancing.

CHAPTER NINETY-SEVEN

Arnav

Arnav gazed at his dreamy wife and sighed, his hand on the fancy steering wheel of his new car. Like all the other joyous transformations in Arnav's life, this car had showed up because of Tara, to fit in her wheelchair. But nearly one year after that dark Diwali at the farmhouse, he had still not been able to bring her justice.

Or to Neha Chaubey and the other women. The case dragged on in the courts. As Tukaram had predicted, even though some papers claimed that Karan Virani had gone bankrupt funding his nefarious activities, a pack of the country's highest-paid lawyers stood behind him, trying to get him an insanity defense. Not many others, though. Not Rehaan, who had dropped out of all his movies and the public eye. Not Namit Gokhale who had lost his cabinet seat as the Home Minister following the newspaper reports. He took every opportunity to mention his lack of association with Bollywood stars. Nor Joshi, who had been suspended and was being investigated by the Anti-Corruption Bureau. Arnav still couldn't believe he'd mistaken Karan for Rehaan. Yes, they were the same height, wore similar beards and clothes, and the smoke had made him queasy, but he was a police officer. He should have known. He was the reason why Tara had not found peace in all these months.

The only sense of closure he could give Neha Chaubey's family was to gather her body together, and arrange her funeral. He'd done the same for all the other women's remains: the bones from the evidence locker, the others Bilal had helped uncover, buried in the farmhouse's courtyard rose garden.

Twelve bar dancers had died. Seven bodies from the cases recorded by the police. Five more, whose skulls were unearthed from Karan Virani's garden, their bodies never located. Rasool's men had confessed, but their boss had escaped to Thailand, running his empire from Bangkok, if Zoya's sporadic calls to Tara were any indication. Vijayan's name had risen on the most-wanted list, his remaining men, arrested at the farmhouse, in jail.

Nandini and her articles had kept interest in the case alive, as had Kittu, Karan, and Rehaan Virani's fans, fighting hashtag battles on social media—relentless in their strident demand for a detailed enquiry by the Central Bureau of Investigation.

The court of public opinion had condemned Karan Virani, especially after Kittu Virani's postmortem report leaked. She'd died of an overdose of vecuronium bromide, exactly like Neha Chaubey. Kittu had lain paralyzed but awake for each moment of her foot being sawed off. She'd died bleeding and unable to breathe, with her heart shutting down in cardiac arrest.

Arnav often had nightmares of that horrific basement, but long drives like this with song and laughter were an equally frequent experience. When they reached the Ravan Dahan, Arnav sent Pia with the others to go up close to watch the Ravan burn. He parked Tara's wheelchair at the grass near the beach with a view of the Ravan Dahan and the sea. His head on her lap, he watched the traditional fierce red demon, with his black handlebar mustache, his evil, tortured eyes, his mechanical arm slicing the air with a tiny, ineffectual sword. He thought of Asha, who used to make fun of his scrambled-Ravan name, and smiled.

Tara crooned under her breath, a sad yet hopeful tune that he didn't recognize at first but turned out to be a rendition of *Har ghadi badal rahi hai roop zindagi*. As darkness descended around them in a comforting embrace, the Ravan caught fire, releasing gunpowder and sulfur smoke, lighting upward from the ground, spitting out a bouquet of firecrackers to the loud cheering for the victory of good over evil from the gathered revelers. Tomorrow, this Ravan would be swept away with the debris.

No endings, though. Only beginnings. Another Ravan would rise again soon—a ritual of nature. As Pia raced toward them, laughing, chased by her friends, Arnav held on to Tara's soft, nerveless hand. *From moment to moment, life changes its face,* he hummed with Tara in Hindi. In this moment, for now, it seemed enough for the demon to keep burning.

ACKNOWLEDGMENTS

Books are magical things that look like they are made of paper and color and ink, but the secret ingredients are the authors' tears and infinite solidarity from the community that surrounds them.

The Blue Bar came into my consciousness in a UEA-India writing workshop by Romesh Gunesekera: Tara in her shimmering blue saree. Its first chapters were written at a workshop by David Corbett.

I wrote the first draft in Kuala Lumpur in a month of isolation facilitated by Sharin Hassan and Karen Pereira.

I was able to research it in Mumbai, owing to the hospitality of Karishma Radhakrishnani and Rohit Mansukhani. Key research also became possible by the grace of the inimitable Satvasheela Prithviraj Chavan, who aided me in speaking with police officers and visiting training facilities to understand the lives of the brave and proud Mumbai Police. I spoke to officers who shall go unnamed because of confidentiality reasons: they described a police officer's life, the realities of patrolling, and the workings of gangs and dance bars. Vaishali Ghorpade made some of these impossible-to-organize meetings happen, as well.

More assistance came from Koral Dasgupta: she introduced me to Deepak Rao, the deeply knowledgeable Mumbai Police historian, who advised me with key location, police procedure, and plot possibilities. So many other friends offered support as I visited slums and dance bar neighborhoods, and walked Mumbai's streets.

Thanks to the generosity of Vandana Shah, I got to visit the movie sets of *Tanhaji* and watch an actual film shoot in progress, where ace director Om Raut shared his insights. Irene Dhar Malik put me in touch with her brother, the maverick filmmaker Onir, who explained how a film production works and the ways of Bollywood denizens. Noted screenwriter Shiv Kumar Subramaniam gave sage advice on writing, acting, and the Bollywood lifestyle.

Very grateful to Neil D'Silva and Sarika Joshi, who verified Mumbai locations and other details. Eric Lahti and Kirsten Moore lent their expertise on the fight scenes and made them so much more plausible.

The narrative is fictional and embellished, and all errors of research are mine.

J. L. Delozier, Sommer Schafer, Rae Joyce, and Zoe Quinton helped read early drafts. My awesome agent Lucienne Diver deserves an acknowledgment page all her own. My wonderful editor Jessica Tribble made the book shine, with help from Charlotte Herscher, Rachael Herbert, Sharon Turner Mulvihill, Elizabeth J. Asborno, Michael Jantze, Sarah Shaw, and others on the dream team at Thomas & Mercer who brought this book into the world. Amanda Hudson at Faceout Studio created the lovely cover.

Special thanks also to the 22 Debuts group, who have provided wisdom and backup, and Sunny Kumar, my yoga guru, who keeps me functional and sane.

The hugest gratitude goes to the readers who have reviewed advance copies, spoken of *The Blue Bar* on social media, and generally made me feel like less of a fraud.

My family has been an enormous source of support, but I wouldn't be an author without Swarup Biswas, my husband, best friend, and the love of my life.

ABOUT THE AUTHOR

Photo © 2021 Swarup Biswas

Damyanti Biswas is the author of *You Beneath Your Skin* and numerous short stories that have been published in magazines and anthologies in the US, the UK, and Asia. She has been shortlisted for Best Small Fictions and Bath Novel Awards and is coeditor of the *Forge Literary Magazine*. Damyanti is also a supporter of Project WHY, a program that provides quality education to underprivileged children in New Delhi. Apart from being a novelist, Damyanti is an avid reader of true crime, a blogger, and an animal lover. Her ambition has always been to live in a home with more books than any other item, and she continues to work toward that. For more information, visit www.damyantiwrites.com.